Praise for the Novels
of Tracy Wolff

Tie Me Down

"All I can say is that it is hot, hot hot! Murder, mystery, and sex that sizzles—what more can a gal ask for? Warning—read this story with a fan ready at hand."   —Sunny, author of *Mona Lisa Darkening*

"An intoxicating blend of suspense and eroticism that will leave readers breathless!"   —Maya Banks, author of *Sweet Persuasion*

Full Exposure

"Wolf ratchets up the tension in her debut novel, a first-rate tale set in the hot and steamy Louisiana bayou. She combines the adrenaline of a psychological thriller with the intensity of an exquisitly sensual romance. . . . Intriguing twists keep the pages turning and pave the way for an unforgettable conclusion."

—*Romantic Times*, 4½ stars, top pick

"This book kept me on the edge of my seat. . . . I recommend *Full Exposure* wholeheartedly."   —Fresh Fiction

"*Full Exposure* is a riveting read that will keep you in the dark until the last frame is fully developed. . . . Tracy Wolff has garnered my attention with her dazzling debut, and I will most assuredly be on the lookout for what she plans to offer next."   —Novel Talk

continued . . .

Also by Tracy Wolff

FULL **EXPOSURE**

TIE ME DOWN

TRACY WOLFF

HEAT

HEAT

Published by New American Library, a division of
Penguin Group (USA) Inc., 375 Hudson Street,
New York, New York 10014, USA
Penguin Group (Canada), 90 Eglinton Avenue East, Suite 700, Toronto,
Ontario M4P 2Y3, Canada (a division of Pearson Penguin Canada Inc.)
Penguin Books Ltd., 80 Strand, London WC2R 0RL, England
Penguin Ireland, 25 St. Stephen's Green, Dublin 2,
Ireland (a division of Penguin Books Ltd.)
Penguin Group (Australia), 250 Camberwell Road, Camberwell, Victoria 3124,
Australia (a division of Pearson Australia Group Pty. Ltd.)
Penguin Books India Pvt. Ltd., 11 Community Centre, Panchsheel Park,
New Delhi - 110 017, India
Penguin Group (NZ), 67 Apollo Drive, Rosedale, North Shore 0632,
New Zealand (a division of Pearson New Zealand Ltd.)
Penguin Books (South Africa) (Pty.) Ltd., 24 Sturdee Avenue,
Rosebank, Johannesburg 2196, South Africa

Penguin Books Ltd., Registered Offices:
80 Strand, London WC2R 0RL, England

First published by Heat, an imprint of New American Library,
a division of Penguin Group (USA) Inc.

First Printing, September 2009
10 9 8 7 6 5 4 3 2 1

Copyright © Tracy Deebs-Elkenaney, 2009
All rights reserved

HEAT is a trademark of Penguin Group (USA) Inc.

LIBRARY OF CONGRESS CATALOGING-IN-PUBLICATION DATA:

Wolff, Tracy.
Tie me down/Tracy Wolff.
p. cm.
ISBN 978-0-451-22788-1
1. Women detectives—Louisiana—New Orleans—Fiction. 2. New Orleans (La.)—Fiction. I. Title.
PS3623.O57T54 2009
813'.6—dc22   20090016913

Set in Sabon
Designed by Alissa Amell

Printed in the United States of America

For my husband, who is the love of my life

Acknowledgments

The folks at NAL, who take such good care of me, especially Claire Zion for taking a chance on me and Scot Biel for giving me the most amazing covers in the business.

Jane Sevier, for her big heart, droll wit and much appreciated ideas for this manuscript.

Emma Clair, Michelle McGinnis, Catherine Morris, Shellee Roberts, Sherry Thomas, Jane Perrine, Lexi Connor, Skye White, Karen Erickson and Lori Borrill—the most talented group of writers I know and ones whose friendship means the world to me.

Austin RWA, which is the best group of romance writers I've ever had the privilege of belonging to.

And finally, to the two most important women in my career:

Emily Sylvan Kim, who is the very best agent a girl could ever ask for. Thanks for putting up with my many and myriad neuroses—and for getting me everything I could ever want.

And Becky Vinter, who has put so much time and effort into me and this book. I am so blessed to have her for an editor and can't imagine doing any of this without her.

TIE ME
DOWN

Chapter One

It was hot as only New Orleans could be.

Hotter than a cat on a tin roof.

Hotter than the Cajun cooking her mother used to make.

Hotter than hell.

And she was burning up, fury and sorrow eating her from the inside out.

More than ready for the day from hell to be over, Genevieve Delacroix slammed out of the precinct on the fly, then cursed as she plowed straight into the sticky heat the city was known for. It rose up to meet her like a wall—thick and heavy and all-consuming.

Pausing to catch her breath, she stared blindly at the planters full of cheerful posies that lined the front of the precinct. Her partner, Shawn, had picked a hell of a time to take a vacation—in the middle of the busiest week homicide had seen in years. After working four homicide scenes in as many days, it was a miracle she could still put one foot in front of the other.

Today, she'd awakened to a ringing phone, news of a brutal sex-related homicide the first thing she'd heard as she surfaced from a sleep so deep it was almost like death itself. Yesterday it had been a murder-suicide. Two days before that, a domestic dispute turned deadly.

Not to mention the bizarre call she'd gotten earlier that afternoon promising her—with sexually graphic delight—that the caller would be seeing her very soon. As the only female on the homicide squad, she got her fair share of calls from weirdos, and this one was nothing unusual—but it still put her back up, as they all did.

Sighing, she rubbed a weary hand over her eyes. This week, the Big Easy was anything but.

Taking the precinct steps two at a time, Genevieve glanced around the French Quarter, where she'd worked and lived for most of her life.

Tonight she could see none of the beauty the Quarter was known for. The architecture, the colors, the history—it all faded beside the sickness she'd witnessed that morning. The most recent in a long line of fucked-up and twisted crimes that ate away at the city's population like a cancer.

Her argument with the lieutenant rang clearly in her head as her long legs ate up Royal Street's narrow sidewalks.

Not enough similarities in the causes of death in the murders.

Not enough similarities in the three victims.

Not enough evidence, in her boss's not-so-humble opinion.

But in the eleven years she'd been on the force, Genevieve's gut had never been wrong, and right now her instincts were screaming that the case she'd caught this morning—the brutal rape and murder of a nineteen-year-old Tulane student—wasn't a freak event. A serial killer was at large.

True, the causes of death in all three murders had been different, as had the body dumps—Jackson Square, Jean Lafitte's Blacksmith Shop, Senator Mouline's house—but the feel of the scenes had felt too similar for it to have been a fluke. The evident full-out rage the killer had been in when he'd inflicted the wounds had been the same, as had the desperate need to cause as much pain and humiliation to his victims as possible.

Without knowing where she was going, Genevieve made a quick left on St. Peter. She knew only that she couldn't face going home and reliving the whole damn day over and over in her head until she wanted to scream—or sob.

The image of Jessica Robbins' body was in front of her eyes, the atrocities done to her burned into Genevieve's brain by the hours and hours she'd spent working the case. By the helpless anger she felt at not being able to stop the crime.

By the failure she was already anticipating.

If this was the work of a serial killer—and her experience and instincts shouted that it was—then he was damn good at his job. Maybe the best she'd ever run across. And she'd need more than a condescending smile and a load of denial from her egotistical boss if she was going to catch the bastard.

Sickness churned in her stomach and turned her legs weak. Chastian couldn't be allowed to sweep this under the rug, like he did so many of the other ideas she went to him with. He couldn't be allowed to discount her ideas just because she was a woman and in his screwed-up opinion didn't belong in homicide. She knew how to do her job, and would be damned if she was going to let his sexist bullshit stand in the way of her doing what she knew was right.

A couple of frat boys cruised by, jostling her, and Genevieve nearly jumped out of her skin. One more sign that she was wound tight enough to break.

"Hey, baby, let me buy you a drink." One of them leered at her, his vacant eyes testimony to just how many drinks he'd already bought.

"I think you've had enough." She started to move away from him.

"Aww, come on, darlin', don't be like that." The second one blocked her way, and Genevieve sighed as she saw her day going from miserable to excruciating in the blink of an eye.

"Guys, you're already drunk off your asses and it's only"—she glanced at her watch—"seven thirty. Why don't you head back uptown and sleep it off?"

"Is that an invitation?" the first one asked, leaning in so close that she could almost identify the brand of beer he'd been slamming back.

"Not the kind you're looking for." Straightening up, she shoved past them. "Now scram."

With much grumbling, they did, and Genevieve started to walk away. But now the idea of a drink had begun to sound entirely too good to pass up. Maybe a hurricane—or three—would help get Jessica out of her head.

Shouldering around the crush of tourists standing in front of Pat O's, she slunk into the much less raucous bar a few doors down. If she couldn't force the memories out of her head, maybe she could drink them away. At least for tonight.

Cole Adams slid onto the barstool next to the blond bombshell with more curves than a baseball and wondered how to start up the conversation he was dying to have.

Should he open with the truth? He wasn't sure how well this beautiful woman would take to the fact that he'd been researching her for months. That he'd followed her from the police station. That he'd been lurking around outside the precinct, waiting for her to come out for nearly an hour.

That he wanted a whole lot more from her than she'd be willing to give.

He'd meant to stop her there, to tell her what he wanted right from the start. But she'd looked so enraged—and miserable—that he couldn't help wondering what had caused the devastation written so clearly on her face.

But before he could decide how to approach her, Genevieve had started off at a walk so fast it was nearly a run, and he'd been forced to follow her or lose his chance.

He couldn't afford to mess this up. Not now, when he'd finally gotten everything set up the way he wanted it.

Glancing at Genevieve out of the corner of his eye, he nearly snorted. Yeah, right. Things were going exactly as he'd planned.

Except that she looked more likely to shoot him than listen to him.

Plus, the speech he'd prepared sounded incredibly stupid now. Like a bad pickup line instead of the appeal to her conscience he'd intended.

Maybe he was just paranoid—and who could blame him? He'd done his homework on the NOPD so thoroughly that the face of every homicide detective on the force was familiar to him by now. But Genevieve's picture hadn't done her justice. On the computer screen, her hair had looked more of a dirty gray than the honey blond it really was, and her ample curves had been hidden under an ill-fitting suit. Now Cole was struggling to deal with the arousal that had wrapped around his gut like a fist at his first sight of her, and had only gotten worse as he'd watched her sinuous glide through the Quarter.

Looking at her from beneath his lashes, he watched her long, unpainted fingernails tap an impatient rhythm on the bar as she leaned back on her barstool in a parody of relaxation. What did it say about him that the guarded accessibility of her frame—combined with the sight of those loose, feminine fingers—had him longing for the feel of her against him? For the feel of her hand on his suddenly—and unexpectedly—hard cock?

Fuck, damn, shit. What was he, a horny teenager who couldn't keep his dick under control? Or a man who knew what he wanted, one with a secret to unravel and could find only one woman to help him do it?

This couldn't be happening. Not now, when he was so close to getting the ball rolling. Not now, when he had Detective Genevieve Delacroix almost exactly where he wanted her.

But it *was* happening, his body spinning rapidly out of control while his mind struggled to find a way to approach her that she wouldn't find threatening—or annoying.

"So, can I buy you a drink?" Her question came out of nowhere, in a no-nonsense tone and a voice that was pure, sugary Georgia peach. Smooth and silky and sweetly delicious, despite the hint of hard-ass he heard just below the surface.

Surprise swept through him, and he wondered if she would taste as good as she sounded. The contrast between her voice and her tone intrigued him, one more example of the numerous contradictions that seemed to make her up.

The lush body covered by that ridiculous suit.

The indolent pose belied by the watchful eyes.

The gorgeous voice with the don't-fuck-with-me tone.

It made him wonder who the real Genevieve Delacroix was. Made him want to fuck with her—to fuck her—and to hell with the consequences.

As he struggled to regain control—to keep his eye on the prize—the wicked curve of her lips kept interfering with his concentration.

"What are you offering?" He kept his voice low as he angled his body toward hers, savoring the rush of arousal pouring through him. Inconvenient or not, it had been far too long since he'd felt this instantaneous reaction to a woman.

Her barely there smile turned into a smirk. "That depends what you ask for."

He nodded to the bartender who had sidled up to the other side of the bar. "A shot of Patrón Silver."

"Interesting choice." Genevieve quirked a brow before turning to the bartender. "I'll take an Absolut and cranberry."

After the bartender moved away, she leveled a pair of deep blue eyes at him and Cole fought the urge to squirm. Genevieve had cop eyes—world-weary, cynical and more than willing to believe the worst.

For a split second, it was like looking in a mirror, his own tormented emotions of the past few years staring back at him. But then a shutter came down, blocking him from seeing anything but a sardonic amusement that sent shivers up his spine.

"So," she demanded as she leaned forward until her mouth was only inches from his own. "Do you often drink alone?"

It was his turn to raise a brow. "I'm new in town. I don't have anyone else to drink with."

"I'd feel sorry for you, but I get the impression that's more by choice than necessity." Her cerulean eyes glowed as they swept over him, and he couldn't stop his body from clenching in response.

"So what about you?"

She inclined her head. "What about me?" Her peaches-and-cream voice was ripe with approval, and he felt his cock throb. Shifting a little, he tried to adjust himself so his hard-on wasn't so obvious—or painful. But a quick glance at Genevieve told him that she was more than aware of his dilemma—and that she was enjoying it.

"Do *you* often drink alone?" He parroted her words back at her, determined to gain control of the conversation.

"Who says I'm alone? I could be waiting for someone."

She was bluffing—pushing him hard with her fuck-off voice and come-hither body language—and normally he'd be more than happy to go along for the ride. But now wasn't the time for this, he reminded himself forcibly.

"Should I leave?" He started to stand.

"No!" For just a moment her facade slipped, giving him one more glimpse of the frustrated, tired, too-pissed-off-to-be-alone woman behind the mask.

He sank back into his chair. "I'm Cole, by the way." He held out a hand.

"Genevieve." She hesitated before placing her hand against his.

"Afraid?" he asked with a smirk, unable to stop himself.

"Of you?" Her hand met his in a firm, no-nonsense clasp, her eyes narrowing in derision.

"Is there someone else here?" She tried to tug her hand back, but he didn't let go. Couldn't let go, any more than he could stop the cocky, shit-eating grin from crossing his face. It was going to be fun as hell testing her, seeing what she was made of.

Seeing just how far he could push before she began to shove back.

It might not be the wisest course of action, but then again, he'd given up being smart when he came to this hellhole of a city, intent on finding a truth that had eluded him for seven long years.

"I don't know." She glanced around the bar, let her eyes linger teasingly on some guy near the door. "Is there?"

As the guy straightened up and made a move toward them, Cole scowled fiercely. Then gave a sharp tug on Genevieve's hand that had her out of her chair and between his legs before she knew what was happening. He wrapped his free hand around her hip and pulled her even closer, so that her thighs rested against his aroused cock.

Those blue eyes sparked with a fury that was cold as ice, and he expected her to struggle—for one brief moment, even wanted her to. His brain was sending all kinds of messages, calling him every name in the book, even as it warned him that he was blowing everything before his plan had a chance to get off the ground.

But for the first time in his life, his body had sole possession of the driver's seat, his suddenly unruly libido shrugging off the warning signs like they didn't exist—even as he fought for control.

For one brief, terrifying moment, he thought about forgetting the whole thing, about saying "Fuck it" and just reveling in the moment.

About taking this woman any and every way he could have her and letting the chips fall where they may.

How had she gotten him so hot so quickly? In the long years following Samantha's death, he'd never let anyone get under his skin. Ever.

And this wasn't how their first meeting was supposed to turn out—with him fantasizing about what she looked like in the throes of one orgasm after another.

He was supposed to be laying the groundwork. Feeling her out. Checking to see if she really was as good as her record said she was. An hour ago her competence—or lack thereof—had been the most important thing on his mind. But now all he could think about was what it would feel like to come in her mouth. In her pussy. In her lush, gorgeous ass.

He tried to tamp down on the arousal, but that was like trying to put out a wildfire with a spray bottle—especially since he could feel the heat and arousal coming off her. Could see her nipples peaking beneath the thin material of her blouse. Could hear the hitch in her breathing as she too struggled for control.

He'd come to New Orleans looking for peace, had sought Genevieve out for just that purpose. But the aroused, out-of-control, gotta-have-her-now feeling that had grabbed him by the balls the second he'd laid eyes on her was anything but peaceful.

Gritting his teeth, he pulled himself back from the edge. It wasn't easy when he wanted to be inside of her more than he wanted his next breath. Almost more than he wanted the answers he'd come here to get.

But the look on Genevieve's face said she'd been pushed—or pulled—as far as she was going to allow. Aroused or not, her next move would be to take a swing at him.

For a minute, he could almost taste the coppery tang of blood in his mouth. It might be worth it.

"You're going to want to let go of me." Her voice was low and hot, a warning if he'd ever heard one.

"I'm not so sure about that." His hands tightened—on her hip and her palm—holding her to him for one endless moment. The image of what she would look like spread-eagled on his bed, her pale skin gleaming against the midnight silk of the sheets, roared through him, and for a second he was afraid he wouldn't be able to let her go.

But his brain was screaming at him, the warning signals having turned into bright red flags of alarm, and somehow he found the strength to release her.

The bartender chose that second to drop their drinks on the bar, and he grabbed the ice-cold shot of tequila like it was a lifeline. Slammed it back and gestured for another one. He was teetering on the brink of madness, his body out of his control. His desire for Genevieve nearly palpable in the small distance she'd created between them.

What was wrong with him? he wondered, tossing back the second shot as quickly as he had the first. He'd never reacted like this to a woman before, had never felt like he would give anything—and everything—just to be inside one.

But Genevieve . . . in a few brief moments, Genevieve had turned him inside out. It was ridiculous, absurd. And he—

"You're not as uncomplicated as you look." Her voice broke into his self-flagellation, had him turning to her with hot eyes he couldn't hope to cool down.

"I could say the same thing about you." He forced a calm into his voice that he was far from feeling.

"Yeah, well, I had a crappy day." She stuck out her chin at him. "What's your excuse?"

"I wasn't aware I needed one."

Very deliberately, she glanced down at where his hands were clenched into fists before taking a long sip of her drink. "It's pretty obvious that you need something."

Her words—cold and taunting—slammed through him. God, she

was amazing—her icy control housed a hot fire, one that was tempting as hell.

"And what is it you think I need?"

For the first time, he saw a flash of uncertainty in her eyes and couldn't help wondering at its cause. A heavy silence stretched between them, long and taut and more than a little uncomfortable. Just when he'd decided that he'd blown it—that she wasn't going to answer—Genevieve took a deep breath.

"Me," she said, in a voice that was as steady as it was unexpected.

Chapter Two

As soon as the word left her mouth, Genevieve wanted to snatch it back. To bury it—and her desires—so deep inside herself that they could never escape. But she didn't.

She couldn't.

Words stuck in her throat, while her body throbbed with a combination of desire and nervousness that all but overwhelmed her.

She knew she would probably regret this in the morning. Hell, she was having second thoughts already; she wasn't in the habit of picking up men and inviting them home with her. But it had been so long since she'd been held, so long since a man had comforted her in the dead of night.

After the week she'd had, she would sell her soul for a little comfort.

Would do anything to avoid knocking around her empty, echoing house in an effort to find sleep.

Would do whatever she had to do to get one night of peace.

It had been months—years—since she'd managed to close her eyes without being haunted by all the violence she couldn't stop.

She glanced at Cole, saw he was as startled by her invitation as she was, and somehow that made the next step easier to take. She didn't know who this man was—what he was—but she wanted him.

Needed him, in a way that was as enticing as it was unfamiliar.

To give her hands and mouth something to do, Genevieve reached for her glass and drained it in one long sip. Then set the glass on the bar with a flourish as she eyed Cole with an unmistakable challenge. "Cat got your tongue?" she demanded. "Or was it something I said?"

He stared down at her from his formidable height—at least six-foot-five—with the blackest eyes she'd ever seen.

The thought caught her unawares, and for long moments she struggled against it, against the need and arousal winding their way through her belly and chest.

Cole kept her waiting—much longer than another man might have, and damned if watching him watch her didn't make her hotter still. She was trapped, ensnared, every cell in her body completely focused on him as she waited for his response.

His strong jaw worked for long seconds, as if he was biting back an instinctual comeback, while his big, rough hands clenched and unclenched in a rhythm that had her nipples tightening and her womb spasming. His heavily muscled body tensed as if to spring, and his arousal throbbed in the air between them.

She felt a shiver work its way up her spine—it was an unbelievable thrill to have this strong, sexy man at a disadvantage. Would be even more of a thrill to have him beneath her in bed.

Or above her, Genevieve acknowledged, as she eyed his broad shoulders and lean waist. With his too-long black hair and too-handsome face, Cole-with-no-last-name struck her as the kind of guy who liked to be on top.

She suppressed another shiver. Tonight, that was more than fine with her—it gave her one more excuse to check her worries at the door and take whatever he could give her. And—if she was lucky—just a little bit more.

Her body quivered, desire a living, breathing animal inside her—so wild that it nearly drowned out the horror, and the sorrow, of her day. And still he didn't answer, just stared at her with eyes the color of midnight.

Then, in a move so fast she would have missed it if she'd blinked, he pulled out his wallet and dropped two twenties on the bar.

"I live uptown." His voice was low, gravelly—filled with sex and promises she couldn't help but respond to.

"I'm closer," she countered breathlessly, as he grasped her elbow and propelled her toward the door.

"We'll go to my place." His voice brooked no argument as he moved ahead of her to clear a path through the crowded bar.

He moved like a jungle cat—each step a smooth, sinuous flexing of long, lean muscle that was no less threatening for its captivating beauty.

And no less perilous.

An unfamiliar fear filled her. Her mouth turned dry as a desert, while her palms ran with sweat. Her heart beat like a metronome on speed, while her breath caught in her throat.

For one long, interminable moment she thought about stopping. Thought about backing away. Thought about doing *anything* but following this man to his house like a lamb to slaughter.

Her empty house rose in front of her eyes, taunting her with one more sleepless night. Morbid pictures blocked her vision, ridiculing her with each new failure. And still she might have changed her mind—might have retreated into the restless, roiling crowd and lost herself.

But Cole chose that moment to turn, to pin her with eyes that were still wicked—still dark, still delicious. Still devastating. She jerked in response, arousal blooming in her belly, and she knew she was going nowhere without him.

The realization should have frightened her, but it didn't.

It should have had her calling out for help, but the words refused to form.

It should have had her backing away, but she kept her feet firmly planted despite the nearly overwhelming urge to flee. Shoving her misgivings down, refusing to do more than halfheartedly acknowledge them, Genevieve returned his stare with interest. And felt the spark all the way to her toes as her temperature shot into the stratosphere and then beyond.

It was too late for second thoughts.

The hunter had just become the hunted.

They hailed an empty cab outside the bar and Cole flung the door open, ushering her in first.

They didn't speak as the taxi crawled through the dark, crowded streets, though Cole gripped her hand like she somehow offered salvation—his thumb stroking her knuckles in a rhythm that was both soothing and seductive.

When they hit a pothole, his fingers tightened instinctively on hers, and she felt herself grow wetter, hotter—until all that mattered was Cole and how he would feel inside of her.

Her sex pulsed at the thought, and Genevieve squeezed her legs together in a fruitless search for relief. *Just a few more minutes*, she told herself as she fought the aching discomfort. Just a little longer and she would finally have Cole exactly where she wanted him.

His hand tightened on hers, as if he sensed her discomfort. But when she glanced up at him, his face was granite hard and expressionless.

A shiver worked its way up her spine, and the voice in the back of her head whispered that she was being stupid. She knew the voice was right—she was being careless and foolish and entirely too trusting—but she couldn't bring herself to back out. To end this thing before it ever got started.

Another glance up at him—into his eyes this time—had her doubts dwindling like so much dust. He wasn't as remote as he would like her to think. His eyes were blazing with a passion that more than equaled her own.

The cab drew to a stop in front of one of the historic homes on St. Charles. As big as it was well preserved, she got a vague impression of stately beauty as Cole paid the driver and hustled her up the steps. But before she could do more than glance at the outside, Cole was slamming through the front door—his hand an unyielding clamp around her wrist.

How could she be this hot, Genevieve wondered dimly, for a man she'd only just met? How could she want anything—anyone—this badly?

She didn't know the answer to the questions, and after a second, didn't care. Her body was literally vibrating with the need to feel Cole against her, inside her. He was a wild man, a sorcerer, and he had bewitched her. There was no other explanation for her behavior. For her desperation to feel his body against hers.

The second he kicked the door shut behind them, she was on him. Her hands around his waist, her lips trailing kisses down his bare back as she struggled with his belt.

"Not yet," he growled, shifting in her arms. Turning her so that her back was against the wall.

She arched against him, felt his cock twitch as she opened her legs so he could settle between them. Grinned at the fact that she could drive him as crazy as he was driving her.

His hands went to the buttons of the shirt she wore and he yanked it off, dropping the ruined silk onto the floor beside them. Then he was slipping his hands into her waistband, tugging. She heard a tearing sound and glanced down just in time to see her favorite pair of work pants fall in tatters around her feet.

Cole stepped back and surveyed his handiwork, noting with appreciation how Genevieve's chest heaved and her body quivered. She was the most beautiful thing he'd ever seen, standing there in nothing but black lace, her back against the wall. A tiger momentarily tamed, but ready to attack at any moment.

His back flexed at the thought, the need to feel her claws digging into him a burning pain that couldn't be denied. Part of him was shocked at what he was doing, astounded at his need to control her. To drive her beyond boundaries, beyond control, until all she felt was him.

All she knew was him.

All she wanted was him.

He'd always been dominant, had always needed to be the one in control—especially after his sister had died—but never had he taken it this far before. Never had he let the dark side of himself go.

He was on wild, uncharted ground.

But seeing the need in Genevieve's eyes—feeling the desperation she couldn't hide—freed the beast inside him, had him slipping the leash in his desperate desire to claim her.

Leaning down, he grabbed her wrists, held them above her head. Then he captured her mouth with his own, using his lips and tongue and teeth to brand her in a way she wouldn't soon forget. A way she couldn't forget.

But, God, was she sweet. Like honey and lavender and warm, sweet sunshine. He nipped at her lower lip, reveled in the moan she couldn't stop. Sucked it into his mouth in an effort to ease the ache.

She went wild, her strong warrior's body bucking against him. Her wrists jerked against his hand, but he wasn't ready to let her go yet. Couldn't let her go, if the truth were known. One touch of her long, slender fingers and he would go up in flames.

So he kept her pinned, using his hand and chest and hips. Made sure every part of her body was covered by every part of his. And then he went about devouring her.

He kissed the softness of her lips, the corners of her mouth. Traced his tongue along her full bottom lip, lingering at the cupid's bow in the center of her upper lip.

"Cole," she gasped, her head rocking back and forth against the wall. "Hurry up, finish it. You'll drive me crazy."

"I like you crazy," he answered, but took advantage of her open mouth to thrust his tongue inside. She was like velvet, softer than he could have imagined. Hotter than he had dreamed. He tried to be gentle, to give her the tenderness she deserved.

But the second he tasted her, he was lost. Lust rose, sharp and terrible and all-consuming. It raked its talons through his belly, got in his head and demanded that he take her. That he fuck her, again and again, until she couldn't remember her own name, let alone any man who had come before him.

And still he kissed her, unwilling to give up her lips. Unable to break the connection when everything inside of him roared that she was his.

He did crazy, wild things to her mouth, reveling in each moan and cry that escaped her lips and entered his. He sucked her tongue, pulled it inside his mouth and nearly fell to his knees when she explored him as he had done her.

Fighting back a yell of triumph, he rejoiced in the fact that her body was nearly as crazed as his own. Ripping his mouth from hers, he ignored her moan of protest and the blind seeking of her lips as she tried to regain his mouth.

Instead he trailed his lips down her cheek, over the long, graceful curve of her neck to the delicate bones of her shoulders. How could she be so fragile and yet so strong? Another contradiction. Another piece of the puzzle he was dying to solve.

Using his free hand, he reached behind her and freed the clasp of her bra. Then let go of her wrists long enough to rip the thing off her. He had to taste her, had to feel her beautiful nipples in his mouth, had to feast on her before he imploded.

Sinking to his knees in front of her, he relished the feel of her hands digging deep into his hair, enjoyed the sharp tug on his scalp. The little pinches of pain only made the pleasure sweeter.

Then he forgot everything but the ecstasy of her body as he buried his face in her breasts in a frenzy of desire. He didn't have the patience, or the control, for delicacy. Instead, he simply latched on to a nipple and sucked it hard into his mouth.

She screamed, the hands in his hair tightening. For a moment he feared he'd been too rough, that he'd crossed the thin line between pleasure and pain. But her hips were moving, shifting, pumping restlessly against his chest. And he knew she was with him all the way.

Genevieve groaned, moving her hips against Cole in a maelstrom of need. He was killing her, *killing* her. Devouring her until she was unsure where she left off and he started.

And, God, was he good—and bad. Oh, so bad. She was going to lose it if he didn't do something, and soon. Trembling on the brink of orgasm, she was ready to fly over the edge at the slightest provocation.

But Cole was a master of suspense, a wicked lover who somehow knew her body better than she did. Who played her like an instrument. Who controlled her and denied her that final pleasure until he was ready to send her over.

As his teeth nipped at her areola, she nearly screamed with frustrated need. Only the knowledge that he wanted her to, that he was trying to drive her completely insane, kept her quiet. But when he soothed the nip with his tongue, taking care to make sure the sting was well and truly gone before moving on to the underside of her breast, she lost the fight.

No man should be so tender and so controlling at the same time—it went against the laws of nature. "Cole," she whimpered, clutching his head to her breast, relishing the soft, delicate sweeps of his tongue. Thrilling in the love bites that sent shivers of desire through her entire body. "Please."

"Oh, sweetheart," he murmured as he moved to the other breast. "I'm just getting started."

"No," she gasped, her fingers clutching at his shoulders as she sobbed out his name. Her body wasn't hers to command anymore, her voice and thoughts and movements taken over entirely by the wizardry of his mouth, of his touch.

He shifted, caught her wrists again in his big hands. Pulled them forward and clasped them in front of her body with one hand. "What are you—"

"Look." His voice was deep, gravelly, unfamiliar in his desire for her. She felt a sharp rush at the thought that she had done this to him, that she had driven this strong, beautiful man so crazy with lust that he could barely speak.

Then she glanced down and was transfixed by the sight in the dim light. He'd captured her wrists in such a way that her arms framed her breasts, plumping the already full mounds up and out for his pleasure.

For her pleasure too, because already she could feel the increase of blood flow to the constricted area. But he wasn't done, the hand on her wrists tightening so that her arms squeezed her breasts even more tightly. They actually stung, the air alone chafing her unbelievably sensitive nipples.

"You're so beautiful like this," he muttered, his tongue darting out to tease and caress.

She whimpered, her knees threatening to collapse beneath her, but he leaned forward again, until the pressure of his chest and shoulders pinning her to the wall was all that kept her upright. Bending his head, he took her nipple in his mouth. She gasped, begging for mercy, but he had none as he bit and licked, sucked and nuzzled her into the most intense orgasm of her life.

Wrapped up in the incredible heat burning through her breasts and the empty aching of her pussy, the climax caught Genevieve by surprise. Though she'd known she was close—so close—she hadn't expected to hurtle over with nothing but the touch of his mouth on her breast.

But as he lapped at her, taking as much of her aching breast into his mouth as he could, she felt herself begin to tremble from the inside out. There was a roaring in her head, a fuzziness that overtook her as pleasure like nothing she'd ever experienced slammed through her body.

She convulsed again and again, wave after wave of ecstasy shooting through her, sizzling along her nerve endings, lighting her up like a bottle rocket until she was flying, soaring, into the endless night sky.

She came back to earth slowly, shocked at the heights she'd scaled. Uncertain about the amount of pleasure Cole had given her. Desperate to feel his body inside of her, to have him anchor her before she spun so far out of control that she'd never find her way back.

She clutched at his shoulders, suddenly needing comfort, and he understood. Standing, he pulled her to him, his arms hard around her newly chilled body. For the first time she realized she was all but naked while he was fully clothed.

"Cole," she whispered, embarrassed. Wondering where the hard-ass detective had gone.

"Don't think," he answered, his lips skimming over her eyelids and across her temples. "Just feel. I need to be inside you, sweet Genevieve."

"Yes," she murmured, because it was what she wanted too. Because there was no way she could turn him away unsatisfied after he'd given her such incredible pleasure. Besides, she needed desperately to be a part of him.

With one fluid movement, Cole swept her against him and into his arms. Despite her height, Genevieve felt too light—as if she'd been starving herself for far too long. Though if he had her job, he might be tempted to give up eating as well. God knew he'd dealt with enough ugly incidents while making his documentaries, and still he couldn't contemplate facing what she did every day of her life.

She shifted in his arms, the softness of her left breast pressing against him, and his thoughts were wrenched forcibly from the gutter to the bedroom.

As he stepped over the threshold into his room, he admitted it was a much better place to be.

He pulled her more tightly against him and she sighed in delight, wriggling as she tried to get closer. Oh, his tough little detective had a soft side, no matter how hard she tried to hide it. One ripe with a sensuality that couldn't be denied.

The thought made him smile even as he burned. It was that sensuality he planned on catering to tonight.

Crossing the room without bothering to turn on a light, he set her on the bed with her feet dangling only inches off the floor. Then he stepped back and watched as she all but melted into the butter-soft comforter, her body relaxed, her eyes closed.

He looked at her for long moments, her figure hazy in the dim light flowing in from the hallway. She was beautiful. Perfect. His cock kicked and twitched at the thought, reminding him that she was the only one who'd come so far.

He had plans to change that, and as she rolled to the side, murmuring, "The light," he figured she was more than on board. A mere glance of his fingers against the base of his bedside lamp had a dim, rosy light filling the room.

"I want to see you," she said, reaching for him.

"Not as much as I want to see you." He settled on the bed next to her, rolled her to her back. Pulled her arms above her head and just looked at her for a while.

Finally—long seconds after he'd expected her to—she jerked against his restraining hands. "Hey," she said. "It's my turn to touch you."

"Soon." But he let go of her wrists, allowed his hands once again to wander to the plumpness of her breasts. "You're amazing." He squeezed a nipple, smiled in delight as it hardened instantly beneath his fingers. "Absolutely unbelievable."

"I could say the same about you." She arched into his hand, her eyes drifting closed as the pleasure once again found her.

But he wasn't letting her go that easy, not this time. "No," he said, tugging insistently at the hard bud. "I want you to watch. To see."

Her eyes opened lazily. "I've already seen it. When you're ready to let me see *you*, let me know. I'll be all eyes."

"Really?" He stood and shed his black T-shirt in record seconds. Then sank to his knees in front of her. "Spread your legs."

"Already?" she asked, jacking up on her elbows. "I want to feel you—"

"Oh, you will, sweetheart. You will." He knew his voice was harsh, strangled by the desire ripping through him with each shallow breath. But he couldn't help it, any more than he could help the hands that moved of their own volition and settled on her thighs. He forced her legs apart, demanding her obedience before she could give it to him. Then he leaned back and simply looked at her.

He never would have figured her for a thong girl, not the tough-as-nails detective he'd researched so carefully. But here was the proof, the black lace Brazilian thong cupping her sex like a lover. Nestling between the folds of her pussy as he was so desperate to do.

Reaching out, he trailed a finger along the edge of the undergarment, relishing each gasp and shiver his journey elicited. "Tell me," he said as he leaned forward until his hot breath was only inches from her beautiful mons, her sexy clit. "Do you have more of these?" He pulled the waistband out and allowed it to snap back against her stomach with a satisfying *smack*.

"Yes." It was a gasp, and a barely coherent one at that.

"Good." He smiled at her, let her see the wicked promise in his eyes. Then leaned forward and with his teeth, ripped the thing to shreds.

Dear God, was all Genevieve could think as she stared at the torn remnants of her most comfortable underwear.

Dear God, what was she doing?

Dear God, how was she ever going to survive this night? Cole was shameless, shameful, and he made her feel the same.

"Please." She lifted her hand to his hair, tangled her fingers in the cool midnight strands. "I need you."

"And you'll have me," he answered, nipping at her inner thighs with his teeth. Electricity shot straight from the bites to her clit, making her crazy. His next words made her crazier still. "Every way you can take me, you'll have me."

His tongue darted out, traced her slit in one long, slow sweep.

She nearly came off the bed, her body out of her control for the first time in her life. "Cole!" The cry was low, keening. A plea for him to stop, to continue, to do something—anything—to relieve her of the sensual misery he had thrust her into.

But he ignored her, simply sat back on his heels and prepared to feast. His need was red-hot now, his cock threatening to burst. But he fought back the desire, sublimated it. She would come for him again, come against his mouth this time. Only then—when she'd lost all control—would he give in to the lust driving him to the brink of madness. Only then would he let himself climax.

Clamping his hands on her upper thighs, he pushed her knees wide enough so that he could wedge his shoulders between them. Whispered to her of everything he was going to do to her. And then leaned forward and thrust his tongue as deeply inside of her as he could reach.

She went wild, her body thrashing against him. Her hands clutched his hair, her legs spasmed and she screamed as she arched against his mouth.

He held her still, stopped the bucking of her hips with a heavy hand on her stomach and continued to take her higher. She was delicious, intoxicating, the sweetest honey he had ever known, and in that moment he wanted her more than he'd ever wanted anything in his life.

"Cole!" It was a plea, a demand, a cry for surcease, but he couldn't stop. He had to have her, had to taste every drop of her sweetness, had to experience every shudder and cry she could give him. Stroking deep, he concentrated on hitting every sensitive spot she had, worked to take her higher than anyone ever had before.

When she was just about there, when she was sobbing and pleading and he sensed she couldn't take any more, he pulled his tongue out of her luscious warmth. Slipping his hands beneath her ass, he lifted her up, opened her wider, and closed his teeth gently around her clit.

Her body arched violently as she came, bucking so wildly that she almost dislodged him. But he held on, used his tongue and teeth and lips to ride her through one climax to another and another.

He was a man possessed, utterly enchanted by, completely addicted to the exquisite feeling he got from giving her pleasure. He could stay like this forever, his cock throbbing, his mouth buried in her hungry, sweet, incredibly responsive pussy. Making her come could be his new obsession.

Sliding first one finger and then another into her, he nearly lost it at the unbelievable perfection of her body. She was tight, hot, her muscles clenching in a rhythm he could feel resonating all the way to his dick.

Genevieve bit her lip, tried to stop the screams rising within her. But it was no use. She was going insane. Cole was driving her completely, around-the-bend, no-holds-barred insane. His tongue was everywhere, pushing her from one orgasm to another and another. And his finger was thrusting inside of her, stroking her G spot and then pulling out while he sucked at her clit until she had gone beyond individual orgasms, was instead moving from one climax to the next in a never-ending stream that became one long orgasm without beginning or end.

She fought to hold on to sanity, to break the hold Cole had on her. But he was pushing her into the bed, the palm of his hand massaging her stomach while his long fingers played over her mons.

She lost the ability to talk, to think, to breathe. He was taking her over completely, making her his in this most intimate, most violent act. Conquering her until she no longer knew who controlled her body, until she gave up everything she was and could be to him.

"Cole, I can't take it. I can't—"

"Yes, you can," he growled, his tongue circling her clit and sending her higher still. "You'll take more and more and more until there's nothing left. You'll take everything."

And then he bit her, and her body went spinning into space, the pleasure beyond anything she'd ever known before. Beyond anything she'd even dreamed existed.

Digging her hands into his shoulders, she held on for dear life. Desperate for something solid to keep her anchored. Desperate for Cole to help her find her way out of this maelstrom of sensation and emotion he had thrust her into.

But there was nothing of the savior in Cole, only the need to brand her in a way he didn't understand. He'd had a lot of women, had used his fame and charm and looks to take whomever he wanted, whenever he wanted.

But Genevieve was different, a primitive voice in the back of his head warned him even as it urged him on. As it pressed him to touch her everywhere, anywhere, to mark her so that she could never forget whom she belonged to. She was more than he'd ever thought he'd find.

Thrusting his tongue inside of her, he sent her over the edge to one final climax before skimming his mouth across the curve of her hip to the flat plane of her stomach and the sunburst tattoo that encircled her navel. Unable to resist, he sank his teeth into the soft flesh of her waist, relished the cry she didn't try to hold back. He soothed the hurt with his tongue and lips before pulling back.

"What—" she asked, dazed. Confused. Her body trembling in the aftermath of so much pleasure.

His balls were on fire, his cock burning with the need to bury itself in all that heat. Flipping her onto her stomach, he reached into his nightstand and snagged a condom. Rolled it on. And then, intertwining his fingers with hers, he wrapped their hands around the iron slats of his headboard—his hands covering hers—and thrust into her from behind.

She cried out, arched wildly, tugged as if to free her hands from his grip. But he held on, covering her with his body. Sinking his teeth deep into her shoulder to hold her still as he pounded into her again and again.

He was rough, as he'd intended to be, any gentleness he'd had in him used up by the long, sexy minutes of eating her out. But he made sure that every cry he pulled from her was of pleasure, made sure that every stroke into her body took her one step higher.

He rode her hard and fast, slamming her into the mattress again and again. Each thrust was a frenzy of raging need, each stroke a declaration of control and ownership.

And she was eating it up, her muscles clenching more and more tightly around him as she begged for more. He kneed her legs apart so he could go deeper, driving his cock so hard and deep inside of her that she'd never forget the feel of him. Never forget who was in control.

Sobbing, Genevieve dug her fingernails into his hands, hanging on for dear life as his powerful thrusts moved her up and down the mattress. "You have to—you have to," she gasped, her body shaking uncontrollably as she clenched her pussy even tighter around his dick.

He saw stars and his body screamed for relief. But he refused to give up, to give in. She would come one more time.

Easing his teeth from her shoulder, he licked the marks and whispered, "No, sweetheart, *you* have to." Then followed the words with a desperate lunge inside of her. "Let it take you, sweet Genevieve. Let it have you."

She screamed, her back arching beneath him like a bow as the waves exploded through her, her pussy clenching around his cock again and again. Gritting his teeth, he kept up the hard, steady strokes until sweat streamed down his body. Until his muscles—and his cock—cried out for relief. Until yet another orgasm whipped through Genevieve and she screamed his name while she came.

Only then did he let himself go, the release that swept through him so strong and violent that for a moment it was like death itself.

Chapter Three

Genevieve woke up slowly, her well-used body aching in places she hadn't known could ache. But Cole had been insatiable throughout the night—they both had—reaching for each other again and again as evening spun into night and night into dawn.

How many times had she come, she wondered as she stretched languidly. More than enough to keep the nightmares at bay. Well, it was hard to have nightmares when your brain was almost complete and total mush.

Was it possible to come too much? She pondered the question as she reached a lazy hand across the bed for her lover. Because she wouldn't mind one more—

Her hand met nothing but cold sheets, and her eyes opened of their own volition. "Cole?" she called, her voice carrying in the silent house.

"Cole?" she tried again as she sat up, but he still didn't answer.

She tried to reassure herself that he was merely downstairs making coffee, that he hadn't given her the best night of her life and then snuck out of his own house before—she glanced at the clock on the bedside table—eight o'clock in the morning. But the house was too still, too lifeless around her.

He *had* left.

Genevieve sighed as her hopes of a quickie before work faded—along with the loose, relaxed feeling she'd awoken with. Climbing out of bed, she saw her clothes and shoes stacked neatly on the chair by the door.

Here's your hat; what's your hurry? she thought sardonically as she crossed the room on legs that were much shakier than she would have liked. Or was this more *Don't let the door hit you in the ass on your way out?*

Definitely the latter, she decided, as she grabbed her clothes with angry hands. He was the one who'd insisted they come back to his place; if he'd wanted to do a disappearing act in the morning, he should have let her take him home instead.

But could she really blame him, she wondered, as she sank into the chair, her legs shaking so badly that they wouldn't support her. She had picked him up in a bar—had behaved like the quintessential one-night stand. Was it his fault he'd given her the best sex of her life—by an amazing margin? Of course not, no more than it was his fault that she suddenly wanted to stick around for more.

Too bad he hadn't felt the same way.

Her gaze wandered to the bathroom, and she wondered if she dared take a shower before she let herself out. Maybe she should just get dressed and head home. . . .

Her gaze dropped to the tattered underwear and shirt in her hands—it would be a miracle if she made it home without her clothes falling off. Cole had really done a number on them the night before, and the idea of wearing them again—especially without a shower—just didn't appeal.

A hot shower was the least he owed her, she decided, as she put the clothes aside and headed into the bathroom. After all, he had shredded more than two hundred dollars' worth of clothing the night before. The fact that she'd enjoyed every second of it was of absolutely no consequence.

It wasn't until she was in the bathroom, shower running, that she glanced at the bathroom vanity and saw the note he'd left between the two sinks.

I had an appointment I couldn't miss this morning, but please stick around. I won't be long. I hope you're still in bed when I get back, but if you're not, feel free to take a shower and start a pot of coffee. I'll be back soon—with breakfast.

Genevieve reread the note three times, a goofy smile on her lips that she couldn't seem to shake off. He hadn't walked out on her—he'd merely gone to get something for them to eat. Her stomach growled at the thought, reminding her of just how many calories she'd expended the night before.

But even hunger couldn't wipe out the rosy glow that surrounded her—it seemed her first one-night stand was working out better than she could possibly have imagined.

After a quick shower, Genevieve slipped into her work pants sans her tattered underwear. The button was missing to the pants, but at least the zipper still worked—though she had no idea how it had survived Cole's brutal handling. Her shirt, however, was another matter—if she tried to wear it home, she was asking for an indecency charge.

After debating with herself for a minute or two, she finally decided Cole wouldn't mind if she borrowed a T-shirt—especially if she washed it and got it back to him in the next couple of days.

Crossing to his dresser, she opened and closed three drawers in quick succession and found underwear, sweatpants and socks, but no T-shirts. She finally struck pay dirt when she turned to his closet, and couldn't help smiling at the neatly folded stack of black T-shirts of all different types and logos. There was one to fit every mood and occasion.

Tugging a shirt randomly from the bottom of the pile, she stepped back, startled, as a large manila folder came with it.

A paper clip from the file had gotten snagged on one of the shirt's arms, and as she pulled them apart, the contents of the file slipped onto the floor.

Cursing, she dropped to her knees and began to pick up the documents and pictures, trying to clean up the mess as quickly as possible. It would be just her luck for Cole to return home to find her apparently rifling through his personal effects. But as she shuffled a group of newspaper clippings together, she froze. Her eyes caught on one of the papers—her name was at the top of the page.

The clipping was over five years old, and showed her receiving an award for valor. She'd still been in uniform then, and more than a little uncomfortable receiving an award she hadn't felt she deserved. She hadn't done anything extraordinary, except to live through the nightmare that had killed her partner and three other cops, but her sergeant had disagreed. Had instead paraded her in front of God and everyone like a puppet on a string.

Anger burned in her gut, and she was shocked to realize it still grated even after all these years.

But what was Cole doing with the picture? She began sorting through the clippings. What was he doing with *all* these pictures of her and other NOPD homicide detectives? Of—her stomach began to churn—photos of homicide scenes that were months and years old?

With an unsteady breath, Genevieve forced herself to look through the entire file when what she really wanted to do was to shove everything back in and forget she'd ever seen any of it.

But she couldn't do that, she acknowledged as she rifled through the rest of the papers. As she came across a second picture of herself and then a third, her entire body began to shake so badly that she could barely hold the photos.

What kind of game was he playing?

What did he want with this information?

What did he want with her?

Panic welled within her as she continued to sift through the papers. There was a ton of research here—and all of it had to do with murder. Clippings of numerous sexual murders that had taken place in the last few years—including the two from earlier this year, open cases that Genevieve was still working.

The two murders she was *sure* were connected to the one she'd been called in on yesterday morning. The serial killings Chastian didn't want to believe in.

Doubts crowded her mind as she relived every second she'd spent with Cole since he'd sat down next to her at the bar last night. *Had he planned the whole thing?* she wondered as she continued to sift through the damning evidence. *Could he have intended for this to happen all along?*

She tried to reject the idea; *she* was the one who had spoken to him first. She was the one who had propositioned him. Surely, if he was the serial killer she was looking for, he wouldn't have been bold enough to accept her invitation.

She stopped at photos of the DuFray crime scene, her blood running cold at the familiar images. Lorelei DuFray had been a teacher—young, pretty, sweet. But by the time her killer had done with her, they had to use dental records to identify her.

Genevieve winced as she traced a finger over one particularly brutal photo. The crime photographer had managed to catch the body so that every jagged slash and tear was visible.

Shaking her head, she shoved the photo to the bottom of the pile, unable to bear the reminder of her failure for one more second. She'd opened this case three months before and had spent weeks working relentlessly as she'd tried to pin down the perp—all to no avail.

About six weeks later, another body had shown up—the cause of death strangulation instead of exsanguination, but to Genevieve's experienced eye, the murder had the same killer's sick and twisted stamp all over it.

The same way it had been all over the case she'd caught yesterday. Of course, she hadn't been able to do much investigating yet outside of the crime scene and the neighborhood the body had been found in. The girl's fingerprints hadn't popped, so even after hours of canvassing the area, they had no idea who she was.

Could Cole have done these terrible things? She closed her eyes, but still the pictures of Lorelei DuFray continued to haunt her. Had she unwittingly let a murderer into bed with her last night?

Had she let a twisted sexual predator inside of her?

Nausea had her stomach cramping, even as everything inside her rejected the notion that Cole could have done these things. He'd been so careful not to hurt her last night, had pushed her to the edge of her control but had never taken her past the point of comfort.

But then, she hadn't protested anything that he'd done either. If she had, would he have stopped? Last night, she would have said absolutely. But now—she glanced down at the incriminating file. Now all she could think was, *What if she'd been wrong?*

Sickness churned in her belly, beating at her brain and heart and lungs until all she could think of was escape. Cole would be back soon and she couldn't face him—not now. Not before she knew who he was and what he wanted.

Glancing around for something that would carry his prints, Genevieve settled on a couple of discarded condom wrappers and the glass he'd left by the bedside last night, after he'd gone to the kitchen for some water. After yanking an extra evidence bag out of her purse, she used the sheet to gingerly pick up the items and slide them into the bag.

Then, desperate to get out of there before Cole made it home, she shoved the file back where she'd found it and yanked the all but forgotten T-shirt over her head. Grabbing her purse and shoes, she ran for the door.

Cole walked away from the small, broken-down house on Magazine with rage in his gut and a cold fear in his heart. The interview hadn't gone as he'd planned; the woman had been so dried up and emotionally closed off that he'd barely learned anything from her.

Her daughter had been murdered seven years before, presumably by the same sick fuck who had killed his sister. But unlike Cole, this woman had put her faith in the police—and had lost a little bit more of her soul each day that her daughter's murderer remained on the street.

With a muttered oath, he glanced at his watch. This had taken longer than he'd thought, and Genevieve had probably woken up—alone. It wasn't what he'd planned for their first morning after. He should have gone with his instincts and canceled the appointment with Mrs. Harlow, but it had been so hard to get her to agree to see him that he hadn't wanted to do anything to spook her.

Now he was the one who was spooked—the utter hopelessness of the woman's face haunting him as he made his way through the humid New Orleans morning.

Ignoring the heat, he started walking back toward his house. It was a couple of miles away and normally he would have taken a cab, but right now the walk felt good. Necessary. The heat touching the part of him that had been frozen since Samantha had died, and had grown even colder as he'd interviewed poor Mrs. Harlow. It wasn't warming him, exactly, but it was keeping absolute despair at bay.

Would he end up like that? he wondered, as he turned left onto St. Charles and continued his trek. Cabs passed him, one after the other, but he didn't raise a hand to flag them down. Simply turned his face as they slowed and kept up his pace. Dried up and miserable, like Mrs. Harlow—a living shrine to the sister who had died so long ago? The world so out of his control that he no longer had a reason to get up in the morning?

For seven years vengeance had kept him going—the need to find Samantha's murderer at all costs. It had fueled the years of monitoring the police, the numerous private detectives, even his latest—and last—plan.

But what would he do if it didn't work?

What if Samantha's killer was never found, never charged?

Would he be able to move on, to live his life with the knowledge that that monster was still free? Still unpunished? Or would he shrivel up, become a soulless entity, just counting down the days until death?

He sped up until he was almost running, as if he could somehow go faster than his fears and the memories that haunted him more each day. What would he do if this stack of cards he was assembling failed? He was out of ideas, almost out of hope and Genevieve was his last chance.

Stopping at the corner market a few blocks before his house, he quickly picked up eggs and bacon, along with some fresh bread and fruit. He'd go home, make breakfast for Genevieve and then lay the whole sordid story out at her feet and pray she would agree to help him. Because if she didn't, he was completely screwed.

But when he opened the door to his house ten minutes later, he knew he had missed her—the warmth she'd brought to the house, and to him, was gone.

Still, he checked the bedroom for her, praying that he was mistaken. He wasn't—Genevieve was gone and she hadn't even bothered to leave him a note.

Cole went back down the stairs to the living room. Mindless of the fact that it was still well before noon, he crossed the huge room and poured himself a shot of Patrón. Tossed it back and wondered, miserably, what he was supposed to do now. What he could do now that he'd screwed everything up so badly.

With the bottle of tequila in one hand and the empty glass in the other, he headed back up the stairs to his office, where he turned on his laptop. While he waited for it to start up, he splashed more Patrón into the glass.

As soon as the computer was ready, his fingers began flying across its keyboard, amassing information at close to the speed of light. God bless the Internet—you really could get anything you wanted on the Web these days. Even information that wasn't readily available was just a few keystrokes away if you knew what you were doing.

Cole knew exactly what he was doing as he eyed the homicide photos that had been taken early yesterday morning. They'd been uploaded into the NOPD database yesterday afternoon, and he had retrieved them last night, before heading out in search of Genevieve.

Tossing back the shot he'd just poured, he reached for the bottle of Patrón he'd set to the right of the computer. Poured another shot into his glass and knocked it back.

What had he been thinking when he'd brought Genevieve home last night? Had he really expected her to sleep with him and then calmly listen—*after* the fact—while he laid out the reasons he'd gone looking for her to begin with?

He was a bigger fool than he'd thought, and now he was stuck between a rock and a hard place. He had to get to Genevieve, which meant he needed to go to the police station. At the same time, his sudden appearance there would seem suspicious to her; they hadn't exactly exchanged job descriptions the night before.

Would she believe him when he told her that bringing her home had had nothing to do with the movie he was making—nothing to do with Samantha? Or would she kick him out before he even got the chance to explain?

The second outcome was much more likely, he acknowledged, his fingers tensing on the keyboard. And if that happened—if that happened, he'd be right back where he'd started. With a bunch of research on dead women and a ton of photos he could barely stand to look at.

Glancing back at the computer screen, Cole ran through the photos of recent homicide scenes. He knew what he was looking for—something, anything, that might connect to Samantha. Something that might point him in the right direction, even after all this time.

But as he scanned the photos, he knew he'd hacked into the NOPD database for no reason—there was nothing here, nothing at all that resembled what had happened to his sister. And yet he couldn't deny a horrified fascination with the pictures. Couldn't help wanting Genevieve to find whoever had done these terrible things. So that some other family could find a modicum of the peace that continued to elude him seven years after his baby sister's brutal murder.

Genevieve could bring him peace. The thought sprang unbidden into his head, even as he snarled at the absurdity of it. She'd done a lot of things to him last night—made him sweat, made him swear, made his body respond in a way it hadn't for a very long time, if ever. But bring him peace—no, he wouldn't describe the riotous emotions she caused in him as anything close to peaceful. Yet she could be the answer to his prayers, the salvation he'd spent so long looking for. *If* he stuck to the plan and controlled his suddenly out-of-control libido.

Shit, fuck, damn. He slammed back another shot as his body tightened uncomfortably. What the hell was Genevieve doing in homicide anyway? She was too hot for this job, too sexy to waste her life investigating the dead. She belonged somewhere far away from all of this—

before she ended up a victim of the very criminals she'd spent her career trying to stop.

The idea of one day staring at homicide photos of his sexy blond cop had him swearing and downing his drink yet again. His hands were shaking, his heart beating wildly, but he ignored them. Stared harder at the broken, bloody bodies on the computer screen. Tried his damnedest not to see Genevieve in the same position as the dead women in the photographs.

He reached for the mouse. Clicked a few times and watched as the current photos were replaced by older ones. Bloodier ones.

As he stared at pictures of his sister's body, he knew he no longer had a choice. There was a compulsion inside of him, a dark and violent need that grew with every day he spent in this city.

It was why he had come back, after all, why he had allowed the studio to talk him into making this movie. And it had only grown worse with every hour he stayed here.

Closing the laptop, he shoved it away from himself with a muffled groan. He couldn't stand to look at it anymore, couldn't stand the images that were branded into his brain. But they were there for good. He'd learned to accept that sometime during the last seven years.

It was ridiculous to be this upset, considering how long he'd spent thinking about doing this. How many times he'd asked himself if he could go through with it before deciding that indeed he could. How often he'd run his plan in his head, looking for any and all flaws.

There hadn't been any.

Focus on the female homicide detective, not just because of her gender but because of her background in cold cases and her higher-than-normal case clearance rate. Get her interested in past cases through the documentary he was working on. Get her to decide to reopen Samantha's case—and investigate it.

The subterfuge burned his ass, but since he'd been all but banned from the precinct, he had no other choice.

After his sister's death—and in the intervening years—he'd gone a little crazy. Had hired private detectives—some of whom caused more harm than good—when he'd been dissatisfied with the police investigation. Had lost his temper and threatened officers when progress hadn't been made.

He'd even gotten himself kicked out of the damn station three years ago, by that prick of a homicide lieutenant, Chastian. He'd told Cole in no uncertain terms that one more inquiry or public confrontation regarding Samantha would end with him burying the file so deep inside cold cases that it would never see the light of day again.

Cole hadn't believed him, had pushed the asshole anyway. And had found out that Chastian didn't make idle threats; Samantha's file had all but disappeared, after erroneously being declared closed. Chastian had even gone so far as to threaten the detectives involved in the case, until each of them had developed an overwhelming case of amnesia when it came to his sister.

Fucking damn corrupt cops. He hated them with a destructive passion that ate at him until he could barely think through the red haze that enveloped him. Hated them enough that he'd planned on using one without a drop of compunction, completely unconcerned that helping him could end her career.

But that was before he'd met Genevieve, before she had stripped everything from him but the primal desire to mate. He wanted her, needed her, in a way he didn't understand and couldn't afford.

She was a distraction, a complication that could keep him from seeing this thing through. Because every time he ran the scenario in his head, with Genevieve as his lover, something went terribly wrong.

How could he lie to her, use her, at the same time he was sleeping with her? He might be a bastard, but that was too far even for him. Besides, the feelings she'd evoked in him last night made it impossible to imagine just fucking her and moving on—he wanted to possess her, to do things to her body no one else ever had.

Leaning back in his chair, he slammed down one last shot, more than a little unsteady from the alcohol he'd consumed but still relishing the burn of the liquor down his throat. The heat that masked the coldness inside of him, even if it couldn't chase it away completely.

So what to do? How to balance his insane attraction to Genevieve with the agenda he just couldn't abandon? How could he have both?

He rolled the shot glass between his hands, watched as the light projected the colors onto the cherry desktop. Shifted his hand and sent the rainbow cascading over his arm instead. Twisted the glass slightly and thought of all the ways he'd failed his sister. Hadn't controlled her wildness as a teenager, hadn't tried to stop her ill-thought-out move to New Orleans, despite his mom and stepdad's objections. Hadn't rushed to her side when his mother had called him and told him she thought something was wrong with Samantha.

He hadn't wanted to seem like he was trying to control her. He'd known how important independence was to Sam, how she'd fought to find a place of her own, separate from the overachieving family she'd always struggled to be good enough for.

As he thought of his sister—of everything he hadn't done for her—he knew he had to tell Genevieve the truth. Had to wait for her to get off work then lay everything on the line—including his too strong attraction to her—and hope that she could see past the deception to help him anyway.

Because if she didn't, he was totally fucked.

Chapter Four

His name was Cole Adams. Genevieve shook her head in disbelief as she stared at the report in front of her. *The* Cole Adams—American documentary maker and Academy Award winner extraordinaire. How had she failed to recognize him?

Maybe because she rarely paid attention to that stuff—even on her good days. Not to mention that his reclusiveness was the stuff Hollywood legends were made of. Of course, the fact that he'd spent most of the night with his face buried between her legs might also have contributed to her lack of recognition.

Feeling her cheeks heat at the memory, Genevieve did her best to convince herself that Cole's profession accounted for the file she'd found at his apartment that morning. Her gut had told her all along that he was innocent, but her brain still wasn't ready to lay it to rest.

If it was something as easily explained as research for a new documentary, why was he hiding it in a bedroom drawer? And why hadn't he said something to her about it right away?

Genevieve read the brief report one more time—seven years before, he'd been arrested for misdemeanor assault, but the charges had been dropped, as the other guy had instigated the fight. Other than that, his record was clean—nothing there to show any signs of sexual or homicidal deviance. With a sigh, she put it aside. She didn't have any more time to waste on this, even though she didn't believe for one moment that he'd sat beside her at that bar last night and not known who she was.

No, that was entirely too coincidental for a woman who didn't believe in coincidence.

Going back to the file she'd started on her latest case, she reviewed everything she'd managed to accomplish that day.

Missing persons had popped on the victim's identity that morning, so she'd started her day by breaking the news to the girl's devastated parents. Her name was Jessica Robbins, and she'd been a freshman at Tulane. Her roommate had reported her missing three days before, when she hadn't come back to the dorm after her evening jog through the Garden District.

Jessica's parents had flown in as soon as she'd disappeared, had hired a private detective to look for her even as they staked out both the Tulane and the Uptown police stations in a desperate attempt to find out what had happened to their daughter.

Once she had a name, Genevieve had called the Tulane Police Department and gotten the parents' information. She'd called them in, told them as gently as possible that their only child was dead.

Not that there was a gentle way to deliver that kind of news—it was the part of her job she hated the most. And the part that haunted her when she lay in bed at night, the lights off and the city finally silent around her. How the people left behind looked when she shattered their world.

In an effort to spare them, she hadn't told Jessica's parents everything she'd discovered. She hadn't told them how the bastard had kept her around for a while. How he had toyed with Jessica almost endlessly in an effort to maximize the pain.

Still, they hadn't taken the news of their daughter's rape and murder stoically. The mother wept uncontrollably while the father simply stared blankly ahead, as if the facts were just too much for him to comprehend. He'd been the one to identify his daughter's body, and he'd been the one to escort his wife from the station when her sobs had died down to occasional whimpers.

And he was the one who had looked straight at Genevieve and demanded to know who had killed his child. She had told him the truth—that she didn't know, but that she would find out.

And she would.

She had promised them justice and she would deliver. Jessica Robbins would be avenged. Her parents' anger and grief would find a focus. Genevieve would make damn sure of it.

But she'd interviewed all the students at the dorm who claimed to know Jessica and none of them had said anything about an irate boyfriend, a stalker or even a guy who'd paid her any extra interest at all.

She'd also spoken with Jessica's professors, classmates, off-campus friends—anyone who could give her a clue into Jessica's daily routine and any problems she might be having.

The picture that was emerging was of a young girl enjoying the freedom that going away to college had given her. She was an above-average student who worked hard but who took time out to have a good time. Well-liked but not insanely popular, pleasant, intelligent—Jessica had been a girl with a bright present and a brighter future. To see it cut so brutally short grated severely; that she had no suspect made it even worse.

That she was convinced Jessica was the latest victim of a serial killer—one Genevieve hadn't been able to catch, though she'd been working on it for months—made it almost unbearable.

Engrossed in her thoughts, Genevieve nearly jumped out of her skin when the phone at her elbow rang. Heart pounding—even as she shook her head at her own skittishness—she reached for the phone with a hand that was not quite steady and answered with a clipped "Delacroix."

There was no answer, only the sound of strangled breathing on the other side of the line.

"Hello?"

More breathing.

"Look, pal, are you kidding me? Do you have any idea who you're calling? This is a police station, for God's sake, and I—"

"I know who I'm calling, Genevieve."

The voice was low, hoarse. Strangely familiar, but somehow muted. "Who is this?" she demanded.

There was a long pause. "There's another one."

"Another what?"

"I think you know. Think of me when you find it."

"Find wha—"

The phone went dead in her hand, leaving Genevieve staring at it much as she would a snake. A chill crept down her spine as she placed the receiver back down. Who was calling her, and what, exactly, was she supposed to find?

Glancing down, she caught sight of the homicide photos she'd added to the folder only an hour before, and the chill became a full-out freeze. Was there another body out there, waiting to be found, or was she over-reacting? Sighing, she rubbed her tired eyes. She'd been working too hard for too long—her mind no longer felt clear.

Was it just another bored kid crank calling, or had it been the killer, calling her to taunt her with his latest success?

The mere thought made her ill. She tried to shrug it off, to put the call down to some idiot just wanting to rattle her chain. But she couldn't shake the idea that it was more than that. That it had been *him* on the phone.

I know who I'm calling, Genevieve. The words played back in her head as she wracked her brain, tried to figure out where she'd heard the voice before. But the answer she was looking for was hovering just out of reach, impossible to retrieve.

Finally, unable to solve the puzzle but unwilling to let it go, she dashed off an e-mail to a friend in the electronic crime division, asking Jose to unofficially look into the call's origin.

If it was nothing—just someone yanking her chain—she didn't want to make a big deal of it. But her instincts were shouting that it was something more, something big, and she couldn't afford to overlook it. Not when her leads were zero and her evidence less.

"Genevieve, you got a minute?"

Looking up from the notes she was making—trying to ignore the nervousness still coursing through her from the call—Genevieve started to snap, then paused as she saw her boss standing at his door. Gritting her teeth, knowing she didn't have a choice, she picked up the file she'd been compiling on Jessica and headed for her lieutenant's office.

"So, where are we with the dead Tulane student?" Chastian asked as soon as the door closed behind her.

Genevieve had worked with Lieutenant Rob Chastian long enough that she didn't even wince at the brusqueness of his tone. He was a big man—though not quite as big as Cole—and good-looking in a Ken doll kind of way. He also had a personality like a Weedwhacker. Which was actually fine with her—better that than the jokes that weren't really jokes that so many of the other squad members leveled at her on a regular basis. With the lieutenant she always knew where she stood—exactly nowhere.

"Not very far." His brows lowered and she held up a hand to forestall the anticipated explosion. "I've interviewed friends, potential witnesses, teachers, strangers and gotten nothing. Jefferson's working on the body as we speak—he promised to have the preliminary report to me by tomorrow at the latest."

"Are you telling me that no one knows anything?" Chastian demanded. "I've got the press crawling up my ass, the commander demanding that something be done, and my homicide detective has nothing. That's just fabulous. At least Shawn is back in a few days."

"It's not that simple."

"Sure it is. But if you can't handle it . . ." He let his voice trail off, but the threat was implicit.

Biting the inside of her cheek in an effort to be civil, Genevieve told herself Chastian would be asking these same questions of any male detective on the squad. Too bad she didn't believe her own bullshit, any more than she believed the lieutenant's.

"I'm handling it just fine, Lieutenant. But, as I told you before, I think we're dealing with a repeat killer. We need to get a profiler and some other detectives involved in this before he kills again."

"So *are* you telling me you can't handle it?"

Her hands clenched into fists as she struggled not to wipe the condescending look off his face with a punch that would show him just how capable she was of handling anything that came her way. The only thing that stopped her—other than the badge at her hip—was knowing that that was exactly what he wanted her to do.

From the moment she'd been assigned to his squad, Chastian had been pushing her. A snide comment here, a public dressing-down there, he'd turned getting under her skin into an Olympic event. Hoping, she assumed, that she'd screw up enough that he'd have no recourse but to throw her off his precious, male-dominated squad.

But that wasn't going to happen. She'd worked too damn hard to get here. So she simply pulled out the ice-cold voice that had saved her so many times in the past and answered, "No, sir. But if we want to catch this guy, we need more people involved."

"You don't have any definitive evidence that links these murders together, yet you expect me to assign a huge amount of departmental resources to a task force that might be totally unnecessary."

"Not a task force, then. Just a few other detectives—"

"No."

Anger shot through her at his shortsightedness, but she kept the Ice Queen facade in place. "Sir, we need to act—"

"We need to not throw this city into a panic. Things are bad enough here right now with the murder rate on such a steep incline. We can't afford to upset the general public until we have proof."

"I have—"

"*Solid* proof," he interrupted. "But if you can't handle it . . ." His voice trailed off.

"Of course I can handle it!"

"Good. Then it's settled." He glanced down at his desk, picked up a file. Started going through it.

She had been dismissed.

Rage simmered just under the surface as Genevieve let herself out of Chastian's office, even as she cursed herself for jumping the gun, for thinking things were getting better. Her gut had told her he would react like that, had known he wouldn't want to see what she saw. Truth be told, she should have waited for Shawn to sell her theory, no matter how painful that truth was.

Grinding her teeth, she snatched up her suit jacket and headed for the exit. She was done tonight, anger clawing at her lungs until she couldn't breathe.

Why the hell did she even bother? She'd known how that briefing was going to go even before she opened her mouth. Chastian might be stuck with her—the only woman on his otherwise pristine homicide squad—but he didn't have to like it. Nor did he have to take her seriously.

Normally, she tried not to let it bother her, but on nights like tonight when she knew she was right, it was hard. Maybe she should just give it up—

But Jessica Robbins' face danced in her mind. No, she wouldn't give up. Those girls deserved justice and she would get it for them, with or without Chastian's cooperation. She was one of the best detectives in the good-old-boy network—despite her gender. To hell with the politics. She would find this killer and prove that she'd been right all along.

Not that it would change anything—those girls would still be dead, their parents would still be wounded beyond recovery. But maybe the next victim and her family wouldn't be as unlucky.

Chapter Five

Genevieve was halfway home before she slowed from the fast clip that had eaten up half the distance between the station and her house. Fury at Chastian burned like bile in her throat, and it was all she could do to keep from screaming in the middle of the Quarter's crowded streets.

Taking a few deep breaths, she tried to concentrate on the world around her. The Quarter was crowded tonight—locals and tourists out in abundance as they searched for a good time.

With a small smile, she passed a group of Goth kids trying desperately to be vampires, then side-stepped a group of Tulane frat boys who had started the party entirely too early. She tossed a dollar into the hat of a young man tap-dancing on the corner of Toulouse, admiring his sense of rhythm when all he had were bottle caps glued to the bottom of a pair of old sneakers.

She wanted to stop and watch him for a while, but she was wound too tight, her body exhausted while her mind raced a hundred miles a minute. Besides, a storm was coming. She could feel it in the cloying heaviness of the air around her, taste it in the teasing, taunting wind that whipped by her. Over her. Around her.

This wasn't just any storm. No, not this one, with its black clouds and rolling thunder just audible in the distance. Its flashes of lightning crisscrossing the afternoon sky. She slipped out her tongue, tasted the sweetness in the water-soaked air.

No, this wasn't just any storm. It was a New Orleans storm—wicked and wild and oh, so restless. And if she didn't move, she'd be caught right in the middle of the violence.

Walking quickly, head down, thoughts still focused inward, she tuned out the world around her. She was locked inside her head, so deep in thought that a freight train could have passed in front of her without garnering notice, when her training finally kicked in—about thirty seconds too late.

It started as a feeling, a realization that all was not as it should be. Continued as her feet picked up the pace even more. Goose bumps rose on her arms, and the hair on the back of her neck tingled before standing straight up. Her breathing quickened; her heart started pounding. And before she knew it, her hand was on the butt of her gun and she crouched low, glancing around her as she looked for the source of her discomfort.

Someone was following her—she felt it in the stare that weighed heavily on her shoulders and the nervous flicker that danced in her stomach. And whoever it was was pretty damn good if she couldn't spot him. But she knew he was there, just as surely as she knew her address and her favorite color.

She straightened, then turned around and picked up her pace. Who was it? And what could he want? Was it the killer, checking up on the case's lead detective? A mugger looking to get lucky?

Her imagination worked overtime as she turned one corner and then another in an effort to lose him. But he stayed with her, got closer—she could feel the menace radiating off him in waves.

Finally, when her nerves were nearly shot and she could take no more of the cat-and-mouse games, she ducked into Pirate's Alley, a narrow passageway off Decatur that housed a few shops and provided great cover. The stores had closed up a few hours before, leaving the alley deserted and almost black, except for the faint glow of light coming from a forgotten sign in a shop window.

Pulling out her gun, she settled against the red brick wall and waited. Time stood still, adrenaline coursing through her body as she readied herself for whatever was to come.

If she was lucky, he'd walk right by and she could shadow him for a while. If she wasn't so lucky, then—

A huge male hand reached out of the shadows and knocked her gun away before she could react. "Hey," she gasped, her heart rate doubling. Scrambling back, she searched the ground for the gun, but her attacker was relentless.

He grabbed her elbow with fingers that felt like steel talons, reached up and tangled another hand on the back of her neck and pulled her up. She tried to fight, to ignore the fear rocketing through her, but his strength was overpowering. Amazingly, he hadn't hurt her yet, his grip inexorable but painless as she struggled against him.

"Hey, stop it!" she said again, as he pulled her against his heavily muscled chest. She started to struggle in earnest, more furious and afraid than she'd been in a long time.

But she'd be damned if she'd be mugged in a back alley because some asshole was jonesing for his drug of choice. Lowering her shoulder, she aimed for her attacker's stomach, but it was like running into a semi in full gear—he was coming, and her only choices were to get out of the way or get pancaked.

Twisting out of his grip, she leapt to the side. Her foot brushed her weapon and she crouched down. Grabbed it. Cocked it and took aim. Then froze as she realized it was Cole coming at her with all the finesse of a berserker on PCP.

"What the hell are you doing?" she demanded as she uncocked the weapon, lowered it. But she didn't holster it, not yet.

"I think that's my question," he growled, starting after her—backing her deeper and deeper into the alley.

"Excuse me?" She used the coldest Ice Queen voice she could muster, tried to hold her ground. But frissons of fear and—God help her—arousal were shooting down her spine. How the hell she could be turned on by his barbarian act she didn't know, but her hormones were bouncing around like jumping beans, despite the fury emanating from Cole.

As she holstered her weapon—afraid she might shoot either him or herself if she wasn't careful—lightning flashed across the sky, illuminating the small alley for one frozen moment. Her eyes locked with Cole's and he looked so angry, so aroused, she actually felt her knees knock together. The harsh planes of his face stood out in stark relief, his mouth tight.

Suddenly, she saw his lips move, saw the demand for information in his eyes, but a huge clap of thunder drowned out the words. Seconds later, the sky opened up and began to pour. She barely noticed the rain as Cole stalked toward her with feral eyes.

"Why'd you leave this morning?" he asked again. His voice was low, guttural.

Though Genevieve told herself not to move, she was backing up before her knees got the message from her brain. The show of fear, of submission, pissed her off, added to the anger that had been simmering since she'd seen his name on those logs hours before.

So instead of answering his question, she shot back one of her own. "What the hell are you doing researching murders that happen in my jurisdiction? What the hell are you doing researching *me*?"

He didn't answer, just kept walking her back until his rock-hard body was flush against hers. Once again she told herself to hold her ground. Once again she found herself backing up. All the way this time, until her back was against the rough stone wall near the end of the alley.

"You don't want to fuck with me on this, Genevieve. Why'd you sneak out like that, without even telling me where to find you?" Cole's voice was lower now, more animal than human as he took advantage of her predicament, closing in until she was utterly surrounded. The wall at her back, his hard, unyielding body hovering only inches from her front. His powerful biceps caging her in from the sides.

His black-magic eyes demanding that she tell him what he wanted to know.

The wind picked up, made her shudder as it whipped around them, as wild and fierce as the attraction she couldn't fight. It lashed the rain against her, against him, as it streamed down their bodies.

He pulled back, looked at her with wicked eyes that proclaimed just how much he wanted her—and just how far he would go to have her—and she became aware, for the first time, of how she must look to him. Her clothes were stuck to her and practically transparent, her nipples showing clearly through the thin lace of her bra, the even thinner cotton of her T-shirt.

Maybe she should have been frightened, with the storm raging around her and Cole burning beside her. But ten years on a male-dominated force had ensured she was not easily cowed.

Resolving to give as good as she got, Genevieve pressed her head back against the wall and glared at him with eyes she knew reflected her own fury, as the storm raged around them. "Answer my question and I'll answer yours."

"Fuck that." He grabbed her wrists with one hand, his long fingers spanning both with ease. Yanked her arms above her head. Moved the last few inches until his body was pressed against hers from chest to thigh.

His breath was coming in short, hot pants against her ear, his heart racing crazily against her breasts. And his erection, his infinitely arousing, unbelievably sexy erection, rested hot and heavy against her stomach. The rain made the barrier of their clothes nearly nonexistent, and she felt his heat against the very heart of her.

Shock raced through her as her brain demanded that she refuse to yield. But her body was firmly in control, the pleasure it took from Cole's unprecedented dominance more than she could fight.

She loved every second of it. Loved the vulnerability of being spread for him. Loved the little frissons of fear working their way down her spine. Loved the idea of being helpless in the face of all this bristling male aggression.

She should have felt vulnerable, but she knew she was safe—she'd trained for years to handle herself against men twice her size. She should have felt uncomfortable, but everything about Cole felt right despite his obvious interest in her case. She should have felt anything—everything— but this overwhelming need to give him whatever he wanted to take. And to take even more for herself.

His grip was firm as he stretched her wrists higher, forcing her to arch her back to relieve the pressure. But as they skimmed down her throat his lips were more gentle than she would have dreamed possible.

"Tell me why," he whispered, running his tongue over her collarbone.

"You already—" Her voice broke and she had to start again. "You already knew where to find me."

"What makes you say that?"

"I found your file." She pushed against him with all the strength she could muster, but he just snarled and pushed back.

"You should have stuck around—I would have explained every-thing. It would have saved me the trouble of hauling you back."

"You wouldn't dare."

His chuckle was low, wicked. "You don't have a clue what I'll dare." He reached up with his free hand, fastened on the collar of her simple silk T-shirt. And then he was yanking, his powerful fist ripping through the material like so much fluff.

She gasped in surprise, her body shuddering as shock ricocheted through her. She started to protest, but he was pushing her bra out of the way, drawing her nipple into his mouth with a suction so strong she couldn't tell where the pleasure left off and the pain began. She knew only that the two were hand in hand as she arched her back, begging for more. Begging for everything.

He lifted his head for a moment, looked at her in the dim light with eyes gleaming. That small break brought her back from the edge of sensual overload, and common sense reasserted itself for a moment. Pushing at his shoulders with firm hands, she said, "Cole, stop. We can't do this here."

"We are doing this here." He bit down on her nipple and she nearly came unglued, her body bucking violently against him.

"But," she tried one more time, clinging to sanity with bloody, battered fingertips. "We're in public."

"Then you had better be quiet," he growled against her breast. "Because we're not leaving here until I feel you come."

Genevieve whimpered, tried once again to shove against his immense shoulders. But it was no use and she knew it, because she wanted this as much as he did. Maybe even more—a walk on the wild side when she'd always been so careful to follow the rules, to do nothing to draw attention to herself.

Shooting a look down the alley, she was comforted by the utter darkness and the knowledge that the tourists were too busy on Bourbon Street—and too scared of the big, bad Quarter at night—to come looking down this alley.

And then she forgot all of her concerns, the need to orgasm rising sharply with each stroke of his tongue on her breast. Her body was spinning out of control, desire taking over completely.

Moaning, panting, she pressed her breast more firmly against his mouth, relishing the feel of his tongue around her areola. Loving the sharp nip of his teeth against her diamond-hard nipple.

"Cole, please," she begged, spreading her legs and pressing her lower body against the hardness of his thigh. She needed him against her, needed him inside her like she'd never needed anything before in her life.

He gave her just a little of what she craved. Slid his thigh between hers and let her rock against him until she was nearly insane with the need to come. Her clit was hot, her womb aching, and she was more than ready for him.

But he was so much better at the game than she, and he pulled away just as the orgasm started rising, her body one thrust away from completion.

She whimpered, tried to follow him, but he held her in place with one hand against her stomach while the other remained anchored to her wrists. "What are you—" She couldn't finish the question, desire so out of control that she had no hope for coherent thought.

"Don't leave like that again," Cole whispered, licking from the valley between her breasts to the hollow of her throat.

"What?" she asked, every part of her trembling with the need for release.

"Promise me you won't walk out like that again—without so much as a note." His teeth sank into her shoulder, hard, and she screamed as pleasure shot through her.

"Genevieve," he prompted, his tongue tenderly licking away the bite marks.

"I won't!" She gave in abruptly, too strung out to fight him anymore. "I'll tell you next time."

Abruptly he lifted his head, stared at her with eyes that glowed red in the twilight shadows. "Thank you."

Before she could figure out how to answer, the hand resting on her stomach moved. Slid inside the waistband of her pants and found her sex. Hot, wet, aching.

"Fuck, sweetheart." He slipped one long finger inside her, curved it so he touched her G spot with the first stroke. Then pulled back and did it again and again. On the fifth stroke of his finger she started to come, wave after wave of sensation swamping her.

He moved his thumb, circled it around her throbbing clit. Once, twice. She glanced up and into his obsidian eyes and shot over a higher, steeper edge, her body completely out of her control as ecstasy whipped through her nerve endings. Her muscles spasmed, clutched at him, wanting to take him deeper and deeper inside her until the pleasure was all-consuming, never-ending.

Cole held her through it, swallowing her cries with his mouth as his fingers continued to work her, controlling her response. Taking her higher. When she couldn't take it anymore, when her body was so stressed out and sensitive that she was almost at a breaking point, she jerked her mouth from his. Laid her head on his broad shoulder and gasped, "No more, Cole. Please, no more."

"There's always more, Genevieve." But he slid his finger slowly out of her, pausing to stroke her labia once, twice. She whimpered, arched against him, so exhausted and shaken that she could barely move.

"Don't worry, sweetheart." He murmured the words against her forehead. "I've got you."

A part of her wanted to argue, but any protest she made would seem pretty stupid, as his arms were the only things keeping her ass from hitting the ground. God knew her legs didn't stand a chance of supporting her.

Slowly, so slowly it was yet another kind of foreplay, he slid her down his wet, denim-covered legs. Held her against him when her feet hit the ground and her knees wobbled. Then he leaned over, brushed her lips in a kiss sweeter and softer than she ever could have imagined.

"Let me come home with you," he whispered, running a hand through her tangled curls. "Let me love you."

A million arguments entered her mind, a million reasons why bringing him home was a bad idea. But as the rain continued to fall, its cool caress touching her everywhere she wanted Cole to, she answered with the only word her aroused brain was capable of forming. "Yes."

His answering grin lit up the dark alley in a way no lightning strike could.

Chapter Six

Later, he would remember little of their walk home. He'd have no recollection of the wind whipping past their soaking bodies, no memory of the rain lashing against their sensitive skin.

But he would remember Genevieve and the way her body fit so perfectly against his own. He would remember the brush of her breast against his torso, and the lush softness of her ass under his hand as he tucked her smaller body into his.

And he would remember that first moment when she stepped over the threshold and invited him into her home. Nothing had ever felt quite so right.

Cole's instincts were screaming at him, his desire to take Genevieve turning him nearly rabid with unfulfilled need. But she looked so dreamy, so sweet, that he found himself going slowly—despite the pounding in his brain telling him to take, take, take.

He took a deep breath—trying to control himself—but her scent was everywhere. A mixture of honeysuckle and summer and dark, delicious night. It turned him inside out.

But still, he was determined to give her sweetness as well as passion, to give her tenderness as well as desperation. Taking her hand, he brought it to his mouth. Brushed his lips over her knuckles before he turned it over and studied the delicate-looking palm.

"You have such small hands for such a capable person."

"They get the job done." Her voice was low, breathless, turning the mundane words into an erotic invitation—one Cole had no chance of refusing.

Lowering his head, he stroked his tongue from her wrist to the top of her palm, lingering for long moments over her chained and broken love line as he licked the raindrops from her skin. She gasped, went perfectly still. And for a moment—just a moment—she was soft and pliant, her body his to command.

He pulled her against him, savored the feel of her soft, lush curves against the hard planes of his own body. Then her arms were around him, pulling him to her, and everything he wanted to say simply faded away as desire—harsh and all-consuming—took over.

He kicked the door closed behind him and took her mouth in an assault that was at once brutal and gentle. Brutal in its intensity and focus; gentle in its execution. With a sigh, Genevieve parted her lips, allowing herself to melt into Cole despite the voice at the back of her head telling her she was making a very large mistake.

But he felt so good against her, their wet clothes only a weak barrier between them. She pressed herself more fully against him and his tongue swept over her lips, exploring every part of them—of her.

Her knees trembled yet again, and she clutched the wet cotton of his undershirt in an effort to get closer. To remain upright.

He gasped his surprise, then pulled her more tightly against him, until she could feel every part of him pressed to every part of her. His arousal was hard as a brick against her stomach and she delighted in it. Moved restlessly in an effort to feel him more fully against her.

He accommodated her, shifted his strong hands until they were cupping her ass. And then he was lifting her, shaping her, molding her against him.

"Put your legs around me," he growled against her lips, and she did. The pleasure—the sweet, soft, incredible pleasure that came from the movement had her gasping in delight.

He took instant advantage, his tongue slipping between her parted lips with all the subtlety of a conquering army. But as he stroked it against the top of her mouth, ran it in one glancing caress over her own tongue, Genevieve couldn't bring herself to care. Not when his invasion sent frissons of delight through her whole being.

She rocked against him, desperate to feel Cole deeper inside of her. To have him anywhere and everywhere he could go. He made a low sound that was half laugh, half growl, and ripped his lips from hers.

"Fuck." It was a curse, a prayer, a statement of intent, and she was more than willing to let him have his way.

"Cole," she gasped, his name suddenly the only word she knew.

He bucked against her, his cock growing harder still. Then he was kissing the corners of her mouth. She waited, lungs burning, body on the brink of an explosion, for him to continue.

But he was moving slowly, his tongue tracing every curve of her lips before he nibbled his way across her cheek, down her chin to her throat. She arched, tilting her head to the side to give him better access. Moaned as he licked at the pulse beating crazily at the hollow of her throat.

Heat sizzled along her nerve endings, burst into flames that seared her from the inside out. She pulled him closer, so close that she could feel his heart beating wildly beneath the firm muscles of his chest. So close that the fine sheen of sweat coating his throat mingled with her own.

Pushing against him, she ran her hands over his pecs. Toyed with his nipples and reveled in the involuntary surge of his hips against hers. She lifted and lowered herself, riding the hard ridge of his erection as she would if there were no clothes between them.

He groaned deep in his chest and went from teasing to dominating in an instant. Claiming her, he bit her lower lip, sucked it between his teeth and brushed against it with his tongue. He delved deeply into her mouth, so deeply that she couldn't remember what it was like to breathe without him there.

His tongue caressed hers, circling, playing, turning her inside out with each touch. He tasted so good—of lime and tequila and dark, sizzling passion—that she knew she'd crave the taste of him for the rest of her days.

"Cole," she moaned again, sliding her hands up to the cool, wet silk of his hair. Tightening her fingers until she knew there was a pinprick of pain. Tightening them more until he erupted with a growl.

And then he was devouring her, his hands squeezing her ass while his denim-clad cock slid back and forth between her thighs. His mouth was everywhere, everywhere, moving down her throat to nudge aside the neckline of the too-big shirt he'd taken off to cover her for the walk home—so he could trace his tongue over the swell of her breasts. Nuzzling the curve of her breast as his tongue swept over her lace-covered nipple with small, velvet strokes that had her burning hotter than she ever had before.

She was on fire, her body aching and heavy and desperate for the feel of him within her. His fingers dipped beneath the drenched waistband of her pants, stroked her skin until all she could feel was him, all she could think of was him.

She was going to regret this in the morning, would hate that she'd let him have her so completely. But she needed him inside her, was desperate to feel his body slide between her bare thighs as he thrust into her again and again.

Cole's teeth scraped against her nipple and she forgot her own name, let alone any reservations she had about being with him. She had never wanted anything the way she wanted him, her entire body tightening until the need to come was a screaming agony within her.

Her hands grabbed on to his shoulders and urged him closer. Urged him to take them all the way. His laugh, low and seductive, brushed against her painfully hard nipple right before he pulled it into his mouth and began to suck.

She moaned, arched her back. Pressed her breast more firmly against his mouth.

"Take me," she murmured, as he skimmed light hands up her arms, over her back. She was adrift, all of her concentration focused on this man and his carefully controlled caresses. "Please take me."

The words were out before she could stop them, a plea she hadn't known she was going to utter.

"I will," he answered, sliding his lips along her throat, and she didn't know if she should be relieved or disappointed at his easy acceptance of the physical meaning behind her words.

Then he was pushing against her with his body, walking her backward as he continued to nibble and lick his way down her neck and shoulder. Caught up in the incredible pleasure of his light caresses, she barely noticed that he had walked her across the foyer to the front parlor she used as a living room.

But suddenly, they were in the dimly lit room and he was shifting her, turning her in his arms so that her back was against his chest.

She reached out and flicked on the lamp near the door and he murmured his approval, his eyes lighting up at the sight of the huge, full-length mirror that ran the length of one wall.

Before she knew what was happening, he'd moved them so that they were positioned in front of the mirror. She felt a flicker of nervousness work through her, but she didn't protest. Tonight—for better or worse—she was in Cole's hands.

"What do you see?" he murmured as he slipped his T-shirt over her head. His hands went to her breasts, cupped them from behind, and his thumbs played gently over her nipples.

"I see you," she answered, and it was no less than the truth. Here in the dim light of her living room, she did see him—all of him. The strong, powerful body. The wary eyes. The gentle heart that beat beneath the rough, domineering exterior.

"You are so unbelievably beautiful," he whispered into her ear. "I can't believe how beautiful you are."

She tried to turn, wanting to wrap her arms around him, but he held her fast, one large hand splaying across her pelvis to lock her in place.

"I want you to watch me take you," he murmured. "I want you to see everything I do to you as you feel it. I want you to watch my hands and lips and body take yours."

Heat spiraled through her, had her pushing her back more firmly against his chest. His muscles rippled at the strong contact, his cock growing even harder and longer against her back. She reached behind her, cupped his ass through his sodden jeans and held him tightly against her. She needed to feel him, to anchor herself in the press of him against her—otherwise she would simply spin away, her body and heart and soul no longer hers to control.

Nothing in her whole life had ever felt as good as Cole did. The feel of his body behind her, the touch of his hands as they glanced over her body again and again. She grew wetter, hotter, lust building in her with each touch of his fingertips.

She moaned, her hands clenching on his ass as she demanded more from him. But he merely laughed. "Don't be so impatient, sweetheart," he murmured against her ear as he slowly slipped her wet pants down her legs. "We'll get there eventually."

"I need you now!" It was a whimper, a plea for mercy, and they both knew it.

But Cole had no mercy in him, and as she watched his eyes darken to blackest obsidian, she knew she was in for it. Tonight, now, Cole would be satisfied with nothing but everything she had to give.

He groaned, his breath coming in hot pants against her cheek for long seconds before he pulled away to yank off his own clothes. "And I need to make you crazy, need to hear you scream my name as you come."

Her legs trembled, but she locked her knees in place, refusing to give up so easily. Refusing to give in.

Cole chuckled low in his throat, as if he sensed her resolve. "Don't fight me, Genevieve."

"Don't push me, Cole." She mimicked the half-amused tone of his voice, even as her body throbbed for his possession.

He caught her eyes in the mirror and for endless seconds there was nothing else—just that one hot, elemental connection. She wanted to jerk away, wanted to close her eyes. It was too personal, everything she felt laid open to him in one blinding instant. But his eyes caught her, trapped her, held her spellbound, and all she could see was him. All she wanted was him.

Then he was moving, his hard fingers cupping her aching breast. She jerked, arched into the sensation. And melted as his fingertips swirled around and around her nipple, each circle bringing him closer to the aching bud, though he never touched it.

It was a double shot of sensation, to watch and feel those long, elegant hands touching her. Heat, rapid and all-consuming, built in her, raced down her nerve endings into every part of her body.

"You have the most beautiful breasts," he said softly as he raised his left hand and cupped her other breast. "Look how pretty they are, Genevieve."

"Cole." It was a protest, a plea, and one he had no trouble ignoring.

"Your skin is such a gorgeous shade of ivory, with just the barest touch of rose. And so soft—you're so incredibly soft here, like the most expensive silk. And these—"

Finally, his hand glanced across her nipples and she moaned, arching into the contact, every cell in her body focused on that one brief moment of contact.

"These are incredible. Sweet, responsive—" Again he ran a finger across her nipple; again she arched against the contact, seeking more. "And so damn sexy I could spend my life right here, loving them.

"Can I do that, Genevieve?" His breath was hot against her cheek, his words even hotter. "Can I suck these gorgeous nipples for hours? Can I slide my cock between your breasts and into that hot little mouth of yours? Can I come in your mouth, on your breasts? On your stomach? In that hot little ass of yours?"

"Cole!"

His breathing was coming heavier, his big body shuddering against hers as his words wound their way around them both, chaining them more and more tightly together. "Can I, Genevieve? I need to be in every part of you, need to know that I've marked you, branded you. Claimed this hot little body of yours until all you feel is me."

His fingers tugged on her nipples and she screamed as fire whipped through her. "Until all you know is me."

"Yes," she gasped, her head thrashing back and forth against his chest as she tried to get closer to him. She wanted to take him every way she could, needed him in every part of her.

He leaned down, bit her neck, and she whimpered, her body going into sensory overload. But he didn't give her time to process her feelings. Instead, he kept moving, his tongue and lips and teeth trailing hot kisses over her shoulders and upper back even as his fingers continued to squeeze and flick and rub against her sensitized nipples.

It was too much, the heat rushing through her body. The lust clenching at her womb. Her eyes drifted closed as she savored everything Cole could do to her body with such little effort.

"Look at me!" he barked, and her eyes flew open, electricity sizzling along her nerve endings.

"You don't own me!" she shot at him, resentment that he could stay so cool while she was so turned on suddenly rampant within her.

But he merely laughed and slid a hand down her stomach to her sex. And shoved two long fingers roughly inside of her. "Don't I?" he asked, as she cried out, her body bucking wildly against his as need—raw and overwhelming—stripped away everything but the desire to be underneath this man as he took her any and every way he wanted to.

"Don't do this to me," she whimpered, even while she moved her hips restlessly against him, seeking more. "Don't make me give you everything."

"I want everything." He circled his thumb around her clit and hurtled her into an orgasm so intense her knees collapsed beneath her. She would have fallen, but he caught her, held her up with one powerful arm against her belly. "I need everything."

"Why?" Once again, she met his eyes in the mirror, saw the heat and lust reflected in his.

"Because I'm giving you everything I can." His teeth sank into her shoulder and she shuddered, her body erupting again.

She couldn't take it—it was just too much. Watching him and hearing him and feeling him—she couldn't think, couldn't catch her breath, couldn't do anything but experience.

Ripping herself out of his arms, she turned and sank to her knees in front of him. "Genevieve!" His voice was low, warning, but she paid no attention to it. She couldn't; all her concentration suddenly focused on the long, hard cock in front of her. Leaning forward, she stroked her tongue up and around his huge length.

Cole's breath slammed out of him, his hands tangling in Genevieve's hair of their own volition. This wasn't how it was supposed to go, wasn't how he'd planned it. But it felt so good, so fucking good, as she ran her tongue over his testicles before taking them into her mouth and sucking gently.

"Fuck, Genevieve." His hands tightened in her hair and he tried to pull her away, but she wrapped her arms around his upper thighs and hung on. And then he couldn't fight anymore, didn't want to fight, as the most incredible pleasure of his life slammed through him.

He glanced into the mirror and nearly came at his first sight of Genevieve's naked back. It was incredible, intense, more arousing than he thought possible to be able to watch her from the back *and* the front as she took him.

When she finally pulled back, giving his balls one last kiss, he didn't know whether to give thanks or howl in disappointment. But she wasn't done—not by a long shot. Now her hot, gorgeous mouth was swallowing him whole.

Fuck, he was going to lose it, his cum boiling up inside of him. What was it about Genevieve, about this cop with the serious eyes and fuck-me mouth, that ripped his control to such shreds?

He didn't know, and in that moment didn't care. He was held in thrall by Genevieve and her hotter-than-hell mouth.

His teeth clenched, his jaw locked as the moist, sexy heat of her mouth drew him in deep. Her tongue ran in circles around his throbbing cock—up and down and around until he was clinging to control by his fingertips.

He looked down, watched as she slid him back and forth between those cherry-red lips of hers. Her eyes were closed, her long, golden lashes resting on her cheeks as she tucked the head of his cock against the roof of her mouth and slid him down her throat.

"Look at me!" His voice was low, guttural, more animal than human. But she understood what he was saying and those beautiful blue eyes flew open. He stared into their cobalt depths as she took him—as he fucked her mouth and she fucked him up—and wondered if he would ever be the same.

But then the pleasure exploded through him, sweeping up from his balls to the base of his cock, taking him by surprise as she sucked a little harder, her tongue wiggling over the sensitive spot on the underside of his cock.

"Fuck!" It was a groan, a plea, a prayer, but his big, bad cop had no mercy in her soul. She took him deeper, her hands clenching his ass as she worked her throat convulsively.

And then he was coming, spurting inside of her, his cum jetting furiously into her mouth. She took it all, swallowed it down, consumed him and left him so damned shaky he nearly fell on her.

And still he burned.

Pulling her up by the hair, he spun her around, shoved her—stomach down—onto the couch. She moved to her knees, wiggling that sweet ass of hers, and it was as if his orgasm of a moment before had never happened.

With a growl, he launched himself at her, slamming himself into her hot pussy again and again. She screamed, pushed back against him. Her fingers tangled in the cushions, her head thrashed from side to side and her vaginal muscles gripped him in fits and spasms that had him seeing stars.

"Genevieve!" he called her name as the orgasm rose sharply in him.

"Cole!" Her voice—her goddamned peaches-and-cream voice—was low, breathless, hotter than hell. And then she was screaming his name, her pussy clenching around him as her climax hit, the waves milking him despite his best efforts to hold on.

With a cry—of thanks, of need, of bone-wrenching fear—he came, emptying himself inside of her. Giving her everything he had in one bone-crushing, mind-numbing, soul-searing orgasm.

And when it was over, when he held Genevieve's trembling body against his own, he couldn't help the feeling that things would never be the same.

What had he done?

What had he let her do?

Chapter Seven

Hours later, they lay in an exhausted heap on her bedroom floor, having fallen out of the bed sometime in the middle of their last encounter—though Cole had no recollection of the fall.

How was it possible, he wondered, for him to have come so many times and still not be sated? He wanted Genevieve and not just sexually, but all the way deep inside of him in a place he barely acknowledged anymore. A place he thought he'd killed off when Samantha had died.

He'd found it tonight when he'd been skulking in the shadows, hanging around the police station, hoping for a glimpse of Genevieve. He'd thought about going in, had even started up the steps a time or two, but he hadn't been able to do it. Every time he thought of going down the hall to homicide, he broke out in a cold sweat. There was no way he'd actually make it down the hall without freaking out—the memories were still too powerful.

So he'd lurked in the shadows, getting angrier and angrier at her the longer he waited. He'd been angry that she'd walked out on him without so much as a phone number, furious that she hadn't felt the same way as he had about the one night they'd spent together.

He'd been thinking about the previous night when she'd finally come out of the station, remembering what it had felt like to taste her while his hands cupped her breasts. He'd been aroused, uncomfortable and more than ready for action.

Which was just one of the many reasons he'd lost it when he'd finally gotten her in his arms. Thank God she hadn't seemed to mind.

Genevieve sighed and wiggled against him. His cock hardened—though he would have sworn it was impossible only minutes before—and he lowered his mouth to the purple bruises that covered her shoulders.

Sneaking his tongue out, he swirled it from one bruise to the next, playing connect the dots with the small hickeys. Slowly, he traced them, moving from her shoulder to her neck to the soft, sweet skin of her breasts. She was covered in the little love bites, no part of her body completely unblemished by his need to brand. To claim.

He'd never felt this possessive before, had never needed to mark a woman so obviously. Part of him was ashamed of his lapse in control, frightened of this desperate need she brought forth so effortlessly from him.

Because he was confused—his instincts demanding that he both dominate and comfort, he took his time soothing the little marks, sliding from one to the next with soft strokes of his tongue. Not an apology, exactly, but an acknowledgment of what he'd done. What he'd been driven to do.

Genevieve started trembling before he'd finished with her right breast, her fingers tangling in his hair. He relished the small pain, tilted his head so that she could grab more. Pull harder. And she did, her actions sending pinpricks of ecstasy cascading through his body.

Shifting a little, he turned her so that he could reach the other bites and bruises. Let his lips trail from her breast down her stomach to her sweet pussy, which was already dripping honey for him.

"Cole, no more." Her voice was hoarse, the hands clutching his hair tighter than they had been just moments before.

"Just one more, sweetheart." He licked lazily up the center of her, let his tongue linger on her responsive little clit. She arched against him, her hands tightening even more. With a flick of his tongue and a thrust of his fingers he sent her careening over the edge again, her cries only making him hungrier.

He could do this all night, all day, he thought as he buried his face in her, took her up again. He loved how she smelled, how she tasted— sweet and spicy and so delicious he swore he could live off her alone.

"Cole!" Genevieve's breath broke and she shuddered against him, her body giving him all the encouragement he could ever need.

Easing to his back, he pulled her slender body over his, relishing the feel of her in his arms. He knew he shouldn't feel like this, not just because it was too soon but because caring for her would probably lead to heartbreak—but he couldn't help it. With a sigh, he lifted her so that she was sitting above him, her legs falling open on either side of his jaw. And set about making her come . . . again.

It was becoming an obsession, this desire to see her climax. This need to make her respond to him. But as he thrust his tongue inside of her—a place he'd already been more times than he could count—she trembled and arched away from him.

Surprised by her reaction—after she'd spent so many hours letting him do whatever he pleased to her—he frowned and slid her down his chest in an effort to see her eyes. But she turned her face away, and though she was sitting on him, her hot pussy poised over his very aroused cock, she suddenly felt far away.

Sitting up, he reached to cup her cheek with a hand that was shaking more than a little. His fingers came away wet and panic raced through him. Grabbing her chin between his thumb and index finger he tried to get her to turn her head to look at him.

But she refused, kept her face steadfastly turned away, and that's when he knew for certain. It wasn't sweat pouring down her face. She was crying.

Genevieve was crying.

Fuck! What had he done to her? Had he somehow hurt her? But he'd felt her response in the hardness of her nipples, in the hands clenching his shoulders, in the rhythmic contractions of her pussy as she'd come again and again. Yes, he'd been rough, but she'd seemed to enjoy it as much as he had.

Springing to his feet, he lifted her in his arms and settled her on the bed. Watched as she curled into the fetal position away from him, tremors shaking her slender body.

Furious, shocked, desperate to understand what he'd done, he settled on the bed beside her. Then, because he couldn't not touch her, he softly stroked a hand over her hair.

But she was struggling, sobbing, her hands clenching into fists as strangled sounds came from her parted lips. Glancing up, he saw her eyes, glazed with pleasure, delirious with it, but also frightened. Wary. He was pushing her too hard, taking everything she had to offer, giving her incredible pleasure in return.

But it wasn't enough. She needed more from him, needed something he wasn't sure he still knew how to give. In those moments when she was utterly lost in her body's response, when the pleasure all but overwhelmed her, she needed tenderness. He only prayed he still had it in him to give it to her.

Moving slowly, he covered her body with his own. She grabbed on to him, her sobs harsh, her body wracked with the aftereffects of the night they'd spent together.

He rolled to his side and gathered her quaking body against his own. Ran a soothing hand down the smooth curve of her spine. Buried his fingers in the soft, strawberry-scented curls that surrounded her face. And let her take as much—or as little—of him as she needed.

It was the hardest thing he'd ever done, lying there while she recovered her equilibrium. He liked to keep his partners off-balance, needed to keep the scales tipped in his favor. But Genevieve was as much a control freak as he was, and he had obviously pushed her too far, too fast.

The thought had him cursing, low and long and mean, as he called himself every name in the book and some new ones of his own invention.

Had he hurt her? Damn it, he'd felt her response, had heard her pleasure as she'd screamed his name. But maybe he'd misinterpreted—maybe he'd given her more pain than pleasure.

"Genevieve, baby—" He broke off, unsure of what to say as his stomach sunk to his toes. Unsure of what to do to make things all right between them.

"I need a minute, Cole," she said as she continued to shake. "It's too much. It's all just too much."

"Did I hurt you?"

"Cole—"

"Just tell me, sweetheart. Did I?"

She would have laughed if she'd been able to work up the energy. But she was empty, strung out, her body so thoroughly used that she wasn't sure if it would ever again feel as if it belonged to her. And he wanted to know if he'd hurt her? He'd shattered her, and she didn't know how to begin to put the pieces back in the right order again.

"Genevieve!"

She finally tilted her head at the barely concealed alarm in his tone, unable to ignore it even as she fought down the panic ripping through her own body. And was shocked at how wild he looked. How fearful. "It's okay, Cole."

"Fuck that!" he snarled, setting her away from him with hands that were shockingly gentle considering the look in his eyes. "Did. I. Hurt. You?"

"No, of course not."

"Fuck." He flopped onto his back, sinking into the mattress as if all the air had gone out of him. Then he lifted his head and eyed her suspiciously. "Are you sure?"

"I'm positive." She told him what he wanted to hear, but it was also the truth. He'd pushed her—fast and furious—beyond every boundary she'd ever had with regards to sex. And up until the end, she'd gone willingly. More than willingly—eagerly. And as soon as it got to be too much, he'd stopped. Instantly.

She'd been a cop long enough to know that a lot of men wouldn't have.

"Then what's wrong, sweetheart?" He grabbed her wrist and pulled her around to face him, shifting so his hard body was wrapped completely around hers. Sheltering her.

It took all her training not to yelp as that last thought occurred to her. It was, after all, the crux of the problem. In one night, he'd managed to get inside of her. To rip her defenses apart and touch the real Genevieve. The one who wasn't such a hard-ass. The one who wanted to believe that such incredible, mind-bending sex meant more than just a good time.

It was too dangerous in the best of times, and around-the-bend crazy with this man she still didn't even know if she could trust. Her body said yes, absolutely, whispered insidious things to her in an effort to take more of the pleasure Cole so easily provided.

But her brain wasn't nearly as accepting. Not with all the warning flags popping out like bare breasts at Mardi Gras. Not with everything she still didn't know about him. But she couldn't bring herself to face the doubts and suspicions while her body still trembled with the last orgasm he had given her.

"Genevieve?" he prompted.

"You're just too much. Too big, too intense, too . . . everything. You want more from me than I can give."

He reached up, stroked a gentle hand down her cheek. "I want you."

"You want too much!" She reached over and grabbed his shirt, shrugging into it as a poor defense for the vulnerability he brought out in her. Then instantly regretted it. Bad enough that her skin smelled like him; now she was surrounded by the tangy, ocean scent. It was enough to drive a sane woman crazy.

Unable to keep still for another second, she stood up from the bed. Started to pace. But she didn't get far.

In a move that was so smooth she almost didn't see it, Cole sprang to his feet. Blocked her path. Began to stalk toward her. "Cole, no." She held up a hand to ward him off, afraid of the frazzled, out-of-control woman she'd become.

"Genevieve, yes." He continued walking toward her, each smooth, deliberate step both a threat and a promise.

"You keep pushing and taking, demanding more and more. I don't know what to do, how to give you what you want."

"All I want is you," he repeated, stopping right in front of her. He stared at her with gleaming onyx eyes she couldn't help responding to.

"You want everything!"

"Damn straight." In a lightning-fast move, he snagged her wrist and pulled her against him. She gasped as she slammed into that hard body—not because she was frightened, but because he felt so damn good.

"Let me show you," he murmured, burying his face in her neck. Licking the spot behind her ear that was guaranteed to set her body on overdrive.

Her laugh was strangled, but the hands pushing against his chest weakened. Began to stroke the firm skin they had resisted only moments before. "You already have. Over and over again."

"Not well enough, obviously." He grabbed the shirt she wore and with one fast tug, ripped it off her so that she was once again naked. Once again laid bare for him.

Even as a nervous tingling skated slickly down her spine, she felt herself opening to him. Her body—so sore and used—preparing to take him. Again. And again and again until he'd used her up. Until she didn't remember what it was like to breathe without him inside of her.

Panic bloomed full out, but she fought it down as she reached for Cole. Took his cock into her hands. Sighed at the look of ecstasy that crossed his face. She would hold her own this time, would refuse to be taken over. Would give as good as she got.

Sinking to her knees in front of him, she ran her tongue up his raging erection. He was hot and hard and so big she didn't know how she'd managed to hold him in her body over and over throughout the long night.

Glancing up, she saw him watching her with eyes that had gone nearly feral in their intensity. But instead of scaring her, the deep, dark look gave her reassurance. She wasn't in this alone. Despite the control he'd exerted all night, he was as affected by her as she was by him.

That knowledge soothed her discomfort, gave her back her equilibrium. With a secret smile, she danced her tongue around the broad head of his cock, then reached between his legs to cup and massage his testicles.

Cole groaned, his fists clenching in her hair. "Do it," he urged, holding her head steady against him.

"Do what?" she teased, flicking her tongue over him again and again. Teasing him, taunting him, giving him only a little of what he wanted. What he needed.

"Genevieve!" His voice was hot, harsh, commanding. The look he shot her just a little bit wild as he thrust against her mouth.

"Is this what you want?" she asked, slipping just the tip of him into her mouth. Sucking gently but never giving him the pressure that he craved.

"Fuck." The fingers in her hair tightened. "You're killing me, sweetheart."

"Payback's a bitch." She laughed low in her throat and then shifted, taking all of him into her mouth.

His cock throbbed as she pulled him deep, letting her tongue run up and down the length of him while she moved her hands until her nails dug into his thighs. Not hard, but just enough to let him know that she meant business.

Then she eased back until only his deep purple head was in her mouth. Sucking him gently, she let her tongue swirl in circles over the small bundles of nerves on the bottom of his tip.

He gasped, clutched at her hair, tried to get her to take more of him. But she refused to give in, refused to be swayed by the wordless pleas of his body. Instead, she lifted a hand and began working his cock with both her hand and her mouth.

"Genevieve." His voice was choked, his hips restless as he thrust against her. "Please—"

The tortured sound of his voice sent her over the edge and she couldn't hold back anymore, couldn't withhold what he so badly wanted when she wanted it too.

Shifting her hands, she cupped his ass to hold him in place. And then slowly, so slowly that she caught every shudder of his strong, virile body, she took all of him.

He was huge, hot, hard—and she loved it. Loved the feel of his body shaking against hers, loved the sharp pain of his hands tugging in her hair. Loved the feel of his cock sliding in and out of her mouth, up and down her throat.

She relaxed her throat, let it milk him as her tongue swirled around him. He tasted like the sea—sweet and salty and storm-tossed—and she couldn't get enough of him. Arousal thrummed through her, making her hot and wet and desperate for the feel of him between her thighs.

But she wasn't ready to let him go, wasn't ready to relinquish the pleasure that came from driving him as crazy as he'd driven her.

Moving again, she brought one hand behind his balls and stroked the sweet spot there. He stiffened, gasped, frantically called her name as he tried to pull out.

She only sucked him deeper, savoring the tangy drop of pre-cum he couldn't hold back. He was on the brink, about to lose control, and she couldn't wait to drive him over. To watch his face as orgasm took him. To feel his body as ecstasy consumed him.

Cole watched her with eyes he could barely keep open, shocked at the intensity of the pleasure Genevieve was giving him. He'd had blow jobs many, many times before, but never had a woman driven him this insane. Never had he lost control of his body, his will. His very soul.

Part of him wanted to stop her, to pull Genevieve up his body and thrust into her until she came, screaming his name. But he had made mistakes with her already, had taken too much power from her, too fast. Had given her pleasure but taken any and all control from her.

And in doing so, he hurt her—something he'd never intended to do. If stringing him out—hurtling him past simple lust and into a primal need to mate—gave her what she needed, then he would let her have it.

For now.

The need to come was urgent, the desire to empty himself into her mouth so intense that it shook him to his very core. But at the same time, he didn't want it to end. He wanted to stay here, in this moment, connected to this beautiful woman forever.

He thrust against her, watched as he slid in and out of her pale pink lips. Did it again and nearly came when she moaned deep in her throat.

"Genevieve, sweetheart," he said, shocked at the gravel in his normally smooth voice. "Stop. I want to be inside you when I come."

Genevieve merely took him deeper, let her tongue run up and down his cock in a rhythm that had his eyes crossing and his balls aching for relief. He was on the brink, orgasm threatening with every strangled breath he took. Just when he was ready to give it up, to let her have her way, she pulled away.

He nearly howled in disappointment, in relief, in desperation. "Fuck," he gasped. "I have—"

He didn't finish the sentence. He couldn't finish it as agony ripped through him. His legs trembled, and his heart beat so fast he was sure it would burst.

But Genevieve seemed oblivious to his plight. Pulling back even farther, she licked her lips. Glanced up at him through her lashes. Then ran her tongue up and down his length in whisper-soft strokes.

He jerked, every muscle in his body tightening as he finally lost all control of his body. Genevieve was taking him, taking everything he could give. And judging from the look on her face, loving every second of it.

"Let me fuck you. Let me come inside you. I want—" He was babbling, incoherent, aware of nothing but the pleasure and pain ripping through him as he fought for control.

Then Genevieve leaned back. Ran her tongue over her sweet, soft lips. Touched the pre-cum leaking from him with one slender finger. "I want you to come," she whispered, slipping the finger in her mouth and sucking it clean before bringing her lips to him once again.

She ran her tongue over his balls, stroked the spot at the back of his balls that she'd found earlier and he'd never known existed. Ordered in a voice breathless with desire, "Come for me, Cole. Come now!"

And swallowed him whole.

It was too much—her mouth on his cock, her hand on his balls, her words in his head. He tried to pull away, to stop the climax flowing through him before he flooded her.

But Genevieve refused to let him go. She slid one arm around his hips and jerked him tightly against her. Her tongue stroked the tender underside of his cock even as she sucked until sanity was a distant memory. She hummed low in her throat, and the ensuing vibrations sent him off the edge of the very high, very jagged cliff he'd been balanced so precariously upon.

With a groan that was almost a shout, he gave himself up to the most incredible orgasm of his life and emptied himself inside of her in long, pulsing jets.

When it was over, when he could think again, he sank gracelessly onto the bed and pulled Genevieve down beside him. He was hot, sweaty. His knees were weak and he was shaking so badly he could barely hold on to her.

He looked down and saw her watching him with such tenderness, he was overwhelmed with emotion. Lying there, looking at him, she was the most beautiful thing he'd ever seen. Her lips were glistening, her cheeks flushed. And her eyes were a bright, shining electric blue—so bright he felt sure she could see all the way to his soul.

The thought should have worried him, should have made him uncomfortable at the very least, considering what he was hiding. Instead, it relaxed him as nothing had in seven long years.

Reaching out, he stroked her tousled curls away from her forehead. Laughed as they wound their way around his fingers. Breathed deeply and inhaled the honeysuckle scent of her into his lungs.

How had he gotten here, to this precise moment? Held tenderly in the arms of this strong, sexy woman?

He didn't know, couldn't fathom how things could have gone so wrong. Or so right. Unsure of what he was doing for the first time in a very long time, he held on tightly to Genevieve. And wondered where on earth they could go from here.

Chapter Eight

Shrugging into her robe, Genevieve stumbled to the kitchen in a stupor, drawn there by the tantalizing aroma of ready-made coffee. Her brain was foggy, her body sore, her libido temporarily sated.

Thank God. How many times had she come last night anyway? Far, far too many to count. It was a miracle Cole hadn't killed her.

Maybe she should have been embarrassed after her meltdown, but Cole had held her so tenderly through it that she didn't regret letting him see her vulnerabilities. And what had happened afterward, when he'd let her take him—in her mouth and in her body—had been worth any of the uncertainties that had come before.

"There you are. I was about to wake you." He skirted the table, handed her a cup of coffee. "What time do you have to be at work?"

"It's my day off." She lifted the cup to her nose, breathed in the life-giving aroma before taking a big sip. It was so delicious she didn't even care that she'd have second-degree burns on her tongue. "You make a hell of a cup of coffee, you know that?"

He snorted. "Don't take offense if I don't hold your opinion in the highest regard. You've been drinking cop coffee for so long, I'd be amazed if you had any taste buds left."

"I've got enough."

"Sure you do." He nodded to the bag on the counter. "I got breakfast, too."

"Well, aren't you just all domestic this morning." She took another sip of coffee, relished the burn as it slid down her sleep-scratchy throat.

"Good sex will do that to a guy."

She lifted an eyebrow, looked him up and down. "*Good* sex?"

He grinned. "Fabulous sex. Amazing sex. Astounding sex."

"Yeah, that's more like it."

Cole grabbed the butter and strawberry jam from the fridge and then settled himself at the kitchen table. In her chair. Which she wasn't nearly as annoyed about as she should have been, but then again, mind-blowing sex could do that to a girl, she thought with a grin.

She watched as he pulled two huge croissants out of the bag, felt her knees turn trembly at the sight. It was really hard to play it cool with a guy who knew all your weaknesses before you even told him, knew them and took care to deliver them to you one after the other.

"How'd you know croissants were my favorite?" she demanded.

He shot her a wicked grin, then licked strawberry jam off his thumb. "Because they're my favorite too."

"I bet. You know," she said, studying him closely over her half-empty cup. "You're awfully domesticated for a big, bad Hollywood type."

His only response was an eye roll, but she'd seen him stiffen. That telltale discomfort had her pushing harder than she might have otherwise. "So did some woman train you to be so thoughtful? A wife? Girlfriend?"

"My mother." His voice was rock steady, but she would have had to be blind to miss the way his hand shook. "I used to have to take care of my half sister—feed her, keep her safe and happy, that kind of thing."

"You must be close to your family."

His eyes turned unreadable in an instant, his jaw clenching so hard she wouldn't have been surprised if he'd broken a tooth. "Not so much anymore."

The tone of his voice made it obvious the subject was closed, and part of her resented his need for privacy. He'd stripped her bare last night, had ripped away every protection she had, yet he balked at answering a few basic questions about his life. It pissed her off, had her wanting to push back just to see if she had the power to make him crack.

But before she could decide from which direction she should push, Cole reached a hand out to her and she took it without knowing why. She should have ignored it, but she didn't. She couldn't. For just a moment he'd looked vulnerable, his pain so real that it took her breath away.

She wanted to ask him about the pictures, to demand an explanation for what she'd seen. But she wasn't ready to go down that road yet. Once she did, she knew the intimacy between them would disappear like it had never been and she wanted—needed—just a few more minutes of it before all hell broke loose. It had been so long since she'd felt this close to another person that she couldn't bring herself to ruin it. Not yet.

When he tugged, she didn't resist, and suddenly she was straddling his lap without being sure how she'd gotten there. Without knowing how she felt about it.

"Open up." She obliged, and he fed her a piece of croissant dripping with jam. She closed her eyes as the sweetness hit her tongue, took her time savoring the rare treat.

"What about you?" he asked.

"What about me?"

"Are you close to your family?"

Opening her eyes abruptly, she found him staring at her, his gaze heavy lidded, his eyes even darker than usual. Her breath caught in her throat, and she felt herself grow wet when minutes before she would have sworn sex was the last thing on her mind.

"I'm an only child," she murmured, struggling to hold on to the conversation. "My parents died in a car crash years ago. Drunk driver."

He stiffened, and the hand on her back turned from sexual to soothing. "I'm sorry—that's terrible."

She shrugged, gave the flip answer she'd been using for years—the one designed to hide her loneliness from the world. "Yeah, well, shit happens. Right?"

"I guess." He paused long enough to make her nervous, then asked, "So is that why you became a cop?"

"I became a cop because there are too many assholes in the world and someone needs to do something about it."

He laughed. "That's the same reason I became a filmmaker."

"I bet."

"No, really," he said as he leaned forward, dropping kisses along the curve of her neck until she relaxed. "So, what are you going to do with your day off?"

She laughed, surprised at how husky the sound was. "Not you." She shoved at his chest. "I've got to work."

He pulled back, looked at her quizzically. "I thought you said you didn't have to work today."

"No, I said it was my day off." She climbed off his lap. "But some psychopath is killing girls on my watch—I can't just kick back and relax while he does it."

"When you put it that way, I guess you can't."

"You guess correctly." She tore off another piece of croissant, popped it in her mouth. "But thanks for breakfast. It was great."

He let her get as far as the doorway before he grabbed a handful of hair and dragged her back against him. "You didn't think it was going to be that easy, did you?" He licked a path up the nape of her neck, smiled as Genevieve shivered and pressed her hips back against his cock.

"I was certainly hoping it wouldn't be."

"That's my girl." He walked her over to the kitchen table, bent her over the chair he had just vacated. Slid a hand under her robe to caress the slick, wet folds of her sex. "Are you sore?" he asked as he slipped a finger inside of her, loving how wet and hot she already was.

"Not too sore, if that's what you're asking." She braced her hands on the nearby table, spreading her legs to give him better access.

"That's exactly what I'm asking." He slid another finger inside her, groaned when she clenched around him. Felt sweat drip down his back as he fought for control. Fuck, she really was the hottest thing he'd ever seen.

Genevieve moved restlessly against him, seeking a deeper penetration. But he kept his touch light, almost playful. Pulled out and stroked a gentle finger over her clit.

"Cole." It was a complaint. A demand. But he merely laughed and brought his second hand up to deliver a sharp smack on her curvy ass.

She jumped, cried out. Turned her head with eyes wide in shock. "What are you doing?"

His only answer was to do it again, this time thrusting two fingers inside of her, hard, as he did so.

She gasped and arched her back, clutching the edge of the table as if she didn't trust her knees to hold her. As she did, his fingers slid deeper, changed angles and rubbed against the sweet spot deep inside of her.

She moaned, her body running like honey around him. She was so responsive it blew him away, so hot that he burned with the need to see just how fast he could send her up and over.

He pulled his fingers out, pinched her clit between his thumb and middle finger. Delivered another, sharper slap to her sweet ass while at the same time tapping her clit with his index finger.

She jerked against him, screaming, her fingers reaching back to grab his cock through the thick material of his jeans. He groaned, thrust against her though he knew better. His dick was on fire, burning for her, and her unexpected touch had taken him all the way to the jagged edge of his control.

She laughed, low and mean, as her fingers worked his zipper down. His cock leapt from between the parted denim and she palmed him, rubbing while he thrust helplessly against her soft hand.

Shit. He was as ready to go off as a sixteen-year-old with his first girl. How could she do this to him so easily? Make him lose control when he'd always prided himself on his staying power?

He pulled away in self-defense, then smacked her harder than he had before. Waited to see how she would react. When all she did was wiggle that luscious ass of hers and press more firmly against him, he swore he'd found heaven.

Fumbling in the back pocket of his jeans, he grabbed a condom. Tore it open with his teeth. Rolled it on in a fever of need. Then sank into her waiting heat with a shudder of relief.

Genevieve came at the first thrust of Cole's cock inside of her. How he'd gotten her so hot so quick, she didn't know, but each tap of his hand on her ass had sent heat shooting through her like fireworks.

She'd wanted to protest on general principle, but it had felt so damn good that she'd kept her mouth shut and let him have his way. That last smack had driven her to the edge, and the utter joy of having him within her again had taken her right over.

Then he was pulling out, robbing her of the last sweet waves of her orgasm. She pressed back, tried to take him again, and he laughed darkly. Then pushed himself inside her, one slow inch at a time.

She shuddered, tried to move back so she could take all of him, but he stopped her with a steady hand on the small of her back. Held her in place so that her screaming nerve endings felt every inch of his invasion.

And it was an invasion, a slow, deliberate conquering that she recognized even through the incredible pleasure. Cole laying claim, establishing dominance, challenging her to deny his possession.

It was the last that had her bucking beneath him, smiling in triumph as she dislodged him.

"Genevieve." His voice was low, warning, as he brought both hands to her hips and pulled her sharply against him until he was as deep inside of her as he could go.

Her muscles clenched involuntarily around him, her body in thrall to his mastery even as her mind rebelled at the limits he set for her. For them. Twisting her hips, she slid away from him again, shimmied until he'd once more slipped from her body.

One hand came down in a sharp crack against the bare skin of her bottom while the other tangled in her hair. He leaned forward until he covered her, until her breasts were pushed tightly against the unforgiving surface of the table and her back was wedged just as tightly against his heavily muscled chest.

"Take me," he demanded, his voice low and harsh in her ear. "Take me now."

He slammed into her so hard she rocketed up onto her tiptoes. Then he was pulling out and slamming into her again and again. He was wild, out of control. She'd challenged him, defied him, pushed him past his limits until the only drive he had was to mark her. To dominate her. To show her who had the upper hand.

And it was delicious, every thrust a shocking invasion. Every slam of his cock a test of her own limits as unimaginable pleasure rocketed through her.

He was moving quickly now, each thrust fast and hard. She closed her eyes, clutched the table, tried to center herself in the maelstrom she'd released. But there was no escape, no control, no salvation. Only Cole and the wicked, inescapable, unbelievable things he was doing to her.

The pleasure rose, tingled, burned, spreading from her cunt to her stomach, up through her breasts, down her arms and legs until no part of her body was unaffected. Until all that she felt, all that she was, was wrapped up in Cole and this unbelievable moment out of time.

Another orgasm rose, sharp and undeniable, yet she tried to push it back. She didn't want this to end, wasn't ready to let this perfect moment slip away.

But Cole's fingers were clenching in her hair, scratching down the delicate skin of her back while his breath shuddered in and out. He was on the edge, holding on through sheer will alone, waiting for his release until he'd sent her careening into her own climax.

It was cruel to make him wait when staving off her own release was nearly killing her. But she shoved the heat down for a few more seconds, reveled in Cole's brutal pounding, in the agony and ecstasy that came with being possessed by this man.

"Come for me, Genevieve." His voice was dark, distorted, and it sent shivers of electricity through her already primed body as he repeated the words she'd used on him last night. "Come for me now!"

And she did, her body shattering into a million pieces, flying far beyond her scope of control as unimaginable ecstasy roared through her.

Cole came about a half second later, his body stiffening and jerking as he pulsed inside of her, his semen coming in forceful spurts that only intensified her own climax. His hands clenched her hips, held her still as he poured himself into her.

"Cole!" She screamed his name as she went under yet again, the contractions building on themselves, over and over until it was both agony and ecstasy. Total fulfillment and complete devastation. She was laid raw and open before him.

Cole collapsed on top of her, his big body covering every inch of her sensitized skin. It was too much and not enough and she went into sensory overload, her body so far beyond her control that it could have belonged to a stranger, for all the attention it paid to her.

And when Cole dragged his teeth along her back, licking his way down her spine, she somehow came one final time. Her body shooting into the stars until all that was left of her was a mindless bundle of sensation.

When she finally came down and managed to catch her breath—not an easy feat with a six-foot-five, 270-pound man on top of her—she said with a grin, "Well, good morning to you too."

She felt his lips curve against her back. "Good morning, Genevieve." Then he was easing out of her, taking off the condom, pulling away and moving toward the bathroom.

Just normal postcoital stuff, so why did she suddenly feel so bereft?

Shoving the ridiculous feeling to the back of her head where she could pretend it didn't exist, she settled into her chair and drew her knees up so that she could rest her chin on them. Picked up a croissant and began to pick at it with studied casualness while she waited for Cole to come back.

Now that her sex drive was well and truly glutted and her brain firing on all synapses, she figured she couldn't put things off any longer.

Which was why, as soon as Cole returned, she shot off, "You never did answer my question last night."

He leaned against the counter, his body suddenly tense as he watched her over the rim of his coffee cup. "Which question was that, sweetheart? 'Where'd you learn to fuck like that?' or 'Could you do it some more?'"

She narrowed her eyes, refused to blush at the reminder of her blatant demands. "The one where I wanted to know what the hell you were doing researching my department and various sexual homicides from the last few years. How'd you even know about them?"

"They're in the newspaper. I found them when I was looking at back issues."

She snorted. "Yeah, well, most of the general public isn't really into researching those kinds of stories. What makes you different?"

He was silent for long seconds, then sighed as he crossed the kitchen and sat down next to her. "I'm doing a documentary on the sexual violence endemic in New Orleans. For centuries, sex and violence have gone hand in hand in this city, and I'm trying to find out why."

"Sex and violence go hand in hand all over the world," she countered. "Not just here."

"True." He inclined his head. "But there aren't many places where it's as blatant as it is in this city. You of all people should know that."

"Why me?"

"You're the only woman working homicide in the entire French Quarter. You can't convince me all the sexual perversity you see on the job doesn't bother you."

"Of course it bothers me."

Silence stretched between them as she contemplated Cole's words. She wanted so much to believe what he was saying, but was afraid the woman was overwhelming the cop. "Do you really expect me to buy that? You looked me up, researched me. What does that have to do with your documentary?"

"I wanted a female perspective on murder in the French Quarter. You're it."

She fought down the hurt his words caused. "So this was all for your movie? Picking me up at the bar, taking me home? What did you do—follow me from the precinct that night? What a brilliant plan to get the *perspective* you needed."

"No, it wasn't like that!" His hands were urgent as he gripped her arms and tried to pull her closer to him. She resisted, but it was more difficult than she would have imagined.

"Then explain it to me, because I don't understand."

"I took you home *despite* my project. I tried to walk away a dozen times, told myself it was stupid even while I was doing it. But I wanted you too much to stop—would have done anything to have you."

"Including hiding the evidence in your closet?"

He flushed, but his eyes never wavered from hers. "I shoved it there before I went out that morning. I was afraid you'd find it before I had a chance to explain and think I'd used you. Which, of course, is exactly what you thought when you did find it."

"Actually, I thought you might be the serial killer I've been looking for for the past few months." She watched him closely as she spoke, wondered how he was going to react to her words.

She didn't have long to wait. Color drained from his face and the look he shot her was full of horror. "You couldn't have."

She shrugged. "I did."

His grip loosened and he shoved away from her, began to pace the kitchen with agitated strides. "Genevieve, you don't honestly think . . ." His voice trailed off, and she could see the last several hours replaying in his head. "You slept with me when—"

"I found out who you were yesterday afternoon and things started to fall into place. But I still wanted to hear it from you."

He stopped, pinning her with his midnight gaze. "Well, you heard it. Now do you believe it?"

She took her time answering, letting him sweat. He'd put her through the wringer yesterday, and—wrong or not—she was more than ready to get some of her own back today.

Finally, when the air between them was so tense she feared one wrong move would shatter them both, she said coolly, "I wouldn't have slept with you if I didn't."

His shoulders sagged in relief. "Well, thank God for small favors. I've seen the pictures from the Robbins homicide. The idea that you thought I was capable of that—"

Cole broke off in midsentence, as if aware that he'd said too much.

"How do you know about Jessica Robbins?" she demanded, everything inside of her running cold. "Her murder hasn't even hit the papers yet."

Anger flashed between them. "Not the way you're implying, obviously. I hacked the NOPD database."

She lifted an eyebrow. "That's illegal, you know."

"So arrest me," he snarled. "If you're going to try and find me guilty of something, I'd rather it be a crime I actually committed."

"Why would you do that?" She lifted her coffee cup to her mouth, then slammed it back down without taking a sip. "Why the hell would you hack the database?"

Something flashed in his eyes and then was gone. It had happened so quickly that she couldn't identify the emotion behind the flash, but she could tell he was hiding something. The knowledge only served to make her angrier. But she bit back the anger—she hadn't been a cop for ten years just to let Cole get the best of her. Even if he was the best lover she'd ever had.

"I knew something big had happened—just from the way you were acting the other night at the bar." He shrugged as he answered her question. "I wanted to know what it was."

She studied him for long seconds, her instincts warring with her logic. He seemed so sincere, so self-assured that she had a hard time believing he was lying. Even more, she didn't want to think he was lying to her—not after last night. But still, his voice was shaking as badly as his hands. . . .

"I can't afford to just let you go blithely on your way about this." She kept her voice and eyes cool, though all she wanted was to fling herself at Cole and beg him to tell her the truth. "Not when I have a serial killer preying on women and killing them in ways that seem particularly interesting to you."

He lifted one eyebrow so high she could barely see it beneath his shaggy bangs. "You think I'm killing teenage girls?"

"They aren't all teenagers."

"Excuse my mistake." He spoke through clenched teeth. "You think I'm killing women?"

She didn't—especially not after his admission of hacking into the NOPD database and the small mistakes he kept making that told her he knew less about the murders than she'd originally thought—but the cop in her wouldn't let her pass up the opportunity to push him just a little further. "Are you?"

His coffee cup hit the counter, hard. "I'm going to pretend you didn't ask that."

"Why?" She stood up, crossed the room until she was in his face. His very irate, very disturbed face. "Hit too close to home?"

"Fuck that. I don't *kill* women. I don't *hurt* women." He pushed past her, crossing the room to where his clothes were crumpled on the floor.

She followed him. "Well, that's not exactly true, is it?" She glanced down at the bruises on her wrists and then back at him. She was hitting below the belt—God, was she ever—but he was hiding something, and she needed to know what it was.

He stopped dead, his hands clenching into fists she could only imagine he wanted to wrap around her throat. "That's a really shitty thing to say."

"The truth often is." She inclined her head.

"You *liked* what I did to you."

"I never said I didn't—merely that you don't have quite the aversion to causing pain that you would like me to think you do."

The look of betrayal on his face had her catching her breath and bile rising in her throat. She hadn't meant to hurt him, had wanted only to get at the truth so that she could relax about him. About them. But from the look on his face as he turned away, there no longer was a *them*.

"Well, fuck you, then, Genevieve. Fuck you."

She scrambled after him with the feeling that her whole world was caving in around her. "Cole, can you see it from my perspective? You have to admit, it looks suspicious."

"Does it?" He yanked on his jeans hard enough to get denim burn in some very uncomfortable places. "Why?"

"Are you kidding me? You have that huge file on the murders. You admit to hacking the NOPD database. How can I not be suspicious?"

"Because you trust me?" He shrugged into his T-shirt, then grabbed his shoes without bothering to button up.

"Trust has to be earned."

The searing look he tossed over his shoulder would have stopped her at two hundred paces if she hadn't just spent the night in his arms. As it was, it still made her more nervous than she liked to admit. Crossing to him, she put a hand on his shoulder, then jumped when he pulled brutally away.

"So does mistrust," he shot back at her as he slammed his feet into his running shoes. "You might think of that the next time you want to throw accusations around."

"Cole—" She didn't know what she was going to say, but he cut her off before she had the chance to get another word out.

"And while you're at it, think about what it says about you that you fucked me while you had even the slightest suspicion that I was involved with raping and killing seven young women. I guess I'm not the only sick bastard around."

"Three," she said, faintly, trust in him coming too late.

"What?" He paused, glared at her.

"To my knowledge, there have only been three connected murders, not seven. Unless you've found something I haven't—" She reached out a beseeching hand to him, but he knocked it away impatiently.

"My mistake. I researched seven murders—and from the way you're acting, I figured they all must be related." Reaching into his pocket, he pulled out a glossy black business card and tossed it on the counter between them. "Here's the Web site the studio set up to pimp the documentary. Kind of a behind-the-scenes thing. Look it up, if you don't believe me. Maybe then we can work on *trust*."

Then he was turning, banging out the back door without a backward glance, letting the small path in her backyard guide him out and into the street. She watched him until he disappeared around the corner. Then wrapped her arms around herself as she sank to the floor.

She needed to get up, to get to work, but her body refused to cooperate. Rocking back and forth, she listened to the sounds of the French Quarter drifting in through the open window, struggling to get control of her emotions. Cole Adams had lodged himself well and truly inside her head and she could no longer think straight. Eventually, she peeled herself up off the floor and moved across to the computer. Logged onto the Internet and found the Web site Cole had told her about. His studio had gone all out as it documented the steps that went in to making his documentary.

It was all true. Guilt gnawed at her stomach and she swallowed down the taste of bile as she switched off the screen. By the time she stepped into the shower, Genevieve was nearly sick. As she soaped up, her mind played over the scene with Cole again and again. She hadn't meant to handle it so badly, had simply been so overwhelmed by him sexually that she'd wanted to prove—to herself and to him—that she could still think like a cop. Still *be* a cop.

After all the shit she'd taken from the guys at the station, after all the innuendoes that had implied she couldn't keep her hormones off the job, it grated that she couldn't help wondering—even for a moment—if they'd been right all along.

Of course, with Cole long gone and her head completely clear for the first time in twelve hours, she knew all that was bullshit. She could compartmentalize just fine; had done so in this case from the very beginning.

She'd known Cole was innocent and now she had the proof—the Web site set up by his studio to follow every aspect of the documentary and his obvious lack of information about the cases.

Still, as lead detective on a string of homicides that were skating dangerously close to being unsolvable, she'd had every right to question him about his involvement. Of course, she acknowledged ruefully as she turned off the spray and climbed out of the shower, she could have handled it better—a lot better. Perhaps waiting for longer than five minutes to pass since he was inside her would have been a good place to start.

Screw that, she decided as she wrapped a towel around her wet hair. She had a killer to catch, and Cole had to understand that. If she ended up stepping on some of his toes in the course of the investigation—or all of them, for that matter—his best bet was to invest in some steel-toed work boots.

Grabbing a lightweight gray suit out of her closet, she headed into the bedroom, only to be brought up short when she caught sight of her reflection in the mirror for the first time.

Was that really her body?

Walking forward slowly, she put a shaky hand against the coolness of the mirror. Stared at the bruises and red marks covering patches of her skin. She looked like she'd been through a war—and lost.

Hickeys lined her throat, dotted her breasts and part of her stomach. Purple bands circled her wrists where Cole had held her arms in place and—she turned—her ass still had the pink imprint of his hand.

Her knees trembled and she collapsed in front of the mirror, staring wide-eyed at the stranger's body reflected back at her. How was this possible? If she'd seen these marks on another woman she would have freaked out, assumed abuse, but there hadn't been any.

Cole hadn't done anything she hadn't wanted—and enjoyed. Every touch, every kiss, every bite had been calculated to bring her the maximum amount of pleasure. And he had succeeded—she'd never known she was capable of the kind of response he drew so effortlessly from her. Of orgasms so intense and plentiful.

Reaching out, she traced a soft finger over a bruise on her upper thigh. She vaguely remembered Cole holding her legs apart as he went down on her, but she hadn't felt any pain. Only the most intense pleasure of her life.

Taking a few deep breaths for courage, Genevieve stared into the mirror as she ran her hands over her breasts, down her stomach and arms. Skimmed her fingers up her thighs and over her buttocks as she tried to come to terms with this new side of her.

Had she really lost it so completely in Cole's arms that she had demanded this kind of response from him? That she'd reveled in it? Had she really driven him so crazy that he'd felt the need to mark her? To brand her?

The evidence that she had was all over her body.

And, bizarre as it was, she loved it—absolutely adored this proof that the Ice Queen could drive a man to such desperate lengths. That she could take him outside of himself to the point that he did *this* to her. That she could go outside herself to the point that she didn't even notice as it happened.

Besides, the bruises didn't hurt—hell, she hadn't even known most of them were there until she'd looked in the mirror. It would be worse than hypocritical to hold them against him, when last night she'd screamed his name more times than she could count.

Turning away, she began to dress. But as she slipped into her underwear, and then the suit that would cover all evidence of the previous night, she couldn't help stealing little glances down at her body and longer looks into the mirror behind her.

She couldn't forget that the love bites were there, nor could she forget the man who had given them to her—as, perhaps, had been Cole's intention all along.

When finally her blouse was buttoned and all her skin was covered up, she slipped into her jacket. Twisted her curls into a loose chignon. Slid her feet into a pair of sensible loafers. And then shifted the collar of her shirt aside so that she could see the marks one more time.

It was going to be a long day, and every second of it would be spent thinking of Cole Adams and his undeniable, unbelievable, highly arousing claim on her body and her soul.

Chapter Nine

Two days later, it was disconcerting to realize just how right she'd been. She was knee-deep in three unsolved homicides, and all she could think of was Cole. Every shift in her chair made her wince as her well-used body protested any sudden movement. Every glance at her watch revealed the lightly bruised skin of her wrist, had her remembering just how fabulous it had been to be restrained by Cole's hands. And still he hadn't called.

She'd spent the last forty-eight hours waiting for the phone to ring, expecting to hear Cole's voice on the other end. But it hadn't—and she didn't know if she was furious about that or relieved. What she felt for him was intense, too intense, and part of her wondered if she was better off without him—even if he did make her feel more than anyone ever had.

Shuffling through Cyndi Priner's file for what seemed like the millionth time, Genevieve scowled in disgust. There was nothing here, nothing she and Shawn had missed. Nothing that might actually connect Cyndi to Jessica and Lorelei's murders.

Not that she'd expected to find anything—she had gone over the file nearly every day since Cyndi had been killed and could quote its contents by heart.

Still, a smoking gun would have been nice—something, anything that might actually convince Chastian to move on this sometime before the next century.

"Hey, partner, you're looking mighty serious there."

Glancing up, she did a double take as her partner, Shawn, swaggered toward her. With his surfer-boy hair and brightly colored polo, he looked more like a San Diego beach bum than a New Orleans cop, but his instincts in homicide were right on and had been for nearly a decade. "What are you doing here? I thought you had a few more vacation days left."

He shrugged, then flashed her the grin that had gotten him everything he'd ever wanted. "I missed you."

"Yeah, right."

"I'm serious. Though the alligators in the bayou did have a sweeter temperament."

She snorted. "Bite me."

"It would be my very great pleasure."

"I don't know about that. The last guy who did said I was pretty bitter."

"Nah." He reached across the desk and picked up the small bag of chocolate chip cookies that was currently passing as lunch. "You're not bitter—just an acquired taste." He popped a cookie in his mouth.

"Oh, really? And you think you've acquired that taste?" She yanked her cookies back.

"More than most of the guys here have."

"Like that's hard?" She shot him a wry look.

"Not really." He stole the last cookie from the bag and hopped off her desk. Then, after settling behind his own desk, said, "So, catch me up. I hear it's been a hell of a week."

"You have no idea."

After briefing him on the cases she'd caught earlier in the week, she slid Jessica's folder in front of him. "Look through it. Tell me what you think."

Shawn spent a few minutes going over her notes and the details of the case. She tried not to watch him, tried not to react to every muffled curse or sigh. But it was hard—she was so wired about this one, so anxious for her partner to see what she saw, that she was afraid she'd jump out of her skin.

But when he raised his eyes to hers ten minutes later, there was no hint of recognition in them. Just an angry disgust he didn't even try to hide. "I swear to God, these guys are getting sicker every fucking day."

"A new day, a new perversion." She repeated the words that were all but a mantra in the precinct.

"Isn't that the truth?" Leaning back in his chair, Shawn studied her for a minute. "What aren't you telling me?"

"Nothing."

"Bullshit. Fess up."

"I don't think she's the only one."

His eyebrows nearly hit his hairline. "You think there's another body out there we don't know about?"

"Maybe." She grabbed her lukewarm Dr Pepper, took a long, slow sip as she formulated what she wanted to say. "I was thinking about those cases we never closed. You know, Lorelei DuFray and Cyndi Priner."

Shawn froze, staring at her as if she'd grown another head. "What makes you think the cases are related?"

"The level of sadism. The obvious humiliation of the victims." She shrugged. "Sheer gut instinct."

"Yeah, well, we can set a clock by your gut instincts, so why hasn't Chastian done anything about this yet?"

"He doesn't believe me. Thinks I'm making things up."

"Yeah, well, don't take his bullshit to heart. The lieutenant wouldn't be able to find his ass with both hands and a mirror the size of the fucking moon."

Genevieve giggled despite herself, and felt her tense muscles relaxing for the first time in days. His sense of humor and ability to call things like he saw them were just two of the many reasons she loved having Shawn as a partner.

"I know. I had the same thought yesterday." She clicked into her e-mail, scrolled through it. "That's what has me so afraid."

Her heart started pounding as she realized she had an answer from Jose. She opened it, felt her stomach cramp at the two terse sentences. *Call made from unregistered, untraceable, prepaid cell phone. What the hell's going on?*

Cursing under her breath, Genevieve sat back in her chair and stared at the computer screen with blank eyes. Shawn was still talking, but she couldn't hear a word he was saying. All of her concentration was focused on Jose's cryptic e-mail.

So her instincts about the phone call had been right on, after all. Not some kids being stupid, but someone who had something to hide. No other reason to use such a deliberately anonymous phone.

But was it the killer—or just someone with a grudge against her? God knew she'd made her fair share of enemies on the job these last few years.

Her gut screamed that the call had come straight from the man she was searching for, and she couldn't ignore it—no matter how much she wanted to.

"Shawn," she said, quietly breaking into his long-winded diatribe. "I think we've got a problem."

"Besides a psychotic killer and no leads?" But his blue eyes narrowed, stared at her with an intensity that belied his laid-back looks. "What is it?"

She told him about the prank call—and Jose's response to it—as succinctly as possible, and wasn't the least bit surprised when he exploded.

"Why didn't you tell me this before now?" he demanded.

"I didn't know if it was important."

"You have some woman-killing psycho calling you and you don't think it's important that he's fixated on you?"

"Two phone calls is far from fixated! What I'm concerned about is what he *said*."

The reminder stopped Shawn mid-diatribe, as she'd intended. "That there's another body out there? Do you believe him?"

"I don't think we can afford not to. Not at this point."

He nodded his agreement, his eyes grim. "So where do we start looking for her?"

"That's the kicker, isn't it?"

They stared at each other for long seconds. Dismay and anger were winding themselves through Genevieve, and she could tell from the look on Shawn's face that he felt exactly the same way.

Some woman was out there right now—either being tortured or already dead—and they could do nothing about it but wait. Wait for the next phone call, wait until the body turned up, wait until it was too late for another girl, another family.

Screw that! She had to do something—*they* had to do something. And at this point, their best chance of catching this sick bastard was to work the cases they already had.

Springing up, Genevieve strode to the large board parked against the back wall. Rolling it back to her desk, she pulled some thumbtacks and dry-erase markers out of her top drawer. "Let's spread it all out, look at the timeline."

Shawn must have had the same thought, because he already had the case files open. "If you're right and this is the same guy, it all starts with Lorelei DuFray."

He grabbed the first folder on his desk, pulled out two pictures. One of thirty-three-year-old Lorelei as she'd been before July fifth—smiling and pretty and alive. And one of her after the killer had gotten done with her.

She'd been laid out naked in Jackson Square, her legs and arms bound behind her with thick rope, her body severely bruised. Her throat had been slashed—not deep enough to kill her instantly, but more than enough to let her bleed out slowly. Next to her in the photo was the long length of black satin she had been covered with when she was discovered.

Genevieve added pertinent details they'd discovered through three months of investigating, including the date Lorelei had gone missing, her approximate time of death and her unusual after-hours schedule, as well as her boyfriend's name and alibi.

"Cyndi came next." Shawn's voice was harsh with anger as he pulled out photos of the forty-five-year-old nurse. Unlike Lorelei, Cyndi had been a blonde—at least until the killer had shaved her head.

Two weeks ago, they'd found her brutalized body in the Dumpster behind Lafitte's Blacksmith Shop—one of the oldest buildings in the Quarter. She'd been fully clothed, her head bashed in. Shawn had originally wanted to call it a mugging gone bad, but the coroner had turned up evidence of rape and sodomy, as well as missing fingertips that indicated she'd gotten in some pretty good licks before the killer had taken her. If he hadn't been afraid of his DNA being discovered, he never would have cut off poor Cyndi's fingers.

They pinned much of Cyndi's file to the board before moving on to Jessica Robbins and doing the same with hers. When they had done all they could, they stepped back and surveyed their handiwork.

"You know, any cop looking at this would think we were insane to believe they were connected," Shawn commented as he leaned against the side of his desk.

"Blonde, redhead, brunette," Genevieve intoned. "Range of ages. Different method of murder in each one."

"The only thing that's the same is the rape—and the beating."

"They were all killed about seventy-two hours after they disappeared," Genevieve said as she stared at Lorelei's vacant eyes. "But they weren't all dumped right away. He held on to Cyndi for a while."

"Or they just didn't find her in the Dumpster until after she'd been there a while."

Genevieve was shaking her head before he finished. It was an argument they'd already had three times since catching Cyndi's case. "You've got to stop harping on that. Jefferson said no way, not with this heat. The rate of decomposition wasn't nearly high enough. They found her within hours of when she'd been put in there."

"So why would he hang on to her and not the others? It doesn't make any sense." Shawn shoved a frustrated hand through his hair, started to pace between his desk and the back of the room.

"Opportunity?" she commented. "The bar's on Bourbon Street, for God's sake. Maybe he couldn't get her there before then."

He shrugged. "I don't know. Maybe." His tone was more than a little doubtful. "But we're talking about a guy who was able to lay a girl out in Jackson Square in the middle of the afternoon and not be seen. Somehow I doubt a Dumpster at the back of a popular bar would give him much trouble."

They fell silent for a few minutes as they studied the board. Finally, Shawn said, "You can see why Chastian's giving us a hard time. These women don't have a thing in common."

"Not even neighborhood or occupation," she agreed, going through the list she'd already run in her head more than a dozen times. "Even the manner of death and distribution of bodies is very different. I know all that."

"You also know that a serial killer has a usual type and method and he sticks to that type religiously. This guy's doing none of that."

She shrugged. "Maybe he's a new breed."

Shawn stared at her in disgust. "Like the old breed isn't good enough?"

"I don't know. But I'm telling you, it's the same guy."

She stepped closer to the photos. "Each of them is cut right here." She pointed to each woman's upper thigh. "Even in Cyndi's case, where he didn't use a knife anywhere else."

Shawn ground his teeth as he followed her finger across the board. "Fuck."

"Yeah, my sentiments exactly."

"Hey, Delacroix, Webster, want a slice of pizza?" called Roberto Torres, another detective who sat a few desks in front of them. "My partner's wife has him on a low-cholesterol diet." He said the last words as if he was describing a fate worse than death.

Genevieve turned and smiled at the suave Puerto Rican detective, and checked out his suit while she was at it. Known among the squad as the best-dressed homicide detective, he took as much ribbing as she did. And that was saying something. He was also one of the few detectives who, like Shawn, looked at Genevieve and saw her, not just a woman trying to crash into the Good Old Boys' Club. She'd always liked him for that.

"How'd you know I was starving, Roberto?" She reached for a piece of the gooey pepperoni pie.

"'Cuz you got that hungry look. I swear, you white girls never eat."

"Sure we do." She laughed and took a huge bite of the pizza. "See?"

"Only 'cuz I brought it to you. Otherwise, you'd be sitting there, wasting away while this no-good loser let you." He nodded at Shawn, who was in the process of snagging a piece of pizza for himself.

"Hey, I'm always up for eating," Shawn protested. He nodded at Genevieve. "She's the one who's always saying she wants to finish one more thing before we go."

"See what I mean? These white girls, they've got no sense of self-preservation." Roberto took another bite of pizza, his eyes wandering over the murder board they'd just set up. "So, what are you guys working on over here?" He glanced at the crime scene photos, winced sympathetically. "Man, three open homicides in three weeks. And such nasty ones."

He nodded at the photo of Jessica. "So what are you thinking about her? A senator's house, man. That's rough—the chief's spent more time talking to the press in the last two days than he has in the last two years."

"We're kind of stumped." Shawn shrugged, then took a bite of pizza. "What do you think?" he asked when he was done chewing, and nodded toward the board.

"She wasn't a piece on the side?"

"If she was, the senator's denying it up one side and down the other. And we can't get anyone—in his camp or hers—to say otherwise."

"Blackmail?"

Genevieve shook her head—she'd spent half of yesterday looking at that angle to please her lieutenant.

"Well, there's got to be something—beyond the normal sadistic crap, I mean. You don't just dump a body in a senior senator's house for no reason."

"That, my man, is exactly what we've been thinking." Shawn pulled a folder off Genevieve's desk. "Look at—"

"Hey, why do you have all three of those girls up on the same board?" Torres' partner, Luc Viglio, asked as he snagged the last piece of pizza from the box.

He was a huge bull of a man and old enough to be Genevieve's father, but he still blushed when she raised an eyebrow at him. "Hey, one piece never hurt anyone."

Torres laughed. "Yeah, unless your wife finds out."

"What she don't know . . ." He glanced again at the murder board. "So are you thinking these three are connected somehow?"

"Don't be stupid," Torres answered. "They've got nothing in com—" His voice drifted off as he saw the grim glance Genevieve and Shawn exchanged.

"Are you kidding me? You think one guy did all three of them?"

"It's looking more and more like it."

Viglio stepped closer, read the timelines and abbreviated notes Genevieve had pinned to the board. "I don't see it. What am I missing?"

"I don't know, just a feeling." Genevieve snatched the folder out of Shawn's hand and laid it open on the desk. Normally, she and Shawn were prone to playing things closer to the vest, but frankly, they could use all the help they could get. Even more, she'd like to have her theory validated by a couple of senior detectives before she took it back to Chastian and got shot down—again.

"The level of torture's the same in each murder," she explained, pulling out the ME's reports and showing them around, along with notes they'd made on the cases.

Torres and Viglio looked over what she and Shawn unearthed. Except for the occasional obscenity, they were quiet as they digested what they were seeing.

Finally, when the silence had stretched Genevieve's nerves to the breaking point, Torres said grimly, "We've got another fucking serial killer on our hands."

"Yeah." Viglio rubbed a hand over the back of his neck. "What's the city coming to when we have a new one of these guys working the area every few months?"

Torres ignored his partner. "What'd Chastian say about this theory?"

"He didn't believe me when I first brought it up."

"Did you show him all this?" demanded Viglio.

"He hasn't been around much the last couple of days."

"He's here now." Torres nodded toward the lieutenant's office. "Get in there. And when he finally gets a clue and gives you backup, tell him we'll be happy to work with you on this."

Shawn nodded, clapped a hand on Torres' back. Seeing as how Genevieve was the social pariah of the department—and had been since she was promoted to it three years before—the offer held a lot of meaning, and they both knew it.

It was nice to know that someone besides Shawn didn't mind working with her.

"Yeah, okay." They headed toward Chastian's office together. "He's going to want to know if we have any suspects."

"I know that, but this guy hasn't made any mistakes yet." She closed her eyes, prayed that the lieutenant would take them seriously. "We've got nothing."

Before Shawn could answer, Chastian's voice barked out, "Webster, Delacroix, get in here!"

"What have you got?" Chastian's voice was more brusque than usual, his annoyance obvious, as they walked into his office.

"Sir." It was Shawn who spoke, since they both knew their boss had a tendency to listen to him much more than to Genevieve.

As Shawn laid the evidence on the table, Genevieve tried to pay attention—hoping to catch something she'd missed in the thousand and one times she'd already gone over it. But her mind kept wandering back to Cole. What was he doing right now? Was he still angry with her?

"Would you care to join us, Delacroix?" Chastian's sarcasm drew her attention, had her flushing before she could stop herself.

"Sorry, sir." Burying her embarrassment, she looked him straight in the eye.

"Shawn seems to think we're dealing with another serial killer and would like to get a profiler on this right away." His eyes dared her to try and take any of the credit for the idea.

Swallowing back her anger, she tried to tell herself that it wasn't important. That as long as she and Shawn got what they wanted, it didn't matter if the lieutenant went the extra mile to antagonize and humiliate her.

But it did matter—not who got the credit, but the fact that no matter how hard she tried or how good she was at her job, she was never going to be accepted the way Shawn and Roberto and Luc were, just because they were men. Even after all these years, it grated much more than she usually admitted to herself.

But she couldn't say what she was thinking, not when it was a guaranteed way to keep her homicides on the track to Nowheresville. So instead, she gritted her teeth and said, "I think Shawn's right, sir. A profiler could really help us with this." She cleared her throat.

He nodded gravely, though his dark eyes mocked her show of subservience. "All right, then." He turned back to Shawn. "And depending what the profiler says, I'll decide whether you need Viglio and Torres backing you up."

"Sounds good, LT." Shawn smiled, his eyes warning Genevieve to stay with the program.

Knowing Shawn was right, she swallowed back the bile scalding her throat and added her thanks to his.

"It's settled, then. I'll call my friend at the bureau and see what he can do for us." Chastian settled behind his desk. "I'll let you know what he says."

"That'd be great."

"Absolutely." Genevieve wanted to puke. She wanted nothing more than to kick Chastian's ass, and instead she was stuck kissing it. What the hell kind of world was it when you needed to beg to get the resources to do your job correctly?

But she waited until they were back at their desks before she made a comment. "That guy is such an asshole."

"Yeah, but he's the boss." Shawn's shrug said it all.

"I still don't know how that happened."

"He didn't used to be so bad." Shawn walked back to the murder board and stared at Jessica's face for long seconds. "He changed after his wife left him, got a lot less human."

She shook her head. "I can't imagine him any other way. The thought of him as a decent guy gives me the shudders."

"Hey, now, I didn't say *decent*. I said *better*."

"Yeah, well, that's not hard. I can't imagine him much worse."

Chapter Ten

Cole lowered his video camera slowly, unhappy with the images he was recording. The crew was going to be here in a few weeks to film and he wasn't nearly ready for them, his mind too full of Samantha and Genevieve to concentrate on the documentary he was being paid to make.

He'd come out today, still miserable over his fight with Genevieve and determined to get some work done, but nothing was going the way it was supposed to. All along he'd planned to do a segment on the topless bars and sex shops that proliferated on the streets of the Big Easy, but he'd wandered from one to the other today—filming and trying out commentary in his head—and nothing had seemed right. He couldn't get Genevieve out of his thoughts enough to concentrate on anything else.

Fuck! He couldn't believe how thoroughly they had managed to blow things the other morning, and he wasn't sure their budding relationship could ever recover. He'd reached for his phone to dial her number on more than a few occasions in the last four days. But each time, he'd hung up before punching in the final digit. What would he say if she answered? What if she *didn't* answer? After what had happened between them, he was pretty damn sure Genevieve would want nothing to do with him. With them.

Shoving a hand through his hair, Cole contemplated his options as he walked the pothole-ridden streets of the Quarter. He should go home—he had a million things to do, starting with finding someone else to help him look at the homicide scenes he wanted to use for the documentary.

Sidestepping the street cleaners rolling down Bourbon, he shook his head in disgust. Could he have handled things with Genevieve any worse? If events were happening the way she'd described, of course she'd have been suspicious of him—she was a cop, for God's sake.

And though he had almost no respect for cops as a breed, Genevieve knew how to do her job and do it well. She rarely let anything stand in her way when she was on a scent, so of course she'd had to ask him about the murders. Add to that the fact that he was omitting things he didn't want her to know, and was it any wonder her bullshit detector was going crazy?

But he hadn't been prepared, hadn't expected it of her right then. He'd left the kitchen after the most intimate sex he'd ever had in his life and returned to find her armored up and on the offense. It had . . . *hurt*, though he felt like a total candy-ass admitting it.

Glancing up, he realized he'd stopped in front of Wild Plums, one of the French Quarter's premier sex shops. He'd planned on starting his film here, with a wide-angle shot of the store amidst the Quarter's craziness, before slowly narrowing in on the posters that covered every available window space—posters that spoke of sex and other, darker pleasures.

He'd been thrilled when the idea had hit him, had spent days getting the timing right. But now that he was here for some preliminary shots, he couldn't work up an ounce of interest.

Probably because he would much rather be having sex with Genevieve than focusing on its darker side. Or maybe the problem was that he wasn't digging deeply enough, that he was simply scratching the surface of a topic that needed to be explored in depth.

Violence was endemic in these sex shops and bars—he'd read enough police reports to understand that. And yet a lot of people in healthy relationships came here too—a fact that made the job of tying everything together that much harder.

With a resigned sigh, he shoved his camera into his case and pulled open the blacked-out door. Maybe a look inside would help him figure out what he was missing.

But as he wandered the rows of magazines and videos and novelties, he found himself at a loss. There was nothing here that he wanted to put in his documentary, nothing here that helped him understand—or explain—the elusive tie between sex and violence that permeated this city like bourbon at Mardi Gras.

Impatient, he turned to leave and was halfway to the door before he caught sight of the largest display of bondage and S-M items he'd ever run across. For a moment, he froze—his mind's eye already taking in what the display would look like on film.

Whips and paddles. Clips and cuffs and satin ties. A truly awe-inspiring collection of leather wear and blindfolds all displayed against dark purple silk. His fingers actually itched with the need to pull out his video camera and record the display—along with the thoughts pouring through his brain. Here was what he'd been looking for—a perfect example of how closely pleasure and pain could be intertwined.

In his head he was already rearranging the documentary, leading off with this display and a voice-over that talked about the violent edge of consensual sex. He could imagine the words clearly, could imagine his voice asking what happened when things got out of hand? When safe words weren't listened to? When pleasure became unbearable pain?

He winced at the thoughts crowding his brain, images of the dead women running through his mind despite himself. *But it doesn't have to be like that*, a little voice whispered in the back of his head.

It didn't have to be black and white.

Good and evil.

Pleasure and pain.

He told himself he was disgusted, that he wanted to focus entirely on the evil that could be done with such "toys." But as he got closer—close enough to touch—he couldn't help thinking of the pleasure they could bring as well.

Reaching out, he ran a hand down a series of satin ties. They were soft, silky—amazingly cool and pleasurable to his touch. Unwittingly, a picture of Genevieve flashed into his head. She was naked, bound hand and foot by the long lengths of black satin as he ran his hands and lips and tongue over every inch of her willing body.

His cock hardened—as much at the idea of overwhelming her with pleasure as at the thought of such blatant dominance. Shuddering, he let the ties fall back into place and wondered what was happening to him.

He'd enjoyed sex for his entire adult life—he didn't know many men in their thirties who hadn't. But until now, his idea of experimentation had pretty much been limited to the places where he made love and a few basic toys. This, he thought, as he ran his hand over a black satin blindfold—this was taking experimentation to a whole new level.

He shouldn't want this—shouldn't need it. He never had before. And sex with Genevieve was already more mind-blowing than anything he'd ever experienced. It should be more than enough for him. It *was* more than enough for him.

Yet even as he told himself that, his eyes fell on a series of Japanese rope bondage items, and he nearly came in his fucking jeans. He wanted to turn away—to walk away—yet he didn't. He couldn't.

He wanted to see Genevieve tied up for his pleasure—for her pleasure. Needed it with an intensity that completely blew him away. He didn't know why—couldn't explain his reasoning to himself, let alone to anyone else. But he needed to dominate Genevieve.

To take her over completely, even as he gave her the most incredible orgasms of her life.

To make her his in every way possible, even as he kept her *safe*.

The whole thing might be a moot point; it was very possible that she'd never speak to him again after how he'd acted that morning. But if she did . . .

He picked up one of the long white satin ropes. If she did, he would die to see her as he'd imagined. To make her come again and again. And to hell with the consequences.

Before he could change his mind, Cole piled a bunch of stuff on the counter and paid for it quickly. Then reached into his pocket for his cell phone as he headed for the door.

He wasn't going to be happy until he'd fixed this thing between Genevieve and himself. Wasn't going to be happy until he was back in her good graces—a feat he deemed nearly impossible after he'd basically told her to go fuck herself.

But he needed to fix this, needed to fix *them*. Sure, this whole thing had started out as nothing more than a way to find his sister's killer, but somewhere in the middle of everything, he'd begun to fall for Genevieve. She was so strong, so self-assured, so innately *kind*, despite the harsh words they'd exchanged the last time they'd seen each other.

He started to dial the precinct number—he still had it memorized after all these years—but again he hung up before the call could go through. Damn it, *she'd* been the one to blow things totally out of proportion. The one who'd refused to trust him. Instead of calling her, he should drag her out of that damn precinct and paddle her sweet ass until she believed that he wasn't the killer. Until she acknowledged that, despite their inauspicious beginnings, there was something between them that couldn't be ignored.

Of course, that probably wasn't the best course of action if his goal was to get her back in his bed. But this silence between them had gone on long enough—he wanted to hear Genevieve's voice, to explain himself better than he had before. To try to convince her to give him another chance.

Hitting redial before he could change his mind, he waited impatiently for the desk sergeant to answer the phone.

Genevieve clicked through her e-mail quickly, her mind whirling with the facts and suppositions associated with the murders she was investigating. The FBI profiler she and Shawn had spoken with yesterday had just e-mailed the profile of the killer—and it was just ambiguous enough to make it feel like they were searching for a needle in a very large haystack.

White male, thirty-five to fifty. Upper-middle class. Successful in his chosen profession, which was probably artistic or service-centered. Above-average intelligence. Had his own ethical code, one that allowed him to commit these murders and still believe he was in the right. Evidence that he'd lost someone very important to him at some point in the last few years led to controlled sadism and the need to be in charge. The rape and sodomy only underscored the anger, the need to control the victim and her world.

Frustration ate at her, even as she told herself she was being unreasonable. The profiler had done his best—had given her exactly what she'd needed to help make her case. But she wasn't satisfied with the report, and probably wouldn't have been with anything short of a map with a huge red X to mark the spot.

Scrolling through a dozen or so messages that had come in since she'd last checked her e-mail, Genevieve searched for anything that had to do with her murders. But there was nothing from Jefferson—nothing that pertained to the murders at all. Just notification of two court dates in cases she'd closed months before, some information about cases she'd recently closed and an invitation to check out a new store opening at Canal Place.

Rolling her eyes, she clicked on the last e-mail on the list. It was addressed to her, and though it was from an address she didn't recognize, the subject line—COMING SOON—made her curious enough to check it out.

Skimming it, her mind still on the killer's profile, Genevieve was halfway down the text before she realized what it was she was reading. Heart pounding, breath shallow, she went back to the top and started again. Read it through once, then again and again.

"Shawn!" she called, her voice low and urgent.

He glanced up immediately from the timeline he was putting together. "What's wrong?"

"I need you to come look at this."

"Sure. Just let me—"

"Now!"

He was around the desk in a flash, his eyes intense. "What's going on?"

"I think this is from him." She pointed at the computer screen, then read along with him as he focused on the e-mail.

Genevieve,

I apologize for my silence the last few days, but things have been quite busy around here. Leaving you hanging after my phone call was inexcusable, but I plead a very full plate, as you will find out soon enough.

I must admit I'm a little disappointed in the progress you've been making. I expected a more worthy adversary. Though you look like a wet dream, I know you are both extremely intelligent and extremely capable. High case-closure rate, strong witness for the defense—for a little while I feared I might have met my match.

But, forgive me for saying so, you seem stumped. No new leads, no evidence, nothing to lead you to my doorstep. Once again, I will confess to being disappointed. I've spent a lot of time imagining you here with me, your body mine to do with as I wish.

I would take my time with you, make it as good for you as it would be for me. After all, we're quite well matched, aren't we? You look like the type to not just tolerate pain well, but to enjoy it too. How fortunate, then, that I am enamored with causing it.

I know what you're thinking. You've seen those poor creatures I've already been to work on. They were nothing, really, simply practice for my greatest work. Practice for you.

I left you clues with the girls, clues that—if you are smart enough—will lead you to me. Of course, you're still missing one. Poor girl, she's been out there, waiting, for nearly three days now. Wondering, I'm sure, how long it will take you to find her.

I hope you find her soon. I'm getting restless, this need I have to feel you under me growing with each hour that passes. And while I want to wait for you, to experience all that you have to offer me when I am at my most passionate, I fear that if you do

not move quickly, I will be forced to secure another
plaything.

    She will, of course, be nothing compared to you,
just a dalliance to keep me busy until we finally
meet.

    Work fast, Genevieve. My craving for you is
growing.

"Son of a bitch!" Shawn's fist hit the desk, and the eyes he turned
on her blazed furiously. "How can you be so calm? That bastard just
threatened you!"

"It seemed more like a promise than a threat," she answered coolly,
proud of how composed her voice sounded when she was shaking apart
inside.

"I don't give a shit what it was. He's not getting his hands on you."

"I certainly hope not." She looked over the letter one more time and
tried desperately to ignore the chill skating down her spine. "Shawn,
you're missing the most important part."

"No, I'm not." His mouth was grim as he looked at her. "There's
definitely another girl out there, one who hasn't been discovered yet."

"We need to find her."

"I know that." He picked up his phone, dialed a quick number.

"Who are you calling?"

"Roberto. He and Luc can get their asses back here and help us
figure out what the hell is going on."

Genevieve stood, strode over to the murder board, where she'd
tacked a map of the French Quarter. The first three dump sites were
clearly marked and, not for the first time, she studied them for some
kind of pattern. There wasn't one, at least not one that she could see.

She traced a finger from Jackson Square to Jean Lafitte's bar to the
senator's house for what felt like the millionth time. "They've all been

on the east side of the Quarter so far," she mused. "So does that mean that this one will be too? Or will he have branched out?"

"There's no guarantee the body's even in the French Quarter, Genevieve."

She glanced at her partner over her shoulder. "Sure there is. He wants me to find her, and I only get cases from the Quarter. Outside, it's a different police station, different homicide squad."

When the phone rang, they both jumped, and Genevieve stared at the receiver as if it was a snake. She knew she should pick it up, to find out if the bastard was calling to follow up on his note, but all she really wanted to do was run away.

But Shawn was having none of her cowardice as he gestured her over to the desk.

"Answer it," he hissed. "And hit speaker so I can hear too."

With a shudder, she followed his directions. "Delacroix." Her voice was clipped, furious, but she couldn't stop it any more than she could stop the fine tremor that shook her normally rock-steady hand.

"Genevieve?"

"Cole?"

"Yeah." She slammed her finger down on the speaker button at the same time she picked up the receiver. Some things Shawn didn't need to hear.

"I was just calling—I wanted to say—" He paused, and Genevieve felt a jolt of surprise. It was a shock to hear Cole sound so uncertain— hell, it was a shock to hear from him at all. It had been four days since they'd argued, and she'd decided he must have written her off. She'd started to call him numerous times to apologize, but had ended up putting the phone down every time, too embarrassed to face him—even over the phone.

She heard him take a deep breath, let it out slowly. And then, before she could say anything, he blurted out, "I wanted to apologize."

It was her turn to take a deep breath as her heart nearly beat out of her chest. There was nothing like going from anger to joy in ten seconds flat.

"Genevieve, are you still there?"

"Yes. But I think I'm the one who owes you an apology." She glanced at Shawn, saw him listening intently to her side of the conversation. Turning her back to him, she lowered her voice. "I made a mistake."

His voice warmed considerably. "I think we both did."

"No, it was mostly me." Her sense of fair play wouldn't let her do anything but take the blame. "I should have called."

"Yes, you should have." Genevieve could tell by his tone that Cole was teasing her, and she couldn't hold back a small smile.

"Sorry, but I've been busy trying to find a killer."

"How's that going?" he asked with concern. "I've been watching the news, hoping to hear that you'd caught him."

"No such luck. But maybe now that he's fixated on me we'll have a better shot."

Cole didn't answer, and the silence stretched between them so long that she wondered if his cell had cut out. "Cole?" she asked.

"What do you mean, he's *fixated* on you?" There was no trace of warmth in his voice now, only a bone-deep fury that shook her to her core.

"Nothing." She watched with relief as Shawn riffled through his desk for some change, then walked towards the vending machines in the hall-way in an effort to give her some privacy. When he was out of earshot she muttered, "He's contacted me, that's all. *Fixated*'s too strong a word—"

"What has he done?" His voice cracked like a whip.

"A couple of phone calls. An e-mail today. It's no big deal."

"It's a very big deal, and you know it." He paused, took another deep breath. "I don't want you near this guy, Genevieve."

"Excuse me?" She couldn't keep the shock out of her voice.

"You heard me. He's dangerous and—"

"It's my job to go near this guy, Cole."

"It's not your job to put yourself on the line for every sick fuck with a dangerous obsession," he argued.

"Maybe not, but that doesn't mean I won't. If it gives me a better chance of catching him, I'd talk to Satan himself."

"Don't say that!"

"Why not? It's the truth."

Silence stretched between them as Genevieve tried to think of some way to make Cole understand. But she was so angry that he'd presume to tell her how to do her job that all she really wanted to tell him was to go to hell.

"Look, Genevieve, this guy can hurt you."

"Really? 'Cuz I thought he wanted to take me to lunch."

"You're being irrational."

"I'm being irrational? You're the one telling me how to do my job."

"It's not like that."

"It's exactly like that, and I really don't have time for it right now." Glancing behind her at Shawn, who had returned with two bottles of soda, Genevieve felt herself grow even angrier. "Good-bye, Cole."

She slammed down the phone with a satisfying thud. How dare he tell her what was too dangerous for her? How dare he tell her anything at all? They'd only known each other a week, and had been angry as hell at one another for most of that time. And he thought he could just call her up and apologize and everything would be okay? Even as he humiliated her in front of her partner?

Over her dead body.

Shawn cleared his throat. "Everything okay?"

The look she shot him should have had him bursting into flames. "Everything's great."

He tapped his hand on the desk. "Sorry. I was—just checking."

She rolled her eyes. "Yeah, well, don't."

"You know, the guy has a point—"

"Don't you start too," she growled. "If one more man tells me I might get hurt, I'm going to hurt *him*."

"All right, then. I'll just, um"—he held his hands up in a gesture of surrender—"come back in a little while."

"Good idea."

Genevieve fumed as she watched Shawn walk away. What was it about the men in her life that made them think she needed protection? She'd been a cop for more than a decade and had always managed to take care of herself. This was no different. He wasn't the first asshole to fixate on her and probably wouldn't be the last. Sure, he might be a bit scarier than the average psychopath she ran into, but that didn't mean she couldn't handle him. Couldn't handle herself.

She still couldn't believe Cole had done that. Who the hell did he think he was? He was the one who stormed out of her kitchen in a snit, and he was the one who hadn't called her for four days. It took a hell of a lot of nerve for him to think that she would hide away like a good little girl just because he said so!

Frustrated, furious, Genevieve started pawing through the papers on her desk in an effort to get her mind off her anger. But as she straightened up the numerous files, her hand fell on the one that contained the results of Cole's fingerprint run.

With rage coursing through her veins, she opened it and spent a long time studying the report of his arrest so many years before. The case had been dismissed, and she couldn't help wondering why that was. Picking up the phone, she called a friend of hers on the LAPD. Maybe Tina could shed some light on the arrest—and subsequent dismissal. Fifteen minutes later, she was scanning the report Tina had e-mailed her, shocked at the amount of information that was attached to a simple misdemeanor assault charge. Skimming the report, she was about three-quarters of the way through the evidence that had led to his dismissal when she found it—a statement from Cole's neighbor claiming that he had been under a lot of stress lately, due to the *brutal murder* of his sister. *In New Orleans.*

Shock ricocheted through her, had her dropping the file as if it had suddenly grown fangs and a long, rattling tail.

Cole's sister had been *murdered.*

Brutally murdered.

Seven years before.

In New Orleans.

The words chased each other around her head, jockeying for position as she tried desperately to wrap her mind around them, her anger draining away in the face of her horror. Cole's sister had been killed here. He was here, doing a documentary on sex and violence—trying to make sense of his sister's death.

Was it any wonder he'd been so offended when she'd admitted she thought he might be a killer? Or that he'd freaked out when she'd told him she was being targeted? Knowing what she now did, she realized he'd exercised great control in reacting as calmly as he had.

Spinning back to her computer, she typed in *Adams* under Old Crimes and waited for something to pop. Nothing did, and then she remembered Cole's comment about taking care of his younger half sister.

Her heart cracked wide open at the thought of him losing her. His clenched fists made much more sense, as did his inability to look at her while he'd talked about his family.

You must be close to your family, she'd said to him.

Not so much anymore had been his laconic reply.

Pulling up cold homicides, she went through all of them from 2002, but nothing popped. Went back to 2001 and forward to 2003 and still couldn't find anything with Cole's name on it. She knew he would have been involved in the investigation, knew the man she'd slept with four nights before would have been right in the middle of the case, raising hell. And yet there was nothing here, in the city. Nothing in the whole state of Louisiana.

Which got her curious enough to double check his case from California. No, the detectives had verified that Cole's sister had been murdered in the French Quarter in July of 2002, a few months before he'd been arrested. The last page of the report listed her name—Samantha Diaz—and Genevieve reared back in shock for the second time.

Though she hadn't been on homicide at the time, she remembered that case, remembered—with perfect clarity—the terrible things that had been done to the young woman. She had been the fourth victim of a serial killer, one who had gone on to claim two more before disappearing. He'd never been caught.

So where the hell was the file, she wondered. Turning back to the computer, she typed in Samantha's name, but nothing hit. Typed in the two other names she could remember from the time period and still got nothing.

Suspicions aroused, Genevieve spent the next hour poking around for some clue as to where the files might have gone, but she could find nothing—not even proof that they had ever existed. Which was bullshit, because she knew the crimes had happened. Had watched the task force assemble every day as they tried to find the killer, all to no avail.

No wonder Cole was so dark and moody and controlling. With this in his past, it was a miracle he was as sane as he was. Murder like this—particularly unsolved—had a tendency to drive even the best-adjusted people to the edge of insanity.

"Hey, I was just talking to Jose." Shawn came back all business, though he kept his distance. "He wants to poke around, see what he can find."

"I'll do that right now." Smiling at Shawn so that he knew it was safe to return to his desk, Genevieve closed Cole's file with a sigh. She didn't have time to deal with his sister's case right now, but she would get back to it. No one should have to go seven years without justice.

Chapter Eleven

I t was nearly six hours later when Genevieve finally shut her computer off for the night. Shawn had already left, claiming he had a lead to check out on his way home. Luc and Roberto had followed closely after.

She had stayed on, running through the files one more time in an effort to find the clues the killer said were there. Then had started on missing persons with the hope of figuring out who he'd chosen for his latest victim.

But without clues and without the body, how could she decide if it was the teenager who looked like a runaway or the divorcée out for a good time? Either way, she hadn't been able to leave—not when some woman's body was out there, just waiting to be discovered.

Enough was enough—her stomach was grumbling, her head was pounding, and all she really wanted to do was crawl under her desk and sleep for about eight hours. But it was too early for bed, and she had something to do first. An apology that needed to be made before she could settle down for the night. It wounded her that she'd accused Cole of being insensitive to victims' families when he himself was the member of one.

Outside, the heat and humidity were still going strong despite the waning sun, and she couldn't help thinking about the body they had yet to find. If it was outside somewhere, they were in huge trouble—any evidence the guy might have left for them would be destroyed by the ever-present rain, humidity and insects that were a part of everyday life in New Orleans. And they'd be right back at square one.

She shook her head, grimaced. Hard to be anywhere else when they'd never left the starting gate. Hard to believe she was waist-deep—and sinking fast—in the homicide investigation from hell, and she still couldn't get Cole out of her mind.

Despite her determination to remain calm, her heart started pounding as she thought of him. Of her destination. It had been four days, more than eighty hours, since she'd seen him—not that the Ice Queen was counting—and since they'd had their blowup, and their conversation today hadn't exactly gone smoothly. It was up to her to make things right.

A cab cruised by and she hailed it, knowing if she walked home for her car she'd end up talking herself out of what she had to do. And she was exhausted, totally worn out—she didn't have the energy to spend another night staring at the ceiling above her bed as she thought about Cole.

After finding out about his sister's murder and rereading that sick e-mail until she was nearly blind, it seemed ridiculous that she had ever thought Cole was the killer. The note wasn't his voice or his style, and believing him guilty of murder seemed utterly ridiculous when she thought back on how tenderly he'd treated her.

Oh, it might not be another woman's definition of *tender*, but Cole had understood her better than she'd understood herself. He'd given her everything she'd always craved in a sexual partner and hadn't known to ask for, but had stopped the second she'd asked him to.

She would apologize and hope that he could forgive her doubts. Her only excuse was the fact that he messed with her head, her need for him so unprecedented—so outside the scope of her experience—that she wasn't able to deal with it.

Yeah, it was lame, but it was also the truth. She didn't know if Cole would believe her, but anything was better than not knowing.

He'd blown it. The first relationship he'd been interested in pursuing in more years than he could count and he'd completely screwed it up. Could he have been more of a jackass?

He hadn't meant to lose his temper when he'd talked to Genevieve— any more than he'd meant to order her around—but the idea of her in danger made him crazy. Losing Samantha the way he did had made him paranoid, particularly about the safety of the women he cared about. Just the thought that some sick asshole had targeted Genevieve made him want to punch his way through a wall.

But she didn't know that, had taken his reaction as proof that he was a domineering asshole. Sitting moodily at his kitchen table, Cole tossed back a shot of Patrón and reached into his back pocket to pull out his wallet. Flipping it open, he stared at the photograph he'd been carrying around for the better part of a decade. Rubbed a finger over the smiling face as he tried to think his way out of the disaster he'd created.

But for the first time in years, he couldn't find a way out. He had pushed Genevieve too far, too fast, and had given her nothing in return. Nothing but bruises and half-truths and bristling masculine outrage. Was it any wonder she didn't trust him?

With a shaking hand, he picked up the wide-bottomed bottle and poured a second shot. He needed to fix this, to go to Genevieve and apologize and hope she was understanding enough to forget about the fiasco of his phone call apology. He owed her that much.

Tossing back the second shot, he followed it with a lime chaser. Normally, he wasn't much of a drinker, but he'd been going through tequila like it was water since hitting this town.

He grimaced. Who was he kidding? It was the situation, not the city. And while getting drunk might not be his first choice of ways to spend the evening, it was currently the best option he had. Because he doubted—severely—whether Genevieve would let him anywhere near her ever again.

His laugh, when it came, was harsh. Yeah, there was no way she'd let him do everything he wanted to her. No way she'd let him tie her up and fuck her hot, luscious body the way he was aching to. Dying to. Not after he'd told her to fuck off—and not in a good way.

When the doorbell rang, he was tempted to ignore it. He had the makings of a hell of a pity party going on and he hated to ruin that by letting some stranger into his lair, even temporarily.

But whoever it was was persistent, hitting the doorbell time and again until he finally gave up any hope of peace and solitude. He headed toward the front door with a growl, prepared to take his displeasure out on whoever was unlucky enough to be on the other side.

He was already cursing when he threw open the door. "What the fuck—" His voice died in midquestion, his eyes running over the familiar figure on his porch in disbelief.

"Can I come in?" Genevieve smiled uncertainly as she waited for him to pick his jaw up off the floor.

"Sure. Of course." He opened the door wider, moved aside so she could enter. And tried to get his alcohol- and lust-fogged brain to function.

But it was no use—he was too overwhelmed by the idea that she was standing in his house of her own volition. That she had spent the time seeking him out when she could easily have forgotten he existed.

He'd certainly been a big enough ass to deserve just that. Not to mention a hell of a lot more.

"I'm sorry I jumped down your throat this afternoon." She said the words quickly, as if they tasted bad.

"I thought that was my line."

She shrugged. "Maybe both of ours?"

He nodded. "Okay."

"So go ahead and say it." She watched him expectantly.

"I'm sorry I was an ass this afternoon?"

"You're not supposed to say it like it's a question."

He grinned because he couldn't help himself. Then reached for her hand and tugged. "Come on in." He dragged her through the living room and down the hallway to the kitchen. "You want a drink?" He nodded to the bottle of tequila on the counter.

She glanced at the discarded lime peels. "It looks like you've been drinking enough of that for both of us."

"Not even close." Then, because he couldn't keep his hands to himself for one second longer, he pulled her into his arms. "I'm glad you came."

"Me too."

He rested his chin on the top of her head for a minute and just breathed in the sweet honey scent of her.

She shoved against his chest, pushed him away. And for a brief moment he felt bereft, though for the life of him he couldn't figure out why.

Striving for control, needing to keep his hands busy with something other than her, he reached into the bar cabinet and pulled out a shot glass. "You ever tried Patrón?"

She wrinkled her nose. "I'm not a big tequila drinker."

"This isn't any ordinary tequila." He poured a shot, handed it to her. But stopped her when she started to sip.

"If you're going to do a shot, you've got to do it right."

Genevieve lifted one cool brow, licked her full lower lip and nearly had him coming in his fucking jeans. "I didn't realize there was a wrong way to do this."

"Sweetheart, there's a wrong way to do everything." And then he was putting his hands on her waist and lifting her up so that her sweet ass was on the center island, her legs just a little bit open.

Stepping between them before she could change her mind, he slipped yet another god-awful suit jacket off her shoulders—he was seriously going to have to do something about her wardrobe. Maybe if he ripped it all off her . . .

Licking a trail from the hollow of her throat to her breastbone, he savored the taste of her.

"Mmm, salty."

She blushed, then leaned back on her hands so that her breasts were thrust forward. "It's a hundred degrees in the shade. Hard not to sweat."

It took all his self-control to take things slowly when all he really wanted to do was to eat her alive.

"I wasn't complaining," he murmured as he trailed his tongue over the curve of first one breast and then the other. Then he slammed back the shot of tequila and finished it off by biting into a lime slice.

Her mouth was slightly open, her eyes wide as she stared at his lips. "*That's* the right way to do a tequila shot?"

He loved her voice, the syrupy sweetness was a turn-on even without the hard-ass tone she deliberately injected into it. With the hard-ass tone, it was irresistible. "It's the best way."

"I bet."

He poured another shot. Handed it to her. "Here. You try."

He shrugged out of his T-shirt and nearly smiled as she did the same. Would have, if his first look at her body hadn't brought him all the way to the edge. She was still covered in little bruises, the love bites he'd given her the last time they'd been together. It was hard to imagine that he'd done that to her, had marked her as he'd marked no other woman. Had claimed her as he'd never had the desire to do before.

Maybe he was a Neanderthal, because looking at her covered in his marks—seeing her proudly wearing the evidence of his desire for her—turned him so hard and fast his vision blurred.

Shit, how he wanted this woman. Was dangerously close to becoming obsessed with her.

Her sexy pink tongue darted out, swiped across her top lip and then her bottom one, as if she couldn't quite decide where to lick. And every thought he had or might have had got lost in the wild need pumping through him.

Groaning, he tangled a hand in her hair and urged her closer. "Come on, sweetheart," he whispered. "Taste me."

And she did, her mouth lowering to his chest so slowly that he wanted to howl. Then her tongue was on him, swirling in circles over his right pec, darting out to tease his nipple. Once, twice. Again and again until it was all he could do to keep from ripping off her pants and sliding into her right there.

"You taste good, Cole." It was a whisper, but he heard it and his body reacted, his arousal ratcheting up another notch. Or twelve. Fuck—who would have thought it was possible to be this turned on and not come?

"So do you, baby. God, so do you." He reached over, put a lime slice in his mouth. Concentrated on the bitterness of it as her sweet mouth fastened on to his neck and began to suck.

When she lifted her lips from his skin, he nearly shouted in disappointment. But it was so damn sexy to see her take the shot glass, to watch as she rubbed the cool glass over one cheek and then the other.

He felt himself grow harder, felt himself leak just a little as she dipped her tongue into the icy cold liquid. He clenched his fists, told himself not to rush her. That it would be sweeter if she took her time.

And was it ever. Her eyes met his, clung, for long seconds before she tossed her head back and slid the tequila down her throat. Then she was reaching up, grabbing the back of his head, pulling his mouth down to hers. And biting the lime he still had between his lips.

He nearly came, had to grit his teeth against the orgasm that rose in him—sharp and clean and demanding. Fuck, this woman was turning him inside out.

And he was loving every second of it.

"You want another one?" Was that his voice? So low and feral, as if all that was civilized had been stripped from him.

"I'd rather have you."

Her bold honesty went straight through him, turning up the raging inferno inside of him until he feared spontaneous combustion.

"The two aren't mutually exclusive, you know." He tipped the tequila bottle slightly, let a few drops dribble onto her breasts and down her stomach.

She gasped as the cold liquid hit her, arched her back so that her nipples were front and center. Because he was dying for another taste of her, he bent down, followed the trail the alcohol had made with delicate flicks of his tongue.

Then, because he couldn't resist, he tilted the bottle so that the tequila coated his index finger. He swirled it first over one of her nipples and then the other before bending his head and circling the hard buds with his tongue. He sucked until all the alcohol was gone, savoring its rich burn as it slid down his throat.

Bringing his hands to Genevieve's shoulders, he pressed her back slowly until she was fully open to him, resting on her elbows, her beautiful breasts bare to him. He paused for a moment, couldn't move, was transfixed by the picture she made.

Her cheeks were flushed, her eyes heavy with desire, her lips slick from the shot she'd taken. Laid out on his counter like the most delectable of desserts, her legs open and dangling over the edge, she was the most beautiful thing he'd ever seen.

"I may never take a shot any other way." He lifted the bottle, poured a steady stream of the liquor over her stomach.

She gasped as it ran down her sides, pooled in her navel, and he bent forward, sipping from her slowly. Savoring the spicy-sweet taste of her that mingled with the smooth heat of the aged tequila.

She moaned, a low, sexy sound that had him glancing up, wanting to see her face. Needing to know that she was as into this as he was.

She had a slice of lime clenched between her front teeth and he groaned as he swooped down, bit it, taking it into his mouth as he longed to take her.

"My turn," she whispered, grabbing his hand and sucking his tequila-coated finger into her mouth.

His knees actually shook as she twirled her tongue around his long finger, stroking it up and down in the same rhythm she'd used four nights before on his dick. His heart was pounding out of control, the need to fuck her an all-consuming ache inside of him.

"Genevieve, baby." He tried to retrieve his hand—along with his sanity—but she lifted her arms and curled her body around his arm, holding him like he was a prize she had won. And then, just when he didn't think he could get any more turned on, just when his knees were locking and his cock throbbing, she bit down, hard, on the tip of his finger and shot his lust-crazed body into overdrive.

He ripped his finger out of her mouth, slid out of her embrace as he strived to get himself under some kind of control. Taking a deep breath, he reached over and grabbed the bottle with a hand that shook so badly it was all he could do to get the tequila in the glass. He handed it to her, but she set it aside. Hooked her fingers in the front belt loops of his jeans and tugged until his cock was right up against her pussy. "I'm more interested in the salt."

Shit. Fuck. Damn. He wasn't going to last. He could feel her heat through her pants, through his jeans. She had barely touched him and already he was going up in flames, his body so far out of his control that he wondered if he'd ever get it back.

And then she put her mouth on him and he knew he didn't stand a chance. Her tongue—her wicked, wild, wonderful tongue—was everywhere at once. Flicking over his collarbone, sliding up his neck to toy with his earlobe. Moving lower to press into his chest.

"Genevieve, baby, stop." He moved his hands to her head, clenched his fists in her hair. Tried to pull her off.

But she was having none of it, her hands slipping around his waist as her nails dug into the muscles of his back. The flickers of pain were exquisite, the feel of her clawing him unbelievably sexy.

"Stop," he gasped again, but even he didn't know if he meant it anymore. All he knew was that he would die if he wasn't inside of her soon, would come in his pants like a teenager with his first girlfriend. The humiliation was almost more than he could take, even as the incredible desire, the unbelievable experience of wanting her this much, only pushed him higher.

She lifted her head, looked at him with passion-dazed eyes. Smiled wickedly and murmured, "Oh, I don't think so," right before she unbuttoned his fly.

Her hand slipped inside, closing around him firmly enough to have him seeing stars. Eyes crossing, hips thrusting, he pumped against her for a few seconds before reaching down and disentangling himself.

"You don't want this to be over before it begins, do you?" he muttered in response to her quizzical look.

"I don't care. I just want to watch you come again."

He groaned, yanked her off the counter so he could strip her of her pants and pink lace underwear. "I like this," he said as he sank to his knees in front of her, twirling the panties around his index finger. "You don't look like a girl who would go for pink lace."

She put her hands on his shoulders, arched against him. "Looks can be deceiving."

"I'll say." He stood, shoved his own jeans down and off, so that he was standing there—in the middle of his kitchen—as naked as Genevieve. And she was taking her time looking him over, her eyes eating him up as if he were a bar of Godiva chocolate. For a moment he felt oddly vulnerable, totally exposed, but then she was pressing her body against his, and everything fled but the need to make her feel as good as he did.

Sinking into the nearest chair, he pulled her onto his lap, had her straddle him so that her hot pussy rested directly over his randy, rioting cock. She gasped and wiggled and he slid between her labia, the tip of his cock resting against her clitoris.

It was his turn to gasp, to shudder as her warm heat enfolded him in a new way. And then she was moving, her slick, hot body sliding against him, and he almost forgot how to breathe.

"You feel amazing," he muttered, his hands digging into her sexy, curvy ass.

"I think it's you." She moved forward and backward slowly, so god-damned slowly he wanted to shout, but it was the most incredible feel-ing he'd ever had—this being in her without being in her, being cradled by her body without the heavy thrusting that would take him all the way inside.

She slid back until the tip of his cock was poised at her entrance, rising on her tiptoes to torment him for a minute with her incredible heat. And then she was moving forward so that his dick rasped at her pussy again.

"You're killing me, sweetheart." He stroked his hands up her back, tangled them in the chignon that was just starting to fall out. Tugged and watched with eyes he knew were turning wild as her hair cascaded around her shoulders and down her back.

God, there really was miles of the stuff—soft and sweet-smelling and so sexy it had him arching against her even as he tangled his fists in it and tugged.

"Cole!" Her voice was low, startled and incredibly excited—so ex-cited that he did it again as he rolled his hips against her.

She whimpered, arched, her eyes closing as the pleasure went through her and he couldn't resist a grin. Or doing it a third time as he realized just how much Genevieve got off on the little licks of pain.

Shifting his hands so that they were at the nape of her neck, he pulled down hard enough to have her tilting her head to the side and opening her eyes. Then he lowered his mouth to hers, sucked her lower lip between his teeth and bit softly.

She cried out, her body shuddering reflexively against his. And she felt so fucking good he wanted to slam inside of her and pound away until orgasm swept through them both.

She opened to him, parted her lips so he could slip inside and explore her. His tongue stroked inside, licked the top of her mouth before stroking down one cheek and then the other. Curling his tongue around hers, he sucked until she was inside him. Relinquishing control for just a moment, he relaxed as she took him as he had taken her.

Genevieve moaned, her tongue tangling with Cole's as she took her time exploring every part of his mouth. She wanted to go on kissing him forever, never wanted this moment to end as she savored the incredible taste of him. Tequila and lime and the deepest, darkest chocolate.

But he was growing impatient. She could feel it in the muscles bunching under her hands, sense it in the restless movements of his hips beneath her own. So she took one more minute to taste him, to slide her tongue over his teeth and the little piece of skin that connected his upper lip to his gums.

He jerked when she touched it, his entire body going rigid, as if electricity had shot up his spine. And perhaps it had—that piece of skin was incredibly sensitive and totally erotic.

Before she could prepare herself, long before she was ready for her exploration to end, he stood and pushed her against the counter. Grasping her hips, he plunged upward, entering her with an urgency that had her trembling on the edge of orgasm.

"Take me," he muttered, plunging deep again and again. "Take all of me."

"God, yes." Twisting her hands in his hair, she smoothed them over his powerful chest. Clutched at the strong muscles of his back. She wanted to touch him everywhere, wanted to feel every part of him against her as he took her higher than she'd ever gone before.

She jerked against him, desperate to get closer. Desperate to take all of him. Cole growled low in his throat, brought his powerful hands to her hips and held her still as he slammed inside of her with what felt like every ounce of strength he had.

She screamed over and over again. She couldn't help it, couldn't control it. His cock was so hard, dragging over sensitive nerve endings, slamming into her all the way to her womb. Turning her on, driving her crazy, making her want more and more of him when he was already giving her everything.

"Cole," she sobbed, her body spinning wildly out of control. "Please, let me come. Let me—"

He reached down and stroked his thumb over her clit. Once, twice, again and again as he continued to thrust furiously inside of her.

And then he was cursing, pulling her up and off of him so quickly that she had no time to prepare. She locked on to the table with desperate hands to keep from falling. "Why—"

He growled something unintelligible at her as he reached for his jeans. Pulling a condom out of his back pocket, he ripped it open with his teeth and started to roll it on. She stopped him.

"Let me." His eyes were blacker than she'd ever seen them as he handed her the condom, and her hands were shaking so badly she wasn't sure she'd even be able to do the job. She knew only that she wanted to touch him, to do this intimate thing for him before she took him back into her body.

So with trembling hands, she slipped the condom over his tip and stroked him—hand over hand—as she rolled it on.

"Enough," he growled, grabbing her hands and pinning them behind her back. "One more touch and I'll come before I ever get inside you."

She purred, arched back so that her nipples were in his face. Luxuriated in the feeling of being taken. Wallowed in the strength he wore so effortlessly.

Then he was leaning down, pulling one of her nipples in his mouth. Her knees buckled and she cried out, reaching for him in an effort to stay upright. He caught her effortlessly, lifted her off the floor and continued to suck as he lowered her slowly—so fucking slowly she nearly screamed—onto his raging-hot cock.

He was huge, long and hard and so wide she felt every inch of him against the walls of her pussy as he slid in. He scraped over delicate nerve endings, took her higher and higher with each inexorable jerk of his hips.

She bucked against him, tried to rush him, but he used his free hand to hold her hips still. "I want to touch you," she gasped, yanking against the tight hold he had on her wrists. Her arms were still pinned behind her and she was completely at his mercy, able to take only whatever it was he chose to give her.

"Not now, sweetheart. I'm too close." He buried his face in the curve of her neck, bit her shoulder in an effort to establish dominance—as if she didn't already know who was in control.

But it grated on her—not the bite, but Cole's need to control every second of their time together. He drove her crazy, took her higher than she'd ever dreamed possible, but that wasn't enough for her. She wanted, needed, to do the same for him.

With that thought in mind, she pushed her knees into his sides and slowly—oh, so slowly—clenched the muscles of her sex around him. She felt his response in the jerk of his cock, saw it in the clenching of his jaw as he fought to maintain control.

She did it again, squeezing a little bit harder, a little bit longer before she released him.

"Stop it," he growled, his free hand coming down hard on her ass.

She threw her head back and laughed, even as she tightened the muscles again and again. "Make me."

"Genevieve." His voice was low, warning, more animal than human as she continued to caress him with her body. He was getting ready to lose it—she could feel it in the thighs that trembled beneath her own and the hand that clenched more firmly around her wrists.

But she didn't care. She wanted him to lose it, wanted him to plunge inside of her with all the darkness and passion and emotion he had inside of him. She wanted him as crazy and out of control as she was.

She wanted him every way she could have him.

"Come on, Cole," she whispered tauntingly. "Fuck me like you mean it."

He released her hands with a roar, his fingers clenching on her ass to keep her in place as he stood. He took two long strides, slammed her back—hard—against the kitchen wall.

"You asked for it," he growled, as his hips began to piston against her. Harder, deeper than before, he pounded into her. Again and again he slammed his cock inside her, until she was overwhelmed. Surrounded. Completely taken over by him.

And still he surged inside of her. Desperately. Furiously. Each quick, hard stroke of his dick a branding that told her exactly who owned her body.

Genevieve moaned as she wrapped her arms around him and held his shaking, furious body against her own. She'd wanted to push him, to see him without his infernal control. To show him that she could take whatever he dished out. And she was taking it, but, God, she'd never felt anything this intense before, not even the last time he'd made love to her. She was completely in his thrall.

Overwhelmed.

Taken.

Dominated.

She was lost in the fire of his possession, explosion after explosion ripping through her as the most unbelievable orgasm of her life tore through her—one that put those she'd experienced four days ago to shame.

Heat poured from her cunt, into her stomach and breasts. Down her legs, up her chest, into her arms and fingers. Radiant, incandescent flames that she couldn't control, only experience. She called his name, her hands tangling in his hair, her legs clenching tightly around his waist.

"Genevieve!" Cole's groan was low, hoarse, his body jerking spasmodically against hers as he emptied himself inside of her in long, jetting streams. His shudders set off another explosion and she was screaming, wailing, burying her face against the heavy muscles of his chest as her body spun onto a whole different plane, one where the pleasure went on and on and on.

They stayed that way for a long time, her back against the wall, Cole's heavy body crushing hers as he leaned against her. His mouth trailed kisses down her neck, over her chest, between her breasts, little nibbles that had her shivering in reaction despite the climaxes that had just seized her.

But he couldn't seem to stop touching her, and she understood, felt the same way. Her hands smoothed over his back, down his arms. Her fingers clenched in the cool silkiness of his hair. She never wanted him to let her go, never wanted her feet to touch the floor again.

Because when they did, all this would be over. She would once again be the homicide detective, and he would be the man afraid to trust her with his secrets.

Chapter Twelve

"I'm starved," Genevieve said more than an hour later, as she stirred against him in bed and pulled away to sit up. "It's almost eight o'clock."

Cole turned to face her, and then almost wished he hadn't. She was wearing an old button-down shirt of his that came almost to her knees, and looking far sexier than the attire warranted. Of course, he'd think she looked sexy in a nun's habit, so maybe he wasn't the best judge.

"Cole?" she prompted again, as she realized his attention was on something other than her stomach.

"Sorry, sweetheart," he said with a nod toward the kitchen. "Come with me while I fix something. I'm hungry too."

"I am *not* going into that room with you," she snapped. "In fact, I think you should be banned from kitchens worldwide."

He couldn't stop the proud grin that came to his mouth as he thought about just what he and Genevieve had been up to in his kitchen little more than an hour before. It had been almost as hot as what they'd done in her kitchen a few days ago.

His dick throbbed, reminding him that thinking about Genevieve and sex was a very bad idea if the lady wanted to get fed. It guaranteed that 90 percent of the blood that was supposed to be in his brain rushed somewhere else.

He got up, then extended a hand to her. "Come on. I promise. I'll keep my fingers to myself."

She snorted. "It's not your fingers I'm worried about." But she took his hand, allowed him to lead her into the kitchen.

"You want something to drink?" he asked, opening the fridge.

"No more tequila."

He raised an eyebrow, deliberately let his gaze run over her breasts. Took great delight in seeing her nipples harden through the thin cotton. "Now, that, sweetheart, is a damned shame. Patrón's never tasted so sweet."

"I bet."

He opened a bottle of white wine, poured her a glass. Let his fingers brush against hers when he handed it to her—not because he was trying to make her nervous, but because he couldn't resist the urge to touch her.

His cock grew hard, a condition that was becoming embarrassingly familiar around her.

"So," she said, after taking a sip of wine. "Tell me about your documentary."

He glanced at her as he pulled a couple chicken breasts and some vegetables out of the fridge. "What do you want to know?"

"I don't know." She shrugged. "How's it going?"

"It's going." He set the food on the counter, began rinsing a tomato. Glanced up to find her staring at him with a look that was half-frustrated, half-confused.

"Are you really going to cook that?"

"I was planning on it. Not being a huge fan of salmonella and all."

"You can cook?"

"You tell me—after dinner."

"You're distracting me."

"Actually, you're distracting yourself. I'm just along for the ride."

He's right, Genevieve thought with abject frustration. She was distracted, so far off her game she couldn't help wondering if she'd ever get it back. But how the hell was she supposed to concentrate when he walked around looking so infuriatingly hot all the time? It was taking all her self-control not to jump him right here in the kitchen. Again.

Ugh. Since when did she have a thing against nice, comfortable bedroom sex? Already she could feel new bruises blooming on her back, souvenirs from when she'd pushed Cole past reason and he'd pushed her back against the wall. Literally.

Just the memory had heat spreading between her thighs, and she squeezed her legs shut in an effort to alleviate the ache. A quick glance at Cole as he sliced and diced told her just how aware of her predicament he was. And that he would be more than happy to help her out with it.

Through sheer strength of will, she forced her mind back to the topic at hand. She knew he had his secrets about his sister, just as she knew he would only tell her about Samantha when—and if—he was ready to. But still, she couldn't help pushing. It couldn't be healthy for him to be carrying all that around with him all the time.

"So." She forced herself back on task. "The documentary."

He popped a piece of zucchini in his mouth, chewed thoughtfully. "It's taking longer than I thought to get everything together. But I think I figured some stuff out the last couple days—got the beginning cemented in my head."

"Well, that's good, right?"

"Yeah." He paused in his slicing and dicing for a minute, stared at her with unreadable eyes. "Have you given any more thought to what we talked about a few days ago?"

She crossed the kitchen, snagged a slice of carrot. "What is that, exactly?"

"I'd love to have you in the documentary, talking about the murders. The city."

"I'm not an actress." She grabbed another carrot.

"I don't want an actress." He finished slicing the vegetables and started on a crusty loaf of French bread. "But I do want the feminine perspective on the whole sex and violence thing. It'll be a nice contrast to my own commentary. Male, female. Dark, light. It'll be a good story."

"A good story?" Fury sang through her veins as he hit on one of her hot buttons—no less dangerous for the fact that it was completely unexpected. "Is that all these women are to you? They're dead, Cole. Some of them brutally murdered—that's not just a good story."

When he turned to her, she saw the banked rage in his own eyes as he dropped the knife on the cutting board. He reached for her and she tried to elude him, but he was too fast, the grip on her biceps too tight for her to do anything but struggle futilely. She refused to give him that satisfaction.

"Who are you to say that to me?" he demanded, shaking her softly. "Who the hell are you?"

"I'm just a woman trying to find justice!"

"Justice?" His laugh was unpleasant as he eyed her with such contempt it had her blood running cold. "There's no justice for what was done to those girls. Nothing that can make what they suffered in their last hours on earth okay. And I find it pretty goddamned absurd that you can think differently—and then stand in my kitchen and accuse me of making light of their deaths."

"Finding their killers is all I can give them and their families!"

"Well, that's just too little too late, isn't it?" His hands tightened on her shoulders, and for one fleeting moment she was afraid. There was such intensity in him, such darkness, that she could almost be afraid of him. Almost think him capable of anything.

"Yes, I write documentaries. Yes, I make movies. But I dare you to find one movie that I've been a part of that treats death as callously as you do.

"Oh, you talk a good game, Genevieve, but that's all it is. Justice? You call spending three years chasing a killer justice? Or plea bargains that let him walk free in three or five or ten years. Is that justice? You call him sitting on death row for twenty years justice? Fuck that; that's not justice. That's a mockery of justice and an insult to the dead."

His grip loosened and then he was thrusting her away from him with enough strength to make her stumble. She threw an arm out to catch herself.

"And then you come here, into my house, into my kitchen, where we have just been as intimate as two people can be, and accuse me of not having the proper amount of respect for the dead? I find that pretty goddamned offensive—not to mention completely beneath you."

When he was finished, the only sound in the house was his harsh breathing as he stared her down. His eyes were fiery, livid. They reached inside of her, set her on fire as his words echoed in her head.

She wanted to defend herself, to tell him that he was wrong. To tell him to go to hell. But he hadn't said anything she hadn't been thinking for years, hadn't accused her of anything she didn't think about regularly.

So what was she supposed to say to him? How was she supposed to defend herself against accusations that were far from baseless? She couldn't believe she'd ever doubted him, couldn't believe she'd ever thought him capable of committing crimes as evil as those she was investigating.

Genevieve reached out a hand and laid it gently on his arm. "I'm sorry. I was out of line. I don't want to have another fight."

His eyes were blacker than night as they met her blue ones. But they were calmer than they had been. "You *were* out of line."

Annoyance danced through her at the snap in his tone, but she pushed it down. She'd accused him of not caring for the victims or their families. For a man like Cole, that was tantamount to a full frontal attack. He had a God-given, constitutional right to be pissed at her.

For a while. Her eyes narrowed as his mouth thinned into an even narrower line. For a very little while.

"Do you see where I'm coming from at all?" The question slipped out before she could censor herself, but once it was asked, she wouldn't have taken it back. "You're not exactly the most forthcoming guy on the block, you know."

"There's a huge leap between not being forthcoming and being completely cold and closed off."

"I know that."

"Do you?" He smirked, an obnoxious twist of his lips that set her blood on simmer.

"You can stop being a sanctimonious prick right about now," she answered. "It doesn't become you nearly as well as the dominant asshole does."

She froze almost before she was done speaking. Had those words actually come from her mouth? Had she tossed such a blatant fuck-you in Cole's face when she'd been sure she just wanted to apologize?

She closed her eyes for a second, prayed that she'd only thought the words. But when she opened her eyes again, Cole had shed any pretense of making dinner. Instead, he was prowling toward her, the predator she'd seen from the very beginning very much in evidence.

She opened her mouth to attempt some damage control, but she couldn't get the words out. Not when he was looking at her like he wanted to throttle her and fuck her all at the same time. But she wouldn't back down. She had a right to her opinions, even if he—

Any and all thoughts she had fled the second his hands made contact with her upper arms. The pressure wasn't hard, just enough to let her know he meant business. As if the gleaming onyx of his eyes and the grim set of his mouth weren't evidence enough.

"You like the dominant asshole, do you?" he asked as he backed her out of the room.

"I didn't say that." She tried to dig in her heels, but he was unyielding as he used his body to keep her moving backward.

"Sure you did, sweetheart." He lifted one hand to her face, stroked it softly down her cheek. "Interesting, isn't it, how the big, bad cop gets off on someone else being in control?"

His hand slipped around to cup her neck. Once again his grip wasn't hard, but the unmistakable dominance of the gesture was obvious—and infuriating. She tried to shrug him off, but his fingers bit into her tender flesh.

"Don't push me, Cole." Again she tried to stand her ground. Again he moved her with nothing but the pressure of his body against hers.

"How can I not, when I know how much you like it?"

They were moving down the hallway now, heading—she was sure—for his bedroom. Panic flitted through her, along with an excitement that nearly shamed her.

How could she get off on his controlling behavior when, before him, she'd always been the one in control? For a brief moment, trepidation turned to fear and she pressed her hands firmly to his chest as she said, "Stop!"

It wasn't the firmest command she'd ever uttered, but it checked Cole instantly. Had him stopping on a dime even as his eyes narrowed dangerously. "You sure that's what you want to say, Genevieve?" He pulled his hand from her neck, and she immediately felt bereft. "Because you don't get a second chance to change your mind."

"Give it a rest! This isn't the world according to Cole, you know."

His grin was wolfish. "My house, my bed, my rules." He stepped aside. "But you're free to leave any time, Genevieve. You know where the door is."

Shit. He'd called her bluff. Called it? Hell, he'd trumped her. Left her with only two choices: leave, which he seemed more than willing to let her do, or surrender herself to him totally. Let him call all the shots.

Could she do that? Could she, who had always prided herself on her icy control, give herself completely to someone else? Could she give herself to Cole, even knowing there were parts of him she was unable to reach?

Glancing behind her, she eyed the hallway that led to the front door. Should she leave? She knew deep down that if she chose to stop things, Cole would walk her to the door like a perfect gentleman. But he'd never touch her again. She would spend the rest of her life without the incredible pleasure he gave her so unstintingly.

The pleasure was insidious, addicting. Even now her body was crying out for his touch, for the sharp bite of his teeth, the slow stroke of his tongue. Could she live the rest of her life without it?

Frustration welled up in her, frustration and need and an overwhelming confusion that was as unfamiliar as it was unwelcome. "Do you have to push me all the time? Can't we ever just be normal?"

She glanced up at Cole's face, saw the softening in his eyes before he steeled himself again. "I'd never force you, sweetheart. You know that as well as I do. But I can't be some guy you sleep with and forget about either. If you give yourself to me, you give all of yourself. You have to trust me that much, at least. Have to trust me to keep you safe."

"And if I can't?" It was a whisper, a cry from her battered, frightened soul.

"Then you can't. And you're better off without me. Without this." He cupped her breast, smoothed his thumb over her hard nipple.

"This isn't fair." She hated the desperation in her tone, hated more that she'd been reduced to a child's argument.

He tilted his head, watched her with those black-magic eyes that had somehow wound themselves into her soul. "No, it isn't. But I can't change that."

"You mean, you *won't* change it."

"Maybe."

She sagged in defeat, knew her decision had been made before she'd ever tried to argue. Reaching a hand out, she placed her palm on his. "Damn you, Cole, don't you hurt me."

He yanked her to him, held her against his chest as he stroked a soothing hand down her hair. "I could never hurt you. Don't you know that yet?"

She merely shook her head, burying her face in his chest. Because she knew the truth, even if he didn't. Cole could do so much more than merely hurt her. He could break her into so many pieces she would never recover.

Chapter Thirteen

t took every ounce of self-control Cole had to keep from showing his relief. For a minute there he was sure she'd call his bluff, tell him that he and his high-handed tendencies didn't have a chance with her. And that would have killed him. He was beginning to think that there was no way he'd be able to let Genevieve go when this was all over.

But he didn't want to think about that now, didn't dare think about it when she was here in his arms. Offering him everything he could ever want from her, more than he'd ever expected she'd give him.

Moving slowly, he propelled her through the doorway to his bedroom before walking her across the carpet and settling her gently on the bed. Then, because he couldn't do anything else, he stepped back and looked at her for a few long moments.

"You are so beautiful." He reached a hand out, stroked it gently down her cheek. "So damn beautiful it blows my mind."

She blushed, nibbled on her lip, and he was shocked at the nervousness of his normally intrepid cop. "I won't hurt you, sweetheart." He crouched down next to her.

"I know." She didn't look him in the eye when she said it.

"Do you?" He toyed with a crazy blond curl, let it wrap itself around his finger for a moment. "Will you do something for me?"

"Yes." For the first time since entering the bedroom, her eyes met his.

"No hesitation?" he murmured, reaching into his nightstand and pulling out one of the things he'd bought last night when he'd been thinking about Genevieve.

"I already agreed to do this, didn't I?" She flicked her hair over her shoulder in a gesture he was already beginning to recognize meant she was annoyed, ready for the action to start. "I don't change my mind halfway through."

"No, you're not a quitter, are you, sweetheart?"

"I wouldn't know how to be." She raised a challenging eyebrow, reached out and stroked her fingers down his chest. He felt his heart beat a little faster at the contact.

"Put this on for me." He slid the silky length of material into her hands.

Genevieve paused, stared at the length of black silk. "Why don't you put it on for me?" The eyes she raised to his were a fuck-you dare. "I thought that was the point of this little game."

"The point is for you to trust me." He leaned forward, nuzzled her cheek before sliding his lips to her ear. "Do it, sweetheart. Give yourself to me."

For a long moment, she didn't move, just let her body rest against his. He could feel her heart beating wildly, feel the increase in her breathing that she didn't even try to hide. And then she was doing it, lifting the black silk to her face with hands that trembled so badly he wasn't sure she'd be able to knot the fabric.

But she managed it, covering her eyes with the fabric and tying it so that the long ends trailed down her back. Her tongue darted out to wet lips that had gone dry with nerves. But her voice was unshaken when she said, "Now what?"

Fuck, the contradictions were going to kill him. So brazen and yet so untried, so hardheaded yet so vulnerable. It made him want to hold her gently, to fuck her uncontrollably. To be everything and anything to her that she needed. To make her do the same for him.

He stood up, moved back from the bed. Made sure his voice was as tough as hers when he said, "Take off your clothes."

"Cole?" She turned her head to follow his voice, reached out a hand to where he'd been and whimpered when it came away empty. "What are you doing?"

"Anything I want. And right now, I want to see you take your clothes off for me."

"I—"

"Don't argue with me." His voice was a whip that flayed at her insecurities. It had her standing and reaching for the buttons on the shirt before she was even aware of moving.

Taking a deep breath, Genevieve slid the first button free. Then the second and the third. Paused when she got to the fourth. It was disconcerting to stand here, completely blind, as she stripped herself for Cole's visual pleasure.

"Don't stop." His voice was harsh—its rasp skated along her nerve endings.

"Why don't you undress?" she asked, her voice trembling as she was.

"Because I'll be inside you five seconds after I drop my zipper."

"Mmm." She moved her fingers, made quick work of the last three buttons. "I like the sound of that."

"I thought you might. But we're not going there yet."

The air-conditioning kicked in and she felt the chill scoot between the open lapels of her shirt. It made her shiver, made her already turgid nipples even harder.

Taking a deep breath, she allowed the shirt to slip off her shoulders, down her arms. Then stood there shivering as the cool air slipped over her body like a caress.

"Take off the panties too."

Amazing how losing her sense of sight had her other senses straining. Would she have noticed how stressed his voice was if she'd been able to see him? Or would she have picked up on other, visual clues—clenched fists, tight shoulders, the wicked gleam he got in his eyes when he wanted to fuck her?

A whisper of movement had her listening intently. Cole had moved, and it was disconcerting, strange, not to know how far away he was from her. Or how close.

"Genevieve?"

The seductive smoothness of his voice drew her back to the task at hand and she slipped her thumbs into the thin straps of her underwear. Shimmied her hips and let the lace fall down her legs. When she felt the panties around her ankles, she kicked them away.

"Do you know how gorgeous you are?" His voice was close, closer than she'd expected. Turning toward it, she held out a hand. She wanted to feel him, needed the reassurance of his strong, hot body next to hers.

Her fingers met nothing but air. "Cole?"

"I asked you a question."

Temper snapped through the uncertainty. "I thought it was rhetorical."

"You thought wrong."

There was a long silence, broken only by the sound of their breathing and the low hum of the air-conditioning.

Finally, Cole spoke. "So do you know how beautiful you are?"

She bit her lip, but the thought of him moving closer to her, touching her, was too tempting to resist. "My breasts are too big and so is my ass."

He laughed, a low, seductive sound that skirted along her nerve endings like the finest wine. "Your ass is perfect. Heart-shaped. Sexy. And your breasts are the stuff fantasies are made of." She felt the air shift around her, heard that soft rustle again. And nearly screamed when Cole licked gently at the underside of one breast and then the other.

She was feeling too vulnerable, too nervous, too out of control. Yanking her arms up, she covered her breasts. And gritted her teeth at Cole's mocking laugh.

"It's a little late for that, isn't it?"

"I don't like this."

He laughed again, thrust a hand between her thighs. Ran a finger over her very slick slit. "Sure you do. I can feel exactly how much you like it."

Her knees trembled, threatened to collapse as he took a second to play with her clit. It was hard and throbbing, desperate for anything he would give it. One, two glancing caresses. A third, longer rub. She spread her legs, arched against the source of the insidious pleasure spreading through her.

And then he was gone, his touch disappearing as rapidly as her mind. She whimpered, reached for him, but again came up with nothing but air. "You're so anxious, Genevieve. So hot." There was that whisper again, just out of reach. "How much hotter can you burn, I wonder?"

"Much hotter and I'll spontaneously combust," she snapped, need drowning out the pride that had kept her relatively still to this point.

"Then we're in trouble, sweetheart, because I'm just getting started."

And then she was falling backwards, caught off guard by the hard push to her shoulders. She cried out, reached a hand back to break her fall and ended up sprawled on the bed.

"Did you think I would let you fall?" His voice was farther away now, and she turned her head blindly, seeking comfort. Seeking him. "I promised I wouldn't hurt you."

She didn't know how to respond. Her heart was still beating wildly, though the active fear had died down to mere apprehension.

She was sprawled half-on, half-off the bed and she wiggled backward, trying to get herself into a more dignified position. But Cole's voice, so deep now that it was barely recognizable, stopped her squirming.

"Spread your legs for me, Genevieve."

Immediately her thighs clamped shut, despite the electricity shooting through her. "Wha-what?" she asked, sounding more dazed than she would have liked.

"You're so damn beautiful there. I want to see you."

She'd never felt more vulnerable. How could he ask this of her? Wasn't it enough that she'd let him blindfold her? Now he wanted more. He wanted *everything*.

"Cole—"

"I said do it, Genevieve!"

"Screw you!" She catapulted into a sitting position. "Stop ordering me around."

There was a long silence, then, "It's not an order if you want to do it."

"I don't!" Her hands clenched, fisted in the soft satin of the comforter beneath her. But she didn't reach for the blindfold, not yet.

"Are you sure about that?" His voice was softly mocking, closer. So much closer than it had been.

"Yes." But suddenly she was anything but. He was touching her again, running one finger down the valley between her breasts, over her stomach, past her navel to her mons. He lingered there, toyed with the little strip of hair she hadn't waxed.

Fire shot through her, had her falling back against the soft comforter even as she reached for Cole.

But he wasn't there, despite the continued contact of that one finger sliding slowly between her thighs. Stroking her clit. Trailing over her labia. Thrusting inside of her.

"Cole!" She arched up, the pleasure of that one thrust so intense she nearly came, her legs falling open of their own volition.

"Genevieve!" he mimicked, but she could hear the strain in his voice. It was the same strain that had her breaking out in a sweat despite the cool air washing over her bare skin.

And then even his finger was gone. She whimpered, arched up, tried to find him again. "Do you want to come?" he asked, his mouth just inches away from her throbbing sex.

"Yes." It was a whisper.

"I'm sorry." His breath was hot against her pussy and she moaned, thrusting her hips up as she desperately tried to get closer to him. "I can't hear you."

"Yes." It was a gasp.

"Then touch yourself. Show me what you like."

"Cole!" she wailed. "I want *you*. Please."

"Oh, you'll have me. Over and over again, you'll take me. But first I want to see you pleasure yourself. I want you to make yourself come."

"I can't." She was on fire, dying, her entire body crying out for him. She wanted to come, needed to with an intensity that bordered on madness. Yet to do as he suggested—while he watched and she could see nothing—was its own kind of madness.

"You will." There was a long pause. "Come on, sweetheart. Touch those beautiful nipples for me. Show me how you like to be stroked."

Her hand trembled against the bedspread as she fought to ignore that black-magic voice. But he was a sorcerer, a demon, each word pulling her more and more under his spell, until all she wanted was to please him.

Slowly, trying to work up the nerve—trying to fight the utter vulnerability she felt—she brought her palm to her naked breast. Cupped it. Stroked it softly and sighed at the sheer relief of the contact.

"That's it, baby," Cole murmured, his voice little more than a growl. "Show me what you like."

She shifted her hand, brushed her nipple once. Twice. Then squeezed it between her thumb and forefinger as Cole had done the night before. Pleasure cascaded from her breasts to her pulsing sex.

Taking a deep breath, caught up in the pleasure, she brought her other hand up. Touched her other breast. Squeezed its nipple. And couldn't stop the small moan from escaping her lips as she arched off the bed.

She wondered what she looked like to him, wondered if he was watching her as intently as she imagined. She listened carefully, tried to distinguish a groan or a shift in his breathing pattern, anything that said he was half as aroused as she was. But there was nothing, only silence from him, as if he'd somehow left the room.

"Cole?" she called out, more uncertain than she could ever remember being.

"I'm here." It was more growl than groan, more animal than human, and it reassured her on a basic level. He was enjoying what she was doing, was as into it as she was.

Taking a deep breath, fighting her inhibitions with each movement of her fingers, she trailed a hand down her stomach. Lingered at her abdomen, smoothing, touching, enjoying the feel of soft skin sliding over softer skin. Ran her hand back up her body, following the path Cole had taken earlier. And slipped a finger into her mouth and sucked gently.

There was a harshly indrawn breath, the sound of knuckles cracking. And she grinned, realizing for the first time the power she wielded in this game.

Relaxing into the bed, letting it take her weight a little more, she ran her finger over her bottom lip. Her top lip. Slipped it into her mouth again to rewet it, and then lowered it to her breast.

She stroked the wetness onto one tight, hard nipple, moaning as the cold air hit it and made it even harder. Brought her finger up to her mouth and sucked again. Brought it to her other breast and repeated the motions. Again and again until her entire body was quivering, until her clit was begging to be touched. Until Cole's harsh breathing echoed in the room.

Only then, when she could feel the heat radiating off his body and hear the insane need in every breath he pulled into shuddering lungs, only then did she move her hand where she'd wanted it to go all along.

Though every nerve ending in her body was screaming at her to hurry, begging her to take herself over the edge, she took it slow. Bending her knees, she let them fall wide so that Cole could see exactly what he was missing with his power games.

She teased her clit, let her thumb glance over it a couple times without ever delivering the firm caress she needed to fly. Then moving lower, she ran a finger over her slit, relishing the dampness waiting for her. She couldn't remember the last time she'd been this wet, this turned on. She knew only that she wasn't ready for it to end, wasn't ready to go over the cliff if she couldn't take Cole with her.

His breathing was harsher, faster, but still he made no move to touch her. Part of her wanted to rip off the stupid blindfold, to gaze at him in the middle of passion. But the game wasn't over—she was no more done with him than he was with her.

Spreading her legs even wider, relishing the pleasure that came not just from her hand but from the knowledge that she was making Cole suffer as she had, Genevieve thrust two fingers inside of herself at the same moment she bent and swiped her tongue over her breast.

"Fuck!" The curse was low and vicious and more than a little slurred, as if Cole was drunk on the mere sight of her approaching orgasm.

He cleared his throat, said, "Do that again."

She took a page from his book and asked innocently, "Do what again?" even though she knew exactly what he was asking for.

"Don't fuck with me!" It was an explosion of sound and then he was there, straddling her hips, his arousal firm against her stomach.

"You've been singing some variation of that line all night, Cole. I thought I was just giving you what you wanted. I sure as hell was giving one of us what we wanted."

"Do it again." His voice was lower, guttural. Knowing he was watching, suddenly loving the attention—and the heady rush of power she got from knowing he was right there with her—she ran her tongue over the slope of her breast a second time.

Paused and whispered, "I wish it was you."

Cole cursed, long and violently, though he slowly untangled himself from where she lay on the bed. "Finish it."

"I can't," she said, tugging against the hand that held her wrist.

"You have to. I have to see—" His voice broke, and she delighted in getting a little of her own back. He might be the one with the blind-fold and bag of tricks, but she had as much power over him as he had over her.

It was a thrilling, beautiful feeling. One that grew as he reluctantly let go of her wrist. She almost whimpered at the loss of his touch, would have if she hadn't felt the pressure of his gaze. He was staring at her, geared up and desperate. She didn't need her eyes to tell her that—she could smell the arousal rolling off him. Hot and salty and so sexy she wanted nothing more than to immerse herself in him.

Restless, aching, she was done with the preliminaries and nearly desperate for relief. Moving her hands once again to her pussy, she thrust two fingers inside of herself as she used her other hand to play with her clit.

It felt so good, especially as she imagined they were Cole's hands on her. Cole's fingers inside of her, searching for her G spot. Finding it. Stroking it as he pinched her clit with his strong, elegant fingers. Cole, with his dark eyes and strong muscles, bending to her. Flicking her clit with his tongue, taking it in his mouth, playing with it.

Sweat rolled between her breasts and she couldn't hold back the moan. Her hips arched, moving restlessly as release beckoned. Cole, she reminded herself as she applied firmer pressure. Cole was inside her, fucking her, having her. Cole—

She whimpered as her body shot to the edge of the cliff. Began to teeter over. One more stroke. Just one more and—

"Stop!" Cole's voice was harsh, violent as it cut into her fantasy. And then he was slamming her hands above her head, leaving her body in an agony of unfulfilled need, balanced precariously on the highest sexual precipice of her life.

Chapter Fourteen

uck! He was going to lose it like a kid in the throes of his first wet dream. How had she done this to him? How the fuck had he thought—even for an instant—that he could control all that heat and fire and rampant sexuality? Genevieve was a time bomb, and he was the one about to go off.

"Cole!" It was a broken cry, one that shot straight to his screaming cock and had him clawing for a control he knew he wouldn't find. "Don't do this to me, don't leave me—" Her voice broke, her body moving restlessly against the navy comforter.

He gritted his teeth, forced the words out when all he really wanted to do was fall on her like a starving man. "Soon, sweetheart."

"Not soon—now!" She nearly screamed the word as she bucked against his hold on her, and the sight of her back bowing, her full breasts standing even more proudly, nearly robbed him of the little composure he still had. "I've got to come. I've got to—"

For a long moment, he sat frozen, staring at her. Unable to breathe, as the world around them shrank to this place and this moment.

He'd meant to drive her out of her mind, had started this as a way to break down the barriers she had against him. But he was the one losing control, the one about to blast through his own barriers in an effort to get to her.

It was a sobering thought, or would have been if he could have thought of anything but Genevieve. There were so many things he wanted to do with her, to her. So many ways he wanted to make her come. They flashed through his mind in an erotic montage as he stared at her in the fading light.

Genevieve on her hands and knees in front of him while he plunged into her. Genevieve screaming, her hands tangled in his hair, as he thrust his tongue into her pussy and ate her like an ice cream cone. Genevieve tied up, her body on fire as he took her places she'd never been before.

"Cole!" This time it was a scream, the sound freeing him from the sensual slide show in his head. With a growl, he reached into the nightstand again, came out with more black satin ties.

Leaning forward, he wrapped one around the wrists he still had pinned together above her head, then tied her to the black iron headboard. She didn't complain as he'd expected, didn't beg to be set free. He glanced down, wanting to make sure she was okay, and that's when she struck. Arching up, her mouth found his pec and her teeth sank in, hard.

"Shit!" he yelled as the threat of coming in his pants became even more real. "You little hellcat."

"You have no idea." Now she strained against the ties. "Fuck me, Cole. Fuck me now before I die of frustration."

His heart was pounding like a fucking rap song, his breath bellowing in and out of his lungs. He had to get away, had to step back before he leapt on her. Before he fucked her and took everything he wanted.

Jumping off the bed, he grabbed more ties. Then bound each of her ankles to the footboard so she was spread-eagled on the bed, her beautiful sex glistening in the evening twilight.

Shit! When he'd bought the ties, he hadn't known if he could actually use them—wasn't sure Genevieve would let him or that he would even want to. But some hitherto unheard-from instinct had him place them on the counter—and never before in his life had he been so glad that he'd listened to his gut.

"Cole, stop!"

"Stop?" he growled, his mouth watering at the sight of her spread out and bound like a sacrifice. He gritted his teeth against the need to taste her. To stroke her. To feel her flow around his tongue as she came. "You don't look like you want me to stop."

His hand moved without his command, stroked up her firm, slender thigh until he reached her drenched pussy. He ran a finger over the slick folds, careful not to touch the hard bud of her clit. "You don't feel like you want me to stop."

"Either fuck me or untie me!" Her heels dug into the bed as she lifted her pelvis, trying to get a stronger pressure on her sex.

But he pulled back, kept his touch deliberately light. Kept her on the brink of madness. "You're not really in a position to give orders, are you?" he asked as he dipped his index finger inside her up to the first joint, felt the warm honey of her response.

"I swear, when you let me go—"

"Who says I'll let you go?" He ignored the trembling in his hands, the weakness in his knees as his cock throbbed for relief. Razor blades of desire were skating down his spine, down his dick, but he was determined to see this through. Determined to give her as much pleasure as she could take—and then more.

"Maybe I'll keep you here, tied up on my bed. I'll come to you in the morning, ease your sleeping body into orgasm so the first thing you think about, the first thing you feel when you wake up, is me."

She moaned, her hips bucking against his hand. "I'll come back in the afternoon, slip my tongue inside this sweet pussy of yours. Stroke you and eat you and fuck you with my mouth until you scream my name. Then I'll slide my cock inside you and fuck you some more."

"Fuck you!" She was trembling so badly that the words were more request than argument, more question than tell-off.

A drop of sweat rolled slowly down her chest and belly, pooled invitingly in her navel. He leaned forward, licked it off. Clenched his teeth until his jaw popped as her vaginal muscles tightened around his finger, pulling him deeper into her endless heat.

He swallowed tightly, struggled to speak over the need consuming him. "I'll come to you at night, spend hours playing with these beautiful nipples of yours." He moved his other hand to her breast, drew circles around the incredibly tight areola.

"Turn you over and spank your delightful little ass. Then fuck you there, where you're so tight." He turned his hand so that his finger could go deeper inside her even as his thumb slid into the tight little hole. The heat of her, the overwhelming, unbelievable heat of her as she clenched around him had his dick spurting little drops of cum he could no longer contain.

"Fuck, Genevieve, you are so my kind of girl." He pressed deeper and she screamed, orgasm rolling through her. He shuddered as she milked his hand, her body clenching and releasing so rhythmically that he felt himself grow wetter still.

But he didn't move, except to wiggle his thumb and finger even deeper into her. To find the sweet bundle of nerves high on her vaginal walls and stroke some more, intensifying her climax. Hurtling her into another one.

"Cole! Oh, my God, Cole!" It was a keening cry, one that shattered the last vestiges of his control. Unbuttoning his pants, lowering his zipper, he sheathed himself in a condom then climbed onto the bed fully dressed and thrust himself inside of her.

She came again, her body shaking and arching and clenching against him. Two thrusts later, maybe three, and he was with her, his body blasting like a freight train before he could even try to control it.

Cock throbbing, pleasure building at the base of his spine and shooting forward, he convulsed again and again as he emptied himself inside of her, giving her more than he'd ever planned to give.

When it was finally over and the first semblance of sanity slowly returned to him, Cole collapsed on top of her, resting his forehead against hers as he tried to catch his breath.

Genevieve wiggled with pleasure, shifted to cradle him as best she could while still tied to the bed. She wanted to see him, to look into his eyes and see if he was as shattered by what had happened between them as she was.

But when she turned her head, started to push against his shoulder in an effort to dislodge the blindfold, he rolled off her. "Not yet," he said as he shifted off her. Immediately she felt bereft—lost, alone in the darkness.

But then he whispered "I'll do it," in her ear, and his hands were there, tenderly lifting up her head as he worked the knot free. Slowly, he pulled the silk away and she could see again.

What she saw nearly blew her mind; the tenderness in his black eyes as he looked into hers shook her to her core.

His fingers trailed across her cheek, toyed with her mouth before sliding tenderly over her breast and down her stomach. Response fluttered deep inside of her, shocking her. She was half-dead, her body so relaxed she feared she might melt into a puddle and run right off the bed, and still she wanted him.

How was that possible?

Cole cleared his throat. "I'll be right back."

If she could have moved, she might have followed him, just to see if he was as affected by her as she was by him. But she was still tied to the bed, her arms and legs bound for his pleasure. And hers.

Oh, God, she'd lose her feminist card for sure, because she'd enjoyed everything Cole had done to her. Worse, she craved more. Not because she wanted to be hurt, to be dominated, but because it was unbelievably exciting to match wits with a man as strong as she was. To lose the battles as often as she won them. To compete with someone who liked to win, to be on top, as much as she did.

She heard the water turn on in the bathroom and imagined him disposing of the condom. Washing his hands. Was he still hard for her, still turned on despite the sex that had nearly killed them? She was, her body hot and aching and more than ready for another round.

When he came out of the bathroom he was naked, and his cock was so long and hard it was almost impossible to imagine he had just come. But when he crossed the room, he didn't climb up on the bed with her as she'd expected. Instead, he grinned, winked at her. And reached into the nightstand next to the bed.

"What are you—"

"Ssh," he said, as he pulled something out, closed his fingers around it. She strained her head, tried to see, but whatever it was fit completely within his big palm.

Then he was sitting on the bed, touching her. Petting her. And she forgot to be nervous as she flexed against his long fingers. Forgot to be wary as pleasure coursed through her.

He moved between her legs, toyed with her until she was soaking wet again. Or still—she wasn't sure if she'd ever stopped flowing. He slid two fingers inside her pussy, stretching her open. And then she felt something else sliding in, something warm but utterly unfamiliar.

"What are you doing?"

"Just enjoy them," he said.

"Enjoy what?" she asked, shifting a little so she could look at him. She gasped as pleasure exploded within her. "What did you do?"

He grinned wickedly. "You'll see." Then stood and headed for the door.

"Wait!" She tried to roll to her side and nearly saw stars as whatever he'd put inside of her clanged together, then rolled over her vaginal walls.

"I have to finish making dinner." He winked and strolled out of the room.

For a moment, time stood still as shock held her immobile. And then she exploded, anger chasing away any thought of another round. "Let me go!" she shouted, bucking and twisting in earnest as she tried to free her hands. "Cole!"

The things inside of her moved with each shake of her hips, rolling over her G spot and a bunch of other sensitive spots she hadn't known existed.

There was no answer, only a silence that spoke louder than words ever could. "Cole, you asshole! Get back here and untie me."

But still he didn't answer. Furious, annoyed, and maybe just a little bit scared, Genevieve strained desperately against her silken bonds. And climaxed as the balls inside of her bounced and rolled around every inch of her pussy.

She moaned as her body exploded, desperately trying to get some semblance of control back. But her nipples were hard, her vagina spasming, and no matter how hard she tried to hold still, she couldn't.

A simple shift of her hips sent pleasure jangling up her nerve endings; an arch of her back had her panting, sweat rolling off her violently hot body in rivers. She tried to move just her arms, to twist her wrists in the silken restraints, but all she did was tangle herself more tightly. Not to mention cause a series of mini explosions to erupt in her sex.

She was going to kill Cole for this. She really was. As soon as he let her go, she would take her gun and—

"Oh, God!"

The pleasure was inescapable, unbelievable. Never-ending. She clenched her vaginal muscles, tried to stave off the exquisite licks of ecstasy that flowed over every nerve ending she had, but tightening up only made the balls feel bigger. Only gave them more area to touch.

"Cole!" Her voice was low, desperate, but she didn't care. She was on the brink of another orgasm, and breathing was becoming impossible. She gasped, tried to suck air down her tight throat, but felt like she was strangling. Tried again, her whole body shaking, and was hurtled into another blinding orgasm.

"Cole!" It was a wail, a cry of desperation and fear. Her body was no longer her own—it was completely out of her mind's control.

"I'm here, sweetheart."

"Get them out," she panted, her body arching, wiggling, twisting as her legs strained against the silken ties. "Get them out now—oh, fuck!" She was coming again—an explosion of pleasure that thrust ecstasy into every part of her body. Her nipples hardened, her back bowed, tears streamed down her face as she tried to escape. But it was unrelenting, insidious, the pleasure everywhere. It took her over, controlled her, trapped her as she pleaded with Cole to end it.

Sobbing, shaking, she flung herself against the ties again and again, unaware of anything but the heat exploding in her womb. And then Cole was there, untying her, slipping his fingers inside of her, searching for the balls.

His touch, his manipulation of the balls, sent her careening over the edge again and she screamed, clutched at him. Desperate for something to hold on to in the middle of the maelstrom that had taken her over.

"I've got you, Genevieve. I've got you." The balls slipped out at the same time Cole pulled her into his arms, rolling so that she rested on top of him. He held her, stroked her, soothed her as her sex continued to spasm.

When she was finally calm and could actually breathe without shuddering, she pulled away from him. "What the hell were those?" she demanded, her voice hoarse and scratchy.

"Just something I picked up for you yesterday."

"Yesterday? After the fight we had, what gave you the idea you'd ever get a chance to use them?"

He smiled wryly, stroked a finger lightly down her arm. She shuddered, her skin so sensitive the contact was almost painful. "I had high hopes."

"Seeing as you were the one to get his panties in a wad, I think it took a hell of a lot of nerve to be out buying sex toys for us."

He shrugged, but his eyes gleamed wickedly. "Maybe."

She snorted. "Definitely." Then started as his hand smoothed over her breast, his fingers pausing to toy with her nipples.

"Oh, no." She jerked away. "We are so not going there again. I'll die."

He ignored her, lowering his head to her breast and flicking her nipple with his tongue.

She raised her hands to push at his head, but her fingers ended up tangling in the black silk instead. "I'm serious. We can't." The arch of her back as she pressed against his mouth made a mockery of her words.

"Why not?"

"Because I'm exhausted. And I'm still hungry. What happened to dinner?" He lifted his head, and she suppressed a moan of disappointment. "Your wish is my command." His thumb and index finger closed around her nipple, squeezed lightly.

She raised one eyebrow. "That's the first I've heard. Are you sure about that?"

He didn't answer, concentrated instead on drawing patterns on her skin with his tongue. She shivered as he skimmed down her abdomen to the tattoo at her navel. Trembled as his tongue swirled around the elaborate design.

Her body was turning on again, responding to his tender ministrations in a way she never could have dreamed about. How could she want him again? How on earth could her body respond after so many orgasms, when usually it took concentration of epic proportions to even get her to one climax?

He was a magician, she decided as she allowed herself to sink into Cole. A sorcerer who could seize control of her body, make it do whatever he wanted. Reaching out, she trailed her hands down his back, felt the muscles bunch beneath her fingers. Sighed as he slipped inside of her.

Maybe one more time wouldn't hurt.

Chapter Fifteen

"Thanks for the ride," Genevieve commented absently as she climbed out of Cole's car and slammed the door behind her. Her mind was already on the crime scene—and on Shawn's warning. *It's really bad.*

She had just drifted off to sleep, her empty stomach finally full, her head pillowed by Cole's chest, when Shawn had called her cell phone to tell her they had discovered the fourth body.

He'd sounded shaken, disturbed in a way that wasn't normal for him. He'd been a homicide detective longer than she and, consequently, had developed a much thicker skin. For him to be this upset . . . she shuddered as she looked up at the Hotel Monteleone. It was the oldest—and most famous—hotel in New Orleans and had been a personal favorite of hers for years because of its fabulous restaurant and beautiful decor.

She'd been here to eat more than once in the past few months; had stayed here with a lover over a year ago. But suddenly, she didn't want to be here. Wanted to be as far away from the historic hotel with its ornate columns and marble floors as she could get. Though she didn't know what waited for her up the steps, she couldn't shake the feeling that it could change her life forever.

Sighing impatiently, she headed into the hotel. Standing out here wasn't doing anything but prolonging the inevitable. Whatever was in there had to be faced, and faced soon. This was her case, and if the killer had left a clue, as he'd promised, that was just one more reason to get a move on.

"Hey," Cole called through the rolled-down window. "Are you sure you don't want me to wait? It's no big deal."

She turned, smiled at him though she knew it didn't reach her eyes. "It's fine—I'll probably be here for hours. I'll just catch a ride back with Shawn."

Cole's jaw tightened, but he didn't protest. Instead, he raised his hand in a wave and said from between clenched teeth, "Be careful."

She laughed. "Look around. There's got to be twenty cops here. I'll be perfectly safe."

He regarded her soberly. "It's the enemy you aren't expecting that often does you in." He rolled up the window and pulled away, leaving her staring after him, mouth agape.

"Delacroix." Chastian's voice cut through the early-morning gloom as he climbed the stairs to stand next to her. "I'm glad you could join us."

Stiffening at the censure in his tone, she turned to face him. "Shawn only called me fifteen minutes ago, sir. I got here as soon as I could."

"Well, I know how you ladies like to primp," he answered, shooting her a patently disbelieving look. "But next time, make sure murder takes priority over makeup, will you?"

Genevieve bit her tongue in an effort to keep from exploding. She was sick of this bullshit, sick of the sexist innuendos and supercilious comments Chastian threw around like candy. She was already pissed enough that Shawn had been called first and had actually made it to the murder site before letting her know what was going on. The last thing she needed was her asshole lieutenant rubbing in that fact. Especially since there wasn't a drop of makeup on her face.

Somehow she managed to keep her cool, and headed through the double doors without another word to her boss. Moving through the hotel's extravagant lobby, she caught the elevator to the fourteenth floor. Exited and followed the signs to the Tennessee Williams suite.

As she walked down the hall, she wondered what had prompted the killer to move so far up the social scale. The Hotel Monteleone was a five-star hotel, and their regular rooms ran hundreds of dollars. The bill for three days in the Tennessee Williams suite would run well into the thousands of dollars.

The door to the room was ajar when she finally found it, but the rookie cop doing door duty didn't give her any trouble—he was the same one who had discovered Jessica Robbins' body and he must have remembered her.

Crossing the threshold, she couldn't help the gasp that escaped her at her first glimpse of the room. It was a scene right out of a horror movie. Bright red blood spattered the pale yellow walls in violent slashes and curlicues, while more had soaked the gold carpet around the body.

"This can't all be hers," she murmured as she stopped next to Shawn, who stood next to the poor girl's body.

"That's what I said. But Jefferson disagrees." He nodded at the ME, who was currently crouched beside the body, doing his damnedest not to get blood on his jeans.

"The human body contains nearly six liters of blood. The perp drained her dry, so this might very well be only her blood."

"But," Shawn said as he leaned down and rolled the body over, "that's not the worst part."

"What is?" she asked, then gasped as her stomach lurched. The room began to spin, and she grabbed on to Shawn in an effort to steady herself.

The killer was getting better at his job, more brutal with each subsequent murder. Genevieve tried to fight down the sickness and horror, but they welled inside of her—combined with lack of sleep—until the room around her began to fade to black.

"I think she's going over!" Jefferson's voice was high with alarm, and she felt Shawn's hands on her elbows as he tried to steady her.

"Don't do this, Genevieve." His voice was harsh. "Stay with me."

But the room was spinning behind her closed eyelids, her knees buckling despite her efforts to lock them in place. Behind her, she heard Chastian's voice exclaim, "You've got to be kidding me!" just before her ass hit the blood-soaked ground, hard.

"Get her head between her knees," Jefferson said. She heard the sound of gloves snapping off, and then gentle hands rubbed up and down her back.

"Look at me, Genevieve. Come on, girl. Open those baby blues and look at me."

She did as Jefferson asked, though her eyelids weighed a thousand pounds. She was careful to focus only on him, careful to keep her eyes off the mutilated body in the middle of the room.

"Good girl," Shawn said. "Now breathe with me."

"I'm okay." She shrugged off Shawn's hand. "It just caught me by surprise."

"Don't worry about it, kid." Jefferson offered a hand and she took it, letting him help her to her feet. "It's pretty bad in here—I nearly lost my dinner, and I've been doing this a hell of a lot longer than you have."

She heard Chastian snort behind her, but he didn't say anything else, thank God. She didn't know if she had enough control right now to keep her mouth shut if he started in on her.

"How long have you been here?" she asked Shawn as she approached the body again.

"I got here about a minute before I called you."

"Have you looked around yet? Tried to find the clues he swears he left for us?"

"I've poked around a little, but haven't found anything yet."

She nodded and stepped carefully around the body, her feet squishing in the wet carpet. Her gag reflex rose, but she beat it back—no way in hell was she losing it twice in one night. Not with her lieutenant looking for any excuse to bust her out of homicide.

"How long's she been dead?" she asked the ME as she leaned against the only wall in the room not coated with blood and let her eyes wander over the crime scene. She'd go through the hotel room in a few minutes—take it apart inch by inch. But right now she wanted the whole picture, wanted to see what the room had looked like when the killer had finished his work.

"About three days is my best guess, at this point. Rigor mortis has already come and gone. But he's had the air-conditioning pumping full blast since he left her here—it preserved her pretty well, but definitely screws with TOD."

"How did they not find her?" Genevieve demanded.

Shawn shrugged. "Do not Disturb sign on the door; it worked until tonight. She was supposed to check out today, and the manager came in to see if she had forgotten to turn in her keys."

"In the middle of the night?"

"Supposedly, some hotshot called up tonight, wants the suite for tomorrow." Luc's voice was less than convinced.

"You think it's our guy?"

"It sure as shit wouldn't surprise me."

Her eyes met Shawn's, and she knew he was remembering the killer's note. *She's been out there, waiting, for nearly three days now. Wondering, I'm sure, how long it will take you to find her.*

"Have there been any murders at this hotel?" she asked abruptly, watching as the crime scene tech painstakingly tried to get prints from the dresser across the room. What a joke—this was a hotel, for Christ's sake. The dresser could have literally hundreds of prints on it.

"I just checked with management," Luc answered her question as he and Roberto crossed into the room. "They said nothing like this has ever happened here before."

"Holy Christ!" she heard Roberto mutter as he got his first look at the vic. "It looks like a *Friday the 13th* movie in here."

"Has anyone checked the bathroom?" she asked, walking toward the room in question as she continued to ponder the incongruities of this case.

It just didn't make sense that the killer had done the vic here; all his other victims had been killed in one place and dumped somewhere else. Strange that he would break his MO so completely.

She looked around the suite. He must have had his reasons, but she'd be damned if she had a clue what they were. At least not yet. She had a feeling, though, that whatever they were, they were tied directly to his identity and motive for committing these murders in the first place.

"I took a cursory look around, but that's it." Shawn answered the question she'd forgotten to ask as he crouched down next to Jefferson and watched the ME work.

"We've already finished with it, so you can do your thing." The crime scene tech currently dusting the table for prints volunteered the information.

"You didn't find anything?"

"Not really. A couple hairs, but they look like they belong to the vic."

"In the bathroom?"

"Yep."

"Do you think they could have been on him?" she demanded.

"Why do you say that?" Suddenly, she had everyone's attention.

"He had to have been covered in blood, right?" She looked around, gestured at the walls. "I mean you don't get this kind of damage without getting some of the blood on yourself. So he had to wash up."

"We sprayed in there—no blood showed up at all in the shower or the sink," Jefferson commented as he went back to cataloging the body.

"Well, how the hell does that happen?" she wondered aloud. "Unless he was wearing a shower curtain, for God's sake, he had to have gotten blood on him somewhere.

"But even barring that, it's strange. Who on earth pays this much for a suite just to kill a woman? Especially since—if the hotel is to be believed—there've been no other murders here. Why change his MO now?"

"Maybe this isn't our guy after all?" Luc suggested.

She thought back on the sadism of the other crimes. "No, this is our guy. But something's off. It just doesn't make sense that he'd choose this suite, this hotel, without a reason."

"When we find him, I'll be sure to ask him," Chastian said sarcastically.

She ignored him. "Her hair was in the bathroom—was this her room?"

"According to the front desk, the vic rented it," Roberto answered her. "Three nights ago. She was by herself on vacation—or at least that's what she told the front desk when she asked about tourist attractions. Her reservation was for the weekend."

"So if she really is a tourist, how'd she hook up with our guy?"

He shrugged. "Bumped into him at the mall? Met him at a bar? At this point, who knows?"

"Run her credit cards and check her purse for receipts. We've got to find out where they connected. Where's she been the last few days?"

"I'm on it," Shawn said grimly.

"Unless she met him here." Genevieve paused as the thought occurred to her. "It would make sense, right? Two tourists hooking up in the hotel bar? He'd seem safer if he was staying at the same hotel."

"That could explain how he got out of here without washing up.

Maybe his room's close by. If he did her at night, it's not that hard to sneak down the hall a few doors . . ." Luc's voice trailed off for a minute as they all pondered.

"That could also explain why he left the body here. Kind of hard to get her out of the place without being seen." Genevieve scanned the room with narrowed eyes. "Where's her bag?"

"Her purse is on the table—we got her BlackBerry, wallet, credit cards, money. We won't know until we talk to her family, but it doesn't look like anything's missing."

"But where's her suitcase?"

"In the closet. We haven't gotten that far yet."

Five long strides and she was at the closed closet doors. She pushed one of the sliding doors open and there it was—a Louis Vuitton resting on a luggage stand. It had been unzipped, but no clothes were hanging in the closet.

She flipped open the lid. There were no clothes inside either, just a large, wrapped box—with Genevieve's name on it.

"He took her clothes." Her voice sounded unnatural, the pitch way too high.

"How do you know that?" Luc headed toward her.

"Because the only thing in the suitcase was this. And I don't think she brought it all the way from"—she checked the luggage tags—"Boston, just for me."

Chastian elbowed his way through the clutch of cops suddenly standing around her. "That thing's addressed to you, Delacroix," he said as he caught sight of the large white envelope on the top of the gift-wrapped box.

"I saw that," she answered dryly, gingerly slipping the envelope from beneath the ribbon.

"What's it say?" Shawn demanded, coming up behind her.

She shuddered, fought the feeling of claustrophobia that came over her as the other cops pressed closer still. With Chastian squeezing her from the right and Shawn from the left, it was hard to convince her lungs she was getting enough oxygen. Of course, her feelings of suffocation were probably caused by the letter from the psychopath and not the other cops' proximity.

"Genevieve," she started to read the pale blue card out loud, but her voice gave way before she got to the first sentence.

I see you've found my present. I hope you like it—I spent a long time looking for just the right colors to match your beautiful hair. But then decided you were right all along.

So, what do you think of my latest masterpiece? She's quite something, isn't she? Her name is Maria, and she reminded me of you—not her coloring, of course, but all those long, beautiful curls. I couldn't resist.

I admit, this was my most challenging creation yet—but then, the most difficult are so often the most rewarding. Do you like her? And the suite? I chose it for you—I know how much you like Tennessee Williams. I never could get into his work, but you, you have every play he ever wrote, don't you?

I'm hungry for you, Genevieve, hungrier than I've ever been. I can't sleep for wanting you, can't eat for thinking of what it will be like to finally be inside you. All the way inside you—with my breath and my tongue. My cock, my hands, every part of me touching every part of you.

I can't wait to open you up, to see your beautiful heart beating just for me. Can't wait to put my hand on it while it pumps, to know that the last thing you'll see in this world will be my face.

She started to tremble, but when Shawn tried to take the note from her, she wrenched it from his grasp. She would finish reading it, she had to, because after this, she never wanted to touch the thing again.

> *So, have you found the clue I left you? I confess to being just a tad bit anxious—I've waited so long to make you mine that I am terribly excited at the thought that if you are smart enough—good enough—you will understand. And then you will come to me.*
>
> *Be smart, Genevieve. And swift—the fate of the next one rests in your beautiful hands.*

For a moment she really thought she was going to puke. Clapping a hand over her mouth, she thrust the letter at Shawn before hightailing it into the hall. She heard Luc call her name, heard Shawn curse as he must have begun reading the letter.

For the second time in an hour, she braced her hands on her knees and concentrated on her breathing. *In through the nose; out through the mouth.*

In, out.

In, out.

She kept up the rhythm for long minutes, worked to keep her mind clear of everything but the need to breathe.

The nausea finally receded, along with her need to flee. What the hell was this guy doing? Why had he fixated on her? And why was he going through this ridiculous game of cat and mouse, when it would be easier—and more expedient—to just snatch her somewhere?

God knew she would prefer it to this endless charade. But then, that was probably why he was doing this. If he knew as much about her as he claimed, the bastard would know that she'd much prefer a direct confrontation. He would know that the idea of women being tortured and raped would hit her hard, especially when he implied that they were stand-ins for her.

Just the idea made her ill—that these women were dying because some psychopath wanted her attention. Well, mission accomplished. He had her attention—and she wasn't backing off until she'd nailed his ass to the fucking wall.

Steadier now that she'd had a chance to think things through, Genevieve headed back into the hotel room. And ran smack-dab into Torres.

"This was in the box," he said grimly, holding up a beaded and fringed scarf in shades of hot pink and purple.

She reached for it reflexively, gasping as her hands touched the gossamer thin silk. "Oh, shit," she said as she held it up to the light and saw the magnificent swirls sweeping out from the center.

"What now?" Luc demanded from the doorway, blatant fury in every line of his body.

"I wanted this scarf." She looked blankly at the two men, watched them tense as they waited for her to explain. "I saw it in the French Market last week, spent a long time debating whether I wanted to spend the money on it. Finally, I decided it was too expensive and I left it there. But I've been thinking of it off and on all week, wondering if I should go back and get it."

Silence greeted her revelation, a silence broken only by Shawn's voice, cursing low and viciously.

Chapter Sixteen

"Delacroix, get in here." Chastian's voice boomed across the bull pen, grabbing Genevieve's attention—and that of every other cop in the room.

She cursed, mentally, even as she slid back her chair and started to cross the room that had suddenly begun to feel like a gauntlet. It had been three days since they had found Maria Varden's body at the Monteleone. Three days with very little sleep and even less progress, as they tried to run this bastard to ground.

Three days since she'd seen Cole. She'd spoken with him briefly this morning, and had been reassured by his quiet assertions that he was getting along just fine without her. Some men didn't understand what it was like to be in the middle of a murder investigation of this magnitude; she'd lost more than one lover through the years because they felt she didn't have enough time for them.

Of course Cole would understand, she told herself as she headed for her lieutenant's office. He'd lived through this from the other side—had dealt with his sister's brutal murder and the ensuing investigation.

Still, she wanted to see him. Her body was aching for him. To have him hold her—just for a minute—and tell her everything was going to be all right. Because with the way she was feeling now—as she hit dead end after dead end in her search for this bastard—she felt like nothing was ever going to be okay again.

She put Cole—and her need for him—out of her mind as she stopped in front of Chastian, knowing she'd need every ounce of concentration she had left, after working almost seventy-two hours straight, to deal with the man.

On some level, she was conscious of Shawn walking behind her, but as she entered Chastian's office, he barked, "Not you, Webster. Go do whatever it is you do." Then slammed the door in her partner's face.

Her heart picked up its rhythm, and a line of sweat—cold and uncomfortable—rolled from her shoulder blades to the small of her back. She'd never seen Chastian look so smug or so grim. Whatever he had to talk to her about wasn't going to be good. That he wanted to do it without Shawn sent her radar on red alert.

Silence stretched between them, long, awkward moments where they did nothing but stare at each other. Genevieve knew he was testing her, waiting for her to speak first. It was just one of the many power games he liked to play, and today she just wasn't in the mood to humor him.

When he finally realized he wasn't going to get a response from her, he reached into the top drawer of his desk and pulled out a large manila envelope. Then tossed it on the desk and nodded for her to take it.

She eyed the thing for a minute, somehow knowing that the contents wouldn't be pleasant. But they both knew she didn't have a choice but to look, so she reached over and picked the thing up, careful not to show her reluctance.

Screw him, she thought as she undid the tabs that held the envelope closed. If he wanted to pull these games with her, he had a long wait coming before he would get a reaction—

Shit.

For at least a minute, the world went black. There was a buzzing sound in her ears, and she swayed alarmingly. But she locked her knees in place, refusing to let them buckle, no matter how weak they had become. She stared down at the pictures in her hands and nearly gagged. Chastian would like nothing more than to watch her fall, to call out for help while the damning photos lay spread out around her on the floor for the entire squad room to see.

Photos of her and Cole—photos of her naked, in his kitchen, him poised over her—tequila flowing freely over her stomach. Photos of him licking it off her breasts.

She flipped through the stack, paused as she saw a series taken with her blindfolded and strapped to Cole's bed. The lines down the middle of the picture made it abundantly clear that it had been taken from outside the half-open shutters that had decorated Cole's bedroom windows. Shutters neither of them had thought to close as the room faced his high-fenced backyard.

She felt violated in a way she had never before experienced. That someone had watched her during the most intimate sexual moments of her life was horrible enough; that he had taken pictures and sent them to her boss was unthinkable.

She wanted to cry, wanted to run away and never come back. But Chastian was counting on that feeling, was exploiting it for all he was worth, and she would be damned if she gave him the satisfaction.

Making sure her voice was as tough as his skin, she demanded, "Was there a note?"

His eyes widened, and she realized that wasn't the question he'd been expecting her to ask. Maybe *Where did you get these?* would have been a more appropriate first question, but she already knew the answer. *He* had taken these pictures. *He* had sent them to her boss.

He was taunting her, humiliating her, paying her back for sleeping with someone else when he'd wanted her for himself. And now that she'd been blindsided by the photos, she realized she shouldn't have been. Of course he'd been watching her, following her, learning her every move. His knowledge of the plays she liked gave proof that he'd already been inside her house, had looked at her bookshelves.

She'd spent the last three days alternating between horror and fury that he'd had the nerve to enter her house, to go through her things. Even though she'd changed the locks, she didn't feel safe in her own home. She stared down at the photos, couldn't repress the shudder that rocked through her. But that—that was nothing compared to what he'd done here.

"Why do you ask?" Chastian's eyes swept over her, and though she assured herself that there was nothing sexual in the look, she'd never felt more naked. How was she supposed to look her boss in the eye and explain how those pictures had been taken? How could she not?

"You know *he* sent these, right?" She was proud of how hard her voice sounded, how completely invulnerable.

"Is that what you think?"

"It's what I know. This has the killer's sick mental fingerprints all over it." She started flipping through the remaining pictures, knowing that if she didn't get through them now, she never would.

Each one was a little more explicit than the one before it, each one a new humiliation for her to endure. The thought of them being logged into evidence, of Shawn and Luc and Roberto seeing them, was more than she could bear.

When she got to the last photo, it was all she could do not to gasp, not to drop the thing and give Chastian exactly the reaction he was looking for. But she was made of sterner stuff, she reminded herself, as she stared at the altered picture of herself. Whoever had developed it had let the developing fluid sit too long on it. Around her body stretched on the bed, there were huge, dark puddles that looked like blood.

Her eyes had been gouged out, her body mutilated almost beyond recognition. She glanced up, saw Chastian watching her with hungry, glazed eyes—as if he was dying for her to fall apart.

Refusing to give him that satisfaction, she said again in her best hard-ass voice, "Where's the note?"

He raised an eyebrow, but reached back in the envelope and pulled out yet another letter printed on pale blue paper. She grabbed it, read the two words with a sinking heart. *My turn.*

She didn't know what to do, what to say. Could barely look Chastian in the eyes as she contemplated how to handle this latest viciousness. If he was a different kind of lieutenant, she might have asked him for help. Might have listened to his suggestions. Might have counted on him to protect her.

But Chastian hated her and always had, and this was the excuse he'd been waiting for to knock her down a peg—or five.

So she simply watched him, waited. He'd already made up his mind on how to handle this before he'd ever called her in—and he would sure as hell tell her what he wanted to do. Better to wait than to humiliate herself all over again.

But when he spoke, his voice was gentler than she'd expected. "This guy's fixated on you, Delacroix."

It was all she could do to keep from laughing. Hysterically. "Yes, sir. That seems pretty obvious at this point."

"What are we going to do about that fact?"

She shrugged. "I don't know. But I figure if you're bringing the topic up, you have a solution."

He sat down hard on his desk chair, drummed his fingers on the desk as he watched her. "I do. I think you should take a leave of absence."

Genevieve felt her mouth drop open. Worked hard to close it so she wouldn't look like a total idiot. But of all the things she'd expected him to say to her, that didn't even register in the top fifty. "A leave of absence? In the middle of a serial homicide case?" She knew her tone implied that she thought he was several cards short of a full deck, but she couldn't help it. Had Chastian gone completely insane?

He held up a hand. "It's dangerous for you to be a part of this case, and I think—"

"It's dangerous for any of us to be a part of this case!" she exploded. "It's ridiculous to say that I'm any more at risk than Shawn or Luc or Torres."

"Don't throw that feminist crap at me, Delacroix." Chastian stood up, got in her face. "This guy kills women, not men. And you are definitely a woman." He waved the photos around. "On top of that, he's obsessed enough with you that he's sneaking around a stranger's backyard to get naked pictures of you. I don't see any of Torres in this pile, do you?"

She gritted her teeth to keep from saying something she'd regret, especially since for once Chastian was actually making sense. "I still don't think a leave of absence is the way to solve that problem."

"Yes, well, that's not actually your call to make."

"Since when? I'm the one who has to put in for the time off."

"Genevieve." Alarm coursed through her as Chastian used her first name for the first time in three years. "You have a choice. Put in for time off or I'll suspend you."

Shock reverberated through her and she gasped, outraged. "Because of a few pictures that had no business being taken?"

"Because I'm trying to protect you!"

"Sir, with all due respect, I find that very hard to believe. You've gone out of your way to make my life difficult ever since I was assigned to your squad. Your concern now is more than just unexpected. In my opinion, it's also suspect."

"Delacroix!" he growled.

"You don't have the right to suspend me because of something I do in my personal time that has nothing to do with this office."

"Maybe not. But this deals directly with this office, doesn't it?" His voice was sharper now, angrier. "The same man you're investigating, the same one who is killing women in my jurisdiction, took these pictures of you."

"Allegedly."

"Don't go there! We both know he did."

"What we know and what we can prove are two different things." She mimicked the words he'd used a few days before on her and could tell her words hit home with him in the most unpleasant manner possible. "And we both know that if this was Shawn being threatened, you'd expect him to suck it up and soldier on. Why should it be any different for me?"

"Because whether or not you and I see eye to eye on anything, the idea of walking into a hotel room and seeing you with your heart cut out and your body massacred is the kind of thought that keeps me up at night. And if you want to call that sexist, go ahead. But the fact of the matter is, this shit isn't happening to men. It's happening to women, and I don't really give a shit if that offends your feminist sensibilities."

His eyes said she had already lost, but she couldn't resist trying to negotiate a truce. "Three more days—if I can't get something together in three more days, I'll take a leave of absence."

"I'm not bargaining with you, Delacroix. I don't want one of my detectives turning up dead in the middle of the Quarter."

"This is my case. These are my bodies—justice for them is on me."

"It's on all of us."

"No, it's not, and you know it."

Chastian's fist hit the desk and he cursed roundly. But Genevieve relaxed because she knew she'd won the battle. The war, however, was another matter entirely.

"I'll give you two days. And you stick close to Webster or one of the other guys. And don't give me any of your bullshit, either. Working with a partner is SOP and you *will* follow the rules or you *will* be out. And it will be a cold day in hell before I let you back into my squad. Do I make myself perfectly clear?"

"Yes. Sir."

"Then get back to work and don't get dead."

"I'll try my best."

He snorted. "Forgive me if I'm not reassured."

Genevieve walked to the door, paused when he called her name.

"I don't really care what you do in your free time, but I don't want these photos getting out. If they were made public, it would be an embarrassment to both you and this department, and that I will not put up with. Do I make myself clear?"

She kept her eyes down, unable to look at him as shame coursed through her. He was right—if these pictures got out, the press would have a field day. "Yes, sir." What went without saying, however, was that it might already be too late. If Chastian had the photos, God only knew who else the sick fuck had given them to.

Her stomach clenched into knots at the thought.

What was she going to do? How the hell was she supposed to deal with Chastian and the evidence clerk and God only knew who else had seen such intimate photos of her?

"Hey," Shawn called as she walked back to her desk. "What'd Chastian want?"

"Just info on the murders," she said with a shrug.

"Without me?"

Guilt swamped her—she'd never lied to her partner before, had always made a point of being scrupulously honest with him. Knew that he felt the same way. But how could she tell him what was really going on? That Chastian knew was bad enough. If Shawn knew, she might as well be suspended, because she'd never be able to raise her head in here again.

Finally settling on a half-truth, she told him, "He wants me to take a vacation. Get me out of the killer's line of sight."

She waited for Shawn to explode, to tell her what an idiot Chastian was for even suggesting it. Instead, he merely regarded her thoughtfully. "That's not such a bad idea, you know."

"What?"

He shrugged. "This guy is gunning for you. Maybe if you weren't around—"

"Shut up! Shut up, shut up, shut up!" She held her hands over her ears. "If I have to hear one more man tell me to run and hide, I swear I'll scream."

"I think you already did that." Torres walked up behind her, carrying a bunch of roses.

"These came for you—they were at the front desk, and I said I'd bring them back to you."

Her breath caught in her throat as she stared at the hot pink roses. They didn't seem like something Cole would send, but the alternative was something she didn't even want to think about.

Reaching for the card, she felt relief swamp her as she read what it said. *Thanks for Wednesday. I miss you. Tonight?* The flowers might not have been to her taste, but at least they were from Cole. Considering what had happened earlier, it was a huge relief.

She looked up to find the others staring at her, their faces so grim that they must have been fearing exactly what she had. "They're not from him," she said, slipping the card into her pocket.

"You're sure?" Torres demanded.

"Yes."

Shawn blew out a sigh of relief. "Well, thank God for small favors."

"Yeah, no shit. Now, can we get to work, please?" Turning to the murder board, she stared at the newly tacked up pictures of Maria. "What's the connection? Why these women in a city full of women and tourists?"

"There doesn't seem to be one," Luc commented.

"There has to be." She tapped a finger on Maria's photo. "We find the connection and we'll find him. I guarantee it."

"You know I thought this was a bad idea from the very beginning, Cole. You can't actually expect yourself to be able to produce a decent documentary with the stress you're under."

"I'm fine, Andrew." Cole pushed away from the computer where he'd spent the better part of the last twelve hours trying to write the script for the documentary that had started this whole odyssey to New Orleans, and tried to focus on what his agent was saying. It was hard, when half his mind was wrapped up in the script and the other half was stuck on Genevieve, wondering if she was okay. Wondering why she hadn't called.

"You don't actually expect me to believe that, do you?"

"I don't really care what you believe at this point. But if you expect a workable screenplay, you need to leave me alone and let me write the damn thing!"

There was a long silence. "You're lucky I know you as well as I do, man. Another agent might take offense."

"Bite me."

"I'd rather not. You're poison mean. God only knows what I might catch."

Cole smiled despite himself. Andrew had been his agent for nine years—well over a year before Samantha had disappeared—and was pretty much the only person still in his life who knew what had made him the way he was. He was a hell of an agent—absolutely cutthroat—and was also the best friend Cole had ever had.

"I'm mellowing in my old age. Didn't you catch the article in *People*?"

Andrew snorted. "Compared to what? A nuclear bomb?"

Cole laughed. "I think I resent that."

"You delicate artist types. You never can take the truth."

"Screw you."

"Sorry, buddy. Lisa might get upset—she's pretty prickly about this whole fidelity thing."

"I can imagine."

Andrew cleared his throat, as if he was working up to something. Then mumbled, "So, have you made any progress? You know, on Samantha?"

Cole's heart dropped to his stomach. He'd known the question was coming, had heard the concern in Andrew's voice the second he'd picked up the phone. But what could he say? That he was sleeping with the cop he'd handpicked to help him solve the case? That he hadn't even asked her about Samantha's death because he was afraid of messing things up with Genevieve?

Or should he mention the guy currently cutting up women in this godforsaken town? And how eerily close his MO seemed to be to the bastard's who had killed Samantha?

In the end, he didn't say any of it, couldn't say it—even to his best friend. Instead, he cleared his own throat. Answered, "I don't know. Everything's completely fucked up down here."

"Isn't it always? That city's never been good for you."

He thought of Genevieve and the trust she'd put in him despite the odds. "It's not all bad."

"Do you need some help? I can hop a plane—"

"Thanks, Andrew. Really. I'm okay, just frustrated as shit."

"Come home, back to L.A. It's a balmy seventy-eight degrees here and everything is looking beautiful. That heat down there fries your brain cells, makes it impossible to think."

"I don't think it's the heat."

There was a long pause. "Yeah. Maybe not."

"Look, I'll call you in a few days. By then I'll have a better idea if the script is working or not."

"Great. And in the meantime, seriously. I can be there in, like, five hours."

"I'm solid. Really."

He hung up the phone a few minutes later, though he didn't immediately get back to work. He couldn't. Thoughts of Samantha were in his head, but hell, that was nothing unusual. She had haunted him for seven years now, and he had become pretty good at compartmentalizing so that he would work, talk, live around her place in his heart and mind.

But Genevieve—she was something else entirely. She took him over, drove almost everything from his head but the need to see her, to talk to her, to be inside her until everything faded away—even his past.

What is she doing now? he wondered. His kick-ass cop with the soft, vulnerable center. What was he supposed to do with her?

What was he supposed to do without her?

Just the thought had his stomach rolling, his fists clenching. No other woman had ever gotten under his skin like this. No other woman had ever touched him so deeply or made him feel so much. He wanted to resent her for it—and the attachment he was forming for her—but he couldn't.

Their relationship was inconvenient, tempestuous, and hotter than hell. It was also more important to him than he could have dreamed possible even two weeks before. With her sassy mouth, deep thoughts and hotter-than-hell body, Genevieve fit him. She made him whole in a way he'd never imagined, in a way he hadn't known he could be after Samantha.

She hadn't replaced his sister in his heart, nor had she made him any less determined to find Samantha's killer. But knowing Genevieve, being with her, had somehow lessened the pain. Had made it easier for him to face each day, when before, getting out of bed to a world without Samantha in it had been unbearably difficult.

Leaning forward, Cole pressed a few computer keys and pulled up the statistics on New Orleans violence. Before Katrina, they had finally made some progress in lowering the homicide rate in the city, but now it was higher than it had ever been—higher than D.C. and Philadelphia, even Compton.

He was building his documentary around it—that even with half its population missing, New Orleans was a city where violence was endemic. Why? What made the dark and deadly so seductive when the motto of the place was *Laissez les bon temps rouler*? Let the good times roll.

The city wasn't having a good time anymore. Oh, the tourists showed up and drank themselves stupid, claimed to be having a blast. But there was something missing in the frivolity—a lightheartedness that had once gone hand in hand with partying in the Big Easy. Like the ladies of the night that she was once known for, New Orleans was beautiful at night, as the stars sparkled against the darkness. In the cold light of day, she just looked cheap and used.

Maybe it was him. He no longer had a lighthearted bone in his body, so perhaps he couldn't see the fun anymore. He thought back to the empty-eyed people he'd seen the other night on Bourbon Street, to the kids who hung out on Decatur near Café du Monde and tried so desperately to be something they weren't. To the women dying such painful, senseless deaths.

No, something was missing from this city now; there was no disputing it. The question was whether it had always been missing. If he found out that answer, he'd have the documentary he and the studio were looking for.

But he couldn't do any more tonight; his brain was fried, his body hot and hard and craving Genevieve. He hadn't bothered her since he'd dropped her off at the Hotel Monteleone a few nights before, had known she'd be immersed in the investigation.

But he wanted to see her, was . . . lonely, if he admitted the truth. For a man who had never needed anything but his own company, it was a hell of an admission.

Screw it. He picked up the phone, dialed Genevieve's cell. The worst she could tell him was to go to hell.

"Delacroix." Her voice—clipped and soft and oh, so exhausted—trailed languorous fingers down his spine. Had his arousal ratcheting up a notch, as well as his need to see her. To take care of her.

"Hey, sweetheart. How are you?"

"Cole." Her voice warmed up instantly, sent a softness spiraling through him that he didn't recognize.

"I miss you." He didn't know where the words had come from, but they felt right.

"God, I miss you too." Her voice caught on what sounded like a sob.

His body went on red alert. Eyes narrowed, breathing shallow, he demanded, "What's wrong? What has you so upset?"

There was a long pause, then a watery laugh. "It's just been a really long day. And it's not done yet."

"Come to me."

Another laugh, sadder than the first. "Oh, God, I can't. I'm stuck here, running out of time, and I have so much more to sort through."

"You're exhausted." It wasn't a question.

"Yes, but I've been tired before. Will be again."

He gritted his teeth, fought against the urge to head to the station and demand that she get some rest. "Come to me," he said again.

"Cole . . ."

She sounded too weary to argue, and that was when alarm and guilt really took hold of him. She was drained—emotionally and physically. He was part of what had drained her, he knew that, and hated that he'd contributed to the sad, broken tears he knew she was fighting so hard to keep inside.

"When you're done—whatever time that is—come to me. Let me take care of you. I'll be waiting." It was a request, not an order, and he held his breath as he waited for her answer.

Another long pause, another shuddering breath. "Okay."

It was a sigh so soft he had to strain to hear it, but it was enough. "I'll see you soon, sweetheart."

"See you . . . soon." Then she hung up, leaving him staring at the phone and fighting the need to go get her and bring her back here with him.

He glanced at the clock—ten thirty—and headed to the kitchen. She wouldn't be here until after midnight; he was sure of it. But still, she deserved a home-cooked meal, a little pampering. And to his everlasting surprise, he was just the man to give them to her.

Chapter Seventeen

For the second time in less than a week, Genevieve stood staring up at Cole's house on St. Charles. This time, however, she wasn't nervous or aroused or any of the other excited emotions that had rioted through her three days ago. Today, she was exhausted—mentally and physically drained—and it was taking all her concentration just to think about climbing the impressive row of steps up to his house.

With an effort born from willpower alone, she put a foot on the bottom step and pressed up. Only twelve more to go.

But the front door flew open before she could try to take the second step, and then Cole was rushing down the stairs. Hauling her into his arms and carrying her the rest of the way into his house.

As he carried her through the foyer, the large grandfather clock near the door clanged once. *Shit,* she thought, laying her weary head on Cole's broad shoulder. It was one o'clock—almost seventy-two hours since Cole had dropped her off at the latest crime scene. How had the days passed in such a blur?

"I can walk," she said, struggling to push against him. It was ridiculous, really, to head to her lover's house when it was too much effort to keep her eyes open, let alone make love to him.

But she'd been so sad, so tired, so fucked up when he'd called, that she hadn't been able to resist his order to come to him when she wrapped up what she was working on. It was a frightening thought—this urge for comfort, for the peace she had been able only to find with Cole, despite the doubt and confusion that had marked so much of their short time together.

He snorted. "I can tell." His steps never faltered as he led her down the hallway to his bedroom. Then he was laying her gently on the bed with the soft command "Don't go to sleep yet."

She watched him walk away, wondered how long it would be before he walked away permanently, when he realized he couldn't protect her any more than he had protected his sister. And fought the urge to weep.

She was no closer to finding the killer, no closer to saving her job. Chastian had spent the rest of the day looking at her like she was a cross between a hooker and an alien, while Torres had skulked after her when she left the station. He didn't think she'd seen him. But she knew when she was being followed. What she couldn't understand—and at that point was too tired to care about—was why.

Cole came back into the bedroom and she blinked away the exhausted tears. He'd already seen her cry twice—which was two times more than she usually did. She'd be damned if she did it again.

He started to undress her, slipping off her work shoes, followed by her pants and blouse. But when he reached for her underwear, she laid a soft hand on his. "I don't know how good I'll be tonight. I'm sorry. I should have just gone home."

The curse that split the air was vile, even for Cole. And then he was ripping her panties and bra off her before divesting himself of his clothes almost as quickly. "Is that what you think of me?" he demanded. "That I would force sex on you when you're nearly catatonic?"

He picked her up, headed into the bathroom. "You don't think very highly of me, do you?"

"It's not—" She struggled to lift her head from where it was pillowed on his chest.

"Ssh, don't talk now. Just let me take care of you."

And then he was stepping into the shower, letting hot water cascade over her from all directions. "Can you stand?" he asked, sliding her slowly down his body.

"Of course I can stand!" She tried to be outraged at the suggestion of her weakness, but as soon as her feet hit the floor, she swayed alarmingly.

Cole cursed again, then settled her on the long bench that ran the length of the shower. Turned the various jets so that they were flowing over her from neck to ankles. "Let's just try this, shall we?"

Her eyes were closed, her head resting against the shower wall as Cole slid soapy hands over her shoulders and down her arms. He was so sweet, his fingers so gentle as they glided over her breasts and stomach, that she had trouble reconciling him with the man who had strapped her to his bed and pushed her body harder than it had ever been pushed before.

As his fingers glanced over her mons before moving between her legs, she felt a flicker of response. Amazing. How could she want him when her body was half-dead, maybe more?

In that moment, when she was so exhausted she could barely hold her head up, she saw their entire relationship as it flashed before her eyes. She saw it, and with one shuddering breath, slipped helplessly over the edge of lust into love.

It wasn't a bad fall, as she'd always imagined it would be. Nor was it terrifying or any of the other things she'd always assumed giving control of her body to another would mean.

With Cole it felt right. Natural. As right as his hands caressing every part of her, as perfect as his eyes lingering on each sweet spot she had.

The words trembled on her lips, the need to share with him what she'd only just discovered nearly overwhelming. But she was beginning to know Cole, to understand how he worked. And she was smart enough to understand that he could not accept how she felt about him—not yet. Whatever his demons were, they were riding him hard. All she could do was hang on and hope to somehow, some way, gentle him into returning her feelings.

With this newfound knowledge burning inside of her, Genevieve felt the body she'd thought too tired to function begin to respond to Cole's tender ministrations.

Arching her hips, she moaned a little, but he ignored the signs. Instead he rinsed the soap from her body slowly, letting the hot water ease aches and pains she hadn't even known were there.

He leaned forward, moving the hand-held shower head up so that water cascaded over first one shoulder and then the other. Little rivulets ran over her breasts, down her stomach, and she arched her back, enjoying the sensual warmth of the water as it touched every part of her.

Soon, too soon, he turned off the water and wrapped her in a huge black towel. She was in a daze, so tired that she could barely hold her head up, so disconsolate that she wanted to crawl into bed and pull the sheet over her head until she could once again face the world.

Cole's hands were gentle as they dried the water from her; gentler still as he carried her back to his bed. After crossing to his dresser and yanking out a huge T-shirt, he pulled it over her head and then slipped her between the covers.

"Cole?" she asked, her hands reaching for him despite the exhaustion.

"Sleep, sweetheart."

"Don't leave me." Her hand clutched at his and she curled herself around it, trying desperately to hold him to her. If she'd been more aware, such neediness would have appalled her. As it was, all she knew was that she didn't want to be alone. Would pull into a ball and sob if Cole left her after taking such sweet care of her.

"I'm right here, Genevieve. I'm not going anywhere."

He climbed into the bed beside her, pulling her into his chest. His warmth seeped into her, and she sighed as she rested her head on his chest, heard his heart beating steadily beneath her ear. She drifted to sleep feeling safer than she ever had before.

Cole smiled as he watched Genevieve sleep, trailed a finger over her high cheekbones and across that lush, relaxed mouth. She looked like hell—dark circles beneath her eyes, tension drawing her skin tight across her forehead and cheekbones, even in sleep. But she was still the most beautiful thing he'd ever seen, this woman who wore herself to exhaustion and beyond in her quest for justice.

She'd say it was her job, and maybe it was, but for Genevieve it was a calling, one she took incredibly seriously. Even if she weren't beautiful and intelligent and the most exciting lover he'd ever had, he would still be intrigued by her, simply because of the way she fought for her victims. For their families. Her raw, unadulterated, uncompromising view of right and wrong—of justice and injustice—appealed to a man who had been forced to see the world in too many shades of gray for much too long.

He brushed his lips over her crazy curls, careful not to wake her despite his need to keep touching her. To feel her against him. To know that she was here, with him, safe in a world that was anything but.

If he'd held Samantha closer, had forced her to— He cut off abruptly, unwilling to take that train of thought any further. Not now, when Genevieve's body was curled so trustingly against his. Not tonight, when his emotions and fears were much too close to the surface.

He squashed a momentary longing for the bottle of tequila in the next room. He'd relied too heavily on the clear liquor since he'd gotten to this godforsaken city, and enough was enough. If he couldn't deal with his problems, couldn't control what was happening now and what had happened seven years before, then what good was he? As a director or a man?

He didn't know how long he lay there like that, watching Genevieve. Winding her curls around his fingers in an effort to hold her to him. Touching her just to reassure himself that she was still alive, still with him.

But dawn was streaking the sky outside his windows before she stirred. He didn't move for long seconds, hoping that she wouldn't wake up. She needed to sleep so badly, needed to heal her tired body and wounded psyche with a little time away from her responsibilities. From the case.

His caution was for nothing, though, as her beautiful sapphire eyes blinked open. She stared at him owlishly for a moment, confusion evident on her beautiful features. He knew the exact moment she realized where she was and how she'd gotten there—a warm, becoming flush crept up from beneath his T-shirt to cover her neck and cheeks.

"Hi there." He tightened his arms around her as he whispered the words, so that she was snuggled—full-length—against him.

"Hi yourself." Her voice was husky with sleep and so sexy he felt the semi-hard-on he'd been ignoring for hours twitch in reaction, growing fuller.

"Go back to sleep." He kissed her eyes, trailed his lips over her soft pink cheeks. "You need more rest."

"I need you." She shifted so that her legs tangled with his and her pelvis was pressed against his suddenly throbbing cock. "Make love to me, Cole. Please."

He stared at her for a long moment, tried to convince himself to leave her alone. To let her get the rest she so desperately needed. But she was wiggling and squirming, her nipples growing hard against his chest, her pussy radiating a heat that called to him.

Telling himself to be gentle with her, he pulled her shirt off, then feathered a trail of kisses from the hollow of her throat to her belly button. His tongue darted out, licked the intriguing lines of her tattoo again and again, until he felt her quiver beneath him, her body softening just a little bit more.

Reaching up, he ran his thumb over and around her nipples. They were diamond hard and so sensitive that each brush of his hand against them had her sucking in her breath and arching her back for a harder pressure.

Licking his way up her body, he stopped at her breasts. Drew her nipple into his mouth and suckled gently. She cried out, buried her hands in his hair, and he reveled in the feel of her fingers on his scalp. She tasted amazing—like the sweetest honey, the softest lavender—and he couldn't get enough of her.

Inhaling deeply, he took her scent into his lungs, loved that the candy sweetness of her was mixed with the wild scent of his own soap. She smelled like him, and that mark of possession, that primitive proof that she belonged to him, lit him up like a rocket. Tightening his arms around her, he rolled until she was above him—her legs straddling him, her hot pussy resting against his dick.

She gasped, her blue eyes darkening to black as she moved her hips gently against him. Rocked until he slipped between the moist folds of her sex, the head of his cock just touching her clit.

He groaned, fisted his hands in her hair and fought for control. How could he lose it so quickly? How could she steal it so easily when he'd been determined to take her with the sweetness and gentleness that he'd previously neglected to give her?

Biting his lip, tamping down on the raging inferno that was his body, he smoothed his hands down her back. Savored the silkiness of her skin, the warm softness of her body. No one had ever touched him the way Genevieve did so effortlessly.

Keeping his eyes locked with hers, he skimmed his hands over her ass, around her hips and up her stomach to her breasts. Cupping the sweet weights in his hands, he rubbed his thumb in small circles on the undersides of her breasts.

"Cole." It was a whisper of sound, a plea for more, but he refused to be rushed. Today, he would savor her, so that when she went back to her hellish job, she would know just what she meant to him.

"Let me love you, Genevieve. No games, no control—just you and me and everything we can give each other."

She bit her lip and her eyes darkened even more as she looked at him. He could see the wariness there, the need to give herself to him but also the desire to keep her battered spirit safe.

He slid his hands up her torso to her face, cupped her jaw in his palms. "I won't hurt you, sweetheart. I already told you that. Trust me to do what's right for you. What's right for us."

He sensed her disquiet, felt her holding her breath as surely as she held him between her thighs. And when she finally nodded, her long, loose curls flowing over her shoulders and breasts in a cascade of gold, he felt his heart melt in his chest.

"I'll make it good for you, Genevieve." He nuzzled her breast, traced patterns on the delicate skin. "I swear I will."

She laughed, the sound low and husky and amazingly feminine. "You always make it good for me."

And then she lowered her mouth to his, caught his lower lip between her teeth and tugged softly, sliding the tip of her tongue over the outside of it before moving slowly, teasingly, over the slickness of the soft inner flesh.

He felt the caress through his whole body, from the soles of his feet and the palms of his hands to his balls, which were already threatening to explode. His hands tightened in her hair, and she laughed.

He took advantage of her open mouth, slipped his tongue inside to tangle with her own. As her teeth parted, he tilted her head so that she was wide open to him, until no part of her mouth was unavailable to his hot, hungry quest.

He slid his tongue beneath her upper lip, played with the soft skin. Relished the moan the little caress drew from her before wrapping his tongue around hers and sucking softly.

She gasped, and he felt her sex grow wetter, hotter against his cock. His hips jerked before he could control them, and his eyes nearly crossed as her legs tightened around him reflexively.

She was so turned on, her body pliant and his for the taking. Part of him wanted to shove her onto her back and thrust inside of her until they were both sweating, both screaming. Both coming.

But that was how he always took her—pushing her to take everything she could. Straining the boundaries of her experience and experimental nature until she took everything he wanted to give her, until she gave all that she was to him.

Today, he wanted to give himself to her. To love her without the tricks and the toys and the walls he'd kept between them until now.

But taking it slow was the hardest thing he'd ever done, when his body was on fire for her, his cock screaming for the chance to slip inside her slick warmth and ride her until ecstasy took them both.

Control, he told himself, as he took her mouth in another soul-searing kiss. Control was the ticket.

Cole had lost his mind, was doing his best to make her lose hers. Genevieve cried out as he nibbled at her lips, his tongue sweeping over and around and inside her lips until she was ready to scream with frustration.

What was he waiting for? How much hotter did she have to be?

Already, her body was trembling, electrified, every nerve ending she had calling out to him, yet he refused to take her. Instead, he kept his mouth on hers, tasting and teasing until she was nearly mad with desire.

"Cole, I need you," she gasped, rocking her hips against his hard cock. He felt so good, so amazingly, heart-wrenchingly good, that she was close to climaxing just from the occasional, glancing caress of his tip against her aching clit.

At that moment, sunlight filtered into the room through the half-open shutters. For a moment, she was dazzled by the play of sun over Cole's strong golden torso, enthralled by each shift and ripple of his muscles.

But then common sense kicked in and she yelped, jumping off Cole as if she'd been burned. His hands were still tangled in her hair and it tugged as she moved away from him, but even that didn't slow her down as she raced across the room.

"Genevieve?" He sat up in bed, stared at her with confused eyes. "What's going on?"

"The shutters. I need to close—" Her voice broke as she rushed from window to window as fast as she could, slamming each shutter closed until the room was once again blanketed by darkness.

Only then did she stop, her back to him as she tried to get control of the panic racing through her system. How could she be so stupid—again? Wasn't once enough of a humiliation?

Horrified, panicked, she tried desperately to remember what had happened after she'd gotten to Cole's a few hours before. They hadn't made love—she'd been too zonked for that—but he had undressed her, showered her, carried her, naked, to his bed.

For a brief moment she thought back to Torres, who had followed her out of the station and through the Quarter. Had he stuck around to see her climb in her car, or had he left once she was safely indoors? Had he been following her to keep her safe, or for some other, nefarious reason?

Luc, Shawn, Chastian, Jefferson, Jose—their faces swam through her head until Genevieve worried she might actually go insane. What was she thinking? They were cops, all of them. Her friends and partners, even her boss. There was no way any of them would do this to her. No way one of them could be this sadistic and manage to hide it so well. She was simply letting paranoia get the better of her.

"Hey, earth to Genevieve." Cole's hands landed heavily on her shoulders, and then he was turning her to face him. "You want to tell me what the hell that was all about?"

"No." Her voice was rusty to her own ears. "I really don't."

"Let me rephrase that." He strode over to the bed, pulling her behind him with a hand around her wrist. "I want to know what that was about. Now."

He switched on his bedside lamp and a soft puddle of light chased away the last vestiges of night. If only he could do the same for the darkness invading her soul. But he couldn't. She smiled sadly. He was just a man—one who spent most of his own life in the shadows. It was unfair of her to ask him to take on her ghosts as well.

"I freaked out." She shrugged, tried to play it off. "I'm sorry—I've got an overdeveloped sense of paranoia. Sometimes it gets the best of me."

The look he gave her was patently disbelieving. "You are the least paranoid person I know."

She snorted. "Don't bet on that."

"Why are you lying to me?" His voice was curiously devoid of the anger she'd expected, and when she finally met his eyes, they were completely blank. As if he'd gone inside himself and nothing she said was going to be able to reach him.

Fear, ice-cold and vicious, whipped through her. *Not Cole too*, a little voice whispered in the back of her head. She was on the brink of losing another victim, her job, and the respect of her colleagues. She couldn't lose Cole too, not when she'd just begun to figure out what he meant to her.

Too humiliated to tell him what was really going on, too frightened not to try to smooth things over, she finally said, "It's work stuff, Cole. Can we leave it at that?"

"You think that sick bastard is following you? That he's out there right now?"

He pulled her into his chest, held her tightly for one long inhalation, then shoved her behind him. He crossed the room in three strides and threw open the patio doors before she could stop him.

His eyes—dark and hyperalert—scanned the backyard, and she knew he didn't miss anything in the early-morning light. But when he strode outside, stark naked, she grabbed a blanket and clambered after him. "Cole, get in here! You can't go out like that."

He didn't even acknowledge that she had spoken, and she knew he wouldn't until he was well and truly satisfied. Time dragged as he walked his backyard, looking behind every tree and bench.

When he finally came back in, he was grim-faced and intense. Slamming the door behind him, he made sure the shutters were completely closed. Then he turned to face her, fury in every controlled line of his body.

Chapter Eighteen

"Tell me." Cole's voice was cold, his eyes colder as he watched her intently.

"It's nothing."

"He's messing with you. That sick son of a bitch is hassling you, and you tell me it's nothing?" His hands clenched into fists. "Worse, you don't even tell me at all."

"It's not like that."

"No?" He stalked toward her, every inch the sleek, sinuous jungle cat she'd thought him at their first meeting. And every inch as deadly. "Then what is it like?"

There was a desert in her mouth, and no matter how hard Genevieve tried to form words, nothing came out but a dry, dusty croak. Shaking her head, she backed hastily away. She'd never seen Cole like this before—he was all predator, all strong male animal on the hunt. And though it was nerve-racking in the extreme to be the focus of all that hostile male energy, it was also arousing as hell.

He stopped mere inches from her, his huge body crowding her from every side. "I'm waiting, Genevieve."

The impatience in his tone set her free, got her back up and her mouth working before she could consider the wisdom of blowing him off. "Back off, Cole! I'm not some plaything to be backed into a corner by the big, hungry cat."

His eyes swept down her nude, trembling body. "I never said you were. But you will tell me what's going on."

"And if I don't?" She raised her chin, glared at him with narrow eyes.

"That's not an option."

Before she could so much as tell him to go to hell, he'd reached out and grabbed her. Yanked her against him. Lowered his mouth to hers in a kiss that was both brand and punishment.

Heat exploded instantly. Hot. Basic. Elemental. It flashed between them, through them, burned them from the inside out and then set fire to the room around them until nothing mattered but the way they made each other feel.

Maybe she should have pushed him away, should have fought against the possession of the gesture. But she didn't. She couldn't. As caught up as he in the conflagration roaring between them, she chose instead to surrender. To let him take her however he wanted to—however he needed to.

Her body went pliant, the fight leaking out of her as she pressed herself as tightly against him as she could get. Her hands grabbed on to his shoulders and hung on, the need to touch him, to feel his strength under her fingers, a compulsion she couldn't begin to fight.

His arms tightened around her, lifting her onto her tiptoes as his mouth devoured hers. Wild, hungry, desperately searching, he took everything she had to give and demanded more. Demanded everything. And she gave it to him, because she couldn't not give it to him. To herself. Her need was that basic. That deep.

That primal.

Cole tore his mouth from hers and she whimpered, her hands grabbing his head and trying to force his lips back to hers. "Don't stop!" she all but sobbed. "Don't leave me like this."

His only answer was a growl as he picked her up and threw her onto the bed. "I couldn't stop if I wanted to," he said as he climbed on top of her.

His lips closed over her nipple, and she felt the sharp bite of his teeth. She screamed, her back arching as her hands grasped onto his head and pulled him even closer. He nipped again and again, but unlike the other times, refused to soothe the little hurts with his tongue. Instead, he left them to burn, to throb, to make her hotter still.

"Cole!" It was a plea, a demand, a cry for mercy, but she had pushed him too far—her refusal to let him protect her sending him over an edge he hadn't known he was balanced on. All he could think of was branding her, possessing her, making her his in a way she could never dispute.

His cock was throbbing, burning, the need for release so urgent he was afraid he'd lose it before he buried himself inside her. But he had to take care of her, had to hang on until he was inside of her.

"I need you, Genevieve. I need you in a way I don't understand." He panted the words in between sharp little nibbles on her belly and inner thighs. "I need to hold you, to feel your body under mine."

"I'm right here!" It was a high-pitched, keening cry, one filled with need and desperation and something he didn't know how to label. Something he was afraid to label.

"I need you to let me protect you." He sank his teeth into her thigh, savoring the strangled scream that came from her. "Trust me that much."

"I'm the cop," she gasped out, her body trembling wildly beneath his. "I protect myself."

He thrust two fingers into her, hard, and she screamed. He gritted his teeth, willed back the orgasm that rose in him with each clench of her pussy around his fingers. But she was so hot—so goddamned hot—that he would die if he wasn't inside her. Soon.

But first, she needed to understand. He knew she was strong and smart and more than capable of taking care of herself—those were the things that had first attracted him to her. But she was also his woman, and if some bastard dared to lay a hand on her, he would annihilate him.

"If some psychopath is after you, I need to know." He curved his fingers, stroked them over her G spot at the exact moment he closed his lips around her hot, hard little clit.

Her only response was a broken moan as her breath hitched in her throat.

Smiling grimly at the sound, he swirled his tongue around the little bud, using his fingers to spread her labia so that she was wide open for him. Pink and wet and so goddamn beautiful, she drew him in like nothing ever had, captured his soul when it had been lost for far too long. Made him ache in ways he'd never thought possible.

Because he wanted more of her—he wanted all of her—he moved on from her sweet little clit too soon. But it wasn't enough for him, the slow lick and swirl. With a groan, he thrust his tongue inside of her, desperate to taste everything she had to offer. Insane with the need to take her in every way imaginable.

She went wild at the first touch of his tongue inside her, bucking and jerking and arching against him as her hands clenched in his hair. They pulled hard, and he saw stars even as he continued his sensual assault on her hot pussy.

Her juices ran over his tongue like honey and he delved deeper, loving the taste of her. It exploded against his tongue—spicy and sweet and so much like Genevieve herself that it made him crazy. Made him desperate to give her the same overwhelming pleasure she gave him just by existing. The same pleasure that burned through all resistance, all excuses. That flamed brighter and brighter with each encounter, until neither of them knew where one left off and the other began.

He pulled her clit into his mouth and rolled it gently between his teeth. She whimpered, tried to reach for him, but he shifted his hips away from her. One touch of those warm hands and he would go up in flames hotter than the ones currently burning through him.

But he wasn't done yet, nowhere near it. Thrusting his hands under her hips, he lifted her so that she was sitting on him, her beautiful sex positioned directly above his mouth.

He'd wanted to do this since the first time he'd touched her, had wanted her above him so that he could kiss and taste and lick her to orgasm while she moved restlessly against him.

His hands moved around to cup her ass, to stroke and mold and squeeze the sweet flesh before slowly, inexorably, he pushed his thumb in between her soft cheeks. She tightened around him, her whole body going rigid at the unexpected invasion.

"It's okay," he whispered against her sex, loving how she trembled at the vibrations from his breath and the soft little licks of his tongue. "Trust me. I'll take care of you."

He sensed her hesitation, her fear of giving him everything. But he was beyond boundaries, beyond separation. He needed Genevieve, had to know she felt the same way about him.

But her muscles were still tight, her body unsure of this new invasion. To relax her, to loosen her up, he licked along her drenched slit, wiggling and pressing his tongue in all the places he'd learned that she liked.

He felt an orgasm hurtle through her, taking her in one spasming, fiery rush, and suddenly she was completely open to him, her body his to do with what he liked.

Working his thumb a little farther into her, he nearly came at the soft, passionate mewl she couldn't hold back. He could stay like this all day, buried in the incredible sweetness of her. Could go down on her for hours even while desperation and desire hardened his cock almost to the point of madness.

Genevieve whimpered, pressing against Cole because there was no other option. He was driving her crazy, and making it so pleasurable that she didn't care that she was absolutely, no doubt about it, going completely, around-the-bend crazy. Why else would she lie here, putting up with his macho bullshit, his need to dominate her and bend her to his will?

What she should do is tell him to go to hell and storm out, but she couldn't move. Her knees were weak from the out-of-control climax that had just whipped through her, and the need for him was building again. Or still—it never really went away anymore, just grew and grew, burning hotter and brighter than anything she'd ever experienced. Taking over everything but her most basic thought processes.

She shouldn't be enjoying this, shouldn't actually like him telling her what to do. But he felt so good, made her feel so incredible, that she couldn't fight him. Not when his mouth was on her pussy and his finger in her ass.

"I need to touch you too," she gasped, her hands reaching behind her to work their way over his heavily muscled chest to his cock. Wrapping her fingers around him, she slid her palm back and forth over the satiny skin, triumph whipping through her as he groaned and thrust helplessly against her.

He felt so good, better than anything in her life ever had. His mouth on her pussy, his cock in her hand; she wished she could stay like this forever. But even as the thought occurred, she knew it was wrong, knew that she wanted more from him.

She wanted everything he could give her, everything he had inside him. But if she couldn't have that, she would take all of him she could get.

Turning, careful not to dislodge him from the wicked, wonderful things he was doing to her body, she wiggled her way down the bed, until her lips were level with his cock. And then she took him in her mouth, relishing the salty hardness of him against her tongue.

He groaned against her, the vibrations sending currents of electricity through her whole body, and it took all her concentration to remember where she was, to remember what she was doing.

Tucking the head of his cock against the top of her mouth, she used her tongue to swirl around his hard length, relishing the near yell the move pulled from him.

It took all of her self-control to keep from coming—again—but she somehow managed to hold back the climax. Instead, she concentrated on him and making him as crazy for her as she so obviously was for him.

She took his balls gently in her hand, rubbed his tight sac and relished the tremors that shot through him at the movement. She loved everything about his body—how he tasted and smelled and felt. Pulling him deeper into her mouth—taking him all the way—she savored the wild ocean taste lingering on her tongue.

She'd never done this before, never imagined how unbelievable it could be to take a guy all the way down her throat as he took her with his tongue and teeth and lips. Every nerve ending she had was on fire, electrified by how unbelievably good it felt to let Cole love her.

When he increased the pressure of his tongue, sweeping it faster and harder against her clit, she gasped and moved her hips faster and faster against him. He did the same, his body instinctively tuned to the rhythm of hers. Moans and strangled screams filled the air, and she was so lost in sensation—drowning in it, really—that she didn't know which of them had made the noises.

He thrust two fingers inside of her, and it was too much. His fingers in her sex, his tongue on her clit, his thumb pressing slowly into her from behind—she was no longer in control of her body. He had claimed her, taken her over, made her his in a way she'd never before imagined.

Sensation rose sharply within her, orgasm threatening with each flick of his tongue. But she was determined to take him with her, desperate to give him the same ecstasy he so generously gave to her.

Reaching under his balls, she touched his most sensitive spot. Pressed her fingers firmly against it at the same time she ran her tongue over and around his cock. He exploded, and with a shout that was her name poured himself into her mouth in long, uncontrolled bursts that sent her hurtling into her own climax.

It was the longest, most intense orgasm of her life, and as he emptied himself into her, his hips thrusting repeatedly against her mouth, she hoped it was the same for Cole. No matter how dominating or controlling he was, he'd given her more in a week than all the other men in her life had given her put together. It was just one more thing to be grateful for.

When the tremors finally stopped and her body was once again her own, she collapsed on the bed. Cole groaned, but shifted so that his head was buried in her breasts, his hands tangled with hers.

She wasn't sure what had happened here between them, knew nothing had been decided in their fight, but still she couldn't let him go. It was as if this latest lovemaking had bonded them together, made them one person instead of two. And she vowed, in the quiet aftermath, that whatever he asked of her, she would be as honest as she knew how to be.

But he didn't say a word for a long time, just held her and worshipped her with soft brushes of his mouth and tongue and fingers against her skin. And when he finally moved, rolling to the side of the bed, she protested with clenched arms around his middle.

He merely laughed, then pulled out a long, black velvet jeweler's case. "I still want to talk about what happened earlier—"

"Cole—"

He stopped her with a hand over her mouth and a tongue in her ear. "Argue with me later. For now, I just want to know if you like it." He flipped open the box lid, showed her the most stunning piece of jewelry she'd ever seen. Made of twisted lengths of platinum, it was shorter than the average necklace, but, she knew, more than adequate to fit around her slender neck. Attached to it was a gleaming sapphire the size of a robin's egg.

"It's beautiful," she said, touching it with delicate fingers. "I've never seen anything quite like it."

"It made me think of you." He lifted the ropelike chain from the box and said, "Here, let me put it on you."

She lifted her hair out of the way and waited, heart trembling in her chest as he fitted the chain around her neck and worked the clasp. He was so close, his masculine power so potent, that she was all but overwhelmed by him. He dropped a kiss on her neck, trailed his tongue along her nape, and she shuddered, desire rising, sharp and unbelievable.

"Let me see." His voice was husky, and when he turned her to face him, she saw evidence of his own arousal in his dark ebony eyes, eyes that grew even darker as he looked at his chain around her neck.

And that's when she knew: It was more than a gift, more than a beautiful memento of their time together. She touched the necklace with trembling fingers, felt the ropelike quality of the platinum. It was a brand, a mark of possession, a claiming of her that could not be denied.

"Cole . . ." Her voice trailed off as she realized she had no idea what to say. Finally, unable to think of anything that was as profound as the look in his eyes as he watched her, she settled for a soft "Thank you. I love it."

"Don't thank me. I like seeing you in something that I bought you."

Unbelievably, she blushed. "I like wearing something that you gave me." Closing her eyes, she rested her head against his chest, tried to savor these last few moments she had with him. The day was starting— she could hear traffic picking up on St. Charles, could see the sun getting brighter behind the closed shutters. Soon she'd have to head to work and face everything she'd been so desperate to forget.

His hands tangled in her hair, massaged her scalp for long moments. Relaxed and more sleepy than she had a right to be, she murmured, "I never thanked you for the flowers. They were beautiful."

She felt him stiffen under her, his chest going rigid beneath her ear. "I didn't send you flowers."

Alarm exploded in her as she shoved into a sitting position. "The roses weren't from you?"

"No." He shook his head slowly, his eyes dark with concern and concentration. "I would have sent honeysuckle."

"Shit." Her mind was already racing, drawing conclusions that made her more than uneasy. "Then I have a very big problem."

Chapter Nineteen

Genevieve hit the station door at a dead run. On some level, she was conscious of Cole pounding down the hallway beside her, but she was totally focused on getting to her desk—and the flowers. Never had the squad room seemed so far away.

Maybe she was jumping to conclusions, but she was afraid that that just wasn't the case. Cole was the only one who should have sent her flowers—if he hadn't done it, then there was a mistake. Or the killer had upped the ante in the sick and twisted game he was playing with her.

Based on everything he'd pulled so far, she had the very sick feeling that it was the latter.

"Hey, Delacroix, where's the fire?" asked Bryce, one of the vice cops she traded information with, as she nearly mowed him over.

"On my desk." But she slowed to a fast walk, aware of the strange looks she and Cole were getting as they crossed the bull pen. Most of the detectives hadn't arrived yet, but a few were around—and looking at her with concern.

When she got closer to her desk and saw the flowers still sitting there in the pretty butterfly vase, she relaxed a little. Some small part of her had been concerned that she'd missed her shot at them—that they would have disappeared as mysteriously as they'd arrived.

Cole made a choking sound as he looked at the hot pink roses in the too-sweet vase. "You thought I sent you those?" The look he cast her was more than a little appalled. "What are we, twelve?"

She shrugged. "I thought you had singularly bad taste."

"Not *that* bad."

She ignored him, reaching into one of her desk drawers and grabbing a pair of latex gloves out of the box she kept there. It was ridiculous to hope for prints, as the asshole had probably never even touched the vase, while she, the florist, the delivery guy and God only knew who else definitely had.

But procedure was procedure, and if the guy was cocky enough to send the lead detective flowers, he was cocky enough to make a mistake. Picking up the vase, she ran her fingers along the lip of it and under the bottom, not sure what she was looking for.

But the message on the card had been too cryptic, the flowers too obvious. No, there was something with these flowers—she could feel it. Besides, the gesture would be useless if he hadn't included something to taunt her with.

She glanced over at Cole for the first time since entering the station. His expression was puzzled and more than a little grim. In fact, he looked like he wanted nothing more than to smash the vase to bits.

"You run across anything having to do with pink roses in your research?" she demanded as she sat back and continued to study the vase.

"No. Not that I recall."

"Anything about flowers at all?"

"I don't think so."

"So what is this all about, then?"

"I have no idea. But I don't like it."

She glanced at him, grinned. "You just don't like the idea of another man sending me flowers."

"While that is entirely true, I still agree with you that this stinks." He leaned over and sniffed a rose. "I'm just not sure why I feel like that."

"There's got to be something." She traced a finger over the swirls on the vase. "Butterflies, maybe?"

"What's in the vase?"

She glanced at him, startled. "What do you mean?"

"Would he put something—"

"In the water?" She finished the sentence for him. Ripping the flowers out of the vase, she dumped them in the trash can next to her desk, then squinted into the murky depths of the vase. "I can't see anything."

She pushed up her sleeves, reached into the vase and felt around.

"Hey, is that a good idea? You don't know what he put in there—" Cole's voice was low with agitation, and a quick glance revealed how desperate he was to rip the vase out of her hands. But he understood the chain of evidence as well as the next guy, maybe more so, and he hung back, let her do her thing.

Which wasn't much, as all she felt was water and a few leaves. About to give up, she stroked her fingertips softly around the bottom of the vase one more time, and that's when she felt it. Something hard and thin.

Grabbing on to it, she pulled it up and gasped when she got her first real look at it. It was a necklace, nearly identical to the one hanging around her neck, except it had a blue, heart-shaped pendant hanging off it.

Shocked, horrified, she turned to Cole. "I don't know what's real anymore."

As Cole stared at Genevieve and the dripping necklace in her hand, fury wound its way through his gut. Someone was fucking with Genevieve, fucking with him, and he really didn't appreciate it.

How could this be happening? He'd worked his ass off planning his return to New Orleans, making sure that everything was in order. Yet from the moment he'd stepped foot in this damn city, things had gone terribly wrong.

First, he'd been unable to find out anything new about Samantha's case. Then he met Genevieve and realized the glaring error in judgment he'd made when he'd chosen her to help him. And now this—someone laying a trail of evidence that led straight to his door, and threatening his lover while they did it. She might have refused to tell him what her little freak-out had been about that morning, but he wasn't stupid. And he'd be damned if some asshole with a God complex got to torment his woman.

On the bright side, he'd managed to step inside this goddamn building without having a nervous breakdown. The knowledge was cold comfort.

Rage ate at him, the need to find whoever had done this and wrap his hands around the bastard's throat until he was no longer a threat to Genevieve. Until he was no longer a threat to anyone.

"Cole?" Genevieve's voice was hard, brittle. "Do you have any idea what's going on here?"

He shoved a hand through his hair, fought down his rising frustration as best he could. But he was out of his element here, and sinking fast. Even he was smart enough to know that. "I don't know."

"You don't know? That's the best you've got?"

"It's the truth, Genevieve. Whether you believe me or not, I'm telling you the truth."

She stared at him for long seconds, those sapphire eyes missing none of his discomfort or anger, despite his attempt to hide both. Ironic, wasn't it, that the reason he'd bought the stupid pendant was because it had reminded him of her eyes—a clear, dark blue that seemed bottomless? Now those eyes were ripping him apart, trying to dig into the soul he'd given up long before now.

Genevieve shook her head, tried to clear it. But there was too much going on in it for her to think clearly, too many things that just weren't adding up. "I know this guy is nuts; I know he's following me. But how can he follow me and you at the same time? It isn't possible."

He shrugged, his mouth grim. "We're on pretty different schedules—if he's willing to sacrifice some sleep, I can't believe it would be that hard."

Blessedly numb, she reached for the phone. Started to dial forensics, when she realized what time it was. The whole shop was shut down until eight a.m.

So nervous she nearly jumped out of her skin, she picked up the pendant with the hand that was still gloved. Ran a finger over it while her other hand went to the stone even now nestling between her breasts.

The one she was wearing felt different, was heavier than the one in her hand. Reality to perception. Worth to smoke and mirrors. Was that what this guy wanted—her questioning Cole, blaming him for something he couldn't have done?

If so, it was a stupid plan. Because no matter how hard he pushed her, no matter how dangerous he looked, she knew Cole wasn't a killer. At least not like this one was—remorseless, vicious, completely without compassion. She would never be able to reconcile the man who had held her while she sobbed with someone who could rape and butcher a woman.

Besides, his intelligence was formidable. His research and planning were the stuff legends were made of. Would he really be stupid enough to jeopardize his freedom for the momentary rush of pissing her off? Scaring her?

Her gloved finger stroked over something that felt unfamiliar, an imperfection in the pendant that hers definitely lacked. Turning over the magnificent stone, she ran a thumb over the back of it again. So clean and shiny, it was hard to imagine that the imperfections she felt were anything but deliberate.

She opened the top drawer of her desk, started searching for the magnifying glass she kept there. It had been a birthday gift from Shawn last year, a Sherlock Holmes joke she couldn't help but be amused by. Who would have thought it might actually come in handy?

"Genevieve." Cole's voice was harsh as he crouched down next to her desk—next to her—and got in her face. "You can't actually believe that I'm messing with you."

She barely processed what he said. Intent on finding the magnifying glass, on figuring out what those scratches were, she was deep in her head. The fact that it was safer there, harder to get hurt, had nothing to do with it, she told herself. It was just better for her to concentrate on the mystery, on the killer—whoever he was—who suddenly seemed to have her in his sights.

But Cole refused to be ignored. His hands wrapped around her upper arms, squeezed until she had to bite her lip to keep from crying out in pain. But two could play his game, and while she let him have his way in the bedroom, out here was a whole different story.

"Back off, Cole. I don't have time for this right now."

"Well, that's just too damn bad, sweetheart. Because whether time allows or not, we are going to have this out."

"I know it's not you, all right? Of course I do." Her grasping fingers finally closed around the handle of the magnifying glass and she pulled it out in relief. "Now, will you back off already?"

His hand closed over the nape of her neck as he leaned so close their breaths mingled, became one. "Hell, no, I won't back off. Because if you know I didn't send this to you, then you know you've got a bigger problem than you originally thought. Some freak has targeted you, is sending you shit he has no business sending you. And as he seems to have a particular fondness for knives and other instruments of torture, I think I've got a right to be concerned."

"We don't know this is the same guy who's killing those women."

"Don't give me your cop bullshit! Just because you can't prove it doesn't mean it isn't true."

"It doesn't work that way. Assumptions aren't going to get us anywhere."

He sneered. There really was no other expression that could capture the curled lip, the insolent eyes. "You, maybe, with your shiny badge and strings of evidence. Assumptions might not get *you* anywhere. But I'm a whole different story." He reached for the magnifying glass.

She knocked his hand away. "I told you to back off."

"And I told you that's not going to happen."

She glared at him for a minute, but he gave as good as he got. Better, and she finally looked away with a sigh of disgust. "Let me do my job, Cole."

"Who's stopping you?"

Refusing to even grace that ridiculousness with a comment, Genevieve focused on the blue and silver pendant in her hand. Stared at it through the magnifying glass and barely made out the impressions of an *S* and a *D*.

She looked closer, ran her finger over the scratches, and realized she was right on. "Someone's carved initials in this stone," she murmured, turning to Cole despite herself.

"What initials?" he demanded.

"It looks like an *S* and a *D*, but I can't be positive until the guys from the lab take a look at it." She bit her lip, ran through what she knew about the three homicides she was already working. Tried to ignore the fact that none of the victims had those initials.

"What are you think—" She turned to Cole and broke off in mid-sentence as she saw the ghastly look on his face. He was frozen, his eyes completely blank as he went somewhere far away in his head.

"Cole?" She snapped her fingers in front of his face, but he didn't respond. Didn't so much as blink. She looked down at the pendant again, ran her fingers over the hastily scratched initials. And realized, for the first time, that they were his sister's initials.

Frightened for him, she called his name again—a little more cautiously than she had before—and was relieved when he finally moved.

"Who the hell is this guy?" he growled, shouldering her aside to pick up the pendant. She knew she should object, but the water would have destroyed any fingerprints, and he definitely didn't look like he was going to take no for an answer.

"If I knew that, I'd be able to sleep at night, instead of imagining his next victim."

"Yeah, well, this is bullshit." He slammed the pendant on the desk so hard that her heart stopped as she imagined explaining to Chastian how the evidence had cracked in half. Thank God it was more sturdy than it looked.

"Cole—" She opened her mouth, unsure of exactly what she wanted to say. Knew only that she wanted to comfort where she should question, soothe where she should antagonize. But every thought in her head went out the window as a shrill scream echoed through the building.

It was quickly followed by another, more bloodcurdling than the first. And another one after that.

She and every other cop in the room leapt to their feet and hit the door running. Following the screams, she wound her way down the hallway until she got to the supply cabinet off the lobby. The screams were loudest there, and a crowd of cops had gathered around the clearly distraught woman.

"Hey, what happened here?" Genevieve leaned forward, asked one of the vice cops she knew a little.

Somebody gagged, rushed away, and then the crowd parted and the desk sergeant on duty looked at her with frantic eyes. "You're homicide, right?"

"Yeah." The sick feeling in her stomach grew until it was all she could do to keep her breakfast down.

"Then you need to see this." He pushed his way through the crowd, yanking her behind him in his wake. And pointed at the open door of the supply closet.

Chapter Twenty

Her own gag reflex kicked in as she took in the scene in front of her. Behind her she heard Cole swear, right before he took off. She wanted nothing more than to turn to him. To comfort him. But she couldn't do that, not now. Clenching her fists until her nails drew blood from her palms, she concentrated on breathing through the pain until she got her emotions—and her stomach—under control.

Then yelled, "No," as someone stepped forward to touch the body.

"She might still be alive!" The cop turned and she recognized Morales, one of the men who had asked her out about a year ago. He was one of the few who hadn't let her rejection get to him.

"She isn't alive, Edgar. And going in there will only contaminate the scene."

"We can't leave her like that!" The anguish in his voice was so real it had her taking another look at the body. And cursing as she realized who it was. Sharon Duval, one of the lab techs. Rumor had it she and Edgar were quite the item.

Sympathy had her glancing at Edgar's face, laying a hand on his trembling back. "I'm sorry," she murmured. "I'm so sorry."

The eyes he turned to her were glazed with shock. "Who . . . what—" He grabbed Genevieve and buried his head in her shoulder as the crowd watched.

Her arms came up of their own volition, rubbed his back as she murmured senseless words of comfort. Everything inside of her was straining to dig into the crime scene, but she took a few moments to hold her friend. To give him what little she could.

She didn't know how much time had passed, but suddenly the forensics guys were there—as shaken and angry as Edgar as they stared at what was left of one of their own. After catching one of the other officer's eyes, she slowly disengaged herself from Edgar as other hands reached out to take him.

Then she moved forward, met Jefferson and the rest of his crew. "What the fuck is going on here?" he muttered in a vicious aside. "Who would do this?"

She understood his anger, felt her own burning in her gut. Sharon had been one of the nicest people Genevieve had worked with—and one of the few other women at the station. To see her like this—naked, strung up, her body mutilated to the point that she was barely recognizable as human—was almost more than she could bear.

When Jefferson gave the okay, she grabbed a pair of gloves from his kit and moved forward. Stared at the incredibly unscathed face. And cursed low and long.

"He wanted us to know who she was right away." She said it softly to Jefferson, felt the other man sway a little before locking his knees.

"Why do you say that?"

She circled the body, stared at the mutilated back. "Her face is the only part of her he didn't ruin."

"Fuck."

As one, she and the crime scene techs put on booties and entered the crime scene. There was blood all over the floor, buckets of the stuff that continued to drip from the long slices on Sharon's body.

Her stomach started to revolt again, but she steeled it. Refused to lose it here. She had a job to do, and by God, she would do it.

On some level, she was aware of her lieutenant showing up, along with Captain Wesley. They got the crime scene cleared, and then entered the closet. She realized, distractedly, that neither one bothered to put on the booties to keep their shoes clean.

"A lot of this was done postmortem." Jefferson said what she'd already been thinking. "Thank God."

"No shit." She crouched down, got a closer look at the victim's feet. She was missing two toes. "But why? That isn't like our guy."

"Our guy?" The captain's voice cut like a whip. "Are you telling me this animal has struck before? And I wasn't notified?"

Oh, shit. Unsure of how to answer him, Genevieve glanced at her lieutenant. Chastian's mouth was tight, his eyes grim, but his anger seemed self-directed. "We think so. But we can't be positive—the MO of each murder is completely different."

"Each?" Wesley's voice was livid. "How many women have died without me being notified?"

"This is the fifth one, sir." Genevieve spoke softly, hoping to diffuse the already tense situation. All she needed was for the captain to explode in the middle of her crime scene.

But all he did was grind his teeth together and say, "When this is over, I want to see both of you in my office." He paused, looked at something over Genevieve's shoulder. "Make that all three of you."

She turned to find Shawn standing there, a look of abject horror on his face as he surveyed the room. He took a minute, then did exactly what she had done. Shrugged it off and said, "Where are we?"

"Just getting started." She went back to looking at the victim's feet.

Something in this one was ringing a bell, taking her back a few years. But she didn't say anything, not yet. She'd work the scene unprejudiced, gather as much evidence as she could. Then she'd check out the database and see if her instincts were as right on as she thought they were.

Oh, shit. Fuck. Goddamn son of a bitch. Fuck, fuck, fuck. Cole dragged air in through his mouth as he searched desperately for a bathroom. He was going to lose it and lose it big, and he really didn't need anyone else to see him when he did.

He found the bathroom at pretty much the exact second his stomach revolted. Slamming through the door, he dashed into the nearest stall and puked up everything in his stomach—and its lining to boot.

And still he wasn't done, the dry heaves racking his body again and again as he struggled for control. But for once, it eluded him—his body and everything else completely out of his power.

The bastard had killed that poor woman the same way Samantha had been killed. Had strung her up, nude and cut all to hell, the same way his sister had been hung. Tears burned behind his eyes, and for the first time in nearly a decade he let them fall.

Fuck, fuck, fuck. How could this be happening again? How could he be expected to live through it a second time? Every instinct he had told him to get his ass up and leave this place, leave this city, and never return.

But he couldn't do that, not now. Not when the nightmare was repeating itself. And not when Genevieve was here, trapped in the middle of everything.

But isn't that what he'd wanted? Her to wade in and get her hands dirty? He thought of the woman he had just seen; it didn't get any dirtier than that.

It was a message and he knew it, even if Genevieve didn't. He might be so twitchy and disturbed that he barely recognized himself, but he was still together enough to realize this whole thing had been done for his benefit.

It had been choreographed, staged, with just this result in mind. He didn't know exactly how he knew that, but he did. It made him even more furious, that he was reacting with such utter predictability that even a murdering asshole like this could figure him out.

But how was he supposed to react? This bastard—this sick, sociopathic fuck—was after her now. Maybe he'd always been, and Cole's interest in her had made the guy snap. He didn't know, and frankly, didn't care. But he couldn't leave Genevieve like this—a lamb for the slaughter.

This son of a bitch was sick, demented. Totally twisted, and he had his eye on Genevieve.

And she knew it.

She'd been shaken by the crime scene—he'd seen it, even if no one else had. She hadn't wanted to go into that closet, hadn't wanted to look at what had been done to that poor woman any more than he had.

But she'd done it.

What kind of strength did it take to do that, he wondered. To walk into that shit day after day, year after year? To look at the dead, and more, to take a stand for them? He didn't think he had it in him—hell, it had taken him close to a decade to take a stand for Samantha, and look what a fine job he was doing of that. Puking his guts up in a police station bathroom, too shaky and too disturbed to get off his knees and try to do some good.

He wanted to stand up, to get back to Genevieve, but he was man enough to admit his legs wouldn't yet support him. While his body might be out for the count, however, his brain was working perfectly well. And he realized that he was going to have to tell Genevieve the truth. Have to give up some control to keep her safe.

And he would keep her safe. Somehow, in the past few days, she'd become more important to him than anything else. She'd become his world, and the idea of her being in jeopardy because of him . . . he shook his head. No, that wasn't going to happen.

Tonight, they would sit down and he would tell her everything. He no longer had a choice. Pushing himself to his feet, he kept his head down as he left the bathroom and headed down the hallway to the nearest exit. He couldn't be here right now, couldn't deal with this newest outrage. Couldn't face Genevieve until he knew how to explain everything to her. Because after today, one thing was clear. He was becoming a liability, and Genevieve had the right to know about it.

Back at her desk, Genevieve stared at her friends and fellow detectives, all of whom looked as sick as she felt. "How did he get in here?" she demanded, more than aware of how wild she sounded. "We need to look at the film. There's a camera aimed directly at the waiting room next to the supply closet. We need it."

Shawn was already on the phone with the front desk. She didn't know what the desk sergeant was saying to him, but it sure as hell didn't look good. "The camera's fried—has been for three days. There's a requisition form in on it, but so far no one's gotten to it yet."

"Are you kidding me?" She stared at him in disbelief. "What about the one by the front door?"

He shook his head. "The whole system is down." Shaking his head, his expression revealing the same impotent fury she was feeling, he said, "This guy is always one step ahead of us."

She snorted. "Don't you mean three?"

"Well, somebody had to have seen him. We'll ask around, find out—"

"Come on, Shawn. A guy good enough to commit bloody murder right under our noses is good enough to keep from being seen."

Shawn looked like he wanted to argue, but in the end he shut his mouth because she was right and he knew it. They were exactly where they had been all along—totally screwed.

"I can't trace the flowers." Luc came up behind them. "Someone dropped an envelope in the mail slot with a hundred bucks in it, asking that the roses be delivered here yesterday afternoon."

She turned to look at him. "What did the guys on duty have to say about last night? How the hell was this bastard able to get Sharon in that closet and mutilate her like that in the middle of a fucking police station? And how the hell did no one hear it going on?"

"They have no idea. I've talked to everyone on duty. According to Jefferson, Sharon was staying late to work on something for one of her cases—apparently, Chastian's in a rush for it.

"Anyway, Jefferson left at nine o'clock, and Sharon was still alive. Edgar called her cell at eleven thirty—I guess they'd had plans—and she didn't answer. He came back here at one to look for her, and found the lab locked up tight."

"Did he get her on the way home, then?" Luc asked. "After she'd left the station?"

"No." Genevieve pictured the crime scene in her head. "That would be impossible. She was taken out by a blow to the head. I don't care how busy or understaffed this place is; if someone carried one of ours—unconscious—through the door, we would have noticed. *Someone* would have noticed."

"So what, then? How the hell did he get her where he wanted her without attracting attention?" Torres demanded.

"He knew her," Luc piped in, his normally ruddy face deathly white. "She trusted him—whoever he is—enough to follow him into a storage closet in an empty police station. He gets her to walk in ahead of him, and pow!" He brought his hand down in a quick slicing motion. "One blow to the head and she's stunned enough to let him do anything he wants to her."

"But where's the satisfaction in that?" demanded Torres. "All his other victims were wide awake for their torture—it's something the bastard gets off on. I know he's mimicked a bunch of past crimes, but he always puts his own twist on it. Why change his MO now? He gets off on the torture."

"Because this wasn't one of his masterpieces," Genevieve answered as her instincts screamed at her that this was an inside job. She beat them down as she glanced into the outraged faces around her. There was no way one of these men was the killer—no possible way. "Sharon was a means to an end, a punishment. Nothing else."

"What the hell does that mean?"

"Almost all the wounds were postmortem—at least, that's what Jefferson believes at this point. And I'm betting that we'll find out that either the blow to the head killed her or something else did very quickly. He didn't want her to suffer. Oh, and there was no sign of sexual assault on the preliminary exam."

"Which reinforces that he knew her." Shawn spoke up for the first time.

"Or that he just didn't want her to scream her head off in the middle of a cop shop," Luc said through gritted teeth.

Genevieve watched him thoughtfully for a minute, and couldn't help thinking that finally the killer had made a mistake. Taking a cop—particularly in her own precinct—was a stupid thing to do. Killing her here and leaving her mutilated body to be found was more than stupid. It was downright suicidal. So either the guy had a death wish and wanted to be caught, or he was too damn arrogant for his own good.

She was betting on the latter.

"Who was he punishing?" Torres demanded, his angry voice drawing her out of her musings. "Who's he pissed at—besides his mother and the whole fucking world?"

Her phone rang before she could answer him. Wondering if it

was Cole—since he'd disappeared once poor Sharon's body had been found—she answered it with a soft, "Delacroix." But it wasn't Cole, and she froze at the whisper at the other end.

It was a recording, and he said only three words, but they had her paralyzed. She stared at her computer like it was a bomb about to go off. "Check your e-mail."

"Why?" she started to ask, hoping to keep the line open long enough to trace him, but a dial tone was her only answer. Bumping Shawn out of her way—as well as the two CSI guys who had just shown up—she logged into her e-mail and skimmed through her in-box.

Buried between an e-mail from the DA's office and one from the lab was a message simply titled READ ME.

She clicked on it, and huge red letters filled the screen. *This one's on you, Genevieve. She didn't have to die.*

Suddenly, loud music blasted from her speakers and photos began popping on the screen—the same photos Chastian had shown her the day before.

She tried to shut it down, to close the e-mail, to turn off the computer—to do something, anything to make the images stop. But nothing was working—her PC had been hijacked.

She was achingly aware of the men behind her, all of whom had averted their eyes after the first few pictures came up. But by then the damage had been done—the bastard had led with the most explicit ones—her naked, blindfolded and tied to Cole's bed, tequila pouring over her nude body with her nipples hard and glistening, a man's hand coming down hard on her bare ass, her masturbating.

The music was drawing attention from others in the room, and though Shawn and Luc and Roberto tried to shield the computer, she knew by the buzz in the room that some of the other detectives saw anyway.

Tears of rage and humiliation burned in her eyes. She saw these men every day, worked with them, took their backs and trusted them to take hers. Now that they'd seen her like this, how could she expect them to ever look at her the same way?

It wasn't that she was ashamed of what she'd done with Cole—she wasn't. The way he loved her was beautiful and exciting and so achingly intimate it made her head spin and her heart ache. But to have others see what she let him do to her was a violation like no other she'd ever known.

Not knowing what to do, wanting desperately for it to stop, she repeatedly hit the computer's off button, but to no avail. Behind her she heard Torres growl, "Unplug the goddamn thing!" and then Luc was crouching next to her, ripping the power cord from the wall.

The music stopped instantly, as did the photo montage as the screen went mercifully blank. For long seconds she stood, paralyzed. Unable to move or think or even breathe, she tried to steady herself. Tried to think of what to say, of what to do.

But there was nothing she could do, the images indelibly burned into her brain—and the brains of her partners, the CSI guys and half the squad room to boot, she was sure. Everything she'd done to fit in, everything she'd done to promote a professional image—strong, self-reliant, as capable as any man—was worthless now. In seconds, she'd been reduced to a joke for the water cooler. Or worse, the locker room.

Her lungs started aching, and Genevieve became abruptly aware of the fact that she wasn't breathing. Opening her mouth, she managed to suck a few strangled breaths into her starving lungs.

But then she heard Torres clear his throat, felt his hand—soft and comforting—on her shoulder. The tears she'd been battling overflowed, sliding down her cheeks in long rivulets she no longer had the strength to hide.

"I need . . . I'm sorry, I need a minute."

And then she was running out of the bull pen. Out of the station house. Out of her mind.

Chapter Twenty-one

She wanted Cole.

Needed him with an intensity that bordered on insanity. Tired, disgusted and more scared than she would ever admit, Genevieve wanted nothing more than to curl against her lover and let him soothe her—body and soul.

But that wasn't going to happen tonight, she told herself grimly, as she fumbled in her purse for the keys to her front door. She hadn't seen him since the body had been discovered that morning, hadn't had a chance to call him as she and the others had worked all afternoon and half the evening trying to get the evidence to pop out a lead—any lead.

Not that she blamed him; that body would have been hard for anyone to take. That it had so closely mimicked his sister's death—she could only imagine how devastated he was.

It had taken her a while to work up the nerve to go back to the station, and when she'd finally gotten there, braced for the worst, it was to find her computer missing, her desk cleaned and the guys deep in conversation about any- and everything pertaining to the case—except what had happened to her earlier that afternoon.

And while she'd been on the receiving end of a couple of hard-tointerpret looks, all in all she was shocked at how good everyone was at pretending nothing had happened. She also couldn't help wondering just what Shawn and Luc and Torres had threatened them with to make such behavior a reality.

The only reference to the e-mail was when Torres growled out of the corner of his mouth, "I had to give the computer to the e-guys—see what they could come up with from it. But I made them promise that Jose would be the only one to look at it. I'm sorry. I didn't know what else to do."

She'd been touched by his concern, by his desire to spare her any and all embarrassment. She'd thanked him, but he'd shaken his head and told her it was nothing. Chastian hadn't seen it the same way; had called her into his office just a little while ago and ordered her to take a week's vacation, or face suspension.

She'd taken the vacation, effective immediately. And the worst part was—after all her fine posturing—that she hadn't even had the nerve to tell him to go to hell. Stressed out over the photos, feeling more violated than she ever had before in her life, she didn't have any fight left in her. She'd just agreed with Chastian and left. What was one more violation on top of all the others?

Her hands locked onto the key ring, and she pulled it out with a sigh. Slid her house key into the lock. Heard it click and then pushed the door open. Before she knew what was happening, Cole grabbed her wrist and yanked her inside before he slammed the door shut behind her.

"What are you—" Her question was cut off when he shoved her face-first into the wall hard enough to have the air whooshing from her lungs.

"I need you." He grabbed her wrists, locked them above her head and pressed his hard, muscular body against her from behind. "I need to be inside you."

He sounded utterly desperate—and her sorrow fled in the face of his obvious pain.

She could feel his arousal against her ass as he molded every inch of his rock-solid body to hers, and she responded instantly as the need to comfort him the only way he would allow welled up inside of her.

She struggled to turn around, to look at him, but he wouldn't ease up. Wouldn't let her go, his hand tightening around her wrists as he leaned even more heavily against her.

"Do you want me to stop?" Cole whispered the question in her left ear, his hot breath making her shiver despite herself.

She wanted to hold him—to soothe him—but she knew him well enough to understand that he couldn't accept that from her now. Wouldn't accept it from her at all. Part of her wanted to stop him, to demand that they talk about this thing that had ripped him inside out, but the other part just wanted to give in to him for a while. To make him feel good. To let him make her feel good in return.

Then he was rocking his hips against her, and any thought of stopping him disappeared. He felt incredible, the hand that gripped her wrists tight but not painful. The pressure of his long, lithe body against her the same.

"Genevieve?" he prompted, licking the delicate skin behind her ear. "Tell me now if you want me to leave."

Closing her eyes, she said the only two words she was capable of forming, the only two words she wanted to say: "Don't leave."

His response was a deep whoosh of air against her cheek, as if he'd been holding his breath, waiting for her answer. And then he was moving, his free hand tangling in her hair. Pulling her head back so that her throat was exposed to his questing mouth.

His raked his teeth down the slender column, then used his tongue to lick away the sweat that had formed as suddenly as her need for him. Up and down her throat, he went, covering every square inch of her neck until there was no place he hadn't kissed. Then he got to the hollow of her throat and began to suck, strong pulls that sent heat and wetness careening into her sex.

She arched against him, stood on tiptoes so that she could press her ass more firmly against his hard cock. He felt so good. Hard and hot and in control, he made her feel like the most desirable woman on earth. Like no one else would ever do for him.

With her hands stretched above her head, her body held nearly immobile by the hard press of his, she felt bound. Helpless. Completely at Cole's mercy. And somehow the vibe worked for her, despite the fact that she had never wanted to give any man this much control over her. Had fought against it her whole life.

But Cole was different. With his hot eyes and hotter body, he brought her more pleasure than she'd ever dreamed possible. He made her crave it—crave him—with a hunger that could not be satisfied.

His free hand fumbled down her back, yanked at her pants until the button popped open and the zipper gave out. Then he was shoving them down her legs, slipping a hand between her thighs to test her readiness.

She knew what he found, knew that the finger he pulled away from her was coated with her juices. So she waited, arms locked above her head, breasts pressed against the wall, pussy wide open and waiting to be filled.

He groaned, slipped the finger that had just been inside her into his mouth and tasted her. One long second passed, then two as she waited for him. Suddenly, he was there, his hard cock shoving into her with one powerful thrust.

She whimpered at the invasion, but pressed back against him and let him ride her to orgasm. It was quick, mind-numbing, a slice of heaven on earth, and as he hurtled her into first one climax and then another, she decided that she would stop fighting. That she would take whatever Cole could give her and just be thankful for the time she had with him.

"Come with me." His voice was still low, still wicked, as he pulled out of her. He held out a hand in the dim light and she didn't hesitate to take it. Wherever he wanted to take her tonight, she would follow. Whatever he wanted to do to her, she would embrace it. And pray that it was enough to satisfy the darkness in his soul.

He led her up the stairs to her bedroom, where long, tapered candles in shades of red and pink and black flickered. "Sit on the edge of the bed and finish undressing." His voice was low, his eyes intense, and she couldn't help wondering why his demons were riding him so much harder tonight.

She almost worked up the nerve to ask him when he pulled a long velvet cord off her nightstand. Her eyes widened as she stared at it, and she couldn't keep the tremble from her voice as she asked, "What's that?"

He didn't answer, just smiled and said, "Do you trust me, Genevieve?"

"Yes," she answered without hesitation, quickly stripping off her shirt and bra. It was true; she knew he would never deliberately hurt her. And if this was what he needed tonight—to feel in control of her, of something, while his life spun completely out of his command—she would give it to him.

"Tell me if you want to stop, or if I do something you don't like."

"You won't."

He grinned at her confidence, his cock twitching between them. And then he was wrapping the cord around her—first over and around her chest, directly above her breasts, then below them, where her bra strap usually rested. Stepping back, he twisted the long lengths of rope still in his hand, so that the pressure was a little tighter and she could feel the ropes digging into her skin.

Pulling her arms behind her, he wrapped the silken cord around first one and then the other, so that her shoulders were pressed back and down, her arms hanging, bound, behind her back.

And it felt good—amazingly good. So good that she looked at Cole in surprise and asked, "What is this?"

He smiled wickedly. "A mild form of Japanese rope bondage." He reached forward and flicked first one of her nipples and then the other. She moaned, arching back a little to give him better access. And felt the bonds constrict pleasurably, her breasts beginning to tighten and throb from the constriction.

She gasped, arched a little more, and nearly came from the sensations cascading through her. "How—" The sensations grew so pleasurable that her voice broke before she could finish the question.

But Cole seemed to understand what she was asking, and answered her slowly while he squeezed her nipples between his thumbs and index fingers. She gasped, trembled, the sensation somehow so much more erotic than it had been before the ropes.

"Japanese bondage isn't just about the psychological pleasure that comes from being bound for your lover's satisfaction." Cole lowered his mouth, teased one red tip with his tongue as she shuddered and cried out. "Although there is that too."

He took her nipple into his mouth and began to suck, and she couldn't disagree with him. Though she longed to run her fingers through his hair, to stroke her hands up and down his back, there was something incredibly exciting about sitting here, unable to move, awaiting whatever pleasure he wanted to take from her.

"But the true pleasure comes from the positioning of the ropes themselves. The dom has to make sure they hit particular pleasure points to ensure the ropes are at their most effective."

He skimmed a finger under first one rope and then the other, massaging each of the points where the ropes touched her body. "Did I get the right points?" he asked teasingly.

Her only answer was her eyes nearly rolling back in her head as pleasure—hot, sweet and out of control—burst inside of her.

"It seems that I did," he murmured, before ordering, "Stand up," in his most commanding voice. He watched with dark eyes as she struggled to her feet without the use of her hands and upper body. Every move-ment pulled the ropes tighter, increasing the pressure and the warm, jetting pleasure she was experiencing.

Her knees trembled, but she locked them in place, determined to handle whatever Cole threw at her. But when he leaned down and took her nipple in his mouth, her control was stretched to the breaking point.

His teeth fastened on her areola, biting and tugging while his tongue soothed the crazy little aches popping up all over her body. He wasn't gentle with her, didn't take it easy on her. But then she hadn't expected him to. He was in pain, his demons completely out of control, and he was desperate to exorcise them.

No, he wasn't easy, but then she didn't want easy. She wanted some-thing that would take her over, consume her, give her unimaginable ecstasy. Something that would take her mind off what had happened at the station today, until all she thought of was Cole. Until all she wanted was Cole. Arching her back to give him better access, she leaned back slightly and relished the electricity that zipped from her breasts to her core, the crazy tightening of the ropes just making it better.

He moved to her other breast, and she looked down at her well-used nipple curiously. It was a deep, dark red, glistening in the candlelight.

He moved to the underside of her breasts, right above the ropes, and nipped sharply. She screamed, shuddered, as she felt that bite all the way to her toes.

Again and again he licked and sucked and nibbled her breasts—until the mere act of standing took more concentration than she could muster.

Collapsing on the bed, her trembling legs unable to hold her any longer, she leaned back on her bound elbows and watched him through heavy-lidded eyes. She longed to touch him, to feel his muscles ripple under her hands. But at the same time there was something liberating about being bound for his pleasure, unable to move or switch. Unable to do anything but simply lay back and enjoy.

"Close your eyes," he whispered, licking a trail from her breasts to her navel to her aching sex.

She did as he requested, arching her hips all the while. But he didn't touch her aching clit, didn't kiss or caress or lick her where she was most desperate for him. Instead he moved away.

She was tempted to open her eyes, but decided to give it a minute, to see what else her lover had up his sleeve. She wasn't disappointed. Within moments, he was pouring something deliciously warm over her stomach. She lay still, savoring the hot water as it ran in rivulets down her sides and onto the bed.

He did it again and again—over her breasts, across her belly, down one leg and then the other, and it felt amazingly good. At some point she realized it wasn't water he was using on her—it dried too quickly and didn't evaporate. She wanted to look, but fought the urge, knowing it would be better to wait for Cole.

So she relaxed and simply enjoyed the unique feeling. Shuddered as whatever it was coated her nipples, increasing their sensitivity to the point that she could barely lie still.

"Cole," she whimpered, eyes closed and body straining. "Take me. Fuck me. I can't stand this."

"Just a little more," he said soothingly, his mouth claiming hers. His tongue tangling and teasing and taunting hers until she wanted to scream with frustrated desire.

"Open your eyes," he said, and she did slowly, glancing down at her body curiously.

What she saw there had her breath hitching in her throat, her eyes widening with shocked pleasure. She'd been right—it hadn't been water he'd been pouring on her at all.

Instead he'd used warm candle wax. Not hot enough to cause pain, but more than warm enough to make her pussy and breasts and clit throb with unrelieved excitement.

"You're beautiful," he murmured, staring at the patterns of red and black and pink on her skin. "Absolutely exquisite."

She reveled in his admiration, in the absence of pain in his eyes, for a minute and let it soothe away the terrible harshness of her day. But then even his gaze was too much, her body starving for him in a way she'd never before experienced.

Burning up, out of control, she let her eyes tell him exactly how much she wanted him. "Does that mean you'll fuck me now?" she demanded.

He smiled slightly, his eyes turning darker. "Is that what you want?"

"God, yes. I'm going to implode if you don't." Already her sex was clenching rhythmically, hungry for his cock.

He moved his hand down to his hugely aroused cock, wrapped it around the base of it and began stroking up and down. She watched him, transfixed, her breathing shallow, her pussy wet, her mouth aching to wrap around him.

Slowly he pleasured himself, settling on the other side of the bed. "Do you want it?" he asked again, his eyes as hot and hungry as hers.

She licked her lips. "Yes."

"Then come and get it." He shuddered, arched into the pleasure he was giving himself. But it was nothing compared to the pleasure they both knew awaited them when he slipped inside her.

Struggling to her knees, she crawled across the bed to him. Threw one leg over his hips and climbed on. Without the use of her hands it was strange, yet somehow even more erotic.

Rising on her knees, she lowered herself onto him slowly. Savored the feel of him slipping between her legs and into the hot recesses of her sex. Her muscles clenched around him, pulled him deeper until he was in her to the hilt and there was nothing more to take.

She felt full, magnificently, sexily stretched by him, until she couldn't breathe without feeling him inside her. And then she began to move, a soft rocking of her hips that had him groaning and clawing the comforter beneath him.

"Faster, Genevieve," he said, his hands moving to her hips to guide her.

But she shook him off, refused to be rushed. And continued the slow, languorous rhythm until they were both panting, sweat dripping off of them as their bodies strained for the climax that was tantalizingly out of reach.

"Sweetheart, you're killing me." He gasped the words between harsh, shuddering breaths. "You have to go faster. You have to—"

She raised her hips until he was almost out of her, then slammed down on him. He groaned, arched his hips and she did it again. And again. Until there was no Cole and no Genevieve, no suspension and no killer. Until there was nothing but two bodies moving as one and an ecstasy that spun wildly out of control.

Chapter Twenty-two

"Are you ever going to tell me the truth, Cole?" Genevieve stared at him across her kitchen island, a glass of white wine in her hand and an outraged look on her face.

He'd had all day to think about how to tell her, but now that the time was here, the words just wouldn't come. Finally deciding to just start at the beginning, he murmured, "I wasn't completely honest about why I'm in New Orleans—why I needed your help."

"No kidding." The glass of wine froze halfway to her lips. "I've only been asking you about your agenda since the first day we met. Forgive me if I have a hard time believing you're ready to just clear the air."

He shrugged. "I don't have much of a choice, seeing as how we're becoming interconnected in this thing."

"Interconnected, huh?" She took another sip of the crisp, cool wine. "Is that what they're calling it these days?"

"Stop it, Genevieve." His voice was dark, his eyes darker. "I want to talk about what's going on, about how I'm afraid I might have something to do with it."

"So talk. If you're the reason these things have been happening to me, then I'm all ears."

So wrapped up in the memories of his past—and the misery that came with them—he almost didn't catch the significance of what Genevieve had said. But then something clicked and sent fury and fear slamming through him. "What's that supposed to mean? Exactly what has been happening to you—besides the flowers?"

"I thought you were going to tell me."

"Don't do that."

She raised an eyebrow. "Do what, exactly?"

"Don't *push* me on this, Genevieve." He crossed the kitchen, grabbed her upper arms and pulled her against his chest—so that he could feel her heart beat and know that she was alive. And that she was going to stay that way, no matter what he had to do.

But her hands shoved against his chest, and the look on her face was angrier than he had ever seen. "No, you don't push *me*. Not after everything I've given you and everything I've done to get you to tell me the truth."

He clenched his teeth, fighting the urge to shake her until she did exactly what he wanted of her. But she was giving as good as she got, and he could tell there was no backup in his little hard-ass tonight. She was all bristling femininity and outraged pride—and he could either go with it or get pulled under.

Gritting his teeth, determined to get through it as quickly as possible, he spit out, "Seven years ago, my sister was murdered. Her name was Samantha Diaz."

The fight seemed to drain out of her as she reached for his hand. "Thank you for telling me that."

"That's it?" he asked, shocked. "That's all you have to say?"

"I'm so sorry for your loss, Cole, and for what you had to see today. But I already knew. I've known almost from the beginning."

Pain, raw and elemental, slammed through him. "How?"

"Your police report. It mentions Samantha."

"Why didn't you say something?"

"Why didn't you?"

"Because I was using you! I wanted to get you to reopen Samantha's case, to look into it."

"I already have." Her eyes were the deep, mysterious blue of the ocean as she told him what he'd waited so desperately long to hear.

He felt tears burning behind his eyes, but refused to shed them. "Why didn't you tell me?"

"I was waiting for you to trust me enough to tell me about her, to tell me that you were really here to find her killer. But after what happened today, I figured we had to get it in the open. I had to force you to tell me, or somehow find a way to tell you that I already knew."

"You know, when the studio talked to me about doing this documentary, I thought maybe it was a sign. If I could come down here and find out who the best detective was, and somehow get him—or her—to look at the case file, maybe we'd find something the other cops had missed. Maybe we'd find out who'd killed Samantha."

"So why did you lie to me? Again and again and again? For a while, I was really afraid you were a murderer—or at least in league with one. This—" It was her turn to shake her head. "This wouldn't have even raised my radar."

"I didn't know if you'd help me; my faith in the NOPD was pretty much nonexistent. And then by the time I'd figured out how different you were from the rest, you'd come to mean too much to me. I was afraid you'd be so offended by the lies that I'd never see you again."

"I'm sorry." He spread his hands. "I was wrong."

"Yes, you were." She stared at him for long minutes, then walked around the island and wrapped her arms around him. "I'm so sorry, Cole. I can't imagine what you've been through—losing your sister in such a brutal fashion."

Her sadness for him was nearly palpable, her sorrow for Samantha just as obvious. But she still wasn't getting it, still wasn't understanding what he was saying. "I let her go. I convinced our mom and her dad to let her come down here on her own. I ignored my mom when she told me something was wrong with Sam, that I needed to come down and check it out."

"You didn't know."

"Do you think that makes it any better? Especially now, when I feel like I'm set to relive it all over again?" His hands clamped convulsively on her shoulders.

But she shrugged him off, shoved at him until he dropped his arms and she could stand. "What is that supposed to mean?"

"He sent you flowers, Genevieve. I've been researching violent crime long enough to know what it means when a serial killer gets fixated on someone. Then the murder like Samantha's—it's because of me."

She stared at him for long moments, her bottom lip clenched between her teeth as if she were debating how much to say. It pissed him off. "Tell me."

"He's been fixated on me for a while, Cole. It's not your doing. This was just one of his newest ideas to get my attention."

The blood rushed from his head so quickly that for a second he was afraid he might actually pass out. "What does that mean? Fixated on you for *a while*?" He reached for her, but she shrugged him off. "Genevieve?" He made sure his voice was as hard as he was, made sure she knew that one way or the other, she was telling him the truth.

"He's done a number of things to get my attention—threats, presents. He's been after me since I figured out what was going on."

"Tell me what he's done."

"It doesn't matter, Cole."

"To hell with that," he snarled, moving toward her like a semi in full gear. "It does matter."

"No, it doesn't." He'd grabbed her wrists and she started tugging, trying to get free. But he was having none of it—this time she would stay put until she told him everything.

He was beyond angry, beyond furious that she had kept this from him. Sure, he hadn't told her the whole truth about what he was doing in New Orleans, but he wasn't putting himself at risk with his omissions. That his woman—for that was what she was, whether she acknowledged it or not—had deliberately chosen not to tell him about this threat was more than maddening. It was completely unacceptable and more than enough to have him tearing at the walls. To have him locking her up so that no one, nothing, could ever get to her again.

Rage, red-hot and explosive, ripped through him as he shoved his face in hers and spoke through clenched teeth. "Tell me what he's done, Genevieve."

"Don't bully me!" Once again she tried to pull away; once again he allowed his grip to tighten.

"Then don't push me—I let it go the other day, but I'm done with that. You will tell me, or you won't like the consequences."

"You can't do this." She tugged at her wrists. "Let me go!"

He was no longer in control, every protective instinct he had was aroused at the thought of her being hurt. At the thought of getting another phone call telling him that a woman he loved was dead.

Protecting her was more than a need, more than his duty. It was a primal obsession that wrapped itself around him and demanded to be heard. She would not be hurt, not this woman. Not this time.

"Tell me what he's doing, Genevieve. Now." His voice was no longer his own—deep, primitive, more animal than human, even as the one small, rational part of his brain that was left warned him that he was going about this all wrong.

But he was too far gone to listen, every part of him straining to find this bastard and rip him limb from limb, until he was no longer a threat to Genevieve. Until she was finally safe and he could hold her, feel her heart beating against his and know that this animal—this sick, fucked-up asshole—would never get his hands on her.

But to protect her, he had to know where the threat was coming from, had to know what was coming next. He knew he was pushing it, knew she wouldn't take much more without fighting back. But he had to try. Shaking her gently, he ordered, "Just tell me, Genevieve!"

She lashed out before he was prepared for it, her foot catching him on the upper part of his shin with more force than he would have thought possible considering her lack of shoes. He stumbled, lost his grip for just a second, but that was all it took for her to spring away from him.

"Don't come near me, Cole," she said from halfway across the room. "You're acting crazy."

"You make me crazy." He stalked toward her, slowly, stealthily. She would tell him what he needed to know to protect her.

"I mean it." Genevieve circled the kitchen warily, watching as Cole mirrored her every movement with his own body. A step to the right from her and he was there. Two steps to the left, the same thing.

She was completely trapped. It didn't bring about the fear it normally did, didn't make her want to run. Instead, she wanted to push back—to see just how far he was willing to let her go and how far past that she could actually take things.

It was stupid, really, to engage in this power struggle when women were dying around her. But she was off the case—on vacation, for all intents and purposes—and to give Cole his way now in this was to breed disaster later on.

And there would be a later on; she was determined about that. He was hers. Despite his high-handed interrogation techniques and crazy need to dominate, to be in charge, he was the man for her. He just didn't know it yet.

"It's a police investigation, Cole. I can't talk about it."

"Bullshit." His voice was lower now, a caress that sent shivers running up her spine and heat spiraling toward her sex. She fought the sensations, kept her eyes on his, but before she knew it, he was two steps closer than he had been before.

Damn it, she had to concentrate. But it was hard to do with a glorious, half-naked man looking at her as if he would gobble her up in a couple of neat bites. Harder to do when she wanted nothing more than to let him.

She tried another tack. "It's no big deal—just some stupid pranks."

"Anything that has you running around our bedroom in a panic, slamming shutters closed and begging me to stay inside, isn't nothing." He took another step closer, but she was so dazed by his voice—and the words coming out of his mouth—that she didn't notice.

"I'm handling it."

"We'll handle it together." And then he was there, in front of her, his wicked black eyes gleaming down at her with a look that said he meant business. He pulled her into his arms, ran his lips softly over her forehead, down her cheeks, across her mouth. "Tell me, Genevieve. Please. Let me protect you."

"I can protect myself."

"Of course you can." It was a groan from his soul, a cry for help she couldn't refuse. "But I need to protect you too. I need to be a part of it.

"After Samantha—" His voice broke, and the hands clutching her trembled.

It was his sorrow that cracked her resolve—it was heart-wrenching to see him so desperate, so shaken, and she knew she could deny him nothing.

"You're making too big a deal out of a few phone calls, Cole." She sighed, then slipped into a kitchen chair, resting her elbows on the table. Waited for him to do the same.

And then told him everything.

*   *   *

With each word that Genevieve spoke, Cole felt himself getting angrier, more wound up. The desire for vengeance was huge, the need to rip this animal apart a living, breathing entity within him. He would kill him for this, would have killed him for much less. But to torment Genevieve like this, to humiliate and scare and taunt her as he had? The bastard had signed his own death warrant—he was just too stupid to know it yet.

"He's not going to get away with this." He growled the words before he could stop himself.

The look she shot him was rife with her own anger, her own frustration. "You're damn right he's not." She shoved a hand through her hair. "He's killed five women in *my* jurisdiction, under *my* watch. There's no way this bastard walks away from that."

His heart stuttered in his chest. "But you're suspended. You can't work—"

"Wanna bet?" She gestured to the backpack she'd brought in with her and that he hadn't paid any attention to until now. "I brought everything home with me, and I will damn sure be working on this—whether Chastian wants me to or not."

"You can't do that." The words were torn from him.

"I am doing it. This guy is going down one way or the other."

"Then let it be the other."

"I can't, Cole. Can't you see that? This is my *job* and I can't just walk away from it."

"What about us?" He pulled her into his lap, smoothed soothing hands over her. "I love you, Genevieve. I love you more than I ever thought it possible to love another person."

She trembled in his arms, her eyes going wide. "Now?" she demanded. "You tell me this now?"

"I can't lose you. I wouldn't survive if this psychopath got his hands on you."

"He won't, Cole."

"You don't know that. You can't." He leaned down, kissed her with all of his pent-up fear and love and anger.

She exploded, her arms going around him as her lips devoured his. On and on and on went the kiss, until every sense he had was clouded by her. But then she was pulling away, her smile sad, her eyes even sadder. "Don't ask this of me, Cole. I would do anything for you, give you everything and anything you asked for. But I can't do this—can't just let this guy go when he's ruined so many lives."

"That's exactly what Samantha said. That it was her job, her career, and she couldn't take the easy way out."

"It's not the same thing."

"No, it's not. She was a random victim. But you, you're taunting the hell out of this guy, making yourself a target. Just waiting for him to make a move." He paused for a minute, studied her with tormented eyes. "Let someone else catch him, Genevieve."

"They can't. This sick fixation he has with me is our best weapon, and it doesn't work if I don't use it to my advantage."

"Goddamn it, Genevieve! You don't always have to be the hero."

"This isn't about being the hero. It's about doing what's right—about bringing this bastard down once and for all. About stopping him before he kills another woman."

As he stared at her, his heart in his throat and his stomach tied into so many knots he feared it would never recover, Cole knew it was a done deal. There was nothing he could say to convince her, nothing he could do that would make her leave this case alone.

He was going to lose her, just like he'd lost Samantha. And there wasn't a damn thing he could do about it.

Chapter Twenty-three

Genevieve woke with a start, thoughts of murder and suspension and Cole chasing each other around in her head. He was pulling back from her, hadn't touched her once after their conversation. He hadn't held her or kissed her or made love to her like he usually did. Just climbed into bed beside her and rolled over so that when she tried to talk to him all she saw was his back.

Her heart was beating much too fast, and as she lay there in the dark, listening to his steady breathing beside her, she thought about what Cole had asked of her.

Could she let this investigation go—for him? Could she just walk away and hope the killer lost interest in her? But it wouldn't work that way. In her heart, she knew that if she didn't find him and shut him down, than he would be coming for her. And in the meantime, another poor woman would die when she didn't have to. When Genevieve could have stopped him.

Willing her heart to calm down, she rolled onto her side to stare at her lover. He really was the most beautiful man she'd ever seen—all long, lithe muscle and dark eyes and gorgeous features.

And inside, he was even more beautiful. This man who had tortured himself for seven years over the loss of his sister, this man who had dedicated his life to exposing corruption and death, who tried so hard to right wrongs that couldn't be righted.

She loved him; how it had happened, she didn't know. What she would do about it, she hadn't a clue. Reaching a hand up to toy with the necklace he'd given her, she couldn't help wondering about its implication. Did he see it as she originally had—as him branding her, claiming her? Or was it just a gift after all—one that was pretty but really didn't mean much?

I love you. He'd said the words last night, but had he meant them? She wanted to believe that he had, but how could she when he was so reluctant to accept her own love for him? When he tried so hard to make her into something that she wasn't?

Because she couldn't go one more minute without touching him, she traced a delicate finger over his eyebrows and down his cheeks. In sleep, he looked almost sweet—all the angst and darkness that possessed him during the day was absent now, leaving only little-boy innocence that tugged at her heartstrings.

How she could ever have thought him a murderer, she didn't know. It embarrassed her that she'd ever doubted him, even when the killer had focused on her. Especially then. He wasn't capable of it, not this man who had tortured himself for nearly a decade, who was so desperate to protect her that he would change his whole life around to save her.

Her cell phone went off in the next room, but she ignored it. No one from the station would be calling her—she was off the case permanently. And she didn't have any friends away from the job—hell, she didn't have many friends on the job. Maybe that was something she needed to work on.

But when the cell phone stopped ringing and the house phone

started, she rolled out of bed and grabbed the cordless on her night-stand before it could wake Cole.

"Hello?" she whispered, scooting out of the room on silent feet.

"Genevieve? It's Roberto. There's another body."

"Where?" She was already reaching for a pen when it occurred to her that she wouldn't be able to do anything about that fact. She ached, literally ached, for the dead woman—she hadn't been good enough to save her. Hadn't been fast enough.

"Dauphine and St. Louis. It's the house on the corner."

"Why are you calling me? I can't do anything about it."

He swore roundly. "Fuck Chastian. You know more about this mur-der than any of us. We're all here. We need you. Even if your name doesn't go on the report, we need your eye. This is what you're good at."

She paused for long seconds, Cole's pleas for her to play it safe run-ning through her head. But she had to do this, had to see it through. Then they would talk—about the future and their expectations for each other. About whether they could make this thing work.

"I'll be there in ten."

"We'll be waiting."

Her clothes from last night were still by the door and still relatively fresh—she'd changed into them after she'd finished Sharon's homicide scene. As she slipped into them—too afraid of waking Cole to chance going back into the bedroom—she fought back the tears that had been burning her throat since she'd heard Torres' voice on the phone.

She'd become such a pariah that they had to sneak her onto a homi-cide case. It was bullshit—total and complete bullshit—but what could she do about it? She was used to fighting, had gotten where she was in the department because she didn't back down when she was sure she was right.

But she didn't have a clue how to fight this. She was demoralized, humiliated, barely able to contemplate looking her partner and friends in their faces.

But she didn't have a choice, she told herself as she shrugged into her blouse. A killer was out there, one she had more than likely spoken to on numerous occasions. From the second she'd seen Sharon hanging in that supply closet, she'd known the killer was one of their own.

All along she'd had her suspicions about it being a cop; things were just too clean for it to be someone else. She'd even had a few suspects in mind, had taken steps to monitor them as best she could without raising any flags. Sharon's body had just proven to her what she'd suspected all along.

And he was probably going to be there tonight, might have been there all along—at each of the crime scenes—and she hadn't known to look for him. But that stopped now. She would get this son of a bitch, with or without her lieutenant's support.

After strapping on her piece, she went to the closet and pulled out the backup gun she rarely carried. Put extra ammunition for both in her back pockets. Scribbled a note to Cole, then let herself out of the house. As she locked the door behind her, she fought back the fear that she would never see Cole again. Never hold him against her, never feel his lips against hers.

Then turned away and focused on what she had to do.

The walk up Burgundy had never taken so long or passed so quickly. Cold sweat trickled down her back despite the heat and nerves jumping in her stomach. She ran through every scenario she could think of, wondered how this whole thing was going to play out. Wondered if she and her friends were going to make it through the night alive.

She'd expected the house to be dark when she got there, had figured Roberto had called her in at the end of the investigation just to look around a little and get a feel for the place without getting written up for disobeying orders. It was the smart thing to do, and she'd told herself she wouldn't resent him if that was, indeed, the case.

Instead, the house was lit up like a Christmas tree and more than a dozen cop cars were parked in front of it. Luc was standing on the front porch and when he saw her, he took the steps two at a time to get to her. "There you are. We've been waiting for you."

For the first time since she'd picked up the phone, the knots in her stomach unwound and the sense of doom that had been plaguing her since the debacle at the station that afternoon drained away, though she was still cautious. "I didn't think Chastian would approve of my being here."

Luc snorted. "What Chastian doesn't know won't hurt us." He led her through the door.

"You don't think any of these guys will talk?" She glanced around at the crime scene unit, busy searching for fibers and fingerprints near the point of entry, a patio door on the side of the house.

"They think this whole thing stinks as much as we do. Who gives a shit what you do on your personal time?" He looked away, as if embarrassed by what he'd said.

"Anyway, it's pretty bad in there. Elements of S and M, not to mention the torture."

Genevieve braced herself as she walked into the room, determined not to react. But her first glimpse of the body stopped her in her tracks. A rope was strapped over and under the woman's breasts, and wound around her arms, so that her entire upper torso was bound—exactly as Genevieve herself had been bound the night before. Except the ropes were harsh and heavy and tied much too tightly. Whereas Cole had bound her with silken cords, for their mutual pleasure, this had been done with one purpose in mind: to cause as much pain as possible.

Candle wax—black and pink—decorated the victim's nipples, stomach and legs in various patterns. But it had been hot—much too hot—when it had touched her, and blisters had formed under the steaming wax.

"How'd she die?" Her voice was hoarse, her fists clenched, as she approached the body.

"We don't know yet." It was Torres who answered, his face grim as he looked at her. "Jefferson"— he nodded at the ME, who was collecting evidence from the body—"can't find any outward sign of trauma. I mean, besides the obvious. But while painful, it isn't the cause of death."

"I'm thinking pills." Jefferson finished cataloging the sample he'd just taken, then stood to look at them with sad eyes. "Or poison. Her eyes and the broken blood vessels near the surface of her skin are consistent with a number of different kinds of poisoning. I'll know more when I get her back to the shop. Of course, the bruising makes it hard to tell."

"If it's poison we can trace it," Shawn said as he walked into the room. He looked exhausted, disgusted, horrified—as they all did. But he managed a quick grin when he saw her. "Maybe we finally got lucky."

"From your mouth to God's ears." Luc had just finished his examination of the outside of the property. "I found a set of footprints about fifteen feet from the house. Looks like a pair of male running shoes."

"Another mistake?" asked Torres. "What's with this guy tonight? Not that I'm complaining, but it just isn't like him to be this careless."

"Maybe it's not him," Shawn suggested. "Maybe we're just chasing our tails here."

"Oh, it's him," Genevieve said as she studied the body with eyes she knew showed too much.

"We don't know that for sure—" Shawn objected.

"Yes, we do." She waited, breath held, wondering if they would trust her. She could see Shawn wanted to argue, took note of the confusion on Luc's face. Only Torres seemed to understand what she was saying, the eyes he turned on her filled with speculation and more than a little concern.

"All right, then. Assuming this is our guy, what's going through his head?" Torres steered the conversation smoothly back to the killer. "It's been less than twenty-four hours since we found the last body—that's fast, even for him."

"Which could account for the mistakes." She leaned forward, looked at the woman's battered face. "Besides, this was a crime of anger. For all the others, he was stone-cold calm. No mistakes. No emotion. But this one—" She pointed to the deep bruises all over the girl. "This one was filled with rage. Look at the way he beat the hell out of her. That's not his normal MO.

"Which, once again, could account for the mistakes. No time to plan; no time to sort things through. This is the one we're going to nail him on, guys. I can feel it."

"Then let's do what we do best." Luc snapped on a pair of gloves. "Delacroix and Webster get the room."

"And we'll take the rest of the house," Torres said as he followed his partner from the room.

"Where are the owners?" Genevieve asked her partner as she crouched next to the body.

"The neighbors don't know much, just that they left three days ago on vacation. Two doors down had a cell number, but there's no answer. I left a message."

"He did her here, in this house."

"Yeah." Shawn cleared his throat, looked at her with suddenly shy eyes. "I'm glad you're back, Delacroix."

"I'm glad to be back, Webster." She flashed him a smile. "Even unofficially. Now let's get to work."

They worked companionably for over two hours, taking the room step by step. About halfway through, Jefferson removed the body and he and his guys took off. Soon after, Torres and Luc came in to see if they were ready to go.

"I want to walk the house one more time," Genevieve said. "See what the killer saw, what the victim experienced."

"Okay." Luc beat back a yawn. "Let's do it."

"You go on. I'll be fine."

Torres snorted. "Like we're going to leave you here alone. Get real, Delacroix."

"It's fine. I'll stay with her." Shawn spoke up. "I wanted to do the same thing. If there's a chance we can nail this bastard here, then I want to do it."

"All right, then. We'll follow the CSI guys in, see what they came up with." Luc patted her shoulder and headed for the door.

"Yeah. And Jose should be in soon. I want to see what he came up with from Genevieve's computer."

Her stomach clenched and she jerked involuntarily. For a minute there, she'd almost felt like one of the guys again. Torres saw her reaction and correctly interpreted it. Shaking his head, he said, "Hey, Genevieve, don't sweat it. We're not."

She nodded, but had a hard time looking him in the eye. "Call us if anything pops back at the station."

"You'll be the first." Torres threw out a fake salute, then headed for the door.

Shawn cleared his throat uncomfortably. "Where do you want to start?"

"Outside. Near the point of entry."

"Okay."

They walked silently through the house, out the side door, into the garden. "So he brought her through here." Genevieve pointed to the path. "But there's no sign of struggle—nothing that said she didn't come willingly."

"Maybe he backtracked?"

"Maybe." She looked around. "But there's nothing—no broken plants, no leaves on the ground, nothing."

"All right." Shawn stepped around her. "So he brings her in here. But wouldn't she notice him jimmying the lock? Be suspicious?"

"Not necessarily. There's the old 'I can't believe I lost my keys at the club. Let's go around to the side entrance. I think I've got a key there. Oops—no key. Let me mess with the lock, see if I can spring it.'"

"Exactly."

"So they come in here, and she still doesn't have any idea what's going on. He takes her to the kitchen, gets her a glass of wine. Does he drug her?"

"We'll know soon enough—the CSI guys took the glass."

"Forget that. Does he drug her?"

"No." Shawn shook his head. "He gets off on pain; he wants to hear her scream."

"You think? What about the neighbors?"

"It's the Quarter—people scream here all the time. Nobody even notices anymore."

She thought about it. "Maybe. So she drinks the wine. One glass or two?"

"One. Once again, he doesn't want to dull her too much. If she's coming from the clubs, she's already pretty loaded."

"I agree. So they move from the kitchen to the family room." Genevieve followed the path. "She kicks off her shoes right here." She stood where they'd found the red stilettos. "Where does she go from here?"

"To the couch. She sits down, kicks her feet up on the coffee table. She's relaxed, feeling pretty good now."

"What's not to feel good about? She's gonna get lucky—and the guy is loaded. Look at this place. It's like she's hit the jackpot." Genevieve sat on the sofa, did as Shawn had suggested and kicked her feet up.

"So does he sit with her?"

"Yeah." Shawn sat next to her on the couch, angled his body toward her. "This is where he makes his move."

"Sexually?" she asked. "Or is this where he gets violent?"

"There're no candles in here."

"Doesn't mean he didn't take them when he left."

"True. But I think he just gets her warmed up in here." He looked around. "There's nothing to tie her to."

Genevieve followed his gaze. "Good point. So, on to the bedroom?"

"Yeah." He offered her his hand, pulled her off the couch and then led the way down the hall to the master bedroom, where the body had been found.

"Absolutely. This is where the action takes place." She looked around the room they'd already spent more than two hours in—stared at the huge mirror that covered one wall. The gigantic white iron headboard that had long scratches gouged into the paint. "Once we find the owners, we need to ask if those scratches are new."

"Oh, they're new, all right. I'd bet my badge on it."

She glanced at him over her shoulder, grinned. They'd always been on the same wavelength from the first day they met.

Shawn didn't smile back, instead stared at her, hard. "Are you happy, Genevieve? With this guy, I mean? Does he make you happy?"

She glanced away, unable to look at the hurt in his eyes. "He does, Shawn. He really does."

"Even with everything he does to you?"

She turned slowly, her heart shifting into overdrive. "How do you know what he does to me?"

"I've seen the pictures. I tried not to look, but . . ." His voice trailed off and he shrugged.

"It's not what it looks like." Had she ever been this uncomfortable? Maybe in the police station when the images were flashing across her screen, but that had been more panicked than anything else. This? This was just plain awkward.

"You sure about that?"

"Yeah, I am." She looked at him impatiently. "Look, I know you're just concerned about me, but I *really* don't want to talk about this. Can we get back to work now, or what?"

"Sure. Sorry."

Genevieve turned back to the bed, stared at it blindly. Tried to focus. Wondered what the hell she was supposed to say now. As she was standing there, too embarrassed to look at her partner, something occurred to her. "You know, I forgot to ask. How did we even know about the body? Who called it in?"

"A neighbor. He heard the scream, saw the light on."

"I thought you said no one paid attention to screams in the Quarter."

"They don't."

"What?" she asked, glancing at him over her shoulder. His voice sounded odd, unfamiliar. But it was too late—something hit her in the center of her back and sent her sprawling onto the bed the dead woman had been on. Before she could react, the shove was followed up with a punch to the face that had her seeing stars.

Shaking her head, she struggled to clear her vision. Then gasped as she caught sight of Chastian looming over her, Shawn crumpled at his feet.

Fear ripped through her and she struggled to get to her feet, even as Chastian shoved her back onto the bed.

Grabbing her wrist, he slipped handcuffs over it, then attached the other end to the headboard. She tried to fight him but she was still dizzy, still off-balance.

Not to mention in shock. "Lieutenant, what are you doing?" she demanded.

"I would think it was obvious. Especially to Supercop herself. I would give you the benefit of the doubt if I still thought you were the original Ice Queen, but I've watched you with him. You're the hottest thing I've ever seen."

It took her a minute to catch on, took time for the shock to slowly give way to understanding, and the understanding to give way to horror.

The whispered voice on the telephone. The sadistic notes. The photographs.

It had been him all along. Chastian had killed all those women, then had gone about terrorizing and discrediting her when she'd gotten too close. He was the one who had brutalized those girls, the one who had taken such delight in torturing her.

Her stomach revolted as she put everything together—the profile, his attitude, little details that she'd previously missed all came together in her head. It seemed so obvious now. How could she have missed it?

She was sure she'd only thought the words, but she must have spoken them out loud, because he laughed. Got closer to her. And stroked one shaky hand down her chest and stomach.

Genevieve recoiled before she could stop herself, her body as horrified as her brain at the thought of Chastian touching her. At the idea of him as a sick, heartless murderer.

Even as her muscles quivered, tried to stay out of Chastian's reach, she knew that it was hopeless. The not-quite-sane look in his eyes promised that he would take her and hurt her, his narrow hips shoving against the legs she couldn't close.

"Not so confident now, are you, Genevieve? Not so full of yourself now that you're not in control?" His breathing was heavy, his eyes darkening a little more with each unsteady rise and fall of his chest.

He tried to grab her second wrist, but she knew that once he caught it she would be completely helpless, a sitting duck unable to move or fight. So when his hands reached for her free wrist, she jerked it away, kicking up and out with her legs instead.

He jumped out of the way, but not quickly enough to avoid a foot to the chest. "Let me go," she demanded. "There's no way for you to win this thing."

His laugh, when it came this time, was brittle. "I've already won, Genevieve. I have you and none of them know—none of them have a fucking clue what I'll be doing to you. They'll be at the station, searching for a suspect and I'll be here, fucking you. Cutting you."

He lunged for her wrist again and again she evaded him with a quick twist of her body. The arm that was locked into the handcuffs on the bed was starting to ache, the sharp twist and pull of her body as she tried to avoid complete capture putting too much pressure on it.

But she ignored it, desperation lending her strength and speed she never would have had otherwise. Chastian lunged for her a third, then a fourth time, but when he kept missing, he grew tired of the game.

Drawing back his fist, he hit her as hard as he could in the face, waited just out of reach as her eyes crossed and she started to go under.

Genevieve fought to stay awake, to ignore the darkness that hovered at the edge of her consciousness. But it wasn't easy—she felt the punch all the way through her body, the crunch of Chastian's fist sending waves of agony reverberating down her cheekbone and throughout her entire face. He'd hit her hard enough to daze her, more than hard enough to have her head ringing. And then he was grabbing her free wrist before she could stop him, dragging it toward the headboard.

He pulled out a second pair of handcuffs and fastened her right hand to the bed in the same fashion he'd already used on her left. As the handcuffs clanged against the iron headboard, fear burned in the pit of her stomach.

Trussed up like a Christmas turkey, there was no way she was going to get out of this now. No way she could fight back against Chastian and whatever he planned to do to her.

For one endless moment, each of his victims flashed into her mind. Lorelei, Cyndi, Jessica, Maria, Sharon and the unknown woman who had dragged them all here tonight. The pain each had suffered had been overwhelming, all-consuming.

And as Chastian leaned over her, a knife in his hand and an insane glint in his eyes, she understood that she would die as the other women had—screaming.

Cole, her angry, battered mind cried out. *Cole, I'm sorry.*

He'd been right after all. She hadn't believed him, and now her arrogance might very well be the death of both of them. For a moment she saw his face—angry, frightened, desperate to save her—and she knew. He wouldn't survive her death. Twice in one lifetime was two times too many.

Chapter Twenty-four

Cole raced around Genevieve's house, panic growing with every second that he couldn't find her. He searched every room, despite the empty feeling of the house, frantic at the thought of some psychopath getting his hands on her in her own house.

He found her note in the kitchen right around the same time his instincts went on red alert. For a minute he tried to think past the sick panic, to tell himself he was overreacting because he was worried. Scared. He was in love for the first time in his life, and it was the 'til-death-do-us-part kind of love. The thought of anything happening to her, of anyone taking her away from him—

Stumbling to a stop, Cole realized what he'd just been thinking. And though his head shied away from it, his heart knew the truth. He would love Genevieve forever—with her formidable intelligence and awe-inspiring temper, with her sweet heart and hot body, he loved her more than he'd ever loved anyone, even his sister. And he would do anything, give up everything, if it meant that she was safe.

With fear a living nightmare inside of him, he reached for the phone and dialed the precinct, only to realize she wouldn't be there. With shaking hands, he tried her cell phone. And waited impatiently, each ring a painful eternity, for her to pick up.

He was about to give up, to slam the phone back on to its charger when the ringing stopped. But it wasn't Genevieve's voice that came on the line. Instead, it was a male voice; high-pitched, a little deranged, it struck terror into his heart like nothing else ever had.

"Genevieve's sorry, she can't come to the phone right now. She's a little tied up. But maybe I can help you?" There was a hysterical giggle followed by a silence that chilled his blood.

"Who is this?" he demanded. "Where's Genevieve?"

"Geez, Cole, could you at least try to play along? Make this a guessing game. I mean, you don't actually think I'll tell you where she is, do you?"

"If you fucking touch her, I'll rip you apart with my bare hands."

There was a long silence, broken only by what sounded like Genevieve's pain-filled scream. "You're a lot dumber than you look, Cole, I've got to say. Issuing ultimatums like that just pisses me off. That one just got your little sweetheart sliced open from sternum to waist. But don't worry, I didn't cut deep.

"At least not this time."

The phone went dead in his hand and Cole stared at it for a good fifteen seconds, horror rocketing through him. And then he was throwing his head back, a bellow of rage like nothing he'd ever felt before rising from within him.

He was going to find that son of a bitch. If it was the last thing he ever did, he would find him and kill him before he killed Genevieve.

Throwing on clothes on the fly, he dialed the police station and her partner. Surely Shawn would know where she was. . . .

Genevieve trembled in horror as Chastian hung up her cell phone and turned it off. Cole was looking for her, trying to find her. Elation warred with a bone-deep fear that he would find her like this—but too late to do anything but torture himself for not getting here in time.

She was spread-eagled on the huge four-poster bed, naked and blind-folded. Completely at Chastian's mercy. He was taking it slow; a slap here, a pinch there. A tightening of her bonds until she lost all sensation in her arms and legs.

He'd keep her like that for a while and then loosen one of the knots so that blood—and painful sensation—rushed back to the body part all at once. And then, once the sensation had returned—painful second by painful second—he would tighten the bonds until the circulation was once again cut off.

And Shawn—Shawn hadn't moved from where Chastian had dropped him. She'd tried to tell herself that he wasn't dead, that he was just uncon-scious, but every minute that passed seemed to make a mockery of her prayers until fear for him and herself was a crazed animal within her.

Part of her wished he would just get it over with—that he would move on to bigger and badder things so that it would all just be done with. But the other part, the one that longed to feel Cole's lips against hers just one more time, wanted to prolong the inevitable. That side of her prayed for Cole or Roberto or Luc to come through that door and realize what had happened.

She knew Cole was aware of what was going on—though Chastian had gone into the next room when he answered the phone, she had heard every word of the conversation. Her only question was whether or not Cole would figure out where she was in time to save her. And what kind of shape she'd be in when he got here.

Suddenly, she felt the cold tip of Chastian's knife against her throat, yanking her out of her thoughts and back to his little shop of horrors. "Sorry to interrupt your daydream," he murmured, "but I was getting bored." She felt the prick of the knife as he nicked her skin for the first time.

"So, is this what you like, Genevieve?" She heard the sneer in his voice. "Does it turn you on?" The knife moved over her right breast, sliced just a little deeper.

"Goddamn it, answer me! I can't believe you let that bastard touch you. Let him tie you up and fuck you like a whore! I would never have done that to you. I would have treated you right!"

She bit her tongue, resisted the urge to point out just what a non sequitur that little trip to Crazytown was. Seeing as how he had barely gotten started and she couldn't find a part of her body that didn't hurt.

"Why won't you answer me?" This time the question was a sob. "I wanted to take care of you, to love you. To treat you right."

Suddenly, the blindfold was ripped away and she was staring into her lieutenant's deranged eyes. "Why did you make me do this to you?" he demanded. "Why couldn't you love me back, just a little?"

"Rob." She kept her voice deliberately gentle when what she really wanted to do was scream at him until she was hoarse. "I'm sorry. I didn't understand—" Her voice broke and she had to try again. "I didn't understand what you wanted from me. I should have listened better."

"Yes, you should have." He shuddered, and the knife came perilously close to her skin.

Fighting back a wave of fear-induced nausea, she murmured, "Tell me now."

The eyes he turned on her were bewildered, like a confused child who couldn't figure out where he was or how he'd gotten there. How could she have missed this, she wondered. How could she have worked for this man for three years and not have a clue he was so far gone?

How could any of them?

"It's too late, Genevieve. Everything's ruined."

"No. No, it isn't. Not everything. Not if you don't want it to be."

"But I saw you with him," he repeated. "You never should have done that. You were mine. Mine!" It was a primal scream of rage, one that had her blood running cold and her body shivering despite the sweat blooming on her body.

"I didn't know." She forced the words out, tried desperately to keep her voice from trembling as her fear seemed only to incite his sadism.

"You didn't want to know. I tried everything to get your attention. Followed you around. Called you into my office every chance I got."

Shock ricocheted through her as the meaning behind his words hit her. He'd made her life a living hell these last years not because he didn't think she could do her job, but because he'd wanted her *attention*.

"I didn't know." She was beginning to sound like a broken record, but she could think of nothing else to say. She felt like Alice, felt like she'd tumbled down a rabbit hole where everything was topsy-turvy. Only instead of Wonderland, she was stuck in hell.

How could this be happening?

How could Chastian be the killer they'd been hunting for months?

How could he have gone so far insane without any of them knowing—or even suspecting?

"That's not good enough, Genevieve. Not knowing isn't an excuse."

She bit back the sharp retort that trembled on her lips, tried to strike a placating tone when all she really wanted to do was rip his fucking eyes out before putting a bullet in his brain.

"I know it isn't, Rob. But I didn't understand."

"Nobody understands," he screamed, and she cringed. She'd meant to draw things out, to calm him down, but everything she said was just inciting him more.

"I'm sorry, Rob." She nearly choked on the words, but she had to keep him talking. Keep him occupied. Cole would find her and Shawn. Cole and Roberto and Luc; she just had to stay alive long enough for them to get here.

It had been nearly twenty minutes since Cole had called—surely he wouldn't be much longer. "Rob—" She opened her mouth to keep the conversation going, but he interrupted her with a scream that was so filled with rage and insanity that it turned her blood ice-cold in an instant.

"Sorry doesn't work, Genevieve! Nothing will ever work again." And then he was reaching for one of the candles he'd lit and set by the bed. Holding it over her stomach and tilting it, so that the searing-hot wax splashed onto her skin.

She couldn't stop the whimper from escaping, her body jerking wildly against the restraints as agony razed her nerve endings.

"Tsk, tsk. I expected better from the Ice Queen. But you're just like the others—nothing but a weak little whore." Chastian's voice was back to that insane singsong, the one that made her blood run completely cold. When he was rational—or at least as rational as he could get—it wasn't so bad. At least she could keep him talking, could distract him.

But when he was like this . . . she shuddered. When he was like this, all she could do was pray to survive whatever he had planned.

Just a little longer, she told herself. *Hold out a little longer, and they would find her.* And Chastian would be dead—if not by her hand, then by the hand of one of her friends.

That thought was the only thing that kept her sane.

But when Chastian unbuttoned his pants and climbed onto the bed next to her, her brain shut down. Disconnected. All the warnings that she'd given herself just disappeared as panic, deep and overwhelming, set in.

She could handle the pain—both emotional and physical. She could deal with the fact that her boss was actually a psychopath bent on her destruction. She could accept all of that. But she could not, would not, die with him inside of her, in a macabre mockery of what she and Cole had shared.

She would rather he kill her now—right now—than live through him killing her as he raped her. She looked into his eyes and knew that this was it; he wasn't going to wait much longer. He was as aware of the clock ticking down as she was, knew that it was now or never.

She was determined that it would be never.

Fear, urgent and uncontrollable, rocketed through Cole as he sat in the police car next to Roberto Torres. They hadn't been able to find Shawn, didn't know if he was lying injured somewhere or if he was dead.

But Genevieve's phone was department issued, and as such was equipped with a GPS chip that let them find her anywhere. According to Roberto, she was still in the house on Burgundy where he'd left her—or at least her phone was.

Hurry up, he urged the cop silently. *Hurry up, hurry up, hurry up.* It had already been almost half an hour since that psychopath had answered her phone. Genevieve couldn't last much longer—he didn't know how he knew this, but he did. No matter how hard he tried to tell himself it was just fear talking, he knew it was the truth. It was almost like he could feel her spirit weakening despite the fight he knew she was putting up.

"Can't you go faster?" he demanded.

"Not without running over a damn pedestrian!" Torres answered grimly. They were going in quiet, sirens silent. They hadn't called for backup, not yet. Roberto had wanted to see if there was anything to Cole's wild accusations.

"Open the glove compartment." Roberto's voice was clipped. "There's a gun in there. Do you know how to shoot?"

He grabbed the gun, relieved by its comfortable familiarity in his hand. But all he said was, "Yeah."

"Don't use it unless you have to."

He nodded, though he knew he would do whatever it took to keep Genevieve safe. If that meant killing this bastard in cold blood, he would do it, and to hell with the consequences. His woman was more than worth it.

Roberto pulled up to the curb, and Cole was out of the car before it even stopped, running toward the house as fast as he could. All he could think of was getting to Genevieve, of holding her in his arms, of never letting her go again.

"Stop!" Roberto yelled, but he didn't listen. He couldn't. He was too far gone, images of Samantha dancing in his head, Genevieve's face superimposed over her mutilated body.

He couldn't lose Genevieve, he just couldn't.

Suddenly, he was flying through the air, taken down by a running tackle from Roberto. He rolled, pulled back a fist and prepared to land it in the other man's face.

"You're going to get her killed! You just can't go running in there like—"

Suddenly, a high-pitched scream, in a voice he recognized immediately as Genevieve's, rent the air. The cop must have drawn the same conclusion, because he stopped fighting him and started moving—silently and low to the ground—around the house.

The side door was open and they slipped inside, more quietly than Cole would have dreamed possible. Roberto gestured for Cole to follow him and he did, even though everything inside of him strained to get to Genevieve as quickly as possible.

Another scream ripped through the house, had him clenching his teeth and shuddering. "Where is she?" he demanded between clenched teeth, his voice almost silent despite the torment ripping him apart with needle-thin claws.

Torres pointed at the hallway and they crept down it, keeping as low as possible. Horror was a sickness inside of him, twisting his stomach into knots as the need to get to Genevieve ripped into him. Only the knowledge that she was still alive kept him sane.

"Just go ahead and kill me, then!" Her voice came loud and clear down the narrow hallway, had him and Roberto freezing in their tracks. "Do it! I'd rather die than spend one second of the life I have left with you inside me!"

For one long second, time stood still. He and Roberto stared at each other in terror, the long hallway looming in front of them as they both wondered if there was any way they could get to her in time.

And then they were running full-out, desperate to reach Genevieve before it was too late. A low scream of insane rage echoed down the hallway, chilled his blood. Nearly stopped his heart.

They all but flew into the room, guns drawn.

"Freeze!" Roberto shouted, but he was too late. Genevieve's lieutenant was on the bed, hovering over her naked, spread-eagled form, a long knife clutched in one hand as he hung, poised, over her heart.

Cole took aim without being aware that he did so, squeezed the trigger one, two, three times. Watched as the bastard's body jerked from the impact of the bullets before falling, lifeless, on top of Genevieve.

For long seconds nobody moved, and then she shouted, "Get him off, get him off! Oh, God, Cole, get him off!"

Chapter Twenty-five

Genevieve shut down her computer with a sigh. It was well past nine o'clock, and she was exhausted—she and Roberto and Luc had been tying up loose ends for nearly twenty-four hours. And not once, in all that time, had she heard from Cole.

Roberto had brought him into the station after the shooting, had let Luc take his statement to keep things as clean as possible. But with both her and Shawn at the hospital, the questioning had been a mere formality. Cole had saved both of their lives, and the entire department knew it. As it was, Shawn was still in the hospital with a concussion, and the doctor had let her go only after it became apparent that keeping her was making her more upset.

She'd needed to see this thing through, had needed to help finish the investigation that had nearly cost her her life.

By the time she'd gotten to the station, Cole was gone—and no matter how many times she called him, she couldn't get him on the phone.

She knew he was shaken up, knew that seeing her strapped down like that had put an image in his head of his sister in the same position. Still, she'd expected him to call her or to answer the hundred and one phone calls she'd given him. But he hadn't; had, in fact, sent each of her calls directly to voice mail.

He was brooding, trying to come to terms with the idea that he'd done all this and still hadn't found Samantha's killer. Roberto and Torres had called him right after they had gotten back from Chastian's house, had told him that there was no evidence Chastian had murdered his sister. They'd also told him that they weren't giving up, that—with Genevieve—they would work the case again, from the ground up.

He'd seemed to accept that, but then her still-shaken friends had blown it. They'd told him of the pictures of him they'd found in Chastian's apartment, of the plans Chastian had had to murder Genevieve and frame Cole for her murder, and the other ones as well. With his bloody history, he'd seemed the perfect fall guy.

According to Roberto, Cole hadn't said a word when they'd told him. He'd simply hung up the phone without a fuss. But no one had heard from him since.

She'd started out being understanding—after all, he'd done everything imaginable to find his sister's killer and his single-minded attention had ended up attracting another psychopath, one with an agenda that had threatened his current lover. That had to be hard to swallow—that all the time he thought he'd been in control, someone else had been pulling the strings.

But after a few hours had gone by, she'd progressed to worried and had now hit downright pissed. He had no right to ignore her like this, not after he'd rushed to her rescue and saved her life in such a dramatic fashion. And from such a monster.

When Roberto and Luc had raided Chastian's house, they'd found every sick and twisted thing imaginable. Photos of each of his victims as he was torturing them, mementos from each of his murders—and there had been a lot of them. In Louisiana and Mississippi, Alabama and Florida. Nearly seventy-five girls through the years, and he'd kept pictures and personal items from each of them.

They'd been so shocked at what they'd found that they'd barely been able to get through the evidence, let alone censor their thoughts. Luc had let it spill that there had also been a slew of pictures of Genevieve, along with a few things she'd thought she'd lost through the years—a gold earring, a scarf, a couple of books, including a collection of Tennessee Williams plays.

The whole place—walls, ceilings, every available space—had been plastered with pictures of women being hurt. Roberto had sworn he'd never seen anything as disturbing in his entire life. Luc kept muttering that he didn't see how it was possible that they'd worked for Chastian for so long—for years—without ever figuring out what a sick bastard he really was.

The entire squad room—hell, the whole precinct—was in shock. Chastian had received numerous commendations through the years, and the idea that he had come to work every day, had talked and laughed and joked with them when he was torturing and killing women on the side, seemed too much for many of the cops to accept.

Genevieve was having the easiest time believing it, but then, she'd gotten a chance to meet his psychoses up close and personal. She couldn't stop the shudder that ripped through her. And she prayed that she would never have to live through something like that again.

But looking on the bright side—if there was one—at least it was finally over. Case closed. Chastian was dead, the paperwork was finished and she was dying to get to her lover. Only now she wasn't so sure that he felt the same way about her.

Genevieve slowly gathered up her belongings as she pondered what to do—how to shake Cole out of whatever self-imposed funk he'd descended into. How to show him that losing control wasn't always the terrible thing he thought it was.

Somewhere between her desk and the front door, the solution finally hit her.

Cole woke from a fitful sleep—one filled with nightmares and what-could-have-beens—to find his arms stretched above his head. With a groan, he started to roll over, only to find that he couldn't move.

Struggling to consciousness, he tried to get his sleep-fogged brain to function. The last thing he remembered was shutting off his cell and house phone and climbing into his bed, where he'd stared at the ceiling for what felt like hours.

He'd been disgusted with himself, furious that he hadn't made it to Genevieve before that psychopath had gotten his hands on her. He'd been so wrapped up in his sister's death and his documentary that he hadn't seen the threat to Genevieve until it was almost too late, and it made him feel like a failure—worse, as if the last seven years of his life hadn't taught him a damn thing.

Again he tried to roll on to his stomach, and again he realized he couldn't move. Alarm shot through the self-pity and disgust, had him raising his head off the bed and looking around wildly.

What he found could have come directly from his fantasies—or his nightmares. Genevieve was standing at the foot of his bed, her golden curls tumbling sexily down her back. Her beautiful body was encased in a black lace thong and see-through corset, while black stockings ran the length of her long legs. In her hands was a bottle of God only knew what.

Not sure if she was real or just the remnant of a dream, he started to reach out for her, only to finally figure out that he was bound—hand and foot—to the bed.

"Hello, lover." Genevieve's voice was low and husky, and it worked its way through his body like an electric shock. "It's about time you woke up."

"What—" His voice was hoarse from sleep, and from the nerves just beginning to set in. "What are you doing? Let me go!"

She shook her head, and he trembled as her silken curls caressed her shoulders and breasts. "Oh, I don't think so. At least not yet."

He strained against the bonds, but they didn't move—in fact, got tighter the more he struggled. Panic exploded in his chest. "Genevieve—"

She shook her head again and the smile she gave him was part siren, part queen. And all predator. "You might as well give it up. I was a Girl Scout, you know. And guess what I got my first merit badge in?"

"Knot tying?" His cock throbbed at the erotic promise of her voice, his early morning erection tightening to the point of pain.

"Bingo."

"Let me up, Genevieve." The words came out as a command. "Don't do this."

Reaching forward, she slid a hand languorously over his abdomen before following the light trail of hair down below his navel. He arched, involuntarily, as her fingers burrowed into the crisp hair at the base of his straining dick—caught between arousal and anger, hunger and hostility.

"I don't think you're in any position to be issuing commands, do you?" She brushed against his erection and electricity shot straight through his dick. Along with a need so strong he had to grit his teeth to keep from begging.

"Why are you doing this?" he asked from between clenched teeth.

She licked her perfect, strawberry pink lips and grinned at him. "Why not?"

"Genevieve." His voice was low, warning. "When I get out of here, I'm going to spank your ass for this."

Smiling wickedly, she leaned over and licked him from navel to collarbone. "Well, that's not much incentive for me to let you go, is it?" she murmured. "Maybe I'll just keep you here, turn you into my own personal plaything."

As she threw his own words back at him, Cole felt his body ratchet up another notch, desire thundering through him until it was all he could do to think. All he could do to breathe without strangling.

"Baby, please," he gasped out as he trembled—fear and fury mixing with a lust so strong he didn't think he could survive it.

Genevieve's lips pursed in mock surprise. "Are you begging already? But I've barely gotten started."

He let out a low, warning growl, but she only laughed. Then sank her teeth into his right pec hard enough to have him shouting. Her tongue darted out to soothe the small hurt before circling first one nipple and then the other.

"Fuck!" he ground out, his body spinning rapidly out of his control. He felt his cock jerk, felt himself leak, and he couldn't believe she'd gotten him so hard, so fast. For a minute he was afraid he was going to embarrass himself and he began to strain against the bonds in earnest.

"Stop fighting, Cole." Genevieve laid a soothing hand against his cheek. "It'll make this so much easier."

"Make what easier?" *Was that his voice?* he wondered. It sounded more animal than human.

"The loss of control. I know how much you *love* being in charge, but tonight it's my turn."

Cole swore, long and viciously, but Genevieve only laughed. "That'll cost you," she murmured as she tipped the bottle in her hands over. A honey-scented liquid squirted out and she rubbed it slowly between her palms.

He watched, mesmerized, as her pink tongue darted out and swiped a taste. And when she murmured, "Mmm, delicious," his mouth actually watered.

What he wouldn't give to be able to get free of these damn ties. He'd swoop her into his lap, paddle her gorgeous ass and then spend the rest of the night showing her exactly who was boss in this—

"Fuck!" It was both a curse and a prayer as Genevieve began rubbing the oil onto his cock in slow, thorough strokes that had his eyes crossing and his back arching convulsively.

"Stop!" he demanded, but it sounded more like a plea. "Don't—" His voice broke and he sucked in huge gulps of air, trying to get enough oxygen to steady his breathing. But Genevieve was only getting warmed up, and as her hands glided down to his testicles, began rubbing the oil into the delicate flesh, he nearly whimpered.

The touch of her hands was amazing, the feel of the oil even more so as it warmed on contact with his flesh. Heat sizzled along his most sensitive nerve endings, nearly burning him alive.

His balls tightened. His cock throbbed. The urge to come was nearly overwhelming, but he fought it back. Genevieve might have the upper hand—for now—but there was no way he was going to give in that easy. No way in hell.

Gritting his teeth, he thought of baseball stats and camera angles and lighting choices—any- and everything to keep from losing it too early.

Genevieve's laugh was low and sultry—as if she knew exactly what he was doing. And when she crawled on top of him, teasing his mouth with her nipple, he nearly said *To hell with it*. Control wasn't that important.

Nothing was as important as getting inside Genevieve and fucking her until neither one of them could walk.

But old habits died hard, and as he fastened his lips around her nipple, he reveled in her moan. Her hands crept around the back of his head to help support his neck as he sucked and licked the ruby red areola, teasing and tormenting her nipple until it was harder than he'd ever felt it.

Her hips started to move against his and he nearly shouted in triumph. He could do this, he could hold on, could stay in control, even tied down for Genevieve's pleasure. He could—

Suddenly, her nipple disappeared from his mouth and he groaned in disappointment. Then nearly choked as her warm, soft, wet mouth fastened around his strained-to-the-breaking-point cock.

"Genevieve, no!" he shouted hoarsely, his hips bucking wildly against her lips.

She pulled away and smiled at him, all temptress now. "Cole, yes!" She mimicked his words, but her voice was full of laughter.

"I can't hold on. I can't—"

"That's the point, baby," she whispered, right before she took him back in her mouth. "You can let go. You *need* to let go."

"I can't." The sweet suction of her mouth combined with the uncontrollable heat of the oil, and he shouted in agonized pleasure.

He strained against the silk ties, his body arching and shuddering as she sucked his cock slowly down her throat. She lingered at the base, swirling her tongue up and around him until it was all he could do to remember his own name.

There was a roaring in his ears, a pounding in his blood that warned him he was on the brink of losing complete control. Biting the inside of his cheek, clenching his fists, he tightened every muscle in his body and fought to hold on.

"Fuck, Genevieve," he groaned in between shudders. "Have mercy."

She only laughed again, sliding him up and down her throat in a rhythm that made his eyes cross and his cock beg for release. When he was at the edge of a yawning precipice, and every ounce of energy he had had been used up in the effort not to come, she pulled back with a long, lingering swipe of her tongue. Then licked him like he was a Popsicle.

"Don't tease, baby." It was a gasp, sweat pouring off him as his body shuddered beneath her. "Let me fuck you. Let me come inside—"

"Let *you* fuck *me*?" Her voice was a low, warm murmur. "You still don't get it, do you, *baby*? It's my turn to fuck *you*."

She slipped lower, her tongue stroking over his balls and behind them, finding a spot that made control a thing of his past and had his blood pressure shooting through the roof.

"Then do it!" His voice was harsh, guttural, his hips unyielding as he slammed them against her. The satin ties grew tighter, dug into his wrists and he tried to relax, to calm down. But he was beyond calm, beyond gentleness, beyond thinking for the first time in his life. Everything he had and everything he was focused on the warm, wonderful woman above him.

"I don't take orders." She pulled away, climbed off the bed. And left him on the brink of madness.

"Where are you going?" he demanded as the liquid on his cock caught fire, began to burn in an incredibly pleasurable way.

She shrugged. "I'm thirsty. I thought I'd head down to the kitchen and get something to drink."

"Genevieve!" It was a roar, the sound of a wild animal pushed past all endurance. His cock throbbed; his balls ached. His entire body was on fire, burning for her. Needing her.

A taunting laugh was her only response as she strolled slowly from the room.

Stressed out, fucked up, he lay there for what seemed like forever trying to get his raging erection under control. But the oil she'd rubbed into his dick and balls was making it impossible. Every breath he took had him throbbing more, every second that passed made his cock grow more and more sensitive, until just the brush of air against it felt like a caress.

"Genevieve," he called again, but this time there was a pleading note he couldn't keep out of his voice. "Come back, baby. Please. Come back."

She appeared seconds later, a glass of ice water in her hand. "Did you miss me, *baby*?" she asked as she approached the bed.

"Fuuuuck." It was a groan, a plea, and she seemed to recognize it as such.

"Good boy," she said. "I think you're almost ready."

"I'm ready." He strained against the bonds. "I'm so ready."

She glanced down at his cock, gave a murmur of approval that somehow made him grow longer, harder, though he would have sworn that was impossible.

She licked her lips and said, "Almost." Then she reached into the glass and pulled out an ice cube.

He shouted as the ice made contact with his rock-hard nipples, cursed as he felt himself grow even wetter. Glancing down, he saw pre-ejaculate glistening on the head of his cock.

Genevieve must have seen it too, because she leaned down and swiped her tongue over his tip, pausing to let those beautiful strawberry lips suck at him for just a second. "Mmm, you taste good."

He groaned when she pulled away, ground his teeth together so hard he swore he could see stars. Writhing, shifting, bucking, he strained against his lover. "You have to . . . Genevieve, please . . . I can't . . . baby, please. I have to—"

There it was, the note of surrender and desperation Genevieve had been waiting for. With a secret grin, she swallowed Cole whole, sucking him all the way inside of her. She used her mouth and tongue and throat on him, then lightly scraped her teeth across his great length. Just like she knew it would, that moment of combined pleasure and pain did it, sent him careening over the edge he'd been clinging to with battered fingertips.

With a hoarse shout, he arched up, thrusting again and again against her seeking mouth. And then he was pouring into her with long, brutal jerks of his hips, and she was loving every second of it.

The orgasm barely slowed him down, his cock still rock hard as he strained against her. Wanting more, begging for more.

Part of her wanted to string him out, to let him suffer more, but by then she was as hot and horny as he was. Maybe more so. Sliding up his body, she came down on him hard—taking him all the way to the pubic bone.

He shouted, his body arching convulsively beneath her. She rode him hard, striving for her own pleasure as much as his, slamming herself down on him again and again until both of them were shaking and covered with sweat.

"Finish it," he gasped from between clenched teeth, his hips rising to meet hers again and again. "I love you, Genevieve. I love you."

His words ripped through her, sent her spiraling out of control as her orgasm tore through her. "Cole!" she gasped as pleasure overwhelmed her. It was wilder and more intense than any that had come before it, and she found herself clinging to him in the middle of the storm.

He came with her, his body spasming as he poured everything he had, everything he was, inside of her. She took it all, took everything he could give her. Because as obnoxious as he was, as domineering and controlling and unyielding, he was also her safety net. Her only security in the craziness that was her life.

She only hoped that after tonight he felt the same way about her.

As her orgasm finally wound down, she rolled off of Cole—settling herself beside him so they could be face-to-face.

His eyes were dark, shadowed—filled with pleasure and a wariness that pulled at her heartstrings. Bringing up a hand, she ran it gently through his wild tangle of hair, smiled as he shifted his head to nuzzle her palm.

"I love you." His voice was hoarse, the words low but certain, and she felt them all the way to her soul. "I know I'm too controlling. I know I want everything my own way. I know—" His voice broke. "I know that I'm not the right fit for you. But I love you, Genevieve, more than anyone else ever has or ever will."

Tears filled her eyes as she fumbled with the knots, blurred her vision so badly that she could barely see to untangle him. "I promise—" he started.

"Shut up," she said as she clawed frantically at the knots. "Shut up, shut up, shut up."

"Genevieve?" He looked at her questioningly, those sinful black eyes filled with uncertainty.

"I want your arms around me when you make promises to me for the first time," she said as the first knot finally unraveled. "I want mine around you."

She yanked and pulled until the second tie gave in and then he was holding her, his strong arms wrapped so tightly around her that she could barely breathe. "Say it again," she ordered as her arms snaked around his neck and she brought her mouth within inches of his.

"I love you, Genevieve Delacroix. And I always will."

Tears bloomed in her eyes—tears of love and gratitude and thanksgiving. "I love you too, Cole Adams. More than I ever imagined possible."

"I know you do." He pulled her so that she was on top of him, his cock nestling in the warmth of her sex as his hands cupped her breasts.

"Hey!" She tried to pull away, but he slid his hands to her hips and kept her in place. "I'm supposed to be controlling this."

"Maybe next time." He shifted his hips until her clit rested against his cock.

She caught her breath as he stroked her with each glide of his hips. "Really?"

Laughing, he pulled her down for a kiss. "Not a chance."

Don't miss Tracy Wolff's next intoxicating erotic tale

TEASE **ME**

Coming from Heat in April 2010
Read on for a sneak peek....

I feel you watching me, feel your eyes through the cold glass of my window and the sheer curtain that does such a poor job of covering it. You don't know that I sense you, that I revel in your burning eyes as they run over me wildly.

To torment you—and myself—I open the pearl buttons of my blouse. I toy with them, sliding each through the buttonhole more slowly than the one before and I can feel your impatience. Your rage. Your need, racing through the humid night until it slams into me as you long to do.

I slide my blouse from my shoulders, then slip out of my skirt, until I stand before you covered only by my lingerie, which is no cover at all.

I cup my breasts, rub my nipples through the stiff lace that has been a torment—and a delight—through the endless day.

You growl, low in your throat, and I swear I can hear you despite the courtyard separating us. I slide my fingers down my stomach, over the lace and silk that barely covers the secret, aching heart of me.

And imagine it is you.

Imagine that it is your hands caressing me. Imagine that it is your mouth upon me.

I rejoice in your strength—in the hardness of your muscles and the sweet seduction of your mouth. I run my hands down your naked back, cup your ass in my hands and pull you to the very center of me so that you can feel my hard nipples and the wild, uncontrollable pounding of my heart.

So that you can feel my damp, heated core and know that you are responsible. That you have done this to me. That it is you, and only you, that I want.

That I need.

That I crave.

"Fuck!" Byron Hawthorne slammed his laptop shut as need ran through him like a goddamn freight train. But closing the computer couldn't make him forget what he'd read—or cool the desire shooting through his veins. But then nothing ever would, he was afraid—save a random case of complete and total amnesia.

Striving to put some distance between himself and the words running rampant through his head, he shoved himself away from his desk with a curse, only to find that his legs were almost too shaky to hold him. Goddamn it. His cock was on fire, his entire body so hard and turned on that it was impossible to breathe without pain.

Why did he continue to torture himself? Why, when he knew he'd spend the rest of the night so hard and horny that he would barely be able to function, did he continue to read her damn blog?

Because he was obsessed—that's why. Obsessed, delusional and completely fucking masochistic. There was no other answer for it. No other excuse as to why he—like the thousands of other morons who were ruled by their dicks instead of their brains—couldn't go a day without visiting her damn Web site.

What had begun as a lark had become the very best—and worst—part of his day. A friend of his who was big into the New Orleans Internet scene had introduced him to the blog months ago, while they were killing time during halftime of one football game or another. Mike had told him that the site was becoming another piece of New Orleans' ever-changing sexually based culture and that, as a newly single transplant to the Big Easy, he should have his finger on the pulse of what the city considered sexy.

At first Byron had made fun of Mike for reading the blog, had laughed at him for being so pathetically wrapped up in the words of a woman he'd never get the chance to meet. Had even wondered aloud what she got out of such a blatant fuck-you to the men of the world.

But he'd logged on. He told himself it was just because he wanted to harass Mike, but as the days passed and he continued to read the fantasies, he had to admit that he was hooked. Hooked on and obsessed with What a Girl Wants—as the mystery blogger had named her site.

It was a place where she could anonymously post her deepest, darkest fantasies. Where she could tell the world—or at least her small corner of it—what she'd never have the guts to tell anyone else. Or so she said . . .

But it was so much more than that. At least to him. It was like she had a window into his soul, like she knew exactly what *he* wanted. What *he* needed. The idea that she needed it too—well, that's what kept him up at night, his body aching for release no matter how many times he jacked off.

It drove him insane—the knowledge that she was out there, that she lived in the same damn city as him, and he couldn't find her. Couldn't even try to find her, unless he wanted to turn into some fucked-up, crazy stalker. Which he wasn't, he assured himself as he strode to the fridge and pulled out a beer. At least not yet. But if this insane sexual frustration kept up, who knew what the hell he'd end up being in a month or two? He could give up his gig as a carpenter and become a full-time psycho instead. He shook his head with disgust at the thought.

As it was, he'd been through five girlfriends in the last four months as he tried, desperately, to focus on a real live woman instead of his fantasies. But he couldn't connect to any of the women he'd dated lately, and while, a year ago, he would have at least tried to forge a relationship with one of them, these days he couldn't be bothered. There was nothing wrong with any of the women he'd seen—they were nice, attractive, smart. But they weren't *her*.

His laugh, when it came, was strangled—and more angry than amused. Of course they weren't. Because really, who could be? Even this woman—who seemed to be the living, breathing epitome of every fantasy he'd ever had—couldn't be real. Her writings were just words, her online personality just a persona that she'd adopted.

Or at least that's what he tried to believe. What he had to believe, he corrected himself as he downed the beer in two long swallows. Otherwise he'd go insane thinking that his perfect woman was out there and that he'd never have more of her than her fantasies. Never have any more of her than thousands of other men had too.

Just the thought of other men reading her words made him feel vaguely homicidal—a surefire sign that he was closer to insanity than he liked to admit. Because he wanted to go back to the laptop and read today's blog entry again, he forced himself to stay on the other side of the room from it. It wasn't nearly as explicit as some of the ones she'd written in the past, yet her list of wants—of needs—was so close to his own that he couldn't help responding to it.

Pissed off, out of sorts, and still more than a little turned on, he grabbed a beer and headed out to his balcony. It was late August in New Orleans, which meant it was already hot as hell and twice as humid, but at least a storm was coming in and the fry-your-brain temperatures of earlier in the day had receded a little bit.

Once he got outside, he felt some of the tension ease—as it always did. There was something about being out here, as day slowly faded to twilight, that relaxed him. In fact, it was this balcony, and the peaceful, narrow courtyard it overlooked, that had sold him on this building when he'd moved to the city last year.

To this day, he didn't know if it was the magnolia-scented air, or the soft trickle of water in the fountain down below, that calmed him. Nor did he care. All that mattered was that for a little while, he had surcease from the painful, clawing need that enveloped him every time he thought about his fantasy woman. The fact that he was pretty much the only one who ever came out here made the whole thing just a little better.

Yet even as the thought formed, he heard the soft snick of a door opening and then closing. A little annoyed at the disturbance, he bent forward until his forearms were resting on the wrought iron of the balcony railing, his beer dangling from loose fingertips.

Scanning the area, where the sound had come from, he finally found the unexpected intruder. It was the little redhead from across the courtyard, the one who had moved into the building last month and had caught his attention from his very first glimpse of her.

For a while, he'd thought about asking her out, about using her to help him get *her* and her dick-twisting fantasies out of his head. But the redhead had never even acknowledged Byron existed, even when they passed in the parking lot or took out their trash at the same time, and he hadn't been interested enough to try to get her attention.

But looking at her now—a little mussed, a little sweaty, and much more than a little sexy—she suddenly seemed worth the effort. With her red hair tumbling down her back and her sheer blouse plastered to her breasts, she looked like a fantasy. Add the pissed-off scowl on her face, and she just might *be* his fantasy. At least for tonight.

Lacey Richards was hot, tired and annoyed. She'd spent all day running down leads on the book she was writing, only to be given the runaround—time and time again. It was ridiculous, really, how the Beauchamp family had closed ranks, especially since so many of them had been willing to talk when she'd interviewed them over the phone a few weeks before.

With a groan of disgust, she flopped down on the upscale chaise longue she'd bought herself last year for her twenty-seventh birthday. It had been ridiculously expensive, but so comfortable that she'd managed to talk herself into the splurge. She hadn't regretted it once—had, in fact, spent many nights out here writing, or simply whiling away the hours when her insomnia was in full swing.

Her long peasant skirt had ridden up to the middle of her thighs when she'd sat down, but she didn't bother to fix the soft cotton. In the evening's oppressive heat, the slight breeze felt nice on her legs. Besides, there was almost never anyone out here. She and the guy across the courtyard were the only two who ever used their balconies. But then, they were also two of the only single people in the entire building.

Because the apartments in the building were large, most of them were taken up by families with small children. And, judging from the amount of noise that came from her neighbors' places, they had plenty to do in the evenings besides hanging out on their balconies—especially in this heat.

And, God, it was hot, so hot that she could actually feel the sweat beginning to bloom on the small of her back. It was stupid to sit out here, baking, when her air-conditioned apartment was only a few steps away. But the frustrations of the day were still looming large, and the idea of sitting in her living room as the walls slowly closed in held no appeal.

Leaning her head against the back of the lounger, she let her eyelids flutter closed and her mind drift. But the heat wouldn't let her relax— the humidity so stifling that it was hard to breathe. She could only hope the rainstorm that was due later tonight would hurry up and arrive.

Without conscious thought, she brought her fingers to the buttons of her blouse and quickly undid them before stripping it off, so that the only thing between her and the sticky air was the ivory silk camisole she'd shrugged into that morning.

With a sigh—of pleasure this time—she picked up her glass of water and took a long swallow, before rolling it slowly down her cheek and across her breastbone.

As the cold liquid bolstered her flagging energy, life suddenly seemed a whole lot more bearable, even if her latest book *was* currently dead in the water. But how could she have known that in a city like New Orleans—which wore its many sins and bad behavior like badges of honor—people would clam up so completely over a prostitution ring? Sure, it was a very large, very high-reaching prostitution ring, but it was *still* just a prostitution ring. Most of the stuff in this city made the midtown madam and her host of happy hookers look like child's play.

Besides, in the years she'd been writing true crime books, she'd found that the payoff of notoriety was often more than enough to convince people to give up their secrets. That same formula had proven true here—at least until today, when all her leads had clammed up tighter than a drum. Of course, all that unexpected silence was setting off her investigative radar, which in turn was making her all the more determined to get the story. When this many people refused to talk, it was usually for a reason. She wanted to find out what that reason was.

Taking another sip of water, she let her eyes wander over the building and balconies across from her. Mrs. Rochet needed to water her flowers—they were dying in the heat, despite the frequent rainstorms. And Mr. Andalukis really should—

Her thought processes shut down as she suddenly realized she wasn't alone. That she was, in fact, being watched—by the darkest, most sinful pair of eyes she'd ever seen. For long moments, she did nothing but return the stare of the man across the balcony, her gaze locked on his like a guided, heat-seeking missile.

There was power in those eyes. Power and sex and an edgy desire that set her blood humming in a way she hadn't felt in far too long. For one endless moment, she wondered what it would be like if she took him up on the blatant offer in his fuck-me stare. If she let him do all the wicked, wild, wonderful things those eyes promised.

It would be good. She knew that much from the way she'd seen him move these last few weeks—when he didn't know she was watching. She'd noticed him right after she moved in—with his broad shoulders, big hands and terrific ass, it would have been impossible not to. Add in the shaggy blond hair and the roguish grin, and he'd been damn near irresistible.

But she had resisted him. For five long weeks she'd ignored the interested glances he'd shot her way, had denied her own interest in him, even as he figured prominently in her most recent fantasies.

But this wasn't make-believe, and she wasn't that woman who trusted every pretty face that came along anymore. And would never be again.

She started to look away—to pretend a disinterest she was far from feeling—but he wouldn't let her, his eyes so steady, and sexy, that she could practically feel them moving over her skin.

She couldn't do this, her sluggish brain tried to tell her body. Not now. Not with him. No matter how out of sorts she was, or how hot he made her, she couldn't start this. Couldn't let him start it. Because tomorrow was only a few hours away and he had the word *complication* written all over him. No wham, bam thank you ma'am for this guy. He'd want to take all night and then start again in the morning, and she just didn't have time for that. Or the inclination. Too messy. Too involved. Too much potential for emotional complications—something Curtis had cured her of once and for all.

Besides, this guy was out of her league, out of her division. Out of her whole fucking stratosphere. She'd watched him enough to know that—and to know that there was no way he'd put up with being a one-shot deal. Too bad that was all she knew how to give.

So they were at an impasse, whether he recognized it or not.

She took another sip of her water, but didn't look away. The sexual magnetism he exuded was amazing, so intense that she could almost feel his fingers stroking down the slender column of her throat despite the courtyard that separated them.

He didn't look away either. Didn't move, didn't blink, didn't shift from that indolent pose against his railing. Just kept her in his sights, his gaze an odd mix of predator and partner.

It was strange and flattering—and oh so arousing—to be the object of that heated stare.

But those were the wrong reactions, she told herself. She should be indignant or wary or at least concerned that he'd been staring at her as she took off her shirt, as she fanned herself with her skirt. She should be annoyed that he'd let her half strip and had done nothing to alert her of his presence.

It wasn't like she was naked, her sense of fair play reminded her, or even showing as much as she would on a public beach. And it wasn't like he'd been skulking in the shadows—no, his stare was a blatant, in-her-face come-on. One she'd been stupid to miss. One she had a sick feeling she wouldn't be able to resist.

Besides, the way he looked at her—like he was the big, bad wolf and she was the most succulent sheep in the herd—intrigued her. More, it turned her on. It had been a long time since she'd paid attention to that look on a man's face—and even longer since she'd given a damn.

One more time Lacey tried to convince herself to leave him hanging. To simply pick up her glass and head inside, where she would make sure to close her blinds behind her.

It was what she should do. What she would *normally* do, as she had absolutely no interest in encouraging any man—even one as hot as this one.

And yet she didn't want to go. Not now, when her toes were curling and her nipples tingling. Not now, when he was smiling a slow, wicked smile that had her fists clenching and her stomach turning somersaults.

Returning his stare with the hottest one she could muster, Lacey sat up and straddled the narrow lounger, placing her feet flat on the ground, but making no move to pull her skirt over her knees. She knew he couldn't see much, if anything at all, but she felt wild sitting there with her pink lace panties exposed.

His eyes flared, grew darker and she felt a little thrill all the way to her toes. Her nipples peaked, and wetness pooled between her thighs. She knew she shouldn't be here, shouldn't be doing this. But it was like something out of one of her fantasies and just once she wanted to be that woman she so often imagined.

Just once she wanted to live in the moment and say to hell with the consequences. Eyes still locked with his, she took a long, slow swallow from her glass, and then tipped it so that a stream of cold water poured onto the hollow of her throat. Ran over her collarbone and trickled down between her breasts, until her nipples hardened even more and her tank clung wetly to her chest.

Then she closed her eyes and let her head loll back on her neck while she arched her back, knowing that she was spotlighting her rock hard nipples. Knowing that even with the courtyard between them, he was close enough to see the dark shadow of her nipples beneath the thin silk.

Wondering if he liked what he saw.

Holy shit, was all Byron could think, as he stared at the siren across from him. She was stunning, more beautiful than he had ever imagined, with her diamond-hard nipples and pink lace panties. More tempting than he had ever thought possible.

He felt his dick twitch, felt himself grow harder still and it was all he could do to keep himself from leaping the two stories to the courtyard below, just so he could climb up to her. So he could bury his hands in those lush, red curls and run his lips over those full, tempting breasts.

He was more than aware that his thoughts echoed those on his fantasy blog—that the situation was eerily reminiscent of the one he'd just finished reading about—but for once, he wasn't imagining doing these things to *her*. No, for the first time in six long months, he was completely in the present. Completely wrapped up in the gorgeous, desirable woman who was, at this very moment, watching him, watching her.

The only question was, what was he going to do about it?